Praise for Jeri Smith-Ready and

*Wicked Game*

### A nominee for the
### American Library Association Alex Award

"Smith-Ready's musical references are spot-on, as is her take on corporate radio's creeping hegemony. Add in the irrepressible Ciara, who grew up in a family of grifters, and the results rock."

—*Publishers Weekly*

"This truly clever take on vampires is fresh and original. The characters have secrets and questionable backgrounds, which makes them intriguing. The use of music as the touchstone for life is sharp and witty. Smith-Ready proves that no matter what the genre, she has what it takes."

—*Romantic Times*

"A colorful premise and engaging characters . . . a fun read."

—*Library Journal*

"Just when I think the vampire genre must be exhausted, just when I think if I read another clone I'll quit writing vampires myself, I read a book that refreshed my flagging interest. . . . Jeri Smith-Ready's *Wicked Game* was consistently surprising and original . . . I highly recommend it."

—A "Book of the Week" pick by Charlaine Harris at charlaineharris.com

DON'T MISS THE SEXY BEGINNING TO CIARA'S TALE. . . .

*Wicked Game*

Available from Pocket Books

# BAD

# TO THE

# BONE

## JERI SMITH-READY

POCKET BOOKS
NEW YORK  LONDON  TORONTO  SYDNEY

Pocket Books
A Division of Simon & Schuster, Inc.
1230 Avenue of the Americas
New York, NY 10020

First Pocket Books trade paperback edition May 2009

For information about special discounts for bulk purchases,
please contact Simon & Schuster Special Sales at
1-866-506-1949 or business@simonandschuster.com.

The Simon & Schuster Speakers Bureau can bring authors to your live event. For
more information or to book an event contact the Simon & Schuster Speakers
Bureau at 866-248-3049 or visit our website at
www.simonspeakers.com.

Manufactured in the United States of America

10  9  8  7  6  5  4  3  2  1

Library of Congress Cataloging-in-Publication Data

Smith-Ready, Jeri
  Bad to the bone / by Jeri Smith-Ready. — 1st Pocket Books trade paperback ed.
    p. cm. — (WVMP Radio ; 2)
1. Vampires—Fiction. I. Title.
PS3619.M59246B33      2009
813'.6—dc22

2008054695

ISBN: 978-1-4165-5178-2

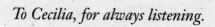

*To Cecilia, for always listening.*

# Acknowledgments

Many thanks to my family for their support, enthusiasm, and understanding during this crazy year. I swear I'll see more of you in 2009. (Well, maybe not the first half, but definitely in the summer!)

Thanks to my beta readers Adrian Pastore, Adrian Phoenix (yes, I collect Adrians), Terri Prizzi, Cecilia Ready, and Rob Usdin for their insights and corrections; to Jana Oliver for her magical brainstorm; and a long-overdue thanks to Shaunee Cole for feedback on the original proposal.

To the WVMP Street Team, for getting the word out in big and little ways. You all rock.

To the hardworking folks at Pocket Books for getting the book from my hands into those of readers: Louise Burke, Anthony Ziccardi, Erica Feldon, Jaime Cerota, John Paul Jones, and Lisa Litwack.

A million thanks to my editor Jennifer Heddle and agent Ginger Clark for their continued brilliance, patience, and support. I'm the luckiest author in the world.

Most of all, thanks to my husband Christian Ready, for his love and faith, and for letting twenty-three dogs come in and out of our lives.

# Playlist

"Wild One," Jerry Lee Lewis
"Flying Saucer Rock 'n' Roll," Bill Riley and His Little Green Men
"Me and the Devil Blues," Robert Johnson
"Bloodletting (The Vampire Song)," Concrete Blonde
"Dragula," Rob Zombie
"Happy Phantom," Tori Amos
"Under Ice," Kate Bush
"Everyday Is Halloween," Ministry
"Lake of Fire," Meat Puppets
"Black Dog," Led Zeppelin
"Babylon's Burning," The Upsetters with Max Romeo
"Stay," Marcia Griffiths
"I'm Free Now," Morphine
"You Know I'm No Good," Amy Winehouse
"I Wanna Be Your Dog," The Stooges
"In My Eyes," Minor Threat
"Beyond the Surf," The Tornadoes
"Mrs. Potter's Lullaby," Counting Crows
"Mother," Pink Floyd
"Whiskey in the Jar," The Dubliners
"Feel the Pain," Dinosaur Jr.
"Fools Gold," The Stone Roses
"Heresy," Nine Inch Nails
"I Can't Be Satisfied," Big Bill Broonzy
"Breed," Nirvana
"Little Saint Nick," Beach Boys
"Father Christmas," The Kinks
"Christmas Sucks," Peter Murphy and Tom Waits
"Where Are You Going," Dave Matthews Band
"Pay to Cum," Bad Brains
"Message in a Bottle," The Police
"Shove," L7
"Doll Parts," Hole
"As Heaven Is Wide," Garbage
"Jet Ski," Bikini Kill
"Jet Black New Year," Thursday
"A Child's Claim to Fame," Buffalo Springfield
"CCKMP," Steve Earle
"Bring Me to Life," Evanescence
"Graveyard Dream Blues," Bessie Smith
"Walk This Way," Aerosmith
"Pressure Drop," Toots and the Maytals
"Hidden Charms," Howlin' Wolf
"Let the Good Times Roll," Roy Orbison

The truth is rarely pure and never simple.

—Oscar Wilde

# 1

## Whole Lotta Shakin' Going On

The things I believe in can be counted on one hand—even if that hand were two-fifths occupied with, say, smoking a cigarette, or making a bunny for a shadow puppet show, or forming "devil horns" at a heavy metal concert. The things I believe in boil down to three major categories:

1. Rock 'n' roll.
2. Vampires.
3. A damn good pair of shoes.

Number two came about when one bit me, in the middle of what could nonskankily be called an "intimate encounter." Number three came later, when I gained the identity and thus the possessions of my dead-undead boss Elizabeth Vasser, owner of WVMP, the Lifeblood of Rock 'n' Roll.

I'm two people, but only on paper. In real life, I'm just

Ciara Griffin, underpaid marketing manager and not-paid miracle worker for a vampire radio station.

On nights like this, marketing is a miracle in itself.

The Smoking Pig is packed with fans who chose to spend Halloween Eve—aka Hell Night, Mischief Night, or Tuesday—in a bar with their favorite DJs, the ones who whisk them through time into another era, and into a world where vampires just might exist.

I lean back against the brass bar rail to avoid getting trampled by a couple dressed as Marilyn Monroe and Marilyn Manson. The guy in the Monroe costume can't be more than twenty-one, but he's twisting to a fifty-year-old tune with as much enthusiasm as his grandfather probably did.

Above me, the station's long black banner hangs on one of the rustic pub's long wooden crossbeams. Draped with fake cobwebs, it features our trademark logo, an electric guitar with two bleeding fang marks.

The two Marilyns jostle me again, and I reach up to check the status of my mile-high dark blond ponytail. Wearing a floral blouse and matching "skort" as twenty percent of the Go-Go's (the Belinda Carlisle percent), I'm glad the crowd provides plenty of heat. October in Maryland shows no mercy to beachwear.

"Excuse me," shouts a voice to my left, straining to be heard over Jerry Lee Lewis's slammin' piano.

I peer over rosy-lensed sunglasses at a young man about my age and height—midtwenties, five-eightish, with a lanky frame verging on heroin-chic thin.

"The bartender said I should speak to you," he says.

I examine his swooping bleach-blond hair, skinny jeans, and faded Weezer T-shirt. The smudged black guyliner makes his hazel eyes pop out behind a pair of round glasses.

"Billy Idol meets Harry Potter. I like it."

He puts a hand to his ear. "What?"

"Your costume," I shout, my voice already raw after only an hour of partying.

He gives a twitchy frown and shifts the messenger bag slung over his left shoulder. "I'm Jeremy Glaser, a journalism grad student at University of Maryland. I came up to do a story on your station."

Oops. I guess it's not a costume.

Jeremy extends a heavily tattooed arm toward the rear wall of the Smoking Pig, away from the stage and the speakers. "Can we talk?"

I reach back to the bar for my ginger ale. "Interviews by appointment only. Give me your e-mail and—"

"It's a freelance assignment for *Rolling Stone*."

My glass slips, and I spill soda down my arm. "Whoa!" I shake the liquid off my hand and grab a bar napkin. "I mean, wow."

He gestures for me to join him at the back of the Pig. This time I don't hesitate.

We weave through the crowd toward a dark corner, my espadrilles sticking in the booze puddles. I take the opportunity to rein in my galloping ambition and figure out how to play my hand.

Why didn't this guy call ahead? Either he's an imposter (always my first guess, due to my own former occupation), or he's committing journalistic ambush to see if we'll embarrass ourselves.

"So what's the angle?" I ask him over my shoulder.

"The first issue of the New Year will focus on the death of independent radio." He turns to me as we reach the back wall. "You guys are putting up a valiant battle against the inevitable."

"Thanks. I guess." I hand him my business card. "Ciara Griffin, marketing and promotions manager."

"I know who you are." He examines my card in the light of

a dancing skeleton lantern, then jots a note under my name. "*Keer*-ah," he mumbles, noting the correct pronunciation.

I keep my smile sweet. "Could I take a peek at your credentials?"

He pulls a handful of folded paper from his bag's outside pocket. "The one with the letterhead is the assignment from *Rolling Stone* editorial. The other pages are e-mails discussing the nature of the story."

I angle the paper to the light. "How does a journalism student snag such a major gig?"

"My professor has a connection." He adjusts his glasses with his middle finger. "Also, I can be pushy."

"I like pushy." I hand him back the papers. "In fact, I'd like to buy pushy a drink."

My best friend Lori swoops by with a trayful of empty glasses and "horrors d'oeuvres" plates. I reach out to stop her—gently, due to her momentum and the breakable items. She's dressed as another twenty percent of the Go-Go's, a small black Jane Wiedlin wig covering her white-blond hair.

"Hey, Ciara." She sends her words to me but aims her perky smile at Jeremy.

"Lori, I know you're busy, but can you get this gentleman from *Rolling Stone*"—I emphasize the last two words—"whatever he'd like to drink? Bill it to the station."

"I can't accept," he says, impervious to her cute. "Conflict of interest."

"Put it on my personal tab," I tell her. "A drink between new friends."

She beams at him. "There's a dollar-a-pint Halloween special on our dark microbrew."

He hesitates. "Do you have any absinthe?"

"Um, I'll check." Lori tries not to laugh as she looks at me. "Another ginger ale?"

"Definitely."

Lori winks before walking away. She knows I always stay more sober than my marks.

I take the last sip of my flat soda to wet my drying mouth. Dealing with the press is usually the jurisdiction of my immediate boss, Franklin, the sales and publicity director. Despite great effort, he's never raised the interest of a national publication, much less *Rolling Stone*. And now they've fallen in our laps, waiting for me to fill them with fascination.

Jeremy crosses his arms and examines me, in a skeptical pose right out of *All the President's Men*. "So what gave you the idea to start this vampire DJ gimmick?"

"It's not a gimmick. They're really vampires." I offer an ironic smile. "They're each stuck in the time they were 'turned,' which is why they dress and talk like people from back in the day." I point to the stage, where a tall man with slicked-back auburn hair surveys his poodle-skirted, pony-tailed groupies through a pair of dark sunglasses. "Spencer, for instance, became a vampire in Memphis in the late fifties. He was around when Sun Records discovered Elvis Presley, Johnny Cash, Carl Perkins, all those guys." He sends the girls a fake-shy smile as he arranges his stack of 45s. "Spencer was there at the birth of rock 'n' roll. You could even say he was one of its midwives."

Jeremy looks at me like I've just recited my grocery list. He hasn't written any of this down. "My research says you came up with this Lifeblood of Rock 'n' Roll thing in a desperate effort to boost ratings."

"It was either that or get bought out by Skywave." I still have corporate-takeover nightmares, where my fanged friends are forced to spin Top 40 hits until they stake themselves in despair. "Something wrong with trying to survive?"

"No, it's genius." He checks out the Lifeblood of Rock 'n' Roll banner. "But how long can it last?"

"Well . . ." I scratch my nose to cover my wince. Despite

our rabid fan base, ratings since the summer have tanked. The public at large is beginning to yawn and look for the Next Big Thing.

It doesn't help that the DJs don't look or act like stereotypical vampires. They wear blue jeans instead of capes. They'd rather guzzle beer, bourbon, and tequila than sip red wine. They don't brood, except about having to record promos for car dealerships and power vacs. They never attend the opera.

And as much as the vampires enjoy their adoring audiences, they want to keep their real nature secret, to avoid the inevitable mass freakout and subsequent stake-fest. Survival is paramount, and without WVMP, our vampires would lose their sun-shielded home under the station. Not to mention their whole reason for "living": the music.

"It can last forever," I tell Jeremy. "Rock 'n' roll will never die. Just like vampires."

A muscle near his eye twitches—the classic journalist spare-me-the-spin facial tic.

Lori arrives with our drinks. "Sorry, no absinthe. Hope beer's okay."

"Whatever." Jeremy accepts his drink and hands her two dollars. "Keep the change."

Ignoring his refusal of my generosity, I raise my new glass of ginger ale. "To the music."

He clinks and sips, then nearly spits the experimental dark microbrew back into the glass. There's a reason they sell it for a buck.

He wipes the foam from his mouth with a bar napkin. "I noticed that after the last ratings report you cut your advertising rates by ten percent. Sounds like you're having trouble holding the public's attention and it's hurting your bottom line."

"Every business has its ups and downs."

"But commercial radio is hopeless. How can you compete

with downloads and satellite stations?" He raises his multi-studded eyebrows. "What's next, werewolves?"

I ignore the jest. "We'll compete the same way radio stations always have—by providing a unique experience and quality entertainment."

Jeremy doesn't record those weasel words. I scan the bar, hoping to see David our general manager, or another DJ—anyone who can impress this guy.

The front door opens, and in walks my savior.

"Come on." I beckon Jeremy to follow me. "Meet our star."

The reporter looks past me and his jaw drops, transforming his face from cyni-cool to little-kid glee. "Yeah, yeah. That'd be great."

As I push through the crowd, I glance back to see Jeremy close behind me, frantically flipping the pages of a small notebook.

By the time I get to the door, Shane is surrounded by a gaggle of college girls. Towering over them at six-five, he greets them with an easy grin, but when his gaze rises to meet mine, his pale blue eyes light up with such force, the groupies' smiles turn to scowls.

The women look over their shoulders at me. One is dressed as Courtney Love, in a white baby-doll dress, black combat boots, and smeared mascara—presumably to appeal to grunge-boy Shane. As I pass through the gauntlet, she gives me and my costume a glare that could melt Teflon.

I take Shane's hand, then pull him close to speak in his ear. "This guy's from *Rolling Stone*."

He tilts his chin to look at me, eyes wide but holding a hint of suspicion. "You're kidding."

"I've never lied to you." He's the only one I can say that about. I turn to introduce the reporter. "Jeremy Glaser—"

"Shane McAllister," Jeremy says, then reaches forward and pumps Shane's hand hard enough to hurt a mere human. "I love your show. I listened to it back when I went to Sherwood College, in your pre-vampire days. Your indie-grunge mix is so eclectic, and yet you tie it all together seamlessly. It's inspiring."

Shane's reticence melts in the face of the reporter's worship. "Wow. I mean, thanks." He sweeps his tangle of pale brown hair off his face in a self-conscious motion. "I mean, good to meet you."

"Would you consider an interview?"

"Seriously?" Shane smoothes the front of his flannel shirt. "Me?"

"He'll meet you over there in a sec." I look at Jeremy and point to the place where we were just talking. The reporter salutes with his little notebook and hurries to the back of the bar.

Shane squeezes my elbow. "You look cute tonight."

"Tonight?"

"Always." He sneaks a kiss, and I can't resist stretching it into an unprofessional public display of affection. Finally, with an audible sigh, Shane pulls away and speaks low in my ear. "So what should I tell this guy?"

"He says his angle is the struggle of independent radio, so give him your authenticity spiel and how radio should be all about the music." I hook my pinky into the belt loop of his faded ripped jeans. "You know, the stuff I find so adorable."

"Adorably naive, right." He chuckles, brushing my ear with a breath warm enough to prove he had his fill of, uh, sustenance before the party. "What about the undead issue? The standard 'pretend to be a human pretending to be a vampire' routine?"

"Yes, with lots of wink-winks. Your usual ironic self."

"Got it." He gives my cheek a quick kiss before heading off to join Jeremy.

Bill Riley's "Flying Saucer Rock 'n' Roll" fades out, and Spencer's honey-smooth drawl comes out of the speakers.

"Ladies and gentlemen, we got two hours left till Halloween. Time for me to say good night, but I'm gonna turn it over to my great friend, Mississippi Monroe Jefferson." The crowd whistles and hollers, especially the older members. Spencer continues, "He'll play you some blues that I guarantee'll send a shiver down your spine."

He steps aside and adjusts the microphone down to the level of Monroe, who has appeared in the chair behind him, like in a magic trick. Another cheer. The stage light makes Monroe's suit glow white, setting off his smooth ebony skin and the lustrous scarlet of his acoustic guitar.

Monroe lets loose with a weepingly beautiful version of Robert Johnson's "Me and the Devil Blues." I smile at the choice; the story of his turning is well known by his fans. Like several legendary musicians of his place and time, Monroe supposedly went to the crossroads at midnight to meet with the devil, to trade his soul for the ability to master the blues. A vampire was waiting for him, and the rest is history.

The blues always makes me want to drink, so I head to the bar and signal to Stuart, the owner of the Smoking Pig, who is making a valiant attempt to look like Simon Le Bon of Duran Duran.

He slides a bottle of my favorite beer across the bar. "How's it going with the reporter?"

"Journalists are a lot harder to impress than the general public." I watch him light a cigarette. "Any luck on that smoking ban waiver?"

Stuart shakes his head in disgust. "I sent the state a photo of the sign hanging over our front door. I said, 'If you look closely, you'll notice that under the words "The Smoking Pig" is an illustration of a pig with a cigarette.' They didn't care." He takes a hostile puff. "Fascists."

"So what are you going to do?"

"Set up an outdoor lounge with space heaters. It'll cost a fortune."

"Hey, Ciara," comes a voice at my elbow. Lori sidles close and adjusts the poof of my ponytail. "I remember that guy Jeremy from my History of the Middle East class senior year. Smart, but kinda intense. He said he hoped the Iraq War lasted long enough for him to be an embedded reporter."

"A thrill-seeker, huh?" I watch him in the corner speaking with Shane, scribbling madly in his notebook. Shane maintains a casual posture against the wall, but his supernatural stillness creates a magnetic field that seems to have snagged the journalist. "I don't like it."

"Why not?" she asks me just as Monroe finishes his song to a rush of applause. "Don't you want the publicity?"

"I want fawning puff pieces about how cool it is to be a vampire. I don't want someone to find out the truth."

Lori hurries off to pick up an order as Monroe begins another song. I watch his fingers glide over the strings like a water bug skimming a pond. He makes it look so easy. Shane tried to teach me guitar last month—I stopped after two days and ten blisters.

A familiar arm slides over my shoulders. I lean into Shane and crane my neck to look behind him. "Where's the reporter?"

"Interviewing Spencer." His jaw twitches in contemplation. "I think he wants to be bitten."

"Lori said he was weird. Are you sure?"

Shane nods. "A vampire can smell an eager donor a mile away."

"Do I need to forbid you to bite a reporter?"

He slants me a gimme-a-break look. "I'm not that dumb. Anyway, I don't think he thinks I'm really a vampire."

"Because that's insane."

"I think he thinks I'm a wannabe."

Ah yes. In the "real" vampire subculture, some humans believe they need to drink blood to thrive, and there are people lined up to oblige them. Lacking fangs, they use razors or needles to bleed their "donors."

Some of those donors find their way to a *real*-real vampire, and if they can be trusted to hide the truth, the two form a symbiotic relationship. The donors exchange blood for money or sex or—most commonly—the masochistic thrill of serving a creature who could rip off their heads.

Not for me. The sensation of being stabbed with a pair of ice picks does nothing for my self-esteem or libido.

At a minute to midnight, my boy takes over the stage from Monroe, who tips his hat to the worshipping crowd on his way out. No one dares to follow. Like Spencer and other older vampires, Monroe's charisma holds an edge of menace that sane people wisely avoid. It's why we ask them to wear sunglasses in public whenever possible.

Shane, on the other hand, exudes humanity, giving his admirers a friendly wave as he moves to the microphone. "Ladies and gentlemen, the time is twelve a.m. It is now. Officially. Halloween."

He hits a switch and a low, hypnotic bass emanates from the speaker—the opening moments of Concrete Blonde's "Bloodletting." The patrons writhe and vamp, reveling in the dark magic the music weaves.

Someone calls my name. I turn to see Lori leaning out of the kitchen, holding on to the edge of the swinging door.

"What's up?" I ask as I follow her into the kitchen.

She takes me behind the salad prep area, where an old boom box sits on a shelf. She turns up the volume. Above the clatter of pans and the sizzle of grease, I hear an angry male voice.

"—'not participate in the unfruitful deeds of darkness, but instead even expose them,' as Paul told the Ephesians." He lets that sink in. "Don't let the secular media and your children's public school teachers convince you that Halloween is harmless fun. Your *tolerance* is their greatest weapon in this culture war. Fact: Halloween is a pagan holiday that glorifies darkness and evil and everything God wants us to fight."

I glance past her at the chef/dishwasher, who's searing a pair of burgers on the grill, then at the ceramic white statue of the Virgin Mary above the prep table. "When did Jorge get born again?"

Lori shakes her head. "It's supposed to be WVMP."

"No, it's just mistuned." I twist the grease-encrusted knob, searching for the station. "The antenna probably got knocked."

"I already tried that. I was here when it happened, just now." She points to the wall clock, which reads a minute after midnight. "Regina was giving her usual creepy intro, then suddenly it was this guy."

I tweak the dial again and again, but there's no Regina, no Bauhaus, no Sex Pistols. Just a whole lotta Jesus goin' on.

"I better get David."

The kitchen door sweeps inward, banging into the stainless steel dishwasher. My boss stalks toward us, dressed as Bruce Springsteen circa *Born in the U.S.A.*, cell phone at his ear. As David passes me, I hear a woman's screech from the earpiece.

"I'll call you back." He shuts the phone as he stomps up to the radio, the bandanna around his ripped blue jeans flapping with each step.

"She's not on," I tell him. "It's some guy nutting off about Satan."

David adjusts the knob up and down, only to get another dose of Ranty Man.

He curses under his breath. "Regina said she's flooded with calls."

"It happened exactly at midnight," Lori offers.

"Strange." David stares at the boom box. "It's like another station was just created on the same frequency."

"Isn't that illegal?" I ask him.

"Extremely." He rubs the dark, uneven stubble on his chin, a look he's been working on for a week (and, if I may say, that has been worth the wait). "If it's a pirate operation, the FCC could slap them with a fine and confiscate their equipment, maybe even throw them in jail."

"Then what are we waiting for? Let's report them."

He gives me a patronizing glare, like I've suggested we call up Santa Claus. "Ciara, the FCC doesn't exactly have a twenty-four-hour emergency number. We'll have to file a report during business hours."

"What if it's not pirates?" I gesture to the radio. "It sounds too high-quality to be coming out of someone's basement. What if it's another real station?" My mind sounds the *cha-ching!* of a cash register. "Can we sue them?"

David turns away, dark brows furrowed. "If it's a real station," he murmurs, "I might be able to find out . . ." He looks at Lori. "Can I use your boss's computer?"

She points to the back of the kitchen. "There's Stuart's office. Sorry about the mess."

David speaks to me as he strides away. "Call Regina, tell her to get the location of everyone who can't hear us."

I return to the bar, where Shane is onstage and on the phone. He pulls his head away from the phone, as if it's delivering electric shocks.

I weave through the crowd to the edge of the stage, then mouth the word "Regina?" to him. Shane nods. Good thing his eardrums are as immortal as the rest of him.

I signal for him to hand me the phone. He shakes his head but obliges. "Be careful!" he shouts.

I move away from the speakers to hear Regina. Unnecessary. Astronauts on the International Space Station can probably hear her.

"Hey, it's me," I say as calmly as I can. "David says to find out the locations of all the callers who can't hear us."

"Don't you think I thought of that?" Regina's voice is even harsher than usual. "They're everywhere—D.C., Sherwood, Baltimore, Harrisburg, every town in between. This isn't some half-assed pirate operation. Someone is fucking with me."

"I doubt it's personal. It's probably just an anti-Halloween demonstration by religious wackos. David says he might find out who it is by looking on the Internet."

There's a long pause before her voice comes back, muted. "Really?"

Regina died in 1987, so her entire experience of the Internet consists of the Matthew Broderick movie *War Games*. To her, the Web is omnipotent, able to produce tragedies and miracles with a few keywords.

"Go on with the show as if nothing's happened," I tell her, "and we'll be at the station after the bar closes at two."

She gives a tight sigh. "I wish I could figure out how to blame you for this."

I hang up the phone as Jeremy approaches me, notebook in hand. "Everything okay?" he asks.

"Of course. Why?"

"The way you and the station manager were running around, it looks like there's a crisis."

"Nope." I adjust my sunglasses. "No crisis."

"You mean, other than the fact that no one can hear your broadcast?" In response to my stunned look, he holds up his own phone. "My roommate just texted me."

Crap. How many other media outlets have noticed already? How many *advertisers* have noticed?

He steps closer, a new gleam in his eye. "Let me help you find the pirate."

"I don't think so." That's all we need, for him to snoop around and discover the real truth. "Thanks, anyway." I pat his arm and turn toward the stage.

"This could be a huge story," he says.

I stop. Visions of the station, the logo, maybe even Shane's face on the cover of *Rolling Stone* form a slide show in my head. Visions of solvency. Visions of survival.

I turn back to Jeremy. "Give us a day to put our own people on it. I'll get you something Thursday morning."

"Exclusive?"

"Through the weekend."

"Good enough." He tucks his notebook back into his pocket. "I'm going to drive back home to College Park and listen myself. I'll call you Thursday."

On my way back to the kitchen, I wing Shane's cell phone toward the stage. He snags it with a deft maneuver.

In Stuart's dim office, I find David leaning close to the monitor, his worried face aglow in the pale white light. He gives me a distracted glance as I pick my way through the piles of papers and stacks of shrink-wrapped Halloween bar napkins.

"Found something odd." David points to the screen. "The FCC keeps a public record of every application. Here's one for a translator construction permit from earlier this month right here in Sherwood."

"A what construction?"

"Translator. It's a two-way antenna that takes a radio signal and transmits it way outside the station's original range. Let's say we wanted to broadcast in Poughkeepsie. We'd build translator stations to relay the signal, and then everyone between here and there could hear us."

"But we couldn't trample on another station's frequency, right?"

"Right. To stay legal, we'd have the translator change our

frequency to one that's available in our target area. If we're 94.3 here, we might be 102.1 in Scranton."

I squint at the browser to see what looks like an application from a Family Air Network, Inc. "But these people didn't bother switching."

"No, they bothered." David highlights a box on the application. "They specifically requested our frequency." He crumples his Springsteen headband in his fist and glares up at me. "They're after us."

"They're after *me*. I knew it!"

Black leather creaking, Regina paces across the small main office of the radio station. As she rants, she stabs the air with a long brown cigarette and shoots hostile glances from her dark brown eyes, outlined in liquid black.

Sitting on either side of my desk, David and I share a glance that mixes relief and confusion. The moment Shane signed on with his *Whatever* broadcast at 3 a.m., the religious screed ended. Maybe Regina *is* the target.

Rob Zombie's "Dragula" pounds out of the speaker that sits under the mounted deer head on the opposite wall. I smile, mentally giving Shane points for every time he plays a song that was released after he died. The DJs stuck-in-time phenomenon isn't a gimmick—it's a sad fact of unlife.

One of their gig posters hangs on the wall above my desk, displaying the six DJs in the garb and attitude of their "Life Times": Monroe, the 1940s bluesman; Spencer, purveyor of '50s rockabilly; Jim, who brings us the dark, psychedelic side of the '60s; Noah, the dreadlocked reggae dude representing the 1970s; Regina, the '80s punk/Goth chick (and the only one who actually looks like a vampire); and youngest of all, Shane, whose broadcast rounds out the twentieth century with whatever music passes his stringent Generation X authenticity test.

"So they're not going to spend the whole day attacking us." I make an unsuccessful attempt to suppress a yawn. "That's good, right?"

"Good for everyone else." Regina yanks on the silver chain dangling from her belt loop, rolling it over her fingers like rosary beads. "What about me?"

"Maybe it was a one-time thing." David holds up a print-out. "Maybe the FCC already shut them down."

Regina scowls at him. "When has any government ever been that efficient?"

"The timing could be a coincidence," I tell her.

"At exactly midnight on Halloween? I don't buy it."

I glance at the clock on the mantel of the bricked-up fire-place next to me, then put my head down on my desk. I have to be back here to work in five hours. Franklin will no doubt want help soothing the tempers of angry advertisers.

David shows Regina the different applications FAN has filed for translators, explaining how this was the only one with a conflicting frequency (ours) and no data on the transla-tor's location. Something's definitely fishy.

I rest my chin on my folded arms. "Have you heard of this Family Action Network?"

David nods. "Religious talk format, some nighttime musi-cal programming. Last year I heard they were going bank-rupt, but the FCC's records show them expanding."

Regina sniffs. "Someone funneled them cash, and it sure as shit wasn't pennies from heaven."

The industrial metal riffs segue into the plinky piano notes of Tori Amos's "Happy Phantom."

I drag myself to my feet. "Whether the piracy was on pur-pose or not, it's over. I'm going home to bed." My feet scuff the rough hardwood floor, because I'm too tired to lift them. I take my jacket off the coat rack, which is currently the hand of a life-size cardboard Elvis.

The song cuts off.

"Like all of Satan's deceptions, the lie of Halloween is subtle." The radio preacher's once raging voice is now soft and cajoling. "It's easy to fool ourselves into believing it doesn't hurt our children . . ."

David, Regina, and I stare at each other.

The man continues and finally says, "God tells us in Deuteronomy . . ."

"Oh, no." I put a hand to my forehead. "Here comes the fire thing."

" ' . . . not be found among you anyone who makes his son or his daughter pass through the fire, one who uses divination, one who practices witchcraft . . .' "

"How'd you know he was going to say that?" Regina asks me.

"I was bathed in that stuff the first sixteen years of my life."

The man's voice takes on an edge again. " 'For whoever does these things is detestable to the Lord.' " I can almost hear his spittle splash the microphone. "There's no arguing with the word of God, people. Are we making our children walk through the fire?"

The phone rings.

"Studio line," David says.

It goes silent, which means Shane answered it, no doubt hearing the bad news from a listener. We hurry downstairs, through the employee lounge, and through the hallway door next to the lighted ON THE AIR sign.

To my right is a corridor leading to the vampires' apartment, blocked by a door that says KEEP OUT. In front of me is the studio, which contains an array of equipment—turntables, tape decks, CD players—some of which dates as far back as the 1940s to maintain "cognitive comfort" for the older DJs.

It also contains one pissed-off vampire.

On the phone, Shane sees us and holds up a finger. He speaks into the receiver, his hand forming a fist on the table and his eyes narrowed to slits.

He punches a switch on his console, slams down the phone, and stalks over to yank open the door.

"What the fuck's going on?" he asks us. "I thought it stopped after Regina's show."

"Now you know how it feels," she says, suddenly calm and smug.

"I don't get it." David rubs the scar on the left side of his neck, which tells me his stress is building to a new level. "Why would they stop for exactly one song?"

They discuss their next steps—mostly David and Shane talking Regina out of violent solutions—while my mind drifts off, listening to the lilting tune and wondering what it has in common with Regina's music.

Shane's gaze flicks to the console, his DJ's sixth sense kicking in near the end of a song. He moves back to the CD player just as a flash of insight hits me.

"Wait!" I scramble into the studio. "What's your next song?"

"Kate Bush's 'Under Ice.' " He sits and adjusts the microphone. "Why?"

"Switch the order and play the next track with a male singer."

With no time to question, he hurries to reprogram the CD player. The song fades, and he hits a switch. "94.3 WVMP-FM. Coming up on ten after three in the morning. I'm feeling a little lonely on my favorite holiday, so phone in and say hey. The ninth caller gets two tickets to this band's upcoming show at Ram's Head Live."

Ministry's "Everyday Is Halloween" slaps out of the speakers. The synthesized New Wave riffs make my heel tap against the floor, long after I thought I had the energy.

The phone is dead quiet.

David turns to me. "I didn't authorize Ministry tickets."

"That's not the point. Shane wanted to see if our listeners could hear him." The phone doesn't ring, no matter how long we stare at it. "Which they couldn't."

Shane reaches for the transmitter console. "Let's see if your theory worked."

He flips a switch to receive our FM signal, so we can listen to what the world is hearing on our broadcast.

"—telling you, this culture war will be fought on the streets of our neighborhoods and—"

I frown at the sound of the evangelist's voice. "Okay, so my theory sucked."

"Wait." Shane switches back to his studio feed so we hear the music. "The instrumental intro lasts fifty-eight seconds." He looks at David. "I know from working at stations where they make you talk over the music."

"What's your point?" Regina says.

"There's no singing yet," Shane says, "so our pirates wouldn't know it's a man and not a woman playing unless they recognized the song."

Regina snickers. "And what are the chances of that?"

We wait for the fifty-eight-second mark, for the vocalist to display his gender. When he starts singing, Shane gives it an extra half minute, then flips the transmitter back to the FM broadcast.

It's "Everyday Is Halloween."

"Whoa," Regina breathes. "Fucking pirates left us alone once they heard a man singing."

"But why?" David asks.

"Ciara was right." Shane swivels his chair to look at me. "It's a girl thing."

\* \* \*

I drive back to Sherwood, listening to Shane's show. He was pissed about changing his carefully crafted Halloween playlist. Unlike the other DJs, nearly half his collection consists of female artists. He's always going off on how "back in the nineties," women found stardom through singing and songwriting, not custody battles and wardrobe malfunctions.

A police siren blasts over the shriek of the Meat Puppets' "Lake of Fire." I ease the car to the side of the road, hoping I wasn't speeding.

The cop continues past, and I pull back onto the street. On the outskirts of town, I pass the green, sloping Sherwood College campus, where two evenings a week I trudge toward a business degree with a concentration in marketing.

The police car's wail is joined by that of the volunteer fire department. I turn down the radio as I come over the hill to Sherwood's central historic district.

Three blocks past my usual turnoff, a fire engine is maneuvering into the tight space of the main intersection, which was clearly designed in the era when such vehicles were pulled by horses.

I slow down at my street, located in what could generously be called the "modest" part of town. A scattering of folks are hurrying down the sidewalk to witness the most exciting thing to happen to this town since—well, since the last time a Main Street business caught fire.

I park the car at the corner near my apartment and follow the crowd. I should at least make sure it's not the Smoking Pig burning down.

My steps slow. Uh-oh.

It *is* the Smoking Pig burning down.

The bottom floor of the building is engulfed in roaring, licking flames. Clay-colored smoke billows from the front window. My heart lodges in my throat at the thought of Lori inside.

I sprint forward, fighting to keep my feet inside my beach

shoes. The emergency vehicles prevent me from getting closer than half a block away.

An ambulance sits to my right, and with relief I notice Stuart sitting on the back bumper, speaking to a cop. A piece of plywood the size of a sandwich board rests against his leg.

I hurry over to him. "Stuart, is everyone okay?" I yell above the sound of rushing water from the fire engine.

"Hey, Ciara," he says in a dazed voice. "I was the only one inside." He gestures to the cop. "I was just telling him, I was in the office doing payroll when all of a sudden I hear car brakes squealing on the street." He puts an oxygen mask to his face and takes a few breaths. "Then there's glass breaking in the bar, like the window shattered. Then an explosion, but not like a grenade. I go out there and the whole place is in flames."

"Someone fire-bombed you?"

"Think so." He wipes sooty sweat from his forehead with the back of his wrist. "No idea why."

I point to the board at his feet. "What's that?"

"Found it on the sidewalk when I ran out the back door. Sitting there like a welcome mat. Figured it'd be evidence."

He turns the sign around. Four words are slathered on the board in crude red paint.

YOUR GOING TO HELL

# 2

## Wild Thing

"Now that's just wrong."

I look up from the shelf of eyeballs to see Franklin glaring at a group of children.

Corporate survival skill number one: Humor boss's moods, especially "cranky." In Franklin's case, there are no other moods.

He points to the line of costumed kids clamoring for candy from one of the Halloween Land sales associates—the lady in the ballerina costume, not the guy dressed as a flesh-eating bacteria victim. "It's bad enough kids are trick-or-treating during daylight savings time. Now they have to do it in the mall? What are their parents afraid of?"

"Vampires, I hope." I turn back to the shelf of party novelties. "Think I'll get brains instead of eyes."

Franklin grabs another package of candy corn, and we make our way over to the cashier, who's sporting half a face.

Tonight's party at David's house is for the DJs—they'll wear costumes, probably get wasted, and the humans will clean up the mess. Only fair, considering the success of last night's Smoking Pig party. Plus, it keeps them off the streets and away from the trick-or-treaters.

We finish our purchase, then wade through a river of sugar-spaced children toward the mall exit.

Franklin shakes his head as the kids bop from one store to the next. "This is too sanitized. Halloween is supposed to be dark and scary and cold."

"Halloween is supposed to be lucrative." I hold up our plastic shopping bag. "You of all people should appreciate that."

"So you think this is better than running from house to house through the dark? Better than waiting for the old man down the street to pop out from behind a gravestone, or wondering which cup of cocoa might be spiked with strychnine?"

"I never trick-or-treated." I shove open the glass door to the parking lot and squint into the setting sun.

"Why not?"

"Because of Satan."

The devil was the excuse for much of my missed childhood. My faith-healer parents fooled a lot of chumps—including their daughter—into swallowing concepts like sin and heaven and hell. Made a great living at it, too. Because crime totally pays. Until it doesn't.

Franklin and I climb into his pickup, where he switches on the radio, tuned to National Public Radio.

"Aw, I'm telling David you're listening to another station." I rip open the bag of candy corn.

Franklin scowls at me as he backs out of the parking spot. "I spend eight hours a day keeping WVMP in the black. Fast-food workers don't eat burgers on their day off."

"Are you comparing my boyfriend's art to a Big Mac?"

"Shane flips switches for a living. He sleeps all day."

"You're just jealous because you're almost forty and he'll stay young forever." I bite the white tip off a piece of candy corn.

"Forever, until he fades. Thanks, I'd rather get fat and bald than turn into a mindless, two-legged leech."

I glare at his pudgy physique and receding hairline. "What do you mean, '*get* fat and bald'?"

Franklin calmly gives me the finger before shifting into first gear.

We reach the stoplight, and he sends me a half-serious look. "You know, in three years you and Shane will both be twenty-seven, but in ten years, you'll be thirty-four and he'll still be twenty-seven, at least on the outside. Then in twenty years—"

"I haven't thought that far ahead. He's already the longest relationship I've ever had, and it's only been four months." Five months if you go all the way back to when we first kissed, but since that encounter resulted in stitches and a tetanus shot, I think it bears exclusion.

"Wow, four months, that's what, a decade in con artist years?"

I pelt Franklin's temple with a candy corn. "This is why I avoid you outside the office."

He smirks as he turns onto the road leading out of Sherwood. We head uphill on the rural highway, and soon the terrain beside us turns from dull gray concrete to bright orange leaves.

Ninety seconds from JCPenney, and we're in Blair Witch country. I love this town.

I lean back against the headrest and close my eyes, hoping a five-minute nap will compensate for staying up until 4 a.m. The fire department extinguished the Smoking Pig blaze before it could spread, but the bar took enough damage to be out of commission for weeks, putting Sherwood College's campus in a state of mourning.

"Holy crap," Franklin says. "Where did that come from?"

I open my eyes to see an enormous white cross at the top of the hill ahead of us, about half a mile away. It's easily three times the height of a telephone pole, bigger than any cross I ever saw growing up in the Bible Belt. The setting sun gleams orange off its surface, giving it a baby aspirin hue.

"That wasn't there the last time we came to David's, for the Ravens opening game. Can a whole church be built in six weeks?"

"It's not attached to a church. Must be a new cell phone tower." Franklin gives a gruff laugh. "Insert obligatory joke about a direct line to God."

We turn onto David's road, leaving the cross behind at the highway intersection.

I crane my neck to examine it. "Weird. They left all the trees standing around the base. Usually construction sites will clear them out to get the heavy machinery in."

"Must be an environmentally friendly church."

"Or they're hiding something."

Franklin utters a noncommittal grunt as he turns onto a roughly paved country lane. I glance at the setting sun, calculating how long before the vampires arrive. Even indirect sunlight can hurt them, so they stay inside the station until twilight—roughly half an hour after sunset and half an hour before sunrise—when the deadly orb is a safe distance below the horizon.

We pull into David's driveway, which is lined with cheesy plastic pumpkin lights.

As we walk up the front pavestones, Franklin says, "Don't make fun of him. It's a thing."

David opens the door, setting off a canned Vincent Price laugh. He's dressed in a complete collection of vampire clichés—tux with black cape, a set of plastic fangs, fake blood dribbling down his chin, and his dark hair slicked back Bela Lugosi–style.

I hold up my shopping bag. "I brought brains, which is good, since you've obviously misplaced your own."

"Brains?"

"You fill them with orange juice and freeze them, then float them in the punch." I hand over the bag as I pass through the door to enter the split foyer house, the kind with stairs leading up and down from the front landing. "By the way, I hired Lori."

He follows me up the stairs to the living room area overlooking the foyer. "Hired Lori for what?"

"As a temp. It'll take weeks to rebuild the Smoking Pig, which means she's out of work."

"You added someone to the payroll without asking me?" The fake fangs make him lisp, robbing his voice of authority.

"You're always saying we need more help with the phones and paperwork." I survey the snacks on the dining room table. "Besides, those grammatically challenged thugs who torched the Pig might have done it because of us."

He sighs. "She can have twenty hours a week. Temporary."

"Thanks." I glance at the clock—6:05. "This party better be worth missing class."

Franklin chuckles. "Tell David which subject you're taking this semester."

I lift my chin and enunciate the words "Business ethics."

David laughs. "Does that count as your foreign language?"

"Hah!" Franklin high-fives him. "I told her she should use herself as a case study. How to stay in business by impersonating your dead boss."

David's smile fades, followed by Franklin's smirk.

"Shit, I'm sorry," Franklin says. "I forgot."

David nods, then extracts his fake fangs. "I need a drink. Help yourselves to—" He flaps his fingers at the table, then walks into the kitchen without another word.

Franklin runs a heavy hand through his thinning blond hair, and I decide not to chide him. We've all made his mistake—mentioning the station's late owner in a less than sensitive manner. Elizabeth Vasser was a vampire, but not a DJ. She was loved by approximately one person: David.

I turn up the radio, as if that will reduce the tension. It's tuned to WVMP, of course. From six to nine tonight, they're rebroadcasting Shane's latest show, with one major difference.

While Franklin empties the candy corn into a plastic skull, I move to the sliding glass door that leads to David's deck. His closest neighbor is half a mile away, on the other side of a large cornfield; the eight-foot wall of dried stalks obscures the view of the distant farmhouse.

Red streaks of light flame the field, then fade as the sun sets. A white cat trots up the stairs of the deck. I slide open the door so it can saunter in.

"Hey, Antoine."

The cat hops over the threshold and drops a dead cricket at my feet.

"Uh, thanks."

Antoine was Elizabeth's cat—named, perversely, after the teenage vampire who made her back in 1997, the vampire David staked in revenge for turning his fiancée into a monster and thus dashing his hopes for growing old with her. When she died permanently, he adopted her cat and has yet to change its name.

The song ends, and a familiar voice replaces last night's preempted Tori Amos tune.

"94.3 WVMP-FM, Sherwood, Maryland. Shane McAllister here, live on this all-too-sunny Halloween evening. In a few minutes I'll return you to the replay of this morning's show. But first I have a special message for the people who interrupted our broadcast at midnight and again at 3:07 a.m."

David comes out of the kitchen and shares a look of trepidation with me and Franklin.

"We're not afraid of you," Shane says. "You don't have God on your side. All you have are deep pockets and a pair of artificially inflated 'nads." His cool voice contains a sharp edge of anger. "You know what we're gonna do when we find your pointy electronic friend, the one that's been chewing up our frequency? We're going to snap it in half, then play nothing but female artists all day, one bitchin' babe after another, while you sit in jail choking on your own hate." After a short pause, he says, "Happy Holiday."

A commercial comes on, filling the show's gap left by last night's pirates.

"That was subtle," Franklin says.

"It gets us attention," I point out, "which means ratings."

"Not if these people get pissed off and decide to throw a twenty-four-hour broadcast blanket over us. It's not like the authorities will do anything."

I can't blame Franklin for his frustration. This morning the FCC told us to fill out a complaint form and fax it to their Enforcement Division. I'm sure we'll hear back from them before the end of the Mayan calendar.

"These people won't cut us off completely." David carefully pours orange juice into a row of brain molds. "They're trying to make a point."

The word "point" reminds me of something Shane said. "David, what would one of those translator thingies look like?"

"All it takes is an antenna and a repeater, which is about the size of a fuse box. Usually they're on a tower at the top of a hill." He wipes up a puddle of spilled juice. "But Sherwood has a lot of hills."

"Does it have to be a radio tower?"

"No. You could attach it to an existing structure, like they do with cell phone transmitters."

I turn to Franklin, whose cheese puff halts halfway to his mouth. Our eyes meet, and a lightbulb dings on between our heads.

A lightbulb in the shape of a big honkin' cross.

At precisely seven o'clock, Jim's blue '69 Charger pulls into David's driveway. We three humans lay our bets on the end table in the corner of the living room, predicting which vampires will be brave enough to investigate the cross.

David opens the door and absorbs the DJs' mockery at his outfit. Shane springs up the stairs.

"Happy Halloween again," he says before kissing me.

"I loved your message to the bastards tonight." I stroke his abs in an exaggerated swoon. "Very macho."

Behind him comes a hiss and a yowl. Antoine is standing at the top of the stairs, his wide yellow gaze fixed on Jim. The cat arches his back, then dashes down the hall in a streak of white fur.

Jim glides up the stairs, shoulder-length brown curls shimmering in the overhead light. "Man, I must be getting old," he says. "Critters all hate me now."

As vampires age, they become less human and more, well, wrong. Animals sense this and act accordingly.

"Any others coming?" David asks the DJs.

"Spencer's finding Travis a quick drink." Regina glares at David as he motions for her to put out her cigarette. "Monroe's at the station manning the booth."

I examine the three vampires' outfits. "I thought you guys were wearing costumes."

"We are." Regina displays her black leather dress, spray of foot-long spiked ebony hair, and silver-buckled combat boots. "I'm Siouxsie from Siouxsie and the Banshees. Duh."

"But you dress like that every day." I study Jim's leather

pants, button-down black shirt, and studded belt. "Jim Morrison?" When he nods, I turn to Shane. "No need to guess there." Except for the greater height and slightly darker hair, my boyfriend is Kurt Cobain reanimated.

Noah comes up the stairs last, his red-gold-and-green knit cap doing little to cover his masterpiece of dreadlocks. "You will guess Bob Marley," he says, "because your grasp of reggae is so superficial I want to weep."

"Actually, I was going to say Peter Tosh."

"Oh." He pats my shoulder and smiles. "Very good."

Franklin picks up my betting sheet and looks at the vampires. "Did you guys see that big white cross?"

"It cannot be missed." Noah goes into the kitchen with his bottle of apple juice—as a Rastafarian, he avoids alcohol (and processed blood). "We'll take the long way home."

"We're going to investigate it," I announce, "to see if it holds the translator."

The house goes quiet except for the radio.

"What do you mean, 'we'?" Regina asks me.

"Come on, the station is under attack by a bunch of chauvinists, and we're a quarter mile from a giant clue."

She twists her studded leather bracelet in a nervous gesture. "So you want us to start playing Cagney and Lacey?"

"More like Scully and Mulder." Shane puts his arm around my shoulder. "I'm in." He gives a broad smile—too broad for him. I can feel the tension in his grip.

As Franklin said, Halloween is supposed to be scary. And not just for humans.


Shane, David, Jim, and I make our way down the dark country road toward the cross, unaccompanied by cowards. Franklin offered to stay by the phone in case we need to call him for bail money after being arrested for trespassing.

But I have plenty of cash after winning our wager. I knew Shane would be game for anything I asked, and Jim is the reckless sort. Noah is the personification of caution, and Regina harbors a typical vampire's pathological fear of religious symbols; so they stayed behind.

The cross shimmers against the starry, moonless black sky. A ground-based spotlight shines on it, changing from red to white to blue every thirty seconds, creating an effect that would make me laugh if it didn't nauseate me. I bet people can see this spectacle ten miles away.

We stumble through a thick copse of trees—or more precisely, David and I stumble. Shane and Jim have the coordination and night vision of natural predators—not that their blood donors ever provide much of a chase.

We come to a small clearing at the base of the cross, about fifteen feet in diameter. It's almost completely dark, since the patriotic spotlight sits on the ground on the other side of the trees.

I sweep the flashlight beam across the clearing. "So where would a translator—"

Two glowing red eyes stare out of the darkness.

"What the—"

In front of me, Jim halts and holds out an arm. "Whoa."

A hunched black shape slouches in front of the white structure. The clank of a chain rises over the sound of the wind in the trees. A low growl stops my breath.

Suddenly the creature roars and leaps forward. I jump back, squealing like a little girl. The chain rattles, then jerks tight.

Shane grabs my arm. "It's just a dog."

Can't be. The noise it makes sounds like a cross between a rabid cougar and a locomotive.

"I've never seen a dog like that." David looks just as scared as I am.

"Don't worry." Shane moves a little closer, stepping sideways. "It's tied up."

I gesture for David to stay back, then follow Shane. The barking grows louder but higher-pitched. Finally the flashlight fully illuminates the dog, and I let myself relax.

It probably weighs twice as much as I do, and my head might fit inside its mouth, but its tail is wagging, and it's play-bowing and clawing the ground at the end of the chain.

"It's okay, buddy," I murmur. "We're here to help."

The dog's bark turns to a whimper as I approach. My light reveals ribs and hip bones showing through patchy black fur. Its head is square, but its legs are long, lending a mismatched, rangy look. Huge eyes reflect the light with a green glow.

When I'm a few feet away, the dog drops to its belly, then rolls over, pawing the air and rubbing its—wait, *his*—back on the gravelly dirt.

"Looks friendly enough," Shane says.

"It could be a trick." David's voice gets fainter as he backs up behind me. "It could be luring you in, looking all innocent."

"Dogs are a lot of things, but they're not con artists." I kneel near the animal, out of range of the chain. He stops groveling and gets to his feet, then shakes off the dust with a horselike shudder of his hide.

"You're all right now." I keep my voice low and even, my gaze on his shoulder instead of his eyes as I extend my hand, palm down and curled, for him to sniff. He licks my fingertips, his tail whipping back and forth like a puppy's. "What a good boy. You're someone's pet, aren't you?" I examine his huge black face, crisscrossed with faded gray scars. "Or maybe bait for a pitbull trainer. You're too nice to be a fighter yourself."

"You know what's freaky?" Jim says. "He's not barking at me."

As if to prove the point, the dog wags his tail at the hippie vampire.

Jim laughs and sings the first line to Led Zeppelin's "Black Dog"—off-key, as usual. The pup wags harder.

"Whoever put him here doesn't deserve him." I stand and dust the dirt off my knees. "So we should take custody."

Shane comes up next to me. "You mean steal him?"

"Not steal, liberate." To avoid threatening the dog, I step past him instead of advancing directly. He pads beside me, panting, as I approach the base of the cross, where the chain is hooked to itself but not locked. "He's not even securely tied up. They probably have a dozen just like him." I look down at the black beast, whose head reaches my waist, as he sits politely at my feet. "Well, maybe not *just* like him."

I squat to unhook the chain, and my hand brushes the white metal of the cross. It's much colder than the air, which isn't even chilly enough to fog my breath.

I place my palm against the cross. It's not only unnaturally cold, but clean, despite the dust in the clearing. It holds the sheen of a china plate that just came out of the dishwasher. (Not that I've ever owned a china plate or a dishwasher. But I've seen them in catalogs.)

The dog whines. I unhook the chain and notice that he hasn't circled the pole, shortening the length and reducing his range like most tied-up dogs would do.

"If you're so smart, then tell me your name."

He just looks at me, eyebrows twitching.

"How about Dexter? You look like a Dexter."

Dexter blinks, then yawns. I notice Shane staring up at the cross's T.

"Can you see an antenna?" I ask him.

He starts. "Uh, no. It's too dark to see from here." He rubs his arms as if he's cold. "Maybe with binoculars."

David clears his throat. "That box could hold a repeater." Standing outside the range of Dexter's chain, he points to the base of the cross.

I jiggle the heavy padlock on the door of the metal box, which is about my height. "Shane, could you pick this?"

He tears his gaze away from the cross and comes over to examine the lock without touching it. "No, it's heavy-duty. And the highway makes too much background noise for me to hear the tumblers click." He straightens up and stuffs his hands deep into his jeans pockets. "You could snap it off with bolt cutters, then replace it with an identical one if you didn't want them to know you'd tampered with it. At least not until they tried to unlock it."

"Sounds like a plan." I ruffle the dusty fur on Dexter's head. "For another night."

# 3

## Stir It Up

In the bedroom of my apartment, I change into a pair of Lycra shorts and a tank top—the fewer clothes the better when bathing a dog. I probably ought to go straight to a bikini, but it would only distract Shane.

In the bathroom I find him bent over Dexter's head with a pair of tweezers. A bowl of rubbing alcohol sits on the pale pink sink.

"Ticks?"

"Just one so far, and it wasn't even attached yet." He holds up a bad guy the size of my thumbnail, then plops it in the bowl of alcohol.

"You'd think a stray like him would have a million. Thanks for doing that." Not many guys would pull ticks off their girlfriend's stinky dog.

"Thank *you*, for not making a crack about professional courtesy."

"Huh?"

"You know the joke about why sharks don't attack lawyers?"

I wrinkle my nose at the fat round tick as its legs slowly stop kicking. "But you only drink from willing donors. And you don't carry Lyme disease."

He laughs, a sound I never get tired of hearing. But it sounds hollow, reflecting the chill of his demeanor since our encounter with the cross.

I push back the shower curtain. "Come on, boy. Let's take a—"

Dexter hops in the tub.

"—bath. Wow." I pull down the shower attachment before he can change his mind about being a perfect dog. Tomorrow I'll call the rescue people and get him a foster home before my landlord finds out he's here and evicts me.

In five minutes we're both soaking wet. Covered in white shampoo suds, Dexter's big black head is utterly marketable.

"Let's take his picture now," I tell Shane, "so the dog rescue can upload it to his adoption page. He looks a lot less scary this way."

He ruffles my hair. "Always thinking of the angle."

I slap his arm with a soapy hand. "Smart-ass, go get my cell phone from my purse."

Shane leaves, allowing me to indulge in doggie talk.

"It's a *good* boy," I squeak. "Yes, it is. Who's your mommy? Hmm? Who's your ever-lovin' momma scratchin' your butt?"

Dexter wags his tail with enough vigor to send the suds flying against all four walls.

Shane returns with my phone. "Who are you calling?"

"No one. It takes pictures, remember?" I flip open my brand-new phone, admiring the maroon chrome surface.

Shane crosses his arms and leans on the wall. "I forgot

they do that nowadays. Give me a little credit for remembering what year it is."

I turn back to Dexter, confused by Shane's sudden testiness. Normally he can laugh at his own "temporal adhesion"— the vampire psycho-phenomenon of being stuck in the era in which they died. After all, he's a lot more normal than the rest of them, due in part to his relative youth—he was vamped only twelve years ago—and in part, I like to think, to my influence.

"Are you feeling weird from being near that cross?" I ask Shane while I take a few photos. "Fever, chills, gut-strafing agony?"

"Nothing physical." He rubs his chest and fails to elaborate. He's wearing that interior look, which has been happening a lot since his dad died last month. My efforts to snap him out of his gloom always backfire, but I can't stop trying.

Soon Dexter's vast geography is rinsed clean and wrapped in a bright pink-and-white towel.

"Aww, he looks like a Good & Plenty." I shroud the dog's head in the towel and mug for Shane.

A reluctant smile creeps over his face, then fades quickly.

"Okay, Dexter-dude, you're done." I help him out of the tub. "Stand back, folks!"

We're sprayed with a shower of fur and water as Dexter shakes himself, jowls flapping, feet flailing. Then the dog dashes out the bathroom door.

We watch as Dexter runs up and down the hall, stopping to roll on the long rug, which is soon balled up at one end of the corridor.

"He looks happy," Shane says with typical understatement.

"That makes one of you."

He gives me a double take. "Is it that obvious?"

"It must be, for me to notice. I'm not exactly the paragon of sensitivity."

He stares past my shoulder, hesitating before he speaks. "You know what the day after tomorrow is?"

"Friday."

"All Souls' Day."

"Is that when the Mexicans do the skull thing?"

"The Day of the Dead, yeah." He runs his finger over the uneven ridges of the bathroom doorjamb. "It's the day vampires are supposed to visit their own graves. Like a pilgrimage."

I freeze in the middle of drying my hands. "You don't have a grave."

"Not yet." He raises his pale blue gaze to meet mine. "But there's one I should visit."

I drape the towel over the rack. "You want to see your father?"

Instead of playing it cool like usual, he comes right out and says "Yes."

"Then we'll go." I step close to him so he has to take me in his arms or be incredibly rude. "Friday night?"

"Tomorrow. It's an odd-numbered day, so Monroe, Spencer, and Jim are working again." He runs a long golden-brown strand of my hair between his thumb and forefinger. "By the time we get to Youngstown, it'll be near midnight, so it counts as November second."

"I admire you for being able to look at your past. Whenever mine comes up, I just blink really fast until it goes away."

He strokes my cheek with his fingertips. "This is the first time I've ever considered going home. I never felt capable before I met you."

I burrow my face into his neck and say nothing. Sometimes the ferocity of his need forces me to breathe deep to avoid passing out. I get the urge to make a lame joke, or excuse myself to go to the bathroom or the kitchen, or find a reason to cancel our next date. I get the urge to do something stupid with the next guy who crosses my path on campus.

But I don't do any of those things. Shane always backs off when I start having these thoughts, as if he can smell my fear. Sometimes our relationship feels like waltzing on a tightrope. One out-of-sync step and we'll come tumbling down.

In the meantime, I'm enjoying the view from such great heights.

"Absolutely not."

"Please? Just for one night?" I clutch my hands before me in the doorway of David's office. "I'll work overtime for free. You know, like I always do."

David glares up at me from behind his desk. "I hate dogs."

"How can you hate dogs? They're man's best friend. You're a man."

"A man who was routinely hunted by the neighbor's Doberman when I was seven."

"Dexter's part black Lab, part Great Dane, I think—both gentle breeds. He's totally chill, as Shane would say. He does everything I ask." I look down and work my boot heel into a moth-eaten hole in his dark gray rug. "Except eat, but he'll get over that. A lot of stray dogs don't eat well at first. They're nervous and scared and . . ." My voice trails off when I see David's expression. "What?"

"He didn't eat dog food?"

"I just told you that's normal, and—"

"He didn't eat dog food, he's preternaturally intelligent, and unlike Antoine, he's not afraid of Jim."

My stomach grows tight with dread. "What are you saying? What's wrong with my dog?"

David checks his watch and mutters, "Five minutes until the next program." Then he gives me a long look as he flips his ballpoint through his fingers, twirling it back and forth. I wait for him to reach the monumental decision he's obviously contemplating.

Finally he rolls his chair to reach the filing cabinet in the back corner of his cramped office. He slides out the squeaky bottom drawer.

Uh-oh. That drawer has nothing to do with radio. As a former agent of the International Agency for the Control and Management of Undead Corporeal Entities ("the Control" for short), David has seen (and staked) his share of vampires. He knows a lot more about them than I do, because some of that information is classified. I'm on what he would call a need-to-know basis, and what I would call a don't-want-to-know basis.

David pulls out a thick green hanging folder and plops it on the desk so I can see the label.

NECROZOOLOGY

Crap. Apparently I need to know.

"Vampire dogs." David flips open the folder with the end of his pen. "They tried it with a few other animals, but so far it's only worked with canids."

"Who's 'they'?"

"The Control." He glances around, as if his office is still bugged by the agency.

"Should you be telling me this?"

"If you have one in your apartment, yes."

I think about Dexter in my apartment, and the strength goes out of my legs. My butt slams the chair.

"What's wrong?" David says.

"I found him in my closet this morning, buried under a pile of blankets. He wouldn't come out, not for anything." My chest turns cold. "Oh my God. Whoever tied him up wanted him to die when the sun rose. If we hadn't found him—"

"But we did, and you saved him. If it helps, vampire dogs aren't vulnerable to things like holy water or crosses. Animals have no free will, so they're morally neutral as far as religion is concerned. They're pure instinct."

So much for *All Dogs Go to Heaven*. "Then why didn't he try to eat me?"

"Because vampires only drink the blood of their own species."

"So I have to feed him dog blood? They don't carry that at PetSmart."

"The Control can probably provide it."

"We can't tell them about Dexter!" I grip the edge of his desk. "They were probably the ones who tied him to the cross in the first place."

"Ciara, be reasonable." He sits back in his chair and spreads his hands. "We have no evidence the Control is working with whoever built that thing. Dexter might've been stolen from the lab, or maybe he escaped. He'd be safer back with the people who know how to take care of his kind."

"No way." I stand up and shove back my chair, catching its leg on the hole-y rug. "I'll get my own dog blood."

David gives me a skeptical look, then glances at his watch. "I've got to get down to the booth and change the program. We'll test Dexter after work and then decide what to do."

I carry the bulky Necrozoology folder back to my desk while David goes downstairs. Franklin's on a sales call over at the other side of the main office we share. His voice shoots up an octave, and his tone lilts as he takes on his *tres fey* public persona.

I plug my ears against his sales-queen routine and flip through the folder. Each page brings a new atrocity: vampire ferrets to be used as stealthy assassins that can slip through tiny cracks in the walls, vampire rats to spread diseases without succumbing to illness themselves. All superstrong, supersmart, and able to survive on a tiny amount of same-species blood.

I slap the folder shut. The Control is capable of anything. I don't want to bring them any deeper into my life.

Which reminds me. I open a browser window on my computer and type my father's name into the news finder, even though I have it set up to ping me with any articles that include the following terms: "Ronan O'Riley," "Travellers," "Irish Gypsies," and "Double-Crossing Jerk Who Almost Got My Boss Killed." Okay, maybe not that last one.

No results. Not that I expect to read about my father's fate in the news. To get early parole from federal prison, he worked as an undercover agent for the Control in the cult compound of Gideon Rousseau, a crazy-evil vampire who almost drained me dry. The only reason Gideon refrained from biting me was because my father had started working for him, too.

To prove his new loyalty, my dad ratted David out for staking Gideon's son and progeny, Antoine (the vampire, not the kitty). Dad's treachery resulted in the death of my Control bodyguard, so if that agency ever finds him, they'll dispense their justice in private.

My stomach squeezes my breakfast at the thought. I've got to find him before the Control does and convince him to turn himself in to the FBI or some other authority that won't kill him.

The phone jolts me out of my morbid reverie. I close the browser window and answer the call with the rote WVMP Lifeblood of Rock 'n' Roll greeting.

A young male voice responds. "Ciara, it's Jeremy Glaser from *Rolling Stone*. I heard Shane's broadcast last night. What did he mean by, quote, 'We're going to play female artists all day, one bitchin' babe after another'?"

I glance at Franklin, who's still on the line with a client. "The signal-jamming only happens when we play women vocalists, or when Regina's on."

"Wow. That's fucked up." He sounds like he needs to wipe the drool from his chin. Journalists.

"I don't know if it's connected, but someone torched the Smoking Pig after our Halloween party."

"I heard. Do you have the original tape of the broadcast?"

"Hell yeah. It's evidence, in the unlikely event the FCC ever wakes up and investigates." I give him a suspicious look, even though he can't see me. "You want it, don't you?"

"Think about it, Ciara. If this keeps up, your ratings will go through the roof."

"Why would people tune in to hear some old fart read Scripture?"

"The story isn't what he's saying. The story is the attack on women in an age when most people think sexism is dead."

"Hmm." I run my fingernails over the edge of my lower lip. "You might have something here."

"So you'll send me the tape? You agreed to give me an exclusive through the weekend." When I hesitate, he adds, "This misogyny narrative could turn it into a huge story—maybe even worth a cover."

My hands curl around my pen. If it were a pencil, it would snap with my spasm of ambition.

"Deal. I'll send you a digital copy of the broadcast. It's yours through the weekend, but Monday the mass press releases are going out. And you share with me any dirt on FAN you can dig up."

"Thanks. I'll let you know what I find."

After I hang up, I search the internal network for the audio file of the piracy.

"They want a culture war?" I murmur. "Well, here's Private Griffin reporting for duty."

# 4

## Youngstown

I pull into the quiet parking lot next to the Sherwood Animal Hospital. Next to the darkened door sits a small white metal box with a green laboratory logo.

I stop the car. "Go for it."

Shane slips out into the darkness, silent as a shadow. I hope the lab workers haven't picked up that day's samples yet. I could've come myself before sunset, just after the office closed, but no one picks a lock like Shane.

I circle around the back of the building, and before I even arrive out front again, Shane is at my passenger door. He lets himself in, and we peel out of the parking lot.

"How much?" I ask him.

He pats the pocket of his gray Steelers sweatshirt. "Ten vials of five cc's each. Hope it's enough."

"David's file says they drink about five cc's a day. It decreases by a milliliter every year they get older." I glance at his pensive face in the dashboard light. "Did you leave the note?"

" 'Dear Doctor: I've displaced all the canine blood in this receptacle. Please draw more for these tests and pass on my apologies to the dogs.' "

"Poor little puppers, having to get stuck again."

"You want me to put it back?"

"Hell no." Dexter's survival could depend on it. Ends justify the means and all.

David is waiting outside my home when we arrive. To my chagrin, my landlord, Dean, is inside the pawnshop under my apartment, even after closing time. Through the shop window I see him standing near the far shelf, probably doing inventory.

I open the door to my apartment and flick on the stairwell light. Clawing noises come from the door at the top.

"Hey, buddy," I call out, struggling to keep my voice steady. David said vampire dogs don't drink human blood, but maybe things have changed since he was in the Control. Maybe Dexter is the omnivorous T-1000 version.

No, I tell myself as I force my feet to follow Shane's battered black Chuck Taylors up the stairs. If Dexter wanted to turn me into a meal, he would've done it last night in the tub.

Shane opens the door, and Dexter is sitting in the middle of the hallway, giant red maw open in a smiling pant. He rushes forward when he sees me, and I grab the doorjamb to keep from fleeing.

Dexter inserts his rough muzzle into my hand, begging for scritchies. I rub his ears. He groans and leans against my leg, eyes rolling up in his head in doggie ecstasy. Shane squats next to him and scratches his back. Dexter's long thin tail whips so fast it creates a black blur.

Suddenly the dog breaks away and stares at David, coming up behind me. Dexter backs up, the fur on his back ruffling into a second spine.

"What's wrong, boy?" I take a step forward, and he runs down the hall into the kitchen. "David, he knows you don't like dogs."

Shane pulls two vials of blood from his sweatshirt pocket and hands them to David. "You do the honors. Make friends."

They follow me to my minuscule kitchen, where Dexter has crammed his butt against the corner cabinet. I pull the dog bowl out of the dish-drying rack while David pops the red rubber stopper off one of the vials. Dexter's ears prick, and his nostrils quiver.

David empties the blood into the cavernous bowl and sets it on the floor. Dexter leaps forward and shoves his face into the bowl.

I cringe at the slurping sounds. "Gross. I mean, good boy."

Dexter cleans the bowl, then looks up expectantly at David, wagging his tail and licking his bloody chops.

David appears oddly pleased. "You want another one?"

Dexter lets loose a booming bark. We all share a horrified look. My landlord definitely heard that, unless he's gone deaf. The dog barks again and again, his forepaws bouncing off the floor with each woof. The sound is loud enough to crack the windows—hell, maybe the building's foundation.

"Quick!" I grab David's arm. "Give him more blood!"

David fumbles with the vial's stopper, and in his haste, the blood sprays across the floor, the cabinets, and my shoes.

Dexter leaps for the life-giving liquid, claws scrabbling over the yellow linoleum. His happy huffs fill the air as he feeds, sucking up every drop of blood as efficiently as a wet-vac.

We hold our breaths, waiting for the knock on the door. My landlord is roughly the size of Shane and David put together.

Dexter finishes his second helping, then, instead of looking for a third, he waddles into the living room and steps up onto the couch.

"I guess he's full," Shane whispers to me.

"My landlord must have gone home."

Just then, a knock comes at the door. Not a knock exactly. The thudding makes the floor shake.

"Shit." I turn to the guys. "Keep him here."

I race down the hall and open the door at the top of the stairs. The pounding continues.

"Coming!" I shut the door tight behind me, then trot down to greet what I hope is a Girl Scout or a Jehovah's Witness or a tax collector. Anyone but my landlord.

Sure enough, Dean is standing on the sidewalk, hands resting on either side of my doorframe. He's the kind of man who commands respect at a glance—if it took only a glance to absorb his six-foot-seven-inch frame, the ace of spades tattoo atop his shaven head, and biceps the size of telephone poles.

"Ciara," he says in a near-whisper. "You have a dog."

I stare up into his ice blue eyes and consider telling him that the source of the booming bark was my television with Animal Planet cranked to the max. But there's honor among pseudo-thieves.

"It's temporary. He's just a stray. I swear I'll get him into a kennel when they open tomorrow morning."

"Now." He taps his fingers against the doorjamb above my head, clicking his thick silver rings against the aluminum frame. "Or you're gone tomorrow night, as in a twenty-four-hour eviction notice."

"Dean, he hasn't done any damage. He doesn't chew. He's housebroken."

"He's loud." Dean lays a thumb against his temple. "I have a migraine."

"Please." I cross one foot behind the other and put my hands behind my back, making myself look small and un-threatening. "I've always been a good tenant, right? Paid the rent on time. Never complained about the way the electric outlets are a tragedy waiting to happen. Or considered reporting it to the proper authorities."

He steps back with a sigh and crosses his arms, which is barely possible over his enormous chest. "I'm coming back tomorrow at five p.m. If that dog's not gone, I'm calling animal control, and you'll be calling a moving company."

I let out a deep breath. "Thank you. Thank you so much. I promise you won't—"

A howl pierces the temporary peace. Something slams the door at the top of the stairs. I turn toward the noise and put out my foot to take the first step.

The door bursts open in a shower of wood and brass. The doorknob bounces down the stairs, then past me onto the sidewalk. Followed by Dexter.

"Holy shit." Dean jumps back, almost to the street.

I grab Dexter's collar as he passes, bracing myself for a dislocated shoulder. But the dog stops, sits back on his haunches, and gives Dean a bloodchilling snarl.

My landlord scurries to put the parking meter between himself and the dog. "Get that thing out, then start packing."

"I'll find him a home." I try to pull Dexter back, but his back claws have dug into a crack in the concrete sidewalk. "I'll pay for the door. Just don't evict me. Please, Dean, I have nowhere to go."

"That's not my problem." He points up at my apartment. "The lease is clear—no pets allowed. Not temporary, not strays, not even a fucking fish."

"Hey, that's my dog!"

Dean and I turn to see David standing on the street corner frantically waving a leash. He runs up to us, breathless, wearing a wide smile. He must have climbed down the fire escape on the other side of the building.

"You found him!" He snaps the leash onto Dexter's collar. "I've been searching for days. How can I ever thank you?"

I put my hands on my hips. "Well, sir, he broke my door, and my landlord here wants to evict me."

David looks up into my apartment and winces. "I'll pay for all the repairs, plus an extra hundred for your trouble. I'm just so glad I got my buddy back." He squats next to Dexter, who licks him on the mouth.

I turn to Dean. "So can I stay?"

My landlord narrows his eyes at each of the three of us in turn. With horror I notice a drop of blood on Dexter's chin. I wipe it off with a tissue from my jacket pocket.

"Heh." I crumple the tissue in my hand. "Looks like a drooler."

Dean points his two forefingers at me. "If you ever bring another animal into that apartment, you're evicted. No notice. No security deposit refund."

"No animals, ever. I promise."

David wraps the end of the leash tight around his wrist. "Come on, Dexter, let's go home."

I tense, fearing the dog will balk. When David tugs on the leash, Dexter tilts his enormous head to look up at me.

"Go on," I whisper. "Have a good life."

He turns and trots alongside David down the sidewalk, occasionally throwing an adoring gaze at his new owner, the guy who brought him blood.

Shane comes out of the apartment and gives Dean a casual nod and a "Hey." He puts his arm around me, squeezing my shoulder as we watch my new best friend walk out of my life.


The trip to Youngstown has a party feel for the first three hours. Shane and I play all our mutually favorite CDs. I keep myself awake with a series of cinnamon-carpeted mochaccinos from Pennsylvania Turnpike rest stops.

Once we pass Pittsburgh, though, Shane grows quieter, and my excitement takes the form of having to pee.

To distract both of us, I ponder out loud the four-legged mystery that is Dexter the Dog.

"Why do you think out of the three humans we've seen him meet, Dexter only liked me, at least initially?"

"Because you're a dog person?" Shane looks at me from the passenger seat. "Or maybe the vampire in him sensed your anti-holy nature."

I grip the steering wheel at the reminder of my secret "specialness"—secret, at least, to those who weren't at David's house the day I accidentally healed Shane's holy-water burns with a mere taste of my blood. If anyone other than Lori and the WVMP staff discovered I had this power, I'd turn into a walking pharmacy for vampires.

I tell myself it's my devout skepticism that kills the magic of holy water, but it's hard to know for sure without controlled experiments. Any experiment that involves me losing blood is an automatic non-starter.

"It must be the dog-person thing," I tell him, "because David said vampire animals aren't affected by holy substances, since they're morally neutral."

I bite my lip as soon as the words leave my mouth, realizing the implication: that vampire humans like Shane are evil, a notion I personally think is bullshit. Just because the church is against them doesn't make them bad. I've known enough shifty preachers (like my parents) to know that morality isn't always on the side of the folks wielding Bibles.

After a long pause, Shane says quietly, "Yeah, that makes sense." His voice's sadness shrivels my heart.

It's past midnight when we cross the Ohio border near Youngstown.

"The cemetery's on the other side, off the interstate," he says. "But if you want to see what my hometown is like . . ."

"Would you like me to drive through the city?"

He taps his fingers on the window as he decides. "Just

down the main drag. Not back to the neighborhood." He adds under his breath, "Maybe next time."

Shane directs me through the downtown area. I don't know what I thought I'd see in the city the steel companies abandoned in the seventies. Was I expecting gang wars? Post-apocalyptic burned-out buildings? Mothers weeping openly on street corners?

Other than the bars near the university, the city seems pretty dead at this hour—but sleepy dead, not slit-wrist dead. Most of the buildings are boxy, mid-twentieth century utilitarian, but a few soar above the skyline with an older, grander ambition. The main street is lined with small leafless trees that have already been decorated with white Christmas lights.

"Lot better than I remembered it," he whispers.

I feel a pang of jealousy. Shane has a hometown, he comes from somewhere. Until I was sixteen and in foster care, I never stayed in the same spot for more than two weeks. My stint in Sherwood is like an eternity at six and a quarter years, but it'll never be where I'm from. There is no such place.

To our surprise, the Catholic cemetery's large iron gate stands wide open. A marquee sign reads NOVEMBER 1– 2: OPEN ALL NIGHT FOR ALL SOULS' OBSERVANCE.

I turn into the driveway, and Shane points out several cars parked near graves. "I guess the immigrant population has gone up, and they've gotten tired of chasing people out."

"Wouldn't most people just come during the day?"

"They're probably shift workers. Youngstown has always had all-night businesses, going back to the steel mill days."

We park next to the cemetery's main office, a squat marble building.

Inside, the lobby is lit with a dimmed chandelier and a scattering of cream-colored candles. Behind a high desk, a middle-aged man in a black suit and white shirt greets us with a polite smile. He's short, plump, and tan, with a set of rimless eyeglasses—hardly the pale, lanky hunchback I was expecting.

Shane approaches the desk. "Hi. Uh, I'm looking for Evan McAllister. His grave, I mean."

"Of course." The attendant taps a few keys on his computer. "Is that Mick or Mack?"

"Mick. With two L's." He shoves his hands inside his sweatshirt pockets. "Evan is spelled—"

"Here it is. Section seven, row six, number four." He pulls out a map of the cemetery and draws the route with a pencil.

Shane gives the attendant a quick nod. "Thanks. I know the way. Looks like he's near my grandparents." He turns and heads for the car, shoulders hunched, hands never leaving his pockets.

I peer through a door on the opposite side of the lobby. "Are there bodies back there?" I ask the man.

"It's the mausoleum, yes."

" 'Kay, thanks." I hurry after Shane, trying not to run. The moment we're in the car, my fingers fumble for the electric lock switch. They snap shut, and I let out a heavy breath.

Shane notices the locks. "Are you scared?"

I squeeze the steering wheel. "I've never been in a cemetery before."

He stares at me. "How is that possible?"

"My mom's mom died when I was two, and we never drove back to South Carolina to visit her grave. My dad's side wanted nothing to do with us after he left his wife to run away with my mom."

Shane shrugs at our surroundings. "We came here almost every Sunday after Mass. My parents had big families, and some aunt or uncle or cousin was always having a birthday or death-iversary or whatever." He points to the gear shift. "Can we go?"

"Sorry." I shove it into drive and pull into the lane, tires squealing. A horn honks. I wave an apology to the passing car and give a nervous laugh. "Heh. If I got killed here, at least I'd have a short trip to the funeral."

"Relax." He puts his hand over mine on the gear shift, the wool of his fingerless gloves scratching my chapped skin. "Not that it matters, but you couldn't be buried here, since you're not Catholic."

Easing down the lane at the posted five miles per hour, we pass a Mexican family spreading out a picnic blanket. "Is this where you would've been buried?" The last word flutters, my breath catching at the thought of his truly dead body.

"Yeah. There used to be a rule that suicides couldn't be interred on hallowed ground, but they changed it."

The silence stretches out, until I can't hold back my question. "Did you leave a note?"

He snorts. "It was pathetic. Regina saved me that embarrassment after she made me. We burned it before we moved to Pittsburgh."

"What did you tell your family?"

"Nothing. I just left."

Cutting all ties—one of the downsides of becoming a vampire. "By order of the Control."

"Not exactly. The Control likes vampires to burn our bridges, not leave them to rot. Skipping town is messy and causes missing-person searches." He shifts his too-long legs under my dashboard for the thirtieth time. "Finally the Control stepped in and got my family off my trail."

"How?"

"My dad and I pretty much hated each other. I wasn't the son he wanted, and he wasn't the father I wanted, since I would've preferred someone who wasn't a total shithead."

"Wouldn't we all?" I cram down my own resentment and keep listening.

"We hadn't spoken in years. So the Control forged my handwriting in a note to my father, asking him to come see me before one of my gigs, saying I want to make peace. He and Mom showed up and found me with a lap full of Regina."

He rubs the side of his jaw. "And probably a table full of drugs, I don't remember."

"I bet Regina and your folks hit it off like old friends."

He grunts. "Yeah. Thirty seconds after they walked in, she and my dad were writing whole new dictionaries of profanity." He runs his fingertips along the seal of the passenger-side window. "My mom didn't say anything. She just cried." He points up ahead. "Turn right. We're almost there."

I obey, fighting the impulse to drive the car straight through the wrought-iron fence. "So that was that?"

"That was that. Another Control mission accomplished. I never heard from my family again."

Until two months ago, as I recall, when Shane's sister called the station to tell him that their dad had terminal cancer and wanted to see him one last time. Colonel Lanham, our main contact at the Control, said no way, not even a phone call. I think Shane was relieved. He never talks about it.

"We're here," he says.

I pull to the side of the lane, and we get out of the car. The light from the newly risen quarter moon makes it easy to see which grave is Evan McAllister's. The soil is freshly turned, still lumpy and grassless six weeks after he died.

Shane closes the car door softly, then pulls up his hood— probably more for privacy than warmth.

I hurry after him, hugging my arms. My eyes flick back and forth, and I regret not having another set in the back of my head. I don't believe in ghosts or zombies with my cerebral cortex, but the lizard brain at the base of my skull turns my blood to ice at the thought of dead bodies under my feet.

I join Shane to stand at the foot of Evan's grave, our toes an inch away from the dug soil. The moonlight glistens on the gray marble headstone.

Something moves in the corner of my eye. My neck twitches, and I see two women, their heads covered by thick hoods to ward off the cold breeze. One of them carries a big wreath looped over her arm. She watches as the other woman lays bouquets of flowers on select graves, crosses herself, then plants a quick kiss on each headstone.

I look up at Shane, whose eyes are closed. I wonder how I'd feel if my own father died. I suppose I'd be sad and angry and relieved, and everything in between.

Shane gets on one knee and reaches out as if to touch the soil. Then he yanks his hand back and tucks it under his other arm. I wonder if the ground is consecrated, if it would burn him like holy water. The two women move closer.

Wind rattles the leafless branches of a nearby tree, and it sounds like the bones of skeletons assembling themselves, ready to rise and greet us. Fallen leaves skittering across the blacktop make me think of corpses clawing the insides of their coffins.

I draw in a deep breath through my nose to calm my pounding pulse. A cemetery is a bad place to have an active imagination.

The women stand a few rows away from us. Shane remains kneeling with his head bowed, though I'm sure his sensitive ears can hear them.

I look up to see the younger woman, the one with the wreath, staring at us. She taps the older woman on the shoulder, interrupting a moment of prayer. They confer for a moment, then the wreath-carrier stalks over.

"Who are you," she says, "and what are you doing at my father's grave?"

Shane stiffens. His head jerks up, and he stares at me, eyes sparking with panic.

Busted.

"Let's go," I whisper. "We can make it if we run."

He slowly stands and turns to her, pulling back his hood.

"Hey, Eileen."

The woman drops the wreath. Her hand flies to her mouth.

"*Shane?*" The older lady runs forward, stopping a few feet away. "Shane, it's you. It's really you."

His face crumples, and his voice cracks. "Mom . . ."

She stumbles the last few steps and flings herself into his arms. He clutches her tight, murmuring incoherent noises of comfort and contrition.

"Shane, let me see you." His mom holds his face between her palms. "Sweet Mary, you're more handsome than ever."

I look at Eileen, who, despite the tear tracking her cheek, glares at her brother with undisguised hostility. The breeze spills her curly hair over the lowered hood of her coat, and the moonlight shines on streaks of silver among the light brown strands.

Shane takes his mother's hands. "Why are you here this time of night?"

"Your sister works the swing shift at the prison." Her words tumble over each other. "She went back to nursing school after the boys were old enough. You have another nephew now." She looks at me, showing in an instant where Shane got his pale blue eyes. "Who's this?"

"My girlfriend Ciara. She drove me up."

"Thank you for bringing my boy home." She wipes a tear from under her glasses and gives me a smile. "Oh!" Her smile widens, revealing laugh lines and crow's-feet in an otherwise smooth face. "Come back to the house, both of you. I'll make some nice—"

"Mom, we can't stay."

For some reason, I share her obvious disappointment.

"But why not?" she asks him.

"Ciara has to work early in the morning."

"You're driving home in the middle of the night?" She turns to me. "With all the crazies on the road?"

"I'll be driving," he says. "I work nights now, at a radio station."

Eileen harrumphs. "We know all about your radio station." She hasn't moved any closer. "We saw you on the Internet, with your monster gimmick and your fancy little MySpace page."

He glances at me. "My what?"

His mother waves her hand at Eileen. "Come give your baby brother a hug. After all these years."

His sister crosses her arms. "Yeah, twelve years. Not a word, not a phone call, even when Dad got sick."

"I couldn't. I can't explain, but—why didn't you tell me he died?" Shane's voice lowers to a rumble. "I had to read the obit on the *Vindicator*'s Web site."

"Because you never called," she snarls. "Too busy playing vampire, and before that? Invisible man." She picks up the wreath. "I got no brother."

"Hush." Mrs. McAllister stamps her foot. "He's here now, and that's all that counts."

"Eileen's right, Mom." Shane takes his hand out of hers. "I shouldn't have disappeared. It's all my fault."

"No." She wipes a flood of new tears with her knit gloves. "We were so worried when we couldn't find you. Especially after you'd tried—" She glances at me.

"Ciara knows about that," Shane says. "And I'm better now."

She makes her plea to me this time. "You sure you can't stay the night?"

"I'm really sorry." I pull a tissue out of my pocket and check that it's not the one I wiped Dexter's chin with. No blood—just lint—so I hand it to her.

"Thank you." Mrs. McAllister wipes her eyes, then wraps her hand around Shane's wrist. "But you'll come back soon? For Thanksgiving? Or Christmas?"

I turn away, not wanting to see her face when he breaks her heart.

"Sure, Mom," I hear him say instead. "Let's plan on it."

# 5

## It's A Man's Man's Man's World

"He said *what*?"

"You heard me." I lower the volume on my cell phone to guard my eardrums against David's shouting.

"He can't visit them for holidays! How will he explain why he can't go out in the sun?"

I turn onto the long gravel driveway leading to the station. "I think he plans to tell them he's a vampire."

"They'll have him committed."

"Unless he proves it. Shows his fangs, drips holy water on his skin, lifts a car above his head with one hand." Okay, he can't actually do that last one, not for another seventy years or so. "Are you going to tell the Control?"

"Of course not."

I brake hard as a squirrel dashes across the driveway ahead of me. The dense woods keep the station and its transmission tower secluded—just the way the DJs like it. Not that it prevents admirers from leaving gifts on our doorstep—flowers, teddy bears dressed as vampires, bags of what often turns out to be real blood.

David continues. "Shane's young enough that the damage of accidentally running into his relatives isn't irreversible. But any further contact is a direct violation of Control rules. Civilians can't learn the vampires' secret."

"Other than the thousands of civilians listening to WVMP."

"Who think they're just pretending. Besides, fans don't pick up on their odd patterns. A vampire's human family would notice them avoiding the sun and never aging."

I slow down to take a tight bend in the lane. "But what if Shane tells the McAllisters the truth?"

"You think they can be trusted?"

"Eileen acted pissed, but deep down I think she was glad to see him. Shane said they used to be really close."

"And his mom?"

"Codependency out the wazoo. She wasn't even mad at Shane, like she should've been." I pause for a moment, recollecting the details. "She wore a crucifix and a Knights of Columbus jacket. If she's high-octane Catholic, she might give religious meaning to his being a vampire." I pull into the clearing, where Franklin is standing in front of the ramshackle building. "Maybe even call for an exorcism."

"Listen. The Control will stop at nothing to protect the vampires' secret. If Shane doesn't make his family go away, the Control will do it for him."

"I'll talk to him." I drive onto the grass to avoid running over Franklin, who appears to be photographing the ground in the center of the tiny parking lot. "How's Dexter?"

"Safe in the basement with the windows covered. No apparent interest in eating Antoine."

"Good. Thanks for saving my ass last night with my land-lord."

He chuckles. "Out of professionalism, I'll avoid any comment on your metaphorical ass."

My face heats, and I clear my throat. "I gotta go. Franklin and I have that early meeting with the, um, people." A second later I think of the word. "Clients."

I hang up and open the car door, almost forgetting to put it in park first (my real car—which is now sort of Shane's car—is a stick shift, but Elizabeth's Mercedes is an automatic), then hurry over to see what Franklin is—

Uh-oh.

Franklin lowers the camera and gives me a sullen glare. "Lovely morning, isn't it?"

Red spray paint covers a large white sign, forming the four familiar words:

YOUR GOING TO HELL

"It's still tacky." Franklin holds up his forefinger, tipped in red. "The paint, I mean, it's not dry. I must've interrupted them by coming to the office early."

"Did you see anyone?"

"Nope, but thank God we had that client schmooze-fest to get ready for." He points to a broken bottle lying on the driveway. "Or we would've ended up just like the Pig."

I approach the bottle and catch the nostril-waxing scent of gasoline. A rag is stuffed into its mouth, which is still intact. The arsonist must not have had time to light it before escaping.

My stomach twists at the image of WVMP going up in flames. The vampires would be safe in their apartment downstairs—temporarily, at least—but the ensuing investigation would raise questions we can't answer.

I turn back to Franklin. "Tell me you didn't call the police."

"I'm not stupid. Travis said he'd investigate after sunset. He's in the office now."

I examine the sign—the "handwriting" is the same as the one at the Smoking Pig. "Hard not to interpret all this as some kind of warning."

"If we didn't back down in the face of Gideon, we're not going to listen to a bunch of Bible beaters."

"But we did back down to Gideon."

"Only long enough for you to kill him." Franklin takes another photo of the graffiti. "These assholes could at least threaten us with proper grammar."

I enter the station via the cellar in the back of the building, since the front door is locked to prevent vampire flameouts. A double-sealed door leads to the downstairs lounge, from which I climb the stairs to the main office.

Typing sounds come from Elizabeth's old office to my left. I turn the corner to find Travis.

"Just the vampire I wanted to see."

He takes out his earbuds and gives me a dull glower. "What?"

"Hate to interrupt your Faith Hill jamfest, but I have a fun job for you, possibly connected to the arson attempt." I tell him about the big honkin' cross. He listens with his arms folded over his chest, his dark green eyes growing more guarded with every sentence. "So can you come with me and David tonight to investigate?" I ask him.

He glances away, clearly freaked by the idea of getting so close to the BHC. "Love to." He focuses on his laptop. "But I'm busy with other cases."

"You have no other cases. You're writing a memoir so you can be as famous as the DJs."

"The Control won't lemme write a memoir, so it's a novel now." He adjusts the angle of the screen. "Autobiographical."

"About a vampire detective. How original."

"It's hard." He scratches the back of his head, ruffling the short dark hair at his nape. "I keep accidentally writing scenes that happen during the day."

"Then it's not very autobiographical."

His eyes narrow. "Don't remind me." He starts typing again, fingers smashing the keys.

Poor Travis is one of those bitter nonvoluntary vampires. On top of the violent attack that turned him into an undead blood drinker—who saw me as his first meal—his maker Gideon left him to starve, in the vampire equivalent of infanticide. The DJs took him in and raised him as their own, thus ensuring his everlasting loyalty, if not his taste in music.

I sit on the corner of the desk. "You knew the day would come when I would call in my favor."

He looks up without raising his head. "I already made up for trying to kill you."

"That's debatable, but it's not what I meant." By reflex, my hand rubs the left side of my neck. "I meant that other favor."

He crosses his arms again, scowling. "I didn't ask for your blood to save my life."

"Then you should have spit instead of swallowed."

Travis sighs and opens a new word processing document. "What do you got?"

I tell him everything we know about FAN and the cross and Dexter and the arsons, both attempted and successful.

From the outer main office, my direct line rings. I hop off the desk and hurry out to my phone.

It's Jeremy from *Rolling Stone*.

"Thanks for the broadcast files," he says. "Anything new?"

I glance at Travis through the open door of Elizabeth's

office. He's already put his earbuds back in and is swaying to what is probably the sensation of the week out of Nashville.

"Maybe," I tell Jeremy. "I'll e-mail you from my personal account. Late tonight."

"Good." He hesitates. "Can I ask you a few specific questions about the vampires?"

"You mean the DJs?" I plop into my chair, ready to bullshit. "Fire away."

"They live at the station, right?"

"Sure." I keep my voice high-pitched to sound like it's part of the PR spiel. "They live in a special underground bunker here that keeps out the sunlight."

"Do they automatically fall asleep at sunrise?"

"The one I'm staring at right now looks reasonably alert." I wave to Travis, and he gives me the finger in return. "They can stay awake all day, just like we can stay up all night. Makes them cranky, though. That's why we repeat their nightly broadcasts the next morning and afternoon rather than have them do live shows during the day. Per their contracts, overtime is paid in blood."

The truth is so fun sometimes.

"And they're immortal, right?"

"Theoretically. They get physically stronger as they age, they can't get diseases, and it takes a lot to hurt them." I remember how in their fight to the death, Shane chopped off Gideon's arm, and it stopped bleeding in about three seconds. "Bullets, cars, poisons—none of them work."

Jeremy pauses. "So what *can* kill them?"

Something in his voice makes me sit up. I try to keep my tone light. "Well, that's a secret, of course."

"What about fire? Fire kills everything, right?"

My stomach tightens. Instead of answering, I decide to let him keep talking.

"Ciara, do you think the arson at the Smoking Pig was

an attempt on the DJs' lives? That maybe someone out there believes they really are vampires, and that this is the only way to kill them all?"

"The Pig was closed when it caught fire. If someone was trying to kill the DJs, wouldn't it help if they were actually present at the time?"

"Maybe it was a warning. Makes sense, considering the tone and content of the pirate broadcasts."

He sounds so self-satisfied, and I wish I could tell him I've already figured all this out, but that would give too much away.

"I have someone working on the case now." I scribble Jeremy's name and phone number on a pink sticky note. "Here's the deal: you get me some info on the Family Action Network like you promised yesterday, and I'll share our findings with you."

"Digging dirt is what I'm best at."

"Have a good weekend." I hang up before he can ask any more questions, then bring the paper with Jeremy's name and number over to Travis.

"What's this?" he asks me.

"Your next subject. I want to know everything about the man who wants to know everything about us."

We'll see who digs the most dirt, Mr. Muckraker, and who gets buried.


"Sorry to drag you along."

"Are you kidding?" Lori grins at me, her face reflecting the red of the stoplight. She gestures at the woods looming next to the highway leading out of Sherwood. "Creeping around spooky spots is my ideal Friday night."

She's not kidding. Lori's passion is Civil War ghosts, a passion she feeds by being secretary/treasurer of the Sher-

wood Paranormal Investigative Team (SPIT). They have yet
to confirm an actual ghost sighting, which I suppose makes
them useful in a different way than they intended.

We pass the cross and park on a turnoff down the road, out
of sight. Lori points to a red pickup as we get out of the car.
"Whose truck is that?"

"Travis. Our staff detective."

"Is he still crazy?"

"No. Shane and Regina make sure he gets his twice-a-
night blood rations so he doesn't attack civilians."

Lori switches on her flashlight as we enter the trees surrounding the cross, which is still flashing red, white, and blue
from the spotlight. "So what's Travis's compulsion?" she asks
me. "Counting? Sorting?"

"Nothing yet. Too young." Shane once explained the
vampires' obsessive-compulsive behaviors to me. The world
moves so fast beyond them, they need to feel like they control
something. It's the only way to feel sane, he says.

David approaches us when we reach the clearing, shoes
crunching over the rocky soil.

"How's Dexter?" I ask him.

"Great. I got him this light-up collar so I can see him in
the backyard at night. And he has a thing for squeaky-balls."

"So you like him now?"

"Do I have a choice?"

"Not until I can find a basement apartment that accepts
pets."

"What about Elizabeth's place down in Rockville?"

"No way." The thought of living in the dead-undead vampire's former home totally skeeves me. "Too long a commute."

Travis is staring at the top of the cross with a pair of binoculars, a long metal tool—a bolt cutter, I assume—resting
against his right leg. A tiny orange glow rises and falls in the
darkness as he takes a drag from his cigarette.

"Hey, what did Shane tell you about smoking?" I stalk up to him. "It could kill you."

"I'm already dead." Travis drops it on the ground and crushes it under the heel of his scuffed black work boots.

"At your age, all it takes is a stiff breeze while you're lighting up, and you'll go poof like a piece of flash paper."

He looks at Lori, and his scowl fades. "Well, hello. Have we met?"

Since Travis rarely smiles around the office, I often forget how his vampiric nature has transformed his formerly dorky expressions. His eyes glint in the light of the cross, his freckled face radiates a magnetic warmth, and the breeze seems made to sweep a few rogue curls across his forehead.

Lori returns his smile and extends her hand. They introduce themselves, even though they met three months ago and damn well know it.

"Can you see anything?" I ask him, to distract his attention from my best friend.

Travis waves the bolt cutter at the top of the structure. "Definitely an antenna up there. It doesn't go too far past the tip of the cross, so it's hard to see."

"If that's an antenna," David says, "then we know what we're going to find in that." He points to the metal box at the base. A thin wire runs from it up the length of the cross.

"Stand back." Travis wraps the bolt cutter's teeth around the loop of the padlock. The lock breaks with a metallic snap that makes Lori jump.

David compares the lock to the new one he brought, then hands the old one to me. Its dull steel feels mundane against my skin—not too warm or too cold.

David uses the bolt cutter to pry open the metal cabinet from a distance, as if he expects something to jump out. Beside me, Lori retreats a step.

Nothing appears but a black box with blinking lights. The

name of a Japanese electronics brand shines in dull silver on the corner of the box.

I pocket the padlock. "I take it that's a repeater."

"Yep." David pulls out a small flashlight. "This is what shifts the original transmission to match our frequency." He draws a gloved finger over the console. "The puzzle is, how are they switching it on and off on command?"

"Let's find out." I dial the station on my cell phone. Noah answers in his velvet voice.

"WVMP, the Lifeblood of Rock 'n' Roll. How may I help you tonight?"

"Hey, Noah. We're ready when you are."

"Most excellent timing. I was about to cue the next song."

"Put me on speakerphone so I can hear when you play it."

"One moment."

Soon I hear his voice echoing within the studio. I acknowledge him, then mute my phone.

While I wait, I notice Lori showing off her electromagnetic frequency reader to Travis. The thing looks like a cross between a *Star Trek* tricorder and a barbecue grill lighter.

"Normally we use EMF to detect ghosts," she tells him, "but it might help here, to see when the remote transmission comes in telling the repeater to turn on and mess up their broadcast."

"You ever seen a ghost?" he asks her with a straight face.

Noah speaks on the air, obscuring Lori's reply.

"That was 'Babylon's Burning' by the Upsetters with Max Romeo. Next we have 'Stay' by Marcia Griffiths, the Empress of Reggae. Lovely lady indeed, and if you ask her about me today, I guarantee she still remember that long night in Kingston."

Yellow lights on the repeater start to glow and blink.

"Look at that." David aims the flashlight on a small black component the size of a pencil sharpener, fastened to the top of the repeater. A steady red light shines in its center. "Must be the transmitter."

"I'm reading an EMF spike." Lori holds her contraption closer to her face. "Something's definitely coming in."

Noah comes back on the phone, off the speaker. "I'll check the FM signal and see if we're on." After a long moment, he sighs. "Bastards, they're on our air. What is wrong with these people?"

"Testosterone imbalance. Probably impotence, too."

Noah chuckles. "I'll switch back to a man on the next song."

I cast a nervous glance at our surroundings. "Might as well do it now. It's not as if anyone can hear you."

"Good point. And good luck."

I put the phone back in my pocket and watch the console with the rest of them.

"Another spike," Lori says.

The yellow lights on the console fade as the radio transmission stops.

The tiny box still glows red. David reaches for it.

I seize his elbow. "What are you doing?"

"Disconnecting it." He shrugs off my grip. "Don't worry, I'll make it look accidental. They can't report it, anyway, since what they're doing is illegal."

"But if we disconnect it," I point out, "they won't be able to interrupt our broadcast."

He rests his hand on the repeater. "That's the idea."

"Then we lose our victim status and all the media attention that goes with it."

David gives me a look of disbelief. "You aren't seriously suggesting we let this continue."

"I've already had calls from reporters wanting the tape of the piracy from Halloween."

"And you said no, right?"

I put my hands in my pockets. "It's free publicity, David."

"You gave the tape to reporters?"

"Just the *Rolling Stone* guy. But I've got press releases waiting to go out Monday with more copies of the broadcast." I shift my feet in response to his stare. "With your permission, of course."

He reaches for the transmitter. "I'm ending this."

"No!" I grab his elbow again. "We can snuff it whenever we want. And they don't know we know about it, which gives us power."

"You don't get it, do you?" He straightens and faces me. "This is about principle, not publicity. They're stealing from us. They want to destroy WVMP."

"And until we find out why, we should let it go on. What's to stop them from building another one of these next week?"

"Money. Time. The law."

I notice Lori and Travis again. He's leaning one hand against the cross, feet crossed in a casual pose as he and Lori converse in a tone too intimate for my liking.

I return my focus to David. "We don't know if money, time, and the FCC are an obstacle to these people, because we don't know who they are."

"And the last thing we need is some ambitious journalist digging a little too deep." He turns back to the repeater. "It's safer to make it all go away."

"Uh, guys?"

Travis is still standing with his hand pressed against the cross. But now he's not leaning on it, he's pulling away.

His hand's not coming with him.

"I'm stuck." He yanks his arm again. "Holy shit, I'm stuck to this thing."

Lori covers her mouth. "Oh my God. What's happening?"

No chains or ties are binding him. His palm is adhered flat to the metal like a kid's tongue on a frozen flagpole.

David grabs Travis's wrist and helps him pull. The skin stretches but doesn't peel away from the cross.

"Ow, stop!" Travis grits his teeth. "You're gonna break my wrist."

David turns to me. "Did you touch it?"

I step back. "I didn't do anything."

"No, I mean, did you touch it without getting stuck? It might be a vampire trap."

"They have those things?"

"If by 'they,' you mean the Control, then yes." He takes my shoulders. "Now think. Tonight, or on Halloween, did you touch the cross?"

I chew my lip while I remember. "The other night." I point at it. "It was really cold. It didn't match the air."

"It's getting colder." Travis's breath rasps shallow and quick. "What if I can't get it loose before sunrise?"

"Don't worry." David holds his palms out, fingers spread, in a calm cool boss pose. "Worse comes to worst, we'll cut off your hand."

"*What?!* No way." He backs away from David, as far as he can. "I need this hand. It's my favorite."

"It'll grow back." David tilts his head in admission. "Eventually."

Travis whimpers. Lori steps up to him, wringing her own hands.

"Does it hurt?" she asks him.

He reins in his panic and squares his shoulders. "Naw, not really. I'll be okay."

While they share a moment, David takes me aside. "If this is a Control vampire trap, we can't get his hand off without a neutralizer."

"I don't suppose you have one lying around your house with the stakes and samurai sword."

"Even if I did, I'd need a special code to release him."

"Can you call the Control and have them come help?"

David frowns. "I could, but if they've booby-trapped this cross, that means they're in league with FAN. Which means we can't trust them anymore."

"We don't have much choice." I lower my voice further. "If we cut him free, there'll be evidence." My stomach tilts at the thought. "His hand would still be attached to the cross, and there'd be blood everywhere."

"But if the Control gets involved—"

"Wait." Thinking of blood reminds me of another possibility. "Maybe I could neutralize it myself." I walk over to the cross, imagining its resentment pulsing against me. "If I'm really the anti-holy—"

Lori pulls me back. "Be careful."

"I've already touched it."

"But that was before. Maybe it wasn't activated then."

She might be right. But my instincts say this thing has no power over me.

I take a deep breath and slap my hand against the cross.

Nothing happens. I keep my palm on the metal for a few moments, then pull it away. Not stuck, at least. I try again, pushing harder against the cold metal.

"Anything?" I ask Travis.

He tugs on his hand. "Nope."

I place both palms, along with my forehead, against the cross. I focus on skeptical thoughts and try to remember the last episode I saw of Penn & Teller's *Bullshit*.

"Hurry up," Travis whines. I turn to glare at him and notice that his fangs are starting to show. Shane told me that very young vampires tend to "sharpen" under stress.

"Put those things away," I tell him, "or we'll leave you—"

I suddenly realize what's missing, the only thing that can save a vampire from holy water. It sure as hell isn't the power of positive thinking.

I curse under my breath, then turn to David. "Is your EMT kit handy?"

"At the house. Why?"

"Get me a sterile blade."

His eyes narrow in confusion, then widen as he realizes what I mean to do. "Are you serious?"

"Just do it before I change my mind."

David nods. "Be back in a minute." He trots into the trees toward the road.

"Ciara, what are you planning?" Lori says.

I slowly sink to sit on the ground against the cross. "Something I'm sure I'll regret."

"Thanks. Again." Travis stares at my neck. "You know, my fangs are sterile."

"Shut up or I'll cut off your hand myself—with the scalpel, not the sword."

After a long, uncomfortable silence, Travis says, "I could really use a cigarette right now."

Lori steps to his side. "Let me light it for you so you won't catch fire."

"Well, thanks, hon." He gives her the lighter and a cigarette, which she puts in her mouth. "Ciara, by the way, I checked out that *Rolling Stone* reporter. He's for real. World's most boring background—not even a parking ticket or a bounced check."

"Why does he want to know so much about vampires?"

"Cuz it's his job?" He looks at Lori, who's burned half his cigarette in her attempt to help. "You have to inhale at the same time as you light the end."

"Is there any chance Jeremy could be involved with FAN?" I ask Travis. "Or whoever's funding them?"

"I could do a deeper background check," he says. "Assuming I survive the night."

Lori erupts into a violent coughing fit, having finally lit the cigarette. Travis pats her on the back, murmuring an apology. I tune them out and try to gird up my courage for what I'm about to do.

All too soon, David arrives with his red EMT bag. Lori holds the flashlight for him while he puts on a pair of latex gloves, then digs out a scalpel and inserts a clean blade onto the tip.

My hands shake as I tear open a foil package of alcohol wipes. I roll up my sleeve and swab the inside of my left forearm. I never noticed how pale it is.

David comes toward me with the scalpel.

"No way." I reach for the blade. "I prefer my pain self-inflicted."

He reluctantly hands me the instrument. "Just a surface slice. Don't open a vein or we'll be taking you to the hospital."

"My best friend in high school used to cut herself all the time. I know how it's done." I grip the scalpel handle. "She said it made her feel better."

I stand up and move closer to the cross. When I lay the blade against my forearm, Lori lets out a whimper, then slaps her hand over her mouth. I can't look at Travis; he's probably drooling.

I close my eyes and lower the blade to my skin.

It doesn't hurt much at all. I hold out my arm toward Travis. "Go ahead. Get it over with."

"Uh, Ciara?" David says. "You didn't break the skin."

"Oh." I open my eyes to see my arm unblemished.

David takes my hand with a gentle touch. "Let me try."

For a moment I consider it, but the act seems too intimate.

I take a deep breath and press the blade against my arm, harder this time. The pain shoots out like lightning in every direction. I draw the scalpel along my arm, one inch, then another, hissing. A dark liquid line appears and swells. Blood, black in the night, oozes from the line and drips over my skin. I stare in fascination, the sight reminding me of the opening credits to a cheesy horror movie, where the words dribble down the screen.

Travis clears his throat.

I look up, the spell broken. "Sorry. Here."

"Wait." David moves behind Travis, withdrawing a stake from his inside coat pocket. He raises the point behind the vampire's back, aimed at his heart. "Don't make me say the 'one false move' line."

Travis rolls his eyes. "I won't hurt her."

I move closer to him and raise my arm. "Remember, no sucking." I turn my head away.

Travis takes my elbow. His lips graze my skin an inch below the wound, where I can already feel a stream of blood. At the first swallow, his grip tightens and trembles. I look at Lori, who watches the procedure with horrified absorption. When our eyes meet, she reaches out and squeezes my other hand.

"It might take a couple minutes," I remind them. "When Shane was burned—"

"Hey, it worked."

I turn to see Travis staring at his liberated hand like he thought he'd never see it again. I tug my arm out of his grip with as little disgust as I can muster.

"Amazing." David moves back to his EMT bag and withdraws a packet of gauze, which he gives to Lori. "Open that for her." He keeps a careful eye on Travis, who seems to be making an effort not to look at my wound.

As am I. "Gotta sit down." Without waiting for help, I sink onto the dirt and put my head between my knees.

Lori crouches next to me and presses the gauze to my arm. "You'll be okay." She rubs my back. "You hardly lost any blood."

"It's not that. All this time I was hoping that healing Shane's holy-water scars was just a fluke, or that maybe he was the special one and not me." I look up at David. "Why am I like this?"

"I don't know." He carefully reinserts the stake in his inside jacket pocket. "In all my days with the Control, I never heard of anyone with this power."

"I bet lots of people have it, but hardly anyone ever meets a vampire, much less gives them blood right after a holy-water injury, so no one would ever know." I point to the sparkly night sky. "It's like what they say about aliens. There's probably tons of them, but the chances of finding them in this huge galaxy are close to zip."

"Maybe." He turns back to the repeater box.

"Are you going to unplug the transmitter?"

"No." He closes the box and puts on the new lock. "While I was fetching the EMT kit, I thought about what you said. How we shouldn't tip our hand until we have more information." He clicks the lock shut and tugs on it to test it. "We can always disable it later, but there's no turning back once we do."

I look up at the cross. "Why didn't it burn Travis up instead of trapping him? It'd be quicker that way."

David grunts. "If they hate vampires, they wouldn't want them to have a quick end. Imagine those hours, sitting there, watching the sky get lighter and lighter."

Lori gives a sympathetic moan and squeezes Travis's freed hand.

I imagine Shane stuck to the cross, awaiting certain death, then turn my darkest scowl on the repeater box. "And they call *us* evil."

# 6

## Basket Case

Late Saturday night, Shane speaks to me just as I'm falling asleep, as he is wont to do. "Ciara, you still awake?"

"Not if you need me to form complete." I rub my eyes. "Sentences."

Standing at my bedroom's stereo, he lowers the volume on a soft, thrumming Morphine tune. "I have the most kickin' idea."

I smile at his outdated slang. "What's that, Sweet Child O' the Nineties?"

With an electronic chirp, he sets our cell phone alarms for an hour before morning twilight, then slides back under the sheets with me. "Come home with me for Christmas. To Youngstown."

I shiver, and not just at the touch of his body, which even at its warmest after a full meal is still a degree cooler than mine. I shiver because I'd hoped to avoid this conversation.

"I figured we could spend Christmas Eve night at my mom's," he continues, "then tell them we have to leave that night to drive to your parents'."

I keep my eyes closed, not wanting to see the hope on his face. "Don't you work on even-numbered days?"

"Then we'll go December twenty-third. Whatever." Just as he settles in beside me, his phone rings. "Shit. Hang on, I know what this is about." He gets up and fetches his phone from my desk. "Hey, Regina." He sounds like he's holding back a sigh when he says, "Yep, daylight savings time, I know. I'll be home an hour early." Pause. "Okay, two hours early." His voice is level and patient, considering the nagging he must be enduring. "See you soon." He hangs up and crawls back in bed. "Where were we?"

"Does Regina know you're not a little kid? Why is she so overprotective?"

"Because being underprotective didn't work out so well for her once."

I open my eyes. "What do you mean?"

"I'll explain some other time." He takes my hand. "Now. Christmas. What do you think?"

"Youngstown is five hours from here. Won't your family wonder why we can't get there until ten thirty or eleven?"

"We could go up the night before and stay in one of those hotels where the windows face an interior courtyard. No sunlight." He slips his fingers between mine, a wordless plea for my concession. "Or I could camp out in the bathroom with a towel stuffed under the door. No maid service, obviously."

"Shane, it's not the logistics." I stroke my thumb over his before continuing. "You can't see your family. Not for Christmas, not ever. The Control won't allow it."

His lip curls. "Fuck the Control."

"No, they'll fuck you, and your family. David says they'll do whatever it takes to maintain your cover."

"They wouldn't—" He lets out a frustrated gasp and rolls on his back, pulling his hand out of mine. "They would. Those bastards would." He rubs his face hard, then darts a sharp glance at me. "You told David we saw Mom and Eileen?"

"I was worried about you."

He turns his glare back to the ceiling. "Goddamn it, Ciara."

"He won't tell the Control, but they'll find out. They have a whole Anonymity Division."

"I know."

"One day when you get too old to look this young, they'll give you a new name and a new identity."

"I know."

"They've done it for all the other DJs except you and Regina."

"I *know* all about the Control." He clenches a fist into the pillow beside his head. "Why do you think I hate them so much?"

"They're just doing what's best for you."

He turns on me, rising to one elbow. "Breaking my mother's heart? Turning my back on my family when they need me?"

"You've been out of their lives for twelve years." I swallow hard. "They don't need you."

His eyes turn cold, followed by his voice. "Do you enjoy hurting me?"

"Shane . . ." My throat constricts. "Of course not. I wish things were different. No one wants you to be normal more than I do."

That didn't come out right.

He stares at me for a long moment. "What the fuck does that mean?" he growls. "Normal? You mean *human*?"

"No, I didn't—"

"You can't have normal. Not with me." He throws back the blankets and starts to get out of bed.

"That's not what I meant." I sit up. "I just want you to be happy."

He stops on the edge of the bed, shoulders hunched. "I can't always be that, either. And there's nothing you can do about it."

Anger wells up inside me, anger at my own helplessness. I can't save him from the darkness, and I want to beat my fists against his back and scream at him to let me make him happy. Because if he just loved me enough, I could make him anything I want.

But I don't punch him. I don't even touch him, because I know it would feel like pity. I just sit here, cold and naked, blankets up to my armpits.

His voice softens. "I've become a monster."

My heart twinges inside my chest. "Why do you say that?"

"I didn't go to my father when he called for me. When he was dying." He spits out the last word.

"The Control said no. If you'd tried, they would've stopped you."

"But I didn't try." He puts his head in his hands, fingers slipping through his tangled hair. "I can't make that same mistake with Mom and Eileen. I have a nephew I've never even met."

"You can't meet him, Shane. It's too dangerous. That's just reality."

"Reality." He scoffs. "Anymore, I don't even know what that is. I'm ordered to pretend I'm a human pretending to be a vampire." He turns halfway and speaks to the wall beside me, face silhouetted against the window's streetlight. "Do you have any idea how fucked up that is, or is that your version of normal?"

My neck prickles at his attack. "How do you think I feel, masquerading as Elizabeth?"

"I think you like it. Living a lie is all you've ever known. That's your normal." His matter-of-fact tone chills me more than any accusation ever could. "We're all operating in the world you've created for us. If I want to keep my job and my girlfriend, then I have to play this game of wink-wink-I'm-a-vampire." His hand tugs the blanket as it closes into a fist. "But I hate it. I hate what people see of me."

I flail for an argument that won't make me sound like a shallow hack. "How can you hate having thousands of fans who love you?"

"They don't know me. It's bullshit for them to love me."

It feels like we're spiraling closer to an unbearable truth. "Do you believe that I know you?"

"I think you try." He finally shifts to face me. "But you're not there yet. You don't want to be there yet."

"I do want to," I whisper unconvincingly.

"My listeners love some ideal of me as this easygoing, uber-cool dude who couldn't possibly drink real blood, or if I did, it would be with the utmost irony. You want me to be that, too." He jabs his fingertips against his chest. "You're trying to change me until I become that person."

"But change is good, right? It keeps you from fading."

His gaze meets mine. "I'd rather fade than become someone I'm not."

My chest feels like solid lead. My mind can't slog through the panic to find the right words.

Shane stands and crosses to my desk, where he picks up my phone.

"What are you doing?"

"Shutting off your alarm so you can sleep in."

"But what about you? What if you doze off and miss—"

"I won't." He slips his own phone into his jeans pocket. "I'm going back to the station."

"Now?"

"I have a lot of work to do." He pulls his shirt on and looks at my surprised face. "What? I leave in the middle of the night all the time. I'm a nocturnal creature with a life of my own, such as it is. I'm not your teddy bear."

"But we're having a . . . a—"

"Fight?"

"Discussion. You can't just walk out in the middle of it."

"This isn't the middle, Ciara." He picks up his shoes. "This is the end."

My stomach plummets as I stare at him. Is he breaking up with me?

I can't breathe, and he's just sitting there on the edge of the bed, tying his shoes, as if the world didn't just skid to a squealing, grinding halt.

"But . . ." My lungs fill with hot fluid that any second now is going to bubble up through my nose and eyes and—

I burst into tears, my chest lurching with sobs. My eyes squeeze out water like twin fire hoses.

Shane's at my side in an instant, his strong arms enfolding me. "Ciara, what? What's wrong?" His voice is urgent, bewildered.

"You said—" I choke on another sob. "You said it was over."

"What? No, I meant the conversation. Not us. Jesus, not us, not ever. I love you." Shane caresses my face and presses his forehead to mine. "How could you even think that?" He kisses my tear-soaked mouth. "I'll never leave you, Ciara, I swear. I swear to God, I won't."

I pull him into a harder, hungrier kiss and shove my hands under his shirt. Though my body is already aching and exhausted, I need to feel him alive against me—as alive as he'll ever be.

We make love like the world just missed an apocalypse, and afterward he doesn't leave, doesn't even move, just strokes my hair and tells me that these arguments are only us working out the kinks, and none of that stuff will ever threaten what we share.

I listen, and try to believe.

Sunday night finds me cramming for tomorrow's midterm exam, a convenient distraction from last night's soul-shaking angst.

Due to my fifty-hours-a-week job as promotions manager and vampire wrangler, I only have time for one course this semester: business ethics. If nothing else, the readings keep me awake. It's hard to doze off while laughing.

I'm sipping my third cup of coffee, feet on the back of my ratty sofa, trying to decipher my handwriting, when my cell phone blasts my latest Amy Winehouse fave.

I stretch out toward the coffee table to answer it, my body stiff and sore from too much vampire sex (note: too much is always just right). The caller ID tells me it's my boss. I open the phone.

"David, you know I don't work Sundays, due to my pious devotion to the Church of the Sacred Slacker."

"Dexter's gone."

My mouth goes dry, and my hand tightens on the phone. "Oh my God." Tears fill my eyes, still swollen from last night's jag of projectile crying. "Was it sunlight?"

"No, he's not dead. Not yet, anyway. He got away from me on our walk. Yanked the leash right out of my hand and took off down the road."

I slap the textbook shut and sit up. "I'm on it. Call the station. Have the DJs do an announcement after every song. Big reward for info—give away all our concert tickets if we have to—but nobody touches Dexter." I shove my feet into my shoes and grab my jacket from the back of the sofa. "Do a phone tree, have all the vampires comb the county looking for him. I'll call Lori. Dole out the vials of dog blood to use as bait for the vamps Dexter doesn't know."

"Ciara, I'm so sorry. If anything happens to him, I'll never forgive myself."

"Yeah yeah." I head down the hall and duck into my bedroom, where I snatch my keys and purse from my desk. "Just tell me where you saw him last."

"I chased him as far as the highway, but I didn't see which way he went."

Highway. With any other dog, that word would give me a heart attack. But Dexter can't be killed by a car. On the other hand, he could cause a nasty accident, and the last thing we need are tabloid reports of a giant self-resurrecting canine.

As I climb into my car, I try not to imagine my furry little dude going up in flames at the first light of day.

"Once again, folks, the lost dog is armed and dangerous." Shane's voice emanates from my car radio at 2:55 a.m., finishing Regina's show. "Do not attempt to capture this beast—he can kick your ass with three paws tied behind his back. Just call me at WVMP if you have any information. Fruitful tips bring your choice of concert tickets or cold hard cash." He pauses. "If Regina were on the air, she would say that Shane McAllister is coming up at the top of the hour to put you to sleep with his *Whatever* broadcast. Then I would come on and we would commit witty repartee. But as you may have heard, Regina keeps getting preempted by the forces of darkness. You can show your support by calling the FCC's Enforcement Division." He recites the phone number. "Tell them we want justice. But more than anything, we want our dog back."

I turn down the volume on the Stooges' "I Wanna Be Your Dog" so I can call Lori again. Nobody's seen one flash of Dexter's stealthy little butt. He could be halfway to Pennsylvania by now. Maybe he'll find a place to dig a hole and stay underground all day.

Or maybe he won't know the sun is coming until it's too late. He may be smart, but he's still just a dog, a species not known for its planning skills.

I turn onto my own street as I hit Lori's speed dial number. I had to come back to town to get gas, and while I was in the neighborhood I figured I'd check my place, just in case Dexter was—

Here.

Even through my closed windows, even over the crash of the Stooges on the radio, I can hear the vampire dog's bellowing bark. A crowd is gathered around my apartment door— mostly people in bathrobes and slippers, dragged out of bed to witness the spectacle.

Lori's voice comes out of the speaker. "Ciara?"

In my horror, I forgot I dialed her number. "I think I found Dexter. Call David and tell him he's about to have two new roommates."

Faces turn in my direction at the shine of my headlights over the crowd. I consider driving away and pretending I don't live here. But only for a second.

I U-turn into the empty spot across the street, then hop out of the car and push through the crowd toward my front door, which stands next to the pawn shop entrance.

Past the shoulder of Mrs. Crosby from two apartments over, I glimpse Dexter's huge form lying on the sidewalk in front of my door. Hmm, I wonder what all the fuss is about.

I sidle past Mrs. Crosby, almost getting poked in the eye with one of her pink curlers, then stop short.

Dexter isn't lying on the sidewalk. He's lying on Dean.

My dog has killed my landlord.

One of the old men from down the street hobbles forward,

brandishing his cane. Dexter snarls like a wolf guarding fresh prey, and the man hustles back into the safety of the crowd.

A woman I don't recognize screeches, "I called the cops!"

I jostle my way to the front of the mob, wondering what the food will taste like in jail. "Dexter, come!"

The dog leaps off Dean's body and runs toward me. The crowd surges back. He makes soft woofing noises as he circles my legs, sniffing my feet as if to confirm who I am. I grab what's left of his leather leash, which is torn ragged from being dragged over five miles of road and woods and hills.

Dean rises slowly from the sidewalk, his face as pale as a zombie's. My landlord stands, using the rusty white downspout to support himself, then slumps back against the building's brick façade. He looks slightly bruised but not bleeding.

He points a shaky finger at Dexter and opens his mouth.

I hold up a hand. "I know. We're gone."

# 7

## God Save the Queen

I trudge down the steep stairs of Statler Hall, my thighs screaming with each step. I must have pulled something during this morning's relocation.

At least I got Dexter out of my neighborhood before the cops arrived. Then I spent the day putting most of my stuff in storage and moving the bare necessities temporarily into David's house, where I'll be living until I can find another apartment.

What I did not spend the last twenty-four hours doing is studying for this midterm, and it showed.

Cursing David and Dexter, I let the younger students shove by on their way to their next class.

At the bottom of the stairs, a man steps in front of me.

"Ciara." The pale hazel eyes of Jeremy Glaser, cub reporter, stare at me through his round glasses and a circle of smudged black eyeliner. So that really wasn't a Halloween costume.

"Right on time." I wanted to meet him in a public place, seeing as he's creeping me out. "Let's talk outside."

The night air is chilly, and I button my coat up to the top. Jeremy deploys his dark gray thrift-store hoodie and shuffles along beside me, his black, thick-soled sneakers scraping the sidewalk as we head for the well-lit fountain at the center of the green.

I sit on the granite edge of the fountain. A couple is cuddling on the opposite side of the circle, but the trickling water will mask our voices.

"So what do you have for me?" I ask him.

"FAN's financial statements." He opens his bag and pulls out a folder. "They came close to filing for bankruptcy last year."

"That's what David said."

"Their third quarter financial report just came out, and look at this." He shines a pen-size flashlight on a revenue line item. "Huge foundation grant."

"Two million dollars?" Pennies from heaven, indeed.

He flips a page. "Their operational budget shot up, too. All those translators." He hands me a stack of FCC applications.

"David showed me these, too. Looks like they're doing a massive expansion."

"Yeah, but for the most part, it's not at anyone else's expense. You guys are the only ones they're targeting."

My fist wants to crumple the applications and shove them down someone's throat. "How can they get away with this?"

"Turns out the FCC chair is a big fan of religious broadcasting."

I scoff. "Go figure."

"So without outside pressure, the complaint you filed will go in the queue with all the rest, handled in an orderly fashion."

"What's orderly?"

He leans away, as if escaping the blast radius. "Two years?"

"*Two years?*" I want to hurl the financial report into the

fountain. "Our advertisers will abandon us. In two years we could be long out of business."

"I said, without outside pressure." Jeremy holds out a pen in the fingertips of both hands, as if he's presenting me with Excalibur. "Don't forget the power of the press."

"Ah." Hope glimmers inside me. "So you write your story, and we not only get better ratings, we also get justice."

"And truth, and the American way." He smiles and shoves the swoop of blond hair out of his eyes.

"Find out the name of this foundation that's giving the Family Action Network two million dollars. Follow the money."

"Hey, who's the journalist here? I'll do what I can, but now it's your turn to answer questions."

I suppose it's only fair. "Fine. Shoot."

"I just have one." Jeremy takes a quick inhale, then the muscles of his face tighten up in a sudden show of tension. "See, I was wondering . . ." He frowns and turns away so that he's facing forward, not looking at me.

"Wondering what?"

He folds and unfolds his hands, intertwining his slim fingers. I notice a tattoo on the inside of his left wrist—a fake slit with a trail of blood drops disappearing under his sleeve. Whoa.

"This is going to sound crazy, but . . ." He stops fidgeting and turns to me again. "Are the DJs really vampires?"

I chuckle in a way that I hope isn't patronizing. I've had this question before, but never so tongue-out-of-cheek.

"Yes."

His jaw drops. "I knew it."

"I mean, yes, it does sound crazy."

His mouth closes and tightens. "Is that a denial?"

"It's not a serious question."

"I sense something about them." He glances at the couple on the other side of the fountain and lowers his voice. "Like we're kindred spirits."

I raise my eyebrows. "Do you think you're a vampire?"

"Of course not. I never thought they existed. It's insane, right?"

"Yep."

"But after meeting your DJs, I started to wonder. They're creatures of the dark, just like me."

"Huh." I place my book bag between us and pretend to search for something inside. Mainly I just want an excuse to scoot farther away. "Well, they do work at night."

"Come on, Ciara." He yanks my backpack strap to get my attention, and I consider acquainting his nose with the heel of my hand. "They never go out in the sunlight."

"Sure they do."

"I can't find anyone who's seen them during the day."

"That doesn't mean it never happens."

"Why do they all live at the station?"

"Because it's free. DJing doesn't pay very well."

"I'd like to see their apartment."

"It's private. I'm not even allowed in there."

My eyelid twitches as I realize my blunder.

Jeremy tilts his head. "Not allowed in your own boyfriend's home?"

I shrug. "They're a tight group. No one raises a stink when the Masons or the Mormons don't allow outsiders into their temples."

"But if they're just a bunch of DJs—"

"Ah, but they're not." I flutter my lashes in a parody of a public relations flack. "They're *vampire* DJs."

He sits back, examining me. "So it's all part of the act?"

"Of course." I lean in, as if sharing a secret. "Our celebrities can't be spotted in the frozen food aisle or the Ruby Tuesday salad bar. We have to pretend they're not like other people. Sequestering them during the day is all part of controlling the message."

"Wow." He blows out a breath. "Your PR machine is hard-core."

"It's my job to maintain the mystique."

He nods. "And it's my job to break it."

"Good luck."

He opens his mouth to reply, but his gaze trips past me, above my left shoulder. His jaw stays agape.

"Hey, Ciara," says a familiar, lazy voice.

I turn to see Jim, whose arm is draped around the shoulders of a petite brunette in a long brown coat with a fake leopard-fur trim. She leans into the hippie DJ, melding her body against his in the distinctively needful posture of a blood donor. I glance at the other side of the fountain and realize they were the couple sitting there earlier. Jim probably heard every word we said.

"Hey." I smile at him, but he's already shifted his dark eyes to look at Jeremy. I introduce them and add, "Jeremy's doing a piece on the station for *Rolling Stone*."

Before I finish the sentence, Jeremy stands and whips out his business card. "Jim, I'd love to, uh, interview you."

Jim slips the card into the front pocket of his bell-bottom jeans without reading it. "Any time, man."

He extends his hand, and I jump up to block it.

Too late. The moment their hands touch, a shiver comes over Jeremy, the kind I get when Shane trails his fingertips down my bare back. His eyelashes flicker.

Jim lets go first, then returns his arm to the girl's shoulders. She sighs hard, as if she had to stop breathing while he wasn't touching her.

"I'll call you." Jim sustains eye contact with Jeremy—or more precisely, eye-to-throat contact. "Soon."

He glides away, his steps synchronized with the woman on his hip so they look like they share one body. Which they do—hers.

Jeremy stares after them. I wave my hand in front of his eyes to get his attention. He reluctantly drags his gaze back to me.

"Don't go alone on that interview," I tell him. "Any of the others, you're probably safe. But Jim, he's—"

"What, a vampire?" His gold-studded brows dip together in a scowl. "Do they exist or not, Ciara?"

"Of course not, but—"

"Then what? The dude does drugs? Big fucking deal."

I let go a frustrated sigh. "Just keep an eye on your drink."

"Duh. I'm twenty-four, not four." He picks up his bag. "And I have a job to do, one that could be my big break. I'll do whatever it takes to get close to the story." He turns away, on the same path as Jim, and speaks to me over his shoulder. "With or without your help."


I carry a hot pizza and a cold six-pack down to David's cozy family room, where I find him decked out in a dark purple Ray Lewis jersey. The Ravens are about to have their Monday Night Football showdown with their archrivals, the Pittsburgh Steelers. I know this because Shane is currently watching the game at the house of his favorite donor, a fellow Steelers fan. I can guess what the halftime snack will be.

I sit next to David on the plush, threadbare brown couch and hand him a beer and a plate.

He waves away the pizza. "I'm too stoked to eat." He takes a swig of beer and hurls a raucous holler at the wide-screen TV as the Ravens cavort and pound their chests in the driving rain of Heinz Field.

I stare at the pod person who has replaced my boss. He glances at me, and I can see his enthusiasm struggle against— and kick the ass of—his dignity.

Two minutes into the game, a Steeler with a mass of long hair head-butts the ball out of the hands of Ravens quarterback

Steve McNair. David's shriek echoes off the wood-paneled walls and makes me wish for earplugs. Antoine the cat runs from the room, but Dexter climbs onto the couch between us and plops his head in my lap. Great, now I can't leave.

When the Steelers quarterback escapes a near-sack to throw a long touchdown, David stomps around the family room, clutching his head. When it happens again a few minutes later, after another Ravens fumble, he sinks onto the couch next to me and reaches for the pizza. He consumes it like a death row inmate eating his last meal.

I pat David's shoulder. "It's just one game."

"It's not just the game." He chews slowly, then swallows. "Shane and I have an ongoing bet. Last year, I was not a gracious winner."

As the game progresses, the room gets very quiet, except for Dexter's snores. David's posture slumps further with each Ravens fumble and Steelers touchdown.

My attention drifts away from the television toward the other side of the family room, where ceiling-high bookshelves face a pair of elegant chairs near the fireplace. It's like a cozy, *Masterpiece Theatre*–type library, a different world from the decades-old couch and electronics extravaganza of the TV area where we're sitting now.

It also looks like a room in a museum—preserved and untouched. I think I see a layer of dust on the chairs' smooth leather arms. Maybe David and Elizabeth used to sit up nights in front of the fire, reading or listening to music, sharing something besides a parasite-host relationship.

"You still miss her, don't you?"

David jerks his chin in response to my question. His brows crinkle, as if he's about to ask me "Who?" but then he shakes his head. The gesture looks more like an admission than a denial.

"It wasn't so bad at first. I guess I was numb from the shock." He takes a long sip of beer. "Now, though, I can't stop noticing the holes. It's like one of those blankets, what do you call them?"

"Huh?"

"With the holes in them." He shrugs. "The ones that grandmothers make."

"I have no idea what you're talking about."

"Never mind." He smoothes back his straight dark hair, which has grown almost past his ears. "It's not as if Elizabeth and I had a future."

"But you were sleeping together, right?"

"No. I mean, sometimes we would . . . do things." He coughs and looks away.

I shift my legs under the dead weight of Dexter's sleeping head, trying not to imagine Elizabeth and David "doing things." Blood tastes better during a donor's orgasm, or so I'm told.

"But no," he continues, "we physically couldn't have sex."

I had no idea. "Was it an injury from your days in the Control?"

"Huh?" His face reddens, and he scratches the back of his neck. "No, I'm fine. Everything's working, last I checked."

I feel my own skin heat, but confusion trumps embarrassment. "Then why couldn't you have sex?"

David hesitates, then half turns to me. "You know how vampires are stronger than humans? Muscle-wise?"

"Sure, but isn't that an enhancement?"

"In some ways. But for a woman, when all her, uh, muscles, sort of contract, they can exert enough pressure to, well—"

I gasp. "No."

"Yeah."

Maybe we're not talking about the same thing. Part of me wants to turn the conversation to the weather, but the skies are clear with seasonal temperatures. Nothing to discuss.

"So you're saying." I speak slowly and avoid eye contact. "While a human guy is penetrating a female vampire, she could accidentally—or on purpose, I guess—perform a sort of penisectomy?"

David cringes. "Yep."

"Wow." I rotate my beer bottle in my hands. "Then female vampires are celibate?" No wonder Regina's so cranky.

"No. Male vampires are, uh, sturdy enough to handle it."

We stare at the TV. Dexter has stopped snoring, accentuating the awkward silence. I wish the game would come back on to distract us, but it's just Peyton Manning appearing in his thirtieth commercial of the night. "So are you seeing anyone now?"

"No. Other than Elizabeth, I haven't had a serious relationship since college."

"That's what, eleven years?"

"Twelve years, since I joined the Control. When you're a member of a clandestine paranormal paramilitary organization, it's hard to get close to anyone. They can never find out what you really do, though some agents tell their families they work for the CIA."

"But you left the Control ten years ago, after Elizabeth . . ." I don't finish the sentence. He's more than a bit sensitive about his former fiancée's fang-out.

"Right, but then we started a radio station with a bunch of vampires. Hard to explain to a potential girlfriend why the windows in my office are boarded up."

"Not to mention the routine puncture wounds."

His mouth drops open, and he stares at me. "How did you know I was feeding her?"

"I guessed." I stroke the jagged scar that lumps the fur over Dexter's right eye. "The way you and Elizabeth acted around each other, plus the fact that she glowed like a power plant even though she claimed she only drank bank blood, which Shane says is nutritionally deficient."

"I see." David rubs the side of his neck. "Yes, as long as

I was . . . sustaining Elizabeth, it was hard to have a steady relationship with another woman."

Convenient. I examine his posture, which, despite his professions of lingering sadness, has been straighter and stronger these last few months. Elizabeth's demise, while causing difficulties for the station, has had its benefits. David's emotional liberation, for one. Me getting to drive her Mercedes, wear her designer suits, and control her bank accounts, for another.

I study his face, wondering when someone last touched those cheeks or kissed those lips. I realize it was probably August second, and that someone was me. Or rather, me as Elizabeth, making out with David for the sake of a phony detective report. But also to give him a way to say good-bye.

Sometimes I wonder how much of the woman he kissed was Elizabeth and how much was me. I don't let myself wonder long, because then I have to ask how much of that Me was Elizabeth and how much of that Me was me.

"I have homework." I set my empty beer bottle on the table. "Dexter, I'm getting up."

He grunts as I lift his head long enough to scoot out from under it, then stretches his legs and closes his eyes again. He's the most phlegmatic vampire I've ever known.

I head for the stairs, but David's voice stops me at the bottom.

"Afghans."

I turn to look at him. "What?"

"That's what those blankets are called. The ones with the holes."

A sudden green-and-yellow image comes to mind. "My mother made one once. I never saw the point in those things. They don't keep you warm at all."

He hesitates, then finally says, "No, they don't." His tone is soft and sad.

I turn away before I can see the weight of grief settle over his face. The fact that he thinks of life without Elizabeth as an Afghan blanket makes my heart twitch and flop inside my chest. It's only supposed to do that for one man at a time.

My cell phone rings in my pocket. Caller ID says it's from the station.

"Hello?"

"What are you doing?"

I recognize Regina's flat, clipped voice. "I was watching football with David, but—"

"American football?"

"Huh?"

"Or soccer."

"NFL."

She gives a quick huff. "Shane says there's still a D.C. hard-core scene."

"Uh, yeah." My head spins from her switch in subject from sports to punk rock.

"When he says 'still,' does he mean in the nineties or now?"

"Now, I think."

"Okay. Pick me up in half an hour."

She wants to go to a club with me? We never—and I mean *never*—hang out. "Can I take a rain check?"

"No, it has to be tonight."

"But I have homework."

"Throw it onto the fire."

"What?"

"You have twenty-nine minutes. Don't dress like an ass-hole."


"Wow, you're like a punk Barbie doll," Regina says when she gets in my car at the station. Before I can answer, she slides a cassette into the tape deck of Elizabeth's—I mean, my Mercedes. It starts playing in the middle of a song with sawing guitars and a driving backbeat.

"Minor Threat!" she yells over the noise.

"Oh!" I shout back.

Those are the last words we speak on the way to our nation's capital (well, *my* nation—as far as I know, Regina's still Canadian). She doesn't sing along to the music, just rests her cheek on her fist, with her elbow on the passenger-side window frame. Her head nods faintly, and her lips move almost imperceptibly, but her black-lined eyes stare straight through the windshield. She doesn't look at me, and I sense that I'm nothing more than a convenient chauffeur.

Maybe she's disappointed in the low ridicule potential of my outfit. She clearly forgot that as a con artist, I can fit in anywhere. My pink-and-black belly shirt says BIG FUCKING DEAL, and the matching skull-bedecked skirt and leggings are ripped in all the right places. My thrift shop black combat boots came prescuffed, but I added the pink laces, which complement the ten Hello Kitty barrettes in my dark blond hair. The ensemble is designed to confuse anyone who might mess with me. They'd figure no one would dress that cute who couldn't defend herself. Psychology.

Even though it's Monday, and the band is D-list at best, the line outside the northeast D.C. club known as Outlander is a block long, consisting of people dressed in enough leather to build an entire herd of cows.

"Don't worry," Regina says in response to my sigh of dismay. "Pull up to the front."

I do as she says, though I don't see a sign for valet parking. She rolls down the window as I ease the car to a stop along the curb. Immediately two bouncers hurry over and confer with her, pointing down the street. I can't hear them over the blast of the stereo, and I sense that lowering the volume would lose me a finger.

When they retreat, practically bowing and scraping before her, she says, "Take the next two rights for the VIP parking lot."

"They know you here?"

She finally turns to look at me. "Don't act so fucking shocked. You're the one who made me famous."

After we park, the beefiest bouncer yet lets us in a back door. His open leather vest displays an anatomically correct tattoo of a heart on his chest. I bet Jeremy would like that one.

Regina leads me down a long hallway lit by a dim red light. When I start to lag behind, she grabs my hand and inserts it into the crook of her elbow.

"Do not let go," she says. "I am your Seeing Eye dog."

"I'm not blind."

"Not yet." She shoves open the door to the club.

The sound waves hit me so hard, I expect my skin to peel off from the guitar riffs. The heavy thump of the bass will probably cause internal bleeding by the end of the night.

Regina drags me toward the bar. On the way, I peer around while trying to look like I've been there a hundred times. It's like walking through a sewer system, and not just because of the smell and the fact that there's enough sweat to sail a small craft upon. Pipes and beams form the walls and ceiling in a monochrome tapestry. The black metal décor is broken up only by an occasional accent of gray.

There's no mosh *pit* here, per se, because the entire floor is filled with crashing, slamming bodies. I wonder if they give out free ice packs and suture kits to patrons as they exit.

The bar area isn't much calmer, it turns out, and if it weren't for Regina weaving us through the crowd, with a combination of brute strength and sheer scaring-the-shit-out-of-people, I'd soon be two-dimensional.

We reach the bar, where a pair of shot glasses await us, filled to the rim with what I assume is whiskey. I pick up my glass and turn around to see all eyes on Regina.

Averted eyes, that is. The jostling patrons watch her over one another's shoulders, and in the mirror shards glued to the wall. It's as if she's the sun, a threat to their retinas. Unlike Shane, whose fans crowd his lanky frame, searching for a piece of him to possess, Regina has an aura that keeps most people at a distance.

Except for one.

"Gina!"

A short, muscular punk dude bounces over to us. His Liberty-spiked candy-apple red hair provides a splash of color against the black and gray background.

He slides his arm over Regina's shoulder and gives her cheek a loud, smacking kiss. I step back to avoid getting hit by whatever limb she's going to tear off in response.

Instead, she hops on her toes like a little girl. "Colin, you wanker! Where've you been the last million years?"

"Right 'ere under your nose." He tweaks the flap of skin between her nostrils, then turns his gaze on me.

Suddenly I realize why she lets him touch her. He's a vampire as sure as the sky is up.

" 'ello, luv," he says, and my feet feel nailed to the floor. Part of my mind notes that he's objectively unattractive—weak chin, crooked teeth, low forehead. But the light in his deep green eyes seems to coat my skin with thousands of tiny steel filings. One blink could switch on the magnet and draw me into his orbit.

"Regina, who's the tasty biscuit?" he asks her without taking his eyes off me.

"Off-limits. She's a coworker."

Colin sighs in the direction of my skirt hem, then turns to Regina. "I was about to step out for a fag." He points his thumb at a red Exit sign.

"Right. Fucking D.C. smoking ban." She yanks me along as they proceed to the door. "The disease is spreading to Maryland in a few months."

"Christ. Well, there's always Virginia, but the clubs out there are crap." He loops an arm around her neck, bringing his elbow up to my nose. I notice that despite the heat, neither of them are sweating.

The door leads to a dark, trash-filled alley, and I balk at the threshold.

Regina tugs my arm. "Believe me, you're safer out here with us."

Colin chuckles. "Said the spider to the fly."

"It's really cold out." I pull back. "Think I'll stay inside."

Regina doesn't let go, but speaks to me in a low voice. "You know what Shane means to me. I know what you mean to him. You think I'd let you get hurt and have him hate me forever?"

I look at Colin, who's unwinding the little gold plastic strip from a fresh red pack of cigarettes. Dunhills, Regina's favorite brand.

"Make up your bleedin' mind," he says. "We've got business to discuss."

Regina jerks her head to look at him. "We do?"

He looks past me into the club as he lights a cigarette. "Either way, you're prey. At least out here you're with ones who can resist." He shakes out the match and grins. "Probably."

Choosing the devil I know (and one I just met) over the ones I don't know, I step into the alley and shut the door behind me. Colin's smile disappears. He picks up the wooden wedge meant to hold the door open and jams it underneath so no one can come out.

"Colin, you're such a drama queen." Regina leans against the brick wall and lights her own cigarette. "What's the big—"

"Listen to me, pet." He seizes Regina's shoulders. "You're not safe here."

"From who?"

He glances at me.

"Just say it," Regina says. "Don't worry about her."

His gaze races over the wall above Regina, as if he's trying to come up with the right words. "There's talk of revenge, for Sara."

Her face flashes vulnerable for half a second, then she scowls. "He's been saying that for two years. It's bollocks. And what's that got to do with this place?" She barks a laugh. "Can you imagine him here at Outlander? He wouldn't get two steps past the door."

" 'e's part of something bigger. And it's not what you think. It's something new." He shifts his weight, still clutching her shoulders. "No, something old. But growing. And this place, they watch it for vampires."

Regina blinks rapidly, glances at me, then stares up at Colin. "It was an accident."

"I know, luv." He kisses her forehead softly. "I know," he whispers against her skin. "But you can't be here, tonight of all nights." Then he turns to me. "Take her home. Now."

"Fucking hell." Regina wrenches away from him and starts down the alley. "Come on, Ciara. No point in staying if Mr. Buzzkill wants to ruin my night."

I hurry after her, fishing in my purse for my keys. Halfway down the alley, I turn to say good-bye to Colin.

Behind him, the door bursts open. The wooden wedge flies across the alley and hits the soot-stained brick wall.

"Run!" he hollers to us.

I obey, grabbing Regina's arm as I pass her. Her eyes go wide with panic, but I don't let her slow down.

"Idiot," she mutters, even as she starts to grin.

As we turn the corner, I look back to see Colin facing down three stake-wielding human men, each of whom is twice his size.

All the way to the parking lot, I can hear his laughter.

# 8

## Light My Fire

Tuesday morning finds me snarling with fatigue and frustration. On the way home last night, Regina refused to tell me anything about Sara and the mysterious vendetta. The only information she offered, when asked if Colin was her maker, were two words: "He wishes."

At the station, Franklin is grumpier than ever.

"Mad about the game?" I ask him as I slump behind my desk with my third cup of coffee.

"Of course," he says, "but don't tell Shane I care. I don't want any part of this rivalry."

"What's the big deal?" Compared to the episode at Outlander, a football feud seems quaint. "It's just sports."

"*I* know that. *You* know that. But to David and Shane, it's war."

The door at the bottom of the stairs opens, and Shane marches up, his chest puffed out like a general on the winning side of a surrender ceremony. His radiance comes from more than his donor's blood—its source is the testosterone surge of vicarious victory.

He comes over and plants a kiss on my lips. "Thank me later."

"For the kiss? It wasn't one of your better ones."

"For the spectacle." He checks the clock. "Any minute now."

Regina, Jim, and Noah file up from the basement and stand in front of Elizabeth's office, looking bored. Regina makes a point of avoiding my eyes.

Shane turns his head toward the parking lot. "He's coming. Can I borrow your phone?"

I pull it out of my bag and hand it to him. "What's wrong with yours?"

"It doesn't take pictures." Shane flips it open, then finds the camera button. "Vengeance is mine, loser."

The door at the bottom of the stairs creaks open, and David walks slowly up from the lounge, wearing a long gray raincoat, tied around the waist. I look up at Shane, whose eyes gleam with triumph.

"Go on." He gestures to David. "Show us what Ravens fans are made of."

Our boss sets his briefcase on the floor. Chin held high, he unties the raincoat and lets it drop to his feet.

My eyes fly open so fast, my lids threaten to cramp.

David stands there dressed in nothing but a pair of shiny black Steelers underwear, though "underwear" is too generous a term, since it's not so much worn as it is painted on.

I'm not normally a fan of Speedos and the like. Few non-models can pull off the look. But David succeeds, partly because his smooth, semi-swarthy skin holds a year-round tan, but mostly because his muscles are developed in just the right way—solid but sleek. My eyes battle over where to linger: on the contoured pecs or the long, wiry thighs. Beneath my desk, I run my fingertips together to stop the tingling.

"Not bad." Regina nods as she checks out David from head to foot. "Makes me wish I could be human for an hour. Or two."

I force my gaze to turn to Shane, whose look of triumph has faded to chagrin. The cell phone is still pointing at David, its camera function forgotten.

"Um," he says, then clears his throat. "David, when'd you start working out?"

"Few months ago." With the maximum dignity possible for someone with approximately 98.7 percent of his skin showing, David bends over and pulls a cardboard sign out of his briefcase. It reads in magic marker, PITTSBURGH 38, BALTIMORE 7.

Shane claps his hands together once and stands up. "Okay, that fulfills the bet. Time to get dressed."

"Nope." David crosses his arms over his chest, and a gasp of admiration floats from Franklin's side of the office (thankfully covering the sound of my own sigh). "The deal was, I'd wear this all day."

"But it's cold in here." Shane picks up David's coat. "At least put this on."

"A man must maintain honor, in defeat as well as victory." David brushes past him on the way into his office. By reflex, my head tilts to keep him in sight.

"It's not appropriate workplace attire." Shane motions to me and Franklin. "It'll bother the other employees."

I shrug. "No, it won't."

"Yeah," Franklin adds, "we're all professionals." He seems to have trouble keeping his mouth closed.

David sits behind his desk with perfect grace. Shane grabs the doorknob and starts to swing the door shut.

"No." David holds up a hand. "It doesn't count as public humiliation if I can hide."

Shane stops, shakes his head, and emits a harsh laugh. "Fine." He lets go of the doorknob and pushes the door wide open.

"Good night." Snickering, Regina clomps back downstairs in her combat boots. Noah follows.

Jim stands at the top of the stairs for a moment. He scratches the back of his head, ruffling the long brown curls. "I thought Baltimore was the Colts."

"Shut up." Shane starts to follow him down the stairs.

"Aren't you forgetting something?"

He turns in response to my question.

"I'll be needing that camera," I tell him.

He looks at my cell phone in his hand, then sets it on the edge of my desk. "I've been outmanned, haven't I?"

"Serves you right for gloating." I aim the camera at David's serene face. "And the word we use these days is 'pwned.' "

It's an unusually quiet day at the office. I occupy myself by updating the DJs' blog entries, transcribing their occasionally rambling treatises on rock history from the tapes they've made for me. Other than Shane, they're so computer-averse, you'd think keyboards were polished with holy water.

At lunchtime, I get up and tiptoe to David's open door. Still mostly naked, he looks up with a Buddhalike smile.

"Yes?"

"Um." I direct my question to his shelf's far corner. "Do you want to see those press releases before I send them out?"

"Ciara?"

"Yeah?" I say to the rubber foot on his desk leg.

"I need you to look at me."

His words send a shock down my spine. "Why?"

"Because I need to know if you're telling the truth."

"Oh." I suck in a slow breath, then meet his gaze. "About what?"

He rests his elbows on the desk and gives me a level look. "You already sent those press releases about the pirate broadcast, didn't you?"

"Yes." When his jaw tightens with anger, I hurry to add, "I had to. Reporters were hearing all sorts of crazy rumors. One of them thought we were the ones breaking the law. I had to set the record straight."

His fingers interlace, creating a two-handed fist. I try not to notice how the action tightens everything from his biceps to his pectorals. I fail.

"I think you're right."

I blink. "Huh?"

"If we can't keep the secret, we need to control the message."

"Right. Of course."

"And the publicity is, as you say, free."

"The best kind."

"But we're not just milking it for the exposure." He sits back in his chair and crosses his bare arms over his bare chest. Once again, I find the ceiling corner fascinating.

"The longer we let this play out," he says, "the more evidence we can gather so we can nail them in the end."

"Absolutely." I should be inspired by his defiance, but my mind is preoccupied. "David?"

"Yes?"

"Do you have to be like that all day?" I wave my hand in his general direction.

"Yes." He opens a drawer and pulls out a folder. "As I was saying, every time they interrupt us, they commit a crime. A crime with thousands of witnesses, including our digital recorder."

"So it's an easy case, right?"

"One would think." He opens the folder. "A pirate radio signal in Brooklyn has been interfering with community stations for years, and the FCC hasn't acted. It's in their queue, they say." He splays four articles across his desk. "Here's one in St. Paul, another in Miami, another in Nashville. This happens all the time, and the government does nothing. It's not a priority."

I think of Jeremy's pen and the power of the press. "It will be if we throw a fit."

"Which is why you're right—we need the media. But we have to proceed carefully." His eyes turn serious, and he lowers his voice. "No more going behind my back."

"But I—"

"First you hire Lori without asking me."

"And didn't she do a great job yesterday?" Nerves are making me babble. "I know I got a lot more done than usual."

"It's not your station, Ciara."

I look at my toes and decide not to mention that legally, as Elizabeth Vasser, it *is* my station. "I know. Sorry."

He clears his throat and speaks in a normal tone again. "Colonel Lanham is coming over tonight to inspect the dog."

My neck goes cold. "Inspect? He won't take him away, will he?"

"Depends. Each of the vampire animals has a subdermal microchip that contains all their information. Lanham can scan the chip and see where Dexter belongs."

"He belongs with me. I'll find a new place where I can keep him." My fists clench. "I'm not letting him go back to the lab."

"Hang on." David holds out his hands palms down in a soothing gesture. "No one said anything about him going anywhere. I promise I won't let Lanham take your dog away."

I can't speak through the lump in my throat. David doesn't have the authority to make that promise.

"Remember, Ciara, Dexter belonged to someone who was working with FAN—that's why he was chained to the cross. He could be the key to finding out who's behind the piracy, maybe even the arson. Our livelihoods—hell, even our lives—might depend on the information he holds. The Control is the only way to get that information."

I frown, knowing he's right. "All right. But whoever let him go doesn't deserve to get him back."

"I'm going out to lunch." Franklin scoots back his chair and grabs his jacket. As he unlocks the front door, he turns and gives me a sly grin. "Behave yourselves."

He shuts the door, and there I am, alone in a tiny office with a nearly naked version of a man with whom I once shared a phony but passionate kiss. I stare at the floor and kick my heel softly against David's doorjamb. An unusually sultry surf rock tune, one of Spencer's favorites, plays over the speakers.

Desperate to break the tension, I decide to tell him about my road trip with Regina last night, though she made me promise to keep it between us. Right now, I'd rather face her wrath than see David looking at me like that.

Just then, the door to the downstairs lounge opens, and in my relief I want to hug Travis, who's taking the stairs two at a time, a small stack of papers in his hand.

"I heard from my guy at the state police." He rounds the corner. "Turns out the—Whoa!" Travis stops at the sight of David. "Remind me never to bet against Shane."

"Don't worry," I tell him. "We'll do anything to keep you out of a Speedo."

"You have new information?" David asks him, as if nothing is out of the ordinary.

"Uh, yeah." He steps into the room and drops the papers on David's desk, then darts back out of the office, keeping me between him and our boss. "Got a copy of the forensics report on the YOUR GOING TO HELL sign and the Molotov cocktail bottle from the Smoking Pig fire."

David examines the pages. I decide to stay away and not indulge my curiosity.

"Anyways." Travis rubs his knuckles over the edge of his jaw. "Near as I can tell, the paint on the sign and the substances in the bottle match the ones left at our station."

"You have your own chemical lab?" I ask him.

"No, but I know a guy."

I nod. Like me, Travis has spent most of his career on the shady side of life, dealing in what my professors might call "the underground economy." Those of us who aren't particular about legalities always seem to "know a guy."

David puts down the pages. "So whoever torched the bar probably did it because of us."

"Not *you* us." Travis slips his hands into his front jeans pockets, hunching his shoulders. "*Us* us. Vampires. Someone wants us to burn."

I look at the YOUR GOING TO HELL sign, which is propped against David's bookshelf, facing the wall.

Someone wants the vampires to burn, all right. In this life and the next.


"This won't work," I tell Shane.

"Are you sure?" he replies, his hand under my shirt. "I think we should try."

I'm lying on my new twin bed, squished between my boyfriend and the wall. "It'd be different if David weren't downstairs."

"He said to make yourself at home." Shane fingers the button of my jeans and nuzzles my neck. "We could be quiet."

I stretch and shiver at the heat of his lips. "I can't be quiet with you."

"Not true. Remember that time in the supply closet at work?" He unhooks my bra with an inhumanly deft maneuver. "And the alley behind the coffee shop? And the parking lot next to—"

"But it feels rude, in David's house, with him here."

"Maybe." Shane's voice turns even sultrier. "But the bed's too small for the three of us."

I stiffen at the sudden sweaty image. After today's Speedo incident, my mind needs no help picturing David's naked body.

"Stop." I push his hands away. "You're driving me crazy."

"Sorry." Shane sits up, shifts to the end of the bed, and pulls my feet into his lap. "We'll figure something out."

"It's just temporary, until I move into a new—Ohhh." My voice drifts into a purr as he starts to rub my feet. "On second thought, let's find a motel right now."

He doesn't laugh. "Ciara, I've been thinking about something."

"Lessons in good sportsmanship, I hope?"

"Dexter stays downstairs here during the day, and he's perfectly safe. Remember Elizabeth's basement apartment?"

"Remember it? I go there every week to pick up her mail." I never venture inside, though—too creepy.

"She had those blackout curtains over the windows to keep out all the sunlight." His grip on my foot tightens. "What if we find a place like that, where we could be together?"

"So you could stay over during the day sometimes instead of running back to the station?"

He stops rubbing. "So I could stay, period."

My eyes fly open as my chest constricts. He can't mean what I think he means. "You want to live with me?"

He nods. "I love you. I want to be with you. I want to take the next step."

I sit up, pulling my feet out of his hands. "Now?" My

heartbeat surges like I just chugged four cappuccinos. "The other night you sounded like you had doubts about us. Now you want to shack up?"

"I think it's what we need." His gaze is steady on me. "The other night we talked about how you don't really know who I am. If we lived together, you'd figure it out pretty fast." His jaw twitches. "Then you can decide if I'm what you want."

The back of my scalp tingles, and I feel a sudden dizziness. What if he decides I'm not what *he* wants?

"Maybe someday. After I finish school." Yeah, that sounds good.

He squints at the ceiling. "But with one class a semester, that'll be more than two years from now, even with summer school."

"So? Can't we wait?"

"Wait for what?"

I hug my knees to my chest. "For me to be ready."

His mouth curves into a half smile. "You think *I'm* ready, Ciara? No one's ever ready."

The doorbell rings. I glance at the clock. Uh-oh.

"What's wrong?" Shane says to the look on my face.

"Promise you'll be nice."

His eyes narrow. "To who?"

I tell him, and his face turns to stone.

When we enter the living room, David has already let Colonel Lanham in. With his impeccable solid black Control uniform and buzz-cut hair that can be measured in micrometers, Lanham exudes a brutal efficiency.

He turns to face us, and his posture stiffens when he sees Shane, the man whose family-reunion dreams he crushed. "Ms. Griffin. Mr. McAllister."

Shane just nods and glares at him as he holds Dexter's leash. The dog growls low in his chest at the colonel. A sadistic smirk crosses Shane's face as he probably realizes Dexter would tear out Lanham's throat if he "accidentally" dropped the leash.

Lanham gives me a contraption that looks like a grocery store handheld scanner. "Point that at the area between the dog's shoulder blades."

I do as he asks. The little machine beeps, and I hand it back to Lanham.

He checks the screen, then pulls out his cell phone. "I'll have my colleague run this through the necrozoology database."

I stand in front of Dexter. "And then what?"

"And then we'll know his status."

My shoulders relax a tad as I realize Lanham just called Dexter "he" instead of "it."

He places the call, relates Dexter's information, and hangs up. "It'll be a few minutes."

David says, "The cross he was tied to was a Control-style vampire trap. It almost killed one of our friends."

Lanham furrows his brow. "How did you deactivate it?"

My heart slams in sudden panic. I send David a look of warning. We can't tell Lanham the truth about my anti-holy blood. I'd be stuck in a lab the rest of my life, like Dexter and his fellow canines.

I blurt the first thing that comes to mind. "We pulled the plug." I mime the action to reinforce the lie.

"That's right," David hurries to add. "I disconnected the repeater, just long enough to release Travis."

Lanham's confusion looks genuine. "Why would that work?"

"Faith!" My voice pitches up. "Faith gives power to the religious symbols your agents use as weapons. They only work in the hands of believers. So David had a hunch that the radio preacher's words were activating the trap."

"Interesting application of the principle." Lanham rubs his chin. "But not one I've heard of in our agency."

"So it could be stolen Control technology," David says.

"Almost certainly stolen. I would know if the agency had deployed a weapon this powerful in my district." He turns to me. "While we're waiting for the results on the dog, I need to speak with you alone."

Shane and David don't move.

"Please," Lanham says to me. "It's about your father."

My throat jolts. "Did you find him?" I don't add, *And kill him?*

Lanham says nothing, just folds his hands in front of himself and waits.

I turn to Shane. "You and David take Dexter outside. See if he'll chase a ball."

"Are you sure?" Shane asks me.

"Go already."

"C'mon, Dexter." Shane tugs the leash, and the dog follows him reluctantly to the back door, watching me over his shoulder, to the point where he bumps into the wall because he's not watching where he's going.

I sit at the farthest end of the L-shaped living room couch. Lanham paces in front of me. I try not to fidget like a kid waiting to see the principal.

"Have you heard from your father?" he asks.

"No." I temper the disappointment in my voice. "Nothing since he left." I don't mention the letter he stuck in my door the day he skedaddled. It had no clues, just some crap about family curses and how sorry he was and blah-diddy-blah.

"If he contacts you, you must inform us immediately." When I don't answer, Lanham turns to me. "It could save his life. He has many enemies, including his own family."

My father helped the feds with a racketeering case against several South Carolina Travellers—or "Irish Gypsies" as they hate to be called. The deal got him out of prison several years early and into the Control's undercover operation, a more exciting alternative to the Witness Protection Program.

"Still," I point out, "the Travellers aren't exactly the Mafia or the yakuza. Con artists take pride in our—I mean, their nonviolent approach."

Lanham straightens a wall-mounted framed photograph of David's family, and says nothing.

I force out the question, "What happens to my father when you find him?"

"He'll go back to federal prison. He broke his early parole deal by turning on us, so he'll finish out his original sentence, plus a few years. But he'll be safe, I assure you." Lanham sits on the couch two cushions over, his posture razor straight. "Internal Affairs is investigating one of your father's Control bodyguards who staffed the safe house this summer. He may have let him escape."

Colonel Lanham's phone rings. He pulls out a notepad and pen as he answers it.

"Right." He jots a few notes, angling away from me as I stand and lean to peer over his shoulder. "Thank you, Lieutenant. Good work." He hangs up.

"Well?"

"The dog appears to have been stolen from the Control lab."

"Stolen?" I plant my hands on my hips. "You can't have him back."

"They don't want him. He was scheduled to be euthanized last month. Someone forged the records to show that it had been carried out. But it obviously wasn't, since he's alive and well." His head quirks. "Not strictly alive."

"Why did they want to put him to sleep?"

"He was a failure." Lanham frowns. "Low aggression

levels, though he didn't show much evidence of that when I showed up."

I rip my mind away from the thought of a dead-undead Dexter, and how they would make him that way. "Why would someone tie him to that cross?"

"Perhaps as a nighttime guard against human trespassers. Though considering the fact that you walked right up to him, he was a failure at that job, too."

"Can I keep him?"

Lanham nods, then points to a small red-and-white cooler at the top of the stairs leading down to the front door. "There's enough blood to last you six weeks. One vial every other day."

"Thank you." I wonder what I'll have to do to get refills.

Lanham answers my unspoken question as he walks to the door. "You can thank me by finding your father."

I mumble my agreement as I see Lanham out. I shut the door behind him and lean my forehead against it.

So now it's my dog versus my dad. I ponder which one has shown more loyalty, and which would stand up for me in my hour of need.

It's a short ponder. Dexter wins.

# 9

## King of Pain

Saturday night Lori and I watch Shane perform an acoustic set at Legal Grounds, the coffeehouse near the courthouse. We sit at a far table on a higher level so we can spectate and drool but still carry on a conversation.

Even after four months of watching Shane perform, I find it hard to tear my gaze away from him. Right now he's in the middle of Luka Bloom's "Ciara," the first song he ever played for me.

"It's so romantic." Lori carves out the graham cracker crust of her cheesecake. "It's like he's reminding those perky little sorority sisters in the front row that at the end of the night, he's going home with you."

"Actually, he's going to work." Another double shift of ninety-five percent male artists. (He sneaks in a female singer once in a while to see if FAN is paying attention. They are.)

Regina supervises his version of her show, but she can't be on the air without the pirates interrupting.

"That's a new one," Lori observes as Shane starts a rendition of "Mrs. Potter's Lullaby" by Counting Crows. "Well, newish. After his time."

"I told you, he can learn. He's not fossilized like Monroe or Spencer." I watch his fingers flash over the strings and fretboard, building complexity into the second verse's instrumentation. "He never will, if I have anything to do with it."

"You'd have a lot more to do with it if you lived with him." In response to my glare, she asks, "How's the apartment hunt?"

"Terrible." I frown at my chocolate-dripped pecan pie—nothing against the pie, of course. "I can't find anything in my price range that takes pets Dexter's size. Credit checks look at my income and student loans and show I can't afford an apartment." I shift my cappuccino mug on the black glass table, missing my old landlord. "Dean never cared where my rent came from, as long as it was on time and in cash."

"Why not apply as Elizabeth? She's got money."

"Too risky. Besides, I won't be her forever. One day the station will make enough to survive without her. Until then, I'm two people."

"One of which your boss is in love with."

I look away, pretending to study the latest series of local artists' prints lined up on the sunflower yellow walls. "David really needs to start dating normal girls."

"Like you?"

"Like you."

She blushes, as I knew she would. "He's not my type."

"He's completely your type." I count off on my fingers. "He's smart. He's sincere. He geeks out over history and magic, just like you."

She crinkles her nose. "Not right now."

I slump to rest my chin on my fist. "I wish you'd been there on Speedo Day. Those camera-phone pictures didn't do him justice."

"It wouldn't have mattered." She picks graham cracker crumbs off her sleeve as her face turns pinker. "It was already too late."

My toe nudges her shin. "Are you hiding a Mystery Dude? Who could be more Lori Koski's type than David Fetter?"

The front door bangs open, hitting the wall and jangling the cowbell attached to the handle. Regina strides in, followed by Travis, whose hand shoots up to catch the door before it bounces into his head.

There's a reason why vampires don't travel in packs in public. One vampire's radiant, magnetic beauty is enough to attract attention. Following Regina, even a fledgling like Travis looks like a predator.

They slide inside the coffee shop, movements coordinated like wolves on the hunt, and though they proceed at normal speed, their graceful swaggers remind me of a slow-motion movie introduction.

They stand together inside the door and scan the joint, as if assessing the patrons' vintage. They see us in the far corner, and Regina gives a cool chin-tilt of acknowledgment.

Travis, on the other hand, breaks into a grin of human warmth. Why is he so glad to see me?

Then I look at Lori. Her face has turned as red as her cheesecake's strawberry sauce.

"Lori, no. Not Travis."

She smoothes a lock of white-blond hair behind her ear. "But he's sweet. And cute."

"He's gross. At his age, he has to drink twice a night. I bet he has blood breath."

"I wouldn't know." She glances back at Travis, who's conferring with Regina. "We haven't kissed yet. I tried last night, but he said he didn't trust himself not to bite me."

I rub the spot on my forehead that feels like it's in a vise. "Don't you see? His vamp eyes'll get you all horny, until you let him drink you just so you can have sex."

She glares at me, sullen-faced, like a teenager with her mom. "I know you two got off to a bad start, what with him trying to kill you—"

"Bit of a speed bump, yeah."

"—but he's been good since then, and so helpful with the investigations."

"Lori, do you want him to bite you?"

She twists the little gold heart pendant on her necklace. "I don't think so. I just like being with him."

"He needs to know that now, not in the heat of the moment with his mouth against your neck or thigh." I lower my voice. "Here he comes."

She gasps. "Is my hair okay?"

Travis climbs the stairs to the second level and gives Lori what I have to admit is a smile of genuine affection.

"Hey there." He squeezes her hand and looks at her like she's the only person in the room. "Your hair sure is pretty tonight."

Lori goes on a mad blushing-and-babbling spree. I wonder if his vampire ears heard her fretting about her hair.

Travis rotates our table's empty chair and straddles it. "Got the goods for you." He opens a vinyl portfolio and lays it on the table so Lori and I can read it. "Colleague of mine over in Frederick County says there's scuttlebutt about a new cult out in the hills. Some local politicians and businessmen are rumored to be members. One guy he talked to said his uncle went to a recruiting meeting. It's all secretive, like the Masons, but they mostly talked about how women were taking over the country."

I scoff. "Which women? The ones who make seventy-seven cents for every dollar a man makes?"

He ignores me and flips to another page, a long list of numerals. "I dug into FAN's electronics purchases and found equipment serial numbers. Maybe one of them matches the one at the cross."

I look at the list. "How'd you find these serial numbers?"

"It's all on their Schedule C's." He winks at Lori. "I got a friend at the IRS."

It occurs to me that Travis is a good person to know. "I thought churches don't pay taxes."

"They still have to file, and a company like FAN is always covering their butts to keep from getting audited." He pats his shirt pocket, probably for his cigarettes, then looks annoyed at their absence. I wonder if Lori has convinced him to quit smoking.

"David and I'll check it out tomorrow." I look past him at Regina, who's glaring at Shane and pointing at her watch. "You guys are here to pick up Shane?"

"She is. We just came from—" He rubs his mouth self-consciously. "We visited a donor."

At least he's not thirsty. According to Shane, the younger vampires usually have their donor visits supervised for their first year. An untrained vampire can puncture an artery and make someone bleed out, or accidentally chomp on nerves and tendons, especially when the thirst is really bad. Why any human would risk such a medical misadventure is beyond me.

"So I'm free the rest of the night." He looks at Lori. "You guys want to get a drink?"

"I'd love to," I tell him, ignoring Lori's grimace. No way I'm leaving them alone. He'll be needing blood again before dawn.

Shane finishes the marathon tune and nods at the applause. He glances at the clock. It's 10:55—enough time for one more song, but Regina clearly wants him to come now. Her posture is rigid, her lips tight with impatience.

He flexes his fingers, gives his guitar case a long look, then sends his gaze my way. I wonder if Regina catches his wink.

He adjusts the microphone closer to his mouth, readies his pick just above the strings, then whispers the first line.

"Mother, do you think they'll drop the bomb?"

The crowd applauds, and Regina's fingers curl into fists. Of course she recognizes the Pink Floyd song from *The Wall* and understands its blatant Oedipal themes.

She yanks a pack of cigarettes from the inside pocket of her black leather jacket, then puts one in her mouth. The coffeeshop manager approaches her and receives a withering glower, stopping him in his tracks. Finally Regina stalks outside, lighting the cigarette a millisecond after crossing the threshold.

Shane continues the song, his plaintive growl embracing and denying the hold this woman has on him. She stares through the front window, her pale face like a moon in the night sky, her cigarette like a star.

I get up and weave through the tables past the tiny corner stage, right up to the window.

With my middle finger extended so that only Regina can see, I tug the lower curtain across the window, obscuring the face of my lover's maker, and the eyes that freeze my blood.


O'Leary's pub is packed, as it has been since the temporary demise of the Smoking Pig. Sherwood has other bars—sports joints attached to strip mall restaurants, or honky-tonks out in the hills—but for the under-thirty crowd, O'Leary's is the only Pig alternative.

An excellent alternative, it turns out. While Lori and Travis flirt with each other, I mitigate my dismay by watching a duo of Irish musicians belt out ballads and reels. I try to enjoy the music for itself, and not let it remind me of my dad or his vast extended con artist family.

Here, in a place where hardly anyone knows my name, it would be easy to succumb to my genetic urge to relieve some poor sucker of an extra ten or twenty dollars. Bar bets like match tossing and "The Swallow" will forever hold a special place in my heart.

I notice my pint of Smithwick's is empty and turn to the bartender to ask for a soda to replace it.

A newspaper slaps down in front of me onto the polished wood of the bar.

CHURCH SUCKS LISTENERS FROM VAMPIRE RADIO

I turn to see Jeremy, who looks pale even in the low light.

"Tomorrow's Sunday edition." His smile is sly.

"How'd you know to find me here?"

"I called the station. Shane told me where you were. He thought you'd want to see the article right away." He sets his messenger bag on the stool next to mine and looks for the bartender. I guess he's staying.

I peruse the *Baltimore Sun* article, the first major piece on the piracy controversy. No one from FAN can be reached for comment. Same goes for the FCC, except to say that the case is under review. As usual, the sensationalistic vampire schtick steals the stage from issues of media freedom. In its attempt to frame the issue as good (church) versus evil (vampires), the article neglects to mention the fact that we're victims of a crime.

I fold up the paper and take the pint Jeremy offers. After that, I could use another drink.

"Could've been worse." He sits on the stool and hooks his thick black sneakers around the lower rungs. "They could've revealed the truth about vampires."

I search for a bar napkin to avoid looking at him. "The truth?"

"You can stop pretending." He leans closer, elbows on the bar. "I fed Jim."

My jaw drops, and it feels like the bartender's sinkful of ice just washed across my back. "You're lying," I hiss at Jeremy. Please let him be lying.

"I've got the marks to prove it." He shoves up the long sleeve of his Dashboard Confessional T-shirt to reveal a bandage on his right arm, stark white against the surrounding blue of his tattoos. The sight turns my mouth dry as sandpaper.

"Jim brought everything we needed," Jeremy continues, "gauze, iodine, razors."

My mind clears at the sound of the last word. I take another sip to hide my relief. Jim didn't bite him—he "just" cut him and drank his blood, something any human could do. Jeremy doesn't know the truth behind the lie behind the truth. He just thinks they're regular humans involved in these kinky "vampire" practices.

Just to be sure: "Did he cut you, or did you cut yourself?"

"I did the first one, but then I almost passed out, so he did the second one." Jeremy seems happy to spill the details. "That way I could just lie back and soak in the experience."

"Why would you do that to yourself? So you can tell the world?"

"It's not about journalism." He rotates his glass. "It's about finding something real. There's nothing more basic to life than blood. Losing it, giving it—that's a sacred act."

"So are you going to write about it or not?"

He thumbs the gold ring on his left eyebrow, contemplating my question. "If I do, only obliquely. I don't want to get Jim arrested."

"Good."

"Because I want to do it again."

I almost smack my forehead in disbelief, then change the gesture to a scratch at the last second. "Doesn't it hurt?"

"Of course it hurts. That's the best part."

"You get off on it?"

He frowns at me. "Not everything is about sex. Pain is real. It's life. It connects us to each other, to the whole universe." He sips his mixed drink, which I don't recognize. "Did you ever watch a bug get caught in a spider's web?"

"No."

"The spider paralyzes its prey so it can't move while it wraps it up. But when it comes back later to feed, the prey is still alive. It feels every bite."

"I don't think insects' nervous systems are—"

"Pain happens everywhere, all the time." He points to the window. "Somewhere in this town, a guy is beating his wife. A little kid is in the last stages of brain cancer. A cat is eating a mouse who has a litter of babies waiting for her to come back to the nest, babies that'll starve by morning."

I stare at him, then grab my pint of ale and take a long gulp.

"You don't think about those things, do you, Ciara?"

I set down my glass. "Not specifically."

His gaze drifts over my neck. "So, then, you and Shane don't—"

"No! No, no. I'm his girlfriend, not his donor."

"Isn't that awkward? That he shares such an intimate act with others but not you?"

"You just said it wasn't about sex. Are you sleeping with Jim?"

"No, I'm totally straight. At least, I think I am." He shifts his glass on the rough wooden surface of the bar. "Honestly, I'm a bit confused about that lately."

"It can't be helped." I squeeze his uncut arm. "We're all a little queer for vampires."

He breaks into a broad smile and raises his glass. I clink my pint against it.

"So who's funneling money to FAN?" I ask him, as much to change the subject as to get the goods.

"Funny thing. The money trail is more convoluted than Watergate. I keep hitting dead ends at offshore bank accounts."

"Whoever it is clearly wants to remain anonymous, and not out of a left-hand-not-knowing-what-the-right-is-doing impulse."

"What do you mean?"

"It's from the book of Matthew. When we do charitable stuff, we should keep our mouths shut, not brag about it on a street corner."

"Or on the radio."

"Now, now." I nudge him with my elbow. "Where's your journalistic objectivity? The Family Action Network is all that stands between this great country and the godless heathens that want to turn our children into gay polar bears." I look over my shoulder to make sure Travis is out of earshot, then lean close to Jeremy. "When you're doing research, keep an eye out for the name Sara."

"Who's that?"

"I don't know." Giving him more details would break my promise to keep Regina's secret. "But let's just keep it between you and me."

He nods. "Sara. Okay."

The Celtic duo breaks into a loud drinking song, and the noise around us puts an end to all rational conversation.

Maybe it's best if Jeremy falls into our web, where we can keep an eye on him.

# 10

## Tempted

**November 11**
David and I visit the big honkin' cross to check the serial numbers of the repeater against Travis's list. Morning fog pools in the tree-enclosed clearing, and the cross's pulsing power is now a steady, inaudible thrum I can feel deep in my chest. I resist the urge to reach for David's hand.

The numbers match, proving the Family Action Network is on a crusade to rid the world of fake vampires.

Or worse, real vampires.

**November 12**
I get my ethics midterm back: an F+. My complete lack of morals is now on my permanent record.

David helps me put it in perspective by showing me the coolest thing in the night sky. An unstable comet, hurtling toward the sun, has broken apart, creating a fuzzy blob that gets bigger each night.

I ignore the jump in my pulse when David puts his hand over mine to point the binoculars, and his other hand on my shoulder to stabilize my viewing experience. No doubt it's just my excitement over the comet.

## November 16

My dream doesn't bother with foreplay. It cuts right to David and me in his bed, our naked skin sliding together, slick with sweat, as we kiss and stroke and grasp each other.

He enters me, and we sigh, as if we've reached the end of a long, hard journey. Our bodies roll and arch and meld, and his arms clutch me close like he fears I'll slip away. But I have no intention of leaving, though I sense there's somewhere else I should be.

Shane's face appears over David's shoulder. I freeze, suddenly remembering who I am and where I belong.

Then he smiles, showing fangs twice as long as I've ever seen them. They shine with the pure silver of moonlight on snow. He strips off his shirt, then disappears from view.

David is oblivious to the incursion, his eyes closed and lashes fluttering as he murmurs my name. My name, not Elizabeth's.

Shane appears again, on the bed with us. He draws his hands up and down David's back, caressing in long, strong strokes. David groans with pleasure and throbs harder inside me.

The sight of both men above me starts a cascade of orgasms, until I feel like my heart will explode. I try to beg them to stop, but I'm laughing too hard from the joy and irony.

David's groans rise in pitch, and his thrusts grow more urgent. He grasps my hands beside my head as he comes, shoving my wrists deep into the pillow.

Shane leans forward and sinks his fangs into David's neck, the same place where Gideon once bit him. David's eyes roll back in elation, and he moans, tightening his grip on my hands.

A drop of blood falls on my chest, just below my collarbone. It's warm and dark, and I have an insane desire to taste it.

Shane's eyes open and gaze straight at me. I hear his thoughts as if he's spoken.

*I love you too much.*

His fangs sink deeper into David's neck, and the trickle of blood becomes a flood. David's mouth opens as if to scream, and his body starts to buck. Shane's grip tightens, and he squeezes his eyes shut, breathing hard through his nose as he swallows.

That's when I notice the silver cross dangling from David's neck. If I could reach it, I'd make myself believe for just one moment, long enough to save him. But his hands are locked with mine, clutching me in the throes of death as his blood pours over my breasts.

A soundless shriek rips my throat. I gulp breath after breath, trying to scream myself awake, but hot, thick blood fills my mouth and nose. David flops and jiggles in Shane's grasp as the death spasms crescendo.

At last a strangled yelp escapes me, and I wake rigid and shaking, lying at the edge of the bed.

A hand touches my shoulder, and someone whispers my name. I sit up quickly, almost knocking my head against David's. I check to make sure I'm not naked in real life. My fingers touch the soft cotton of my sleeveless sleep shirt.

He sits on the bed. "Nightmare?"

It's too dark to see him, so I reach out and run my fingers over the smooth, intact flesh of his throat. "You're okay."

"It's me," he says, and for a moment I wonder what he means. Then I realize he thinks I thought he was Shane, because I touched him, and am still touching him, even though—oh God—he's not wearing a shirt.

Now I'm not touching him.

"I know it's you, David. You were dead." I rub my upper arms to smooth the goose bumps. "It was so real. So much blood."

He sighs, and I hear his hand running over his neck in that familiar new tic. "You dreamed about Gideon."

I remain silent until I come up with words that are true. "I don't want to talk about it."

"Can I get you anything?"

"A new apartment."

He doesn't laugh. "I'm sorry you don't like it here."

"It's fine." I touch his arm in what I hope is a friendly, casual manner. "But I don't want to be a burden."

"I like having you here, Ciara." He clears his throat, as if to mute the force of his sincerity. "Much more than I thought I would, anyway."

I laugh louder than his comment warrants, just to relieve the tension. "You can go back to bed now."

"You sure?" He puts his hand over mine, provoking a flashback to my dream. "You're still shaking."

What does that mean? That I should let him stay and make me stop shaking? His hand is so warm—I forgot how much heat a human body holds—if he put them both on my body, the chill would vanish.

My mind swirls with the effort to separate dream from reality, fear from lust. The darkness magnifies my disorientation, but turning on the bedside lamp would force me to pull my hand from his. And again, it's so warm.

A spotlight shines on one fact, leaving the rest in obscurity: if I curl my thumb over his, so that I'm holding his hand in return, that tiny motion could set off a chain reaction that would change our lives forever. One thumb.

I hold my breath, frozen with indecision. The tension spikes with each passing second, because David is waiting for an answer to a not-so-simple question. I need to pull away, but right now it seems like it would rip off my own skin.

I force myself to breathe. The flood of oxygen to my brain gives me a sudden strength.

"Yeah, I'm sure." I pull my hand from under his— miraculously leaving my skin intact—and shift my legs over the edge of the bed. "I'll get some chamomile tea and go back to sleep."

"Me, too—the sleep, not the tea."

"Good. I mean, thanks." I shove myself off the bed. "I mean, good night," I say as I stumble to the door. "Again."

Dexter gets up from his position at the foot of my bed and follows me to the kitchen.

After I make the tea, I grab my cell phone and head down to the basement to call Lori. Midnight on a Friday is definitely within the realm of best friend semi-emergency calls.

Her phone rings as I shut the door at the bottom of the stairs. She doesn't pick up until the fifth ring.

"Hey." She stretches the word into two syllables, which means she's either sleepy or drunk or both.

"Did I wake you?"

"Nope. What's up?"

"You won't believe the dream I just had."

"Hold on while I get a pen."

"No! Promise me you won't jot a single note."

"Okay, okay. No jotting."

"Believe me, this one needs no interpretation." I glance at the closed door to the stairs, then decide I need more insulation between my mouth and David's ears. I go down the hall and into the storeroom, most of which is occupied by the oil-burning furnace and shelves of homeowner-type items.

I sit on a large, sturdy toolbox and tell Lori the whole

thing, leaving out none of the details. She doesn't comment, except with the occasional "Uh-huh" or "Then what?"

When I finish, she says, "Hm. So what do you think that's all about?"

I slap my forehead. "Lori, this isn't abstract Freudian symbolism. I didn't dream about David offering me a cucumber. Obviously I'm attracted to him, and I think he feels the same way. We live together. This is a powder keg, and it could get him killed."

"Oh, I doubt that last part."

"About the killing?"

"Mmm-hmm. That person just isn't the type."

*That person?* Suddenly I realize why she's being cryptic. "Is someone with you?"

"Uh, sort of."

"Who?"

"No one."

"It's Travis, isn't it?"

"Maybe."

I kick my heel against the toolbox. "Where are you?"

"At my place, watching a movie."

"Which movie?"

"Ciara . . ."

"Sorry." My hand tightens on the mug handle. "But tomorrow you call and tell me all about it."

She makes an ambiguous noise that contains no actual words, then says good night.

I finish my tea on the toolbox. A familiar duffel bag sits on the floor to my left, near the door leading to the backyard. The day Gideon attacked David, Shane and I used the bag's contents to destroy the ancient vampire. I can still hear his screams and smell his flesh burn as I shot him with a holy-water Super Soaker. At least he only suffered for about ten seconds before Shane sliced off his head.

Until that day, Shane had never killed anyone, living or undead. He refuses to talk about it; I think it damaged him, even though he was defending my life and David's.

Lori's probably right—now that Shane knows what it's like to take a life, he wouldn't do it again out of petty jealousy.

But if I ever cheated on him, the guilt would make me wish for death.

I go upstairs, set my empty mug in the sink, then start packing.

# 11

## Creep

I wait at the door of Elizabeth's condo while Shane enters the darkness inside, checking for intruders. Every week since her death, I've been making the forty-five-minute drive here from Sherwood to pick up her bills, but only got as far as the square metal mailbox inside the door of the building. I told myself it was because I was always in a hurry, but the fact is, I didn't want to be in this place alone.

Shane prowls the apartment—all senses tuned, no doubt—then turns on the light, a simple chandelier over the black, ultramodern dining room table. A thin layer of dust on the table mutes the reflection of the chandelier's bulbs.

From the door I can see the living room area, too, as well as the kitchen and a dark hallway. The air smells stale. I shiver and hope my reaction is only from the temperature.

"First we need heat." I spy a digital programmable wall thermostat not far from the door. I tap menu squares on the flat screen at random until the word "heat" comes on and warm air blows from the floor vents. I smile with satisfaction, though I have no idea how I made it happen. It's an improvement over my old apartment's hissy radiator, which would stop working if I made direct eye contact with it.

Shane moves into the living room and clicks on the stereo. The soporific voice of a female National Public Radio announcer crawls out of the speaker, entreating us to pledge seventy-five dollars in exchange for a coffee mug and a year-long lapse in guilt.

He snorts and changes the station to WVMP. Monroe's *Midnight Blues* program fills the room with notes of spirited loneliness. Oddly, the sound of a vampire radio show makes this place feel less creepy.

Shane nods approvingly at the speakers. "Nice system."

"It doesn't feel like home." I sit on the edge of Elizabeth's white leather couch, which isn't nearly as cushy as it looks. "Maybe I should sell all this nice furniture, then go Dumpster diving for new stuff."

"I have a better idea." Shane kneels on the floor in front of me, easing himself between my thighs. "Let's celebrate your new home." He gives me a deep kiss, pulling me into his arms. I return his passion for a few moments, trying to psych myself into the mood.

Finally I let go of him. "This feels weird."

"Not for long." He starts unbuttoning my shirt. "Think of all the new horizontal surfaces we can explore. Not to mention a few vertical ones."

"Maybe later." I gently push his hands away. "It feels like she's still here."

He studies my face. "But you don't believe in ghosts."

"Not real ones." I glance past him down the hall. "She's on my mind a lot lately, maybe because of all the time I've been spending with David."

"I knew Elizabeth Vasser. I worked with Elizabeth Vasser."
He brushes my hair off my cheek. "Senator, you're no Elizabeth
Vasser."

"Huh?"

"Sorry. Eighties humor." Shane kisses my forehead, then
takes my hand. "Let's move you in."

Sunday evening I roam the aisles of the local discount store,
examining the list Shane and I made of the housewares I need.
As a vampire, Elizabeth didn't eat, so plates, bowls, and forks
are at the top of the list. (Technically, only bowls are at the
top, since Shane ordered the items alphabetically.)

I stop in front of an endcap of ten-dollar throws. Hmm,
maybe a cheap-ass blanket would warm up Elizabeth's couch
and give it that college-student grunge factor I've been missing. I wonder if they sell prestained slipcovers.

"Ciara?"

I raise my head before I turn. It can't be. Please don't let
it be.

A man steps out of the area-rug aisle behind me. "It *is* you.
How have you been?"

"Fine. Uh . . ." I snap my fingers, pretending I don't remember the name of the squirrelly bald guy who saved my life.

"Ned!" He pats his chest. "Ned Amberson. From Gideon's
Lair. Remember?"

"Of course. Ned. What are you doing"—*Outside an
asylum?*—"in Rockville?"

"I live here. Well, I live with my parents for the moment,
which is pathetic, I know, for a thirty-five-year-old man. *But*."
He gestures to the cart parked halfway down the aisle. "I just
found a new place, looking to spruce it up."

"Are you, uh—" *Sane?* "Do you have a job?"

He laughs melodically, blue eyes sparkling. "No, but I'm

getting help." He shakes his head as he stops laughing. "I needed a lot of help, as you can imagine, after leaving that place. I went through the whole de-culting process, and let me tell you, I learned so much about myself."

"I bet." I check my watch. "I'd love to hear more about it, but—"

"Then let's go get coffee."

"Now?"

"Come on, it'll be fun. The store has a little food place up front."

My mind scrambles for an excuse and somehow finds the truth. "I have homework."

"Well, I don't want to stand in the way of that." He takes my shopping list and jots an address on the back. "I'll be here for the foreseeable future. It's sort of a halfway house for ex-cult members. They keep an eye on us, make sure we're consorting with the right people." He holds up a hand. "Don't worry—even though you work with the monsters, you get bonus credit for getting rid of Gideon." He leans closer and whispers. "Tell me, did all of him disappear, or just his body? Rumor says your boss has Gideon's head in a meat freezer."

I step back from him. "Um, let's save that story for another time." Like during the intermission of a hockey game in hell.

"Okay, Ciara." He puts his hand next to mine on my shopping cart handle. "But I encourage you to call us soon, before it's too late."

"Too late for what?"

His face turns somber. "To save you from hell."


At the discount store's "café," the chairs are all bolted to the frames of the orange acrylic tables—as if someone would walk off with one.

"So tell me," I say to Ned with an encouraging smile, "how

did you find this organization?" The going-to-hell statement could be just a coincidence, or there might be a connection to the wackos who tried to roast the station. It's worth spending a few more minutes with Ned to find out.

"My younger brother is one of the leaders," he says. "After Gideon's compound was raided by the Control, those of us who were in thrall to Gideon and his three progeny were taken away." He lowers his voice. "With him and Lawrence dead, and Jacob and Wallace in custody, it would've been too painful for us to stay."

I nod. Lanham had explained to us that the Control placed the compound under the agency's supervision rather than shutting it down. They figured the remaining two dozen ancient vampires posed less danger in a place where they could be monitored than if they were roaming the streets and countryside looking for food. Practical to the core, the Control. I have to admit I admire that.

"How many of the compound's, uh, guests stayed behind?"

Ned shakes his head sadly. "We called ourselves that, didn't we? 'Guests'? We were prisoners, plain and simple. Walking blood banks."

"But you told me last summer that the vampires didn't hurt you. That you had medical care and shelter and food. Even a home school for the kids. It was like a commune, you said."

"I was in denial. I was trying to impress you, per my orders, convince you to stay. Show you we were sane." He gives an embarrassed smile. "You weren't fooled, were you?"

"You weren't crazy," I tell him, though to be honest, he still has that cult light in his eyes. "You were manipulated. I'm sure if I'd stayed longer, I would've been a willing guest, too."

"That's sweet of you to say." He smiles down into his cup, rotating it with one hand while the other hand holds the stirrer straight up in the middle of the coffee. "But looking back on those years, it sure seems nuts."

"Were you bitten a lot?"

"One hundred seventeen times." Ned winces, as if the admission alone pains him. "What about you?"

"Just the once so far." Not true (it was twice). "Hurt a lot." Totally true (it was agony).

"It gets easier. Too easy." He shakes the ice in his empty water cup. "So who was it?"

I flick the salt crystals off my stale soft pretzel, choosing my words carefully. "This guy. He wants to be my boyfriend."

"He only says that so he can drink you. There was a woman once who had me fooled. Before I found out that we could never, you know." His voice dips as he stares into his coffee. "They all lie."

To keep him on my case, I say, "No, this guy's different. I think he loves me."

"Of course you do." Ned puts his hand on the table near mine. "They're so persuasive."

I try not to feel sleazy as I cash in on Ned's newfound concern for me. "So tell me more about this group. What are they called? Where did they come from?"

He hesitates, probably wondering whether he can trust me.

I push the sympathy card. "For me to feel comfortable asking you guys for help, I need to know more about you."

He gives a quick nod, his savior complex kicking in. "The Fortress has been around a long time, I think a hundred years. There are chapters all over the world. Secret, of course. Most of us would be carted off to the funny farm if the authorities heard our stories."

"What do they do besides run these halfway houses?"

He looks uncomfortable, and begins to fold his paper napkin in a way that reminds me of Shane. "I can't really tell you."

"But I need guidance," I say in my best imitation of a confused, frightened female. "Can you help me?"

Ned snaps open a bag of chips and eats one, then another, as if mulling over his next words. "I help run a support group you should join. The leader is a psychologist, so it's not just a bunch of us sitting around talking about being bitten. Though that is the name of the group."

"What is?"

"The Bitten."

I almost spew my coffee.

Ned rolls his eyes. "I know, kind of a dorky name. I wasn't there when they formed the group. Our next meeting is Tuesday night in Frederick."

Hmm, that's where Travis said the new cult was located. "I'll be there."

He brightens. "Fabulous!" His voice lowers. "There's just one thing. To keep out the posers and reporters, they ask newbies to show their wounds."

I gape at him. I hope he means metaphorical wounds.

"Your fang marks," he says. "The fresher the better." He angles his head. "Did he bite your neck? I don't see it."

That's because it healed months ago. "No, it was, uh, somewhere else."

Ned blushes. "Don't feel embarrassed. You can show Dr. Shelby in a private room. She's seen everything." He looks away and wipes his mouth with his paper napkin. I bet his skin looks like a topographical map.

"So if I join the group, can I find out more about the Fortress? It sounds exactly like what I need."

He hesitates. "Just come to the meeting, and if you like what you hear, we can let you in on more of the agenda. It's important to protect the Fortress at all costs."

I chuckle. "Aren't fortresses built to protect people instead of the other way around?"

Ned looks unamused. He leans forward. "When I was forced out of Gideon's Lair, I lost my will to live, until the

Fortress saved me. Some of us need to serve something larger than ourselves to feel complete." His fingers clutch at the napkin, ruining its careful folds. "What's the point of living if it's just for yourself?"

I nod solemnly, letting my eyes go soft and vulnerable, with a tinge of moral righteousness. It's a hard look to pull off, but he seems convinced, especially when I add, "I've never met anyone like you, Ned."

He blinks. "Really?"

"Everyone I know, they only think about getting ahead, taking what they need. No one really cares about anyone else." I let the back of my hand brush his palm. "But you're different."

He wraps his hand around mine. "I guess we're sort of soul mates."

I try not to think about his 117 bites. "How long were you at Gideon's compound?"

"Five and a half years. When I got out, it was like the world had passed me by." He pulls out his cell phone. "These things take pictures now."

"Yeah, a lot's happened. So where is this Fortress—"

"Hold still."

I realize he's taking my picture with his phone. "No!" I lunge forward to grab it, but he yanks it out of reach.

"Too late." Ned examines the screen. "Oh, that's a nice one." He snaps it shut and leans in his seat to insert it in the belt clip on his khakis.

Whoever these Fortress people are, I don't want them with a free mug shot of yours truly. For a moment, I consider throwing coffee on him, then stealing the phone while he's distracted.

Oh, what the hell. It wouldn't be the first time.

I point behind him. "You think that girl behind the counter's a vampire?"

He turns, and I tip my cup across the table into his lap. Ned shrieks and leaps up.

I gasp. "Oh my God, I'm so sorry. Are you burned?"

"No, it wasn't hot anymore." He shakes the coffee off his hands. The front of his pants are soaked. He makes to put his phone in his pocket before realizing it would get wet, so he sets it on my side of the table, away from the puddle.

"I'll buy you another pair of pants right now."

"No, that's okay—"

"I insist." I grab a stack of napkins from the empty table beside us and hand him several. I wipe the tabletop with the rest, swiping the phone into my other hand while he carefully blots his soaking crotch.

Phone safely in pocket, I crouch in front of him and dab the napkins against his thighs.

"Really," he says, somewhat breathless, "you don't have to do that." He puts his hand over mine, though not to remove it. "But thank you."

Ha. I was pretty sure he wasn't gay.

From my knees, I give him my sauciest gaze. "You sure I can't put you in another pair of pants?"

His eyes widen. "Uh . . . on second thought, that'd be real nice."

"Think nothing of it." I stand, hook my arm through his, then turn us toward menswear. "Join me in the fitting room?"

He gives me an amazed smile, then glances back at the table. "Where's my phone?"

"I'll hold on to it until we get you changed." I risk a quick brush of my fingertips over his hip, a move he could interpret as an accident.

"Thanks, Ciara."

We reach the menswear fitting room, where I wait outside Ned's cubicle until he tosses his pants over the door.

I grab them and scurry out. "Be right back!"

It takes about twenty seconds to find a replacement for his generic khaki trousers, then another five minutes to delete my photo from his phone, search fruitlessly for other pictures, and copy the numbers of his entire contact list and recent calls on the back of my store receipt.

He declares the trousers a perfect fit and invites me inside the cubicle to give him a second opinion.

I decline.


Dexter greets me at the door, knocking the large shopping bags of cheap housewares out of my hand and spilling their contents. He grabs one of the blankets and shakes it, hard enough to dislodge the cardboard wrapper.

"Glad you approve." I scratch his head, sparking a butt-wiggle seizure. "How much have you destroyed your new home?"

A quick inspection of the apartment reveals no chewed furniture, though the kitchen floor is covered in an eviscerated box of cereal. Hundreds of Cheerios—which comprised my entire food supply—lie uneaten but crushed into a fine oaty powder.

On the shopping list on the refrigerator, I write MORE DOG TOYS and BABY LOCKS FOR CABINETS.

The cold, damp night air coats my skin as I take Dexter out for a walk. I tug up the hood of my coat to warm my ears, then shove it back down when I realize it blocks my peripheral vision. After two weeks of living with David, I find myself spooked at being alone again.

A car door slams behind me, making me jump. I turn to see a bulky man get out of a black Lexus about twenty feet away. My heart starts to pound as I wonder why someone with an expensive car would be in my neighborhood.

Wait. This isn't my neighborhood. It's Elizabeth's. Rich people are supposed to be here.

The man gives me a casual wave, then engages the car alarm with a chirp. I wave back, and we continue our mutual anonymity.

When he disappears, I pull up my hood again. This is a safe area. The condo association probably has a neighborhood watch, or can afford to pay for its own private police force.

Dexter drags me over the shiny wet sidewalk toward a large shade tree at the corner of the parking lot, where my apartment building ends and another begins. In the space between the buildings is a small playground with a swing set and sliding board. It's empty now, of course, glowing in a sulfurous orange light.

Dexter circles the tree three times before choosing the perfect place to leave his mark. He doesn't have much ammunition, due to his low levels of liquid intake. He lifts his leg just as a car drives by on the road, its tires swishing through the puddles.

The sound fades, and in the silence, I hear a creak behind me, steel against steel. I turn my head, but the hood cuts off my vision. In front of me, Dexter freezes, leg raised.

Another creak, louder, from the playground. I turn quickly.

One of the swings is swinging in a wide arc, its seat empty.

The wind, right? But then wouldn't both swings be moving?

The swing's momentum slows, and its seat sways and turns on its chain in such a way that tells me someone pulled it up and let it go.

But who? And where the hell are they now?

I step back, fear zinging over my skin like static electricity as I sense I'm being watched. It's not the cold, slithery feeling I got when Gideon stalked me. It could be a younger, less sinister vampire, or "just" a human attacker.

Something bumps into me from behind, and I let out a yelp before realizing it's Dexter.

Or, at least, what used to be Dexter. He stands rigid, one forepaw slightly raised, his muzzle pointed at the playground. Nostrils flaring, ears twitching, he takes a stiff step forward. My grip tightens on the leash so hard, the leather pinches my skin.

"What is it, boy?" I whisper, as if he can tell me.

A rumble starts deep in his chest, so low in tone I can barely hear it. Beneath his black coat, the muscles of his back and legs bunch into tight, trembling cords.

His lips curl back into a snarl, arranging the scars on his face into a fearsome war mask. He steps forward, pressing against me as he brushes by, putting himself between me and the playground. My gaze darts back to the swing, which continues to slow.

Dexter lunges, but I'm ready for him. He hits the end of the leash, then rears on his hind legs and lets loose his booming bark, the one that must be registering on the Richter scale at a distant geological research center. Every snarl and growl reverberates through the leash to my hand, and I feel a surge of invincibility.

Feet crash over dry leaves, and a shadowed figure races away through the wooded area behind the apartment buildings.

Dexter barks a few more times, then reduces his voice to an indignant growl. Lights flicker on in windows around us.

"Good boy." I tug his leash, grateful that he didn't tear off my arm. "Let's go inside."

He shakes himself hard, then gives me a broad doggy smile and wags his tail. We return to our building at a brisk pace, before anyone can yell at us.

Back in our living room, I give Dexter an hour-long belly rub while we watch TV. He might be a monster, but in this world, maybe a monster is just what I need.

# 12

## Time the Avenger

Monday morning I meet with Lori, David, and Shane in the station lounge to report the latest.

Shane paces as he listens to my stories of Ned and the stalker. "You think it's a coincidence?" he asks me.

"I don't believe in coincidences." I slouch over to the coffee pot on the credenza, exhausted from a poor night's sleep. Dexter kept me up with his constant patrolling, his nails clicking over the hardwood floors. "But it might not be Ned stalking me. It could be anyone from the Fortress. Or there could be another secret nut-job organization out there who wants to mess with me. But I'll send Travis the contacts I got out of Ned's cell phone and see if he can find any connections."

"Wait a minute." David turns to me from the card table, where he's been sitting, deep in thought, since I began. "When did Ned say the Fortress was formed?"

"About a hundred years ago." I finish pouring the coffee

and reach for the sugar. "But who knows if they told him the truth?"

"I wonder . . . " He rubs his knuckles against the side of his face. "That would have been around the time of the schism."

"What schism?" I snap the three sugar packets before ripping them open.

"The Control."

We all stare at him. "The Control schismed?" Shane says finally.

He spreads his hands. "It wasn't a major split. About five percent of the organization resisted the changes that took place around the turn of the twentieth century."

Shane narrows his eyes. "Changes like not hunting and slaughtering every vampire they see?"

"Exactly." David looks at me. "It was around the same time they started allowing female agents—though they weren't called 'agents' until the Control changed its name. Before that we were all 'warriors.' "

My shoulders sag. "So these schism people blamed the policy change on the influx of women."

David nods. "They said the Control had gotten soft. They said there were some places women just didn't belong. Namely, in power."

"Jerks," Lori says.

David puts his hands on the table. "Here's the kicker. The people who schismed from the Control called themselves the Citadel. I'm not a walking thesaurus, but a citadel is a lot like a fortress."

"Music gives women power," Shane adds. "This fits with their attacks on our programs, why this Family Action Network only blocks our signal when women are on the air."

"So FAN is connected to the Fortress." I turn to David. "Which explains why they used Control technology for that booby-trapped cross. Maybe they still have a connection inside the Control."

"A sympathizer." David frowns. "Maybe a disgruntled agent, someone who's not happy with the way the Control operates. Or an ex-agent with a vendetta."

This is getting more complicated by the minute. I stir the sugar into my coffee. "Colonel Lanham said someone stole Dexter." Another memory pings my brain. "He also said they suspected my dad's bodyguard of helping him escape."

David frowns in his automatic response to any mention of my dad. "Maybe that guy's a double agent for the Fortress now."

"I'll try to learn more about them at that Bitten meeting."

"You're not going alone." Shane folds his arms in a rare don't-argue-with-me pose. "It's not safe."

"You can't come with me. These people know vampires. They'll sniff you out in a second."

A small, high voice says, "I'll go with you."

I turn to Lori. "But Ned says they need to see wounds—"

"I know."

"—and you haven't been . . ." My voice fades as I notice her avoiding my eyes.

She let that bloodsucking redneck get his fangs into her.

"Lori." I fight to keep the anger from my words. "You said you didn't want Travis to bite you."

She shrugs, looking at her toes. "I changed my mind."

"You have no idea what—"

"Leave her alone." David's tone is deadly sober. "It's not your place to judge."

Lori gives him a tiny smile. A look of understanding passes between them. They like being prey.

"Just be careful." I swallow my self-righteous disgust and squeeze her shoulder. "I'd love it if you came with me to the meeting."

She brightens. "We'll be undercover, like another con job."

The door to the studio opens, and Noah glides in. "Good morning," he says as he retrieves a bottle of water from the fridge. "What's new?"

We bring him up to speed on the situation. He listens with concern, then turns to me.

"How will you infiltrate these people without a bite?"

"I've been bitten."

"Four months ago," Lori points out. "How are you going to convince them you have a habit you can't kick?"

"Clever makeup application?" I look at each of them for encouragement. "Removable vampire bite tattoo?"

Noah screws the cap back on his water bottle. "I'll do it right now."

I take a step back. "Uh, do what?"

"Do you mind?" he asks Shane, who shakes his head.

"Not if I'm here." Shane looks at me. "You'll barely feel it. Noah's like the master phlebotomist of vampires."

A cold heat sweeps over my scalp. "I don't want to be bitten."

"We did it before," Shane says.

"And it hurt!" My breath shortens just thinking about it. "I said, never again."

Lori crosses her arms. "I can't get into the Bitten meeting without you. You're the one who knows Ned."

I dig my nails into my palms. I don't want to do this, but Lori's right—I'm the only avenue to the Fortress.

"Fine. But not in the neck. And it has to be Shane." I turn to him and touch my waist, right below my rib cage. "Here, like you did to Deirdre." My voice gives out at the mention of the woman I once watched him drink. They were so helpless in each other's arms.

Shane nods. "It won't be deep, just enough to make it convincing."

"And no drinking."

"Promise." He points to the door. "Everyone else out."

David stops next to me on his way to the stairs. "Thanks. I know this isn't easy for you."

I glance at Shane, conferring with Noah in the corner of the lounge. "It's for a good cause, right?"

David pats my shoulder as he passes. It's a casual, friendly gesture, like the kind we used to share before the weirdness began.

Lori follows David upstairs, and Noah exits into the hallway by the studio. Then it's just me and my biter.

Shane kisses me lightly on the lips. "They should give you a bonus in your paycheck."

"Just get it over with." My muscles feel like they could snap from the tension. "Forget the hypno-eyes and the pretty words of comfort."

"Okay, but it's easier if you relax." He brushes my hair behind my neck on one side. "Hey, are those new earrings?"

"No, I've had them for years." I finger one of the small fake garnet studs. "Do you like them?"

"I always like red." He massages my shoulder with one hand and slips the other under the hem of my shirt, shifting it up on one side. "But you usually go for something a little funkier."

"Well, now that it's cold, I'm wearing my hair down, and I don't want to get it caught in—"

A third hand rests on my hip, and a sudden warm pressure touches my waist.

"What the—Ow!" Something just pricked me, like a bee sting. I look down to see Noah withdrawing his fangs from my flesh. "Hey!" I try to move away, but Shane holds me fast. "What the hell are you doing?"

"Nothing now." Noah stands and dabs his mouth with a tissue while his other hand holds a piece of gauze to my side. "All finished. Here, apply pressure."

"That's not—how did you—" I slap my hand over the gauze, where a small bloodstain is spreading, then look up at Shane. "You set me up."

"Sorry, but I thought this was better than hurting you." He nods at Noah over my shoulder. "Thanks. Nice stealth."

"How could I be so stupid?" I smack Shane in the chest with my free hand. "You never talk about jewelry."

"Are you mad at me?"

"I should want to kill you." I shake my head in amazement at the wound. "But you were right. It hardly hurt at all." I look at Noah. "How do you do that?"

He shrugs. "It is a gift." Noah touches the edge of his red-gold-and-green knit cap and saunters toward the hallway. "Good night, lady and gentleman."

When the door shuts behind him, I turn back to Shane, who's staring at the wound on my waist. The blood flow hasn't slowed at all.

"Why does it take so long to stop?" I ask him.

"We have anticoagulants in our saliva." He blinks, but doesn't look away. "Like mosquitoes."

"Ha." I attempt a joke to lighten the growing tension. "They should make anti-artery-clogging drugs from you guys."

"Hmmm." He rubs his hands along the sides of his jeans, still staring.

"I'll need another pad," I tell him. "Hello?"

Shane jerks his gaze back to my face. "Sorry? I mean, yeah, okay. Gauze." He turns away, then scans the room, as if he's already forgotten what he's seeking. Then he lurches to the credenza and opens the second drawer.

"You want to drink me, don't you?"

"Of course I do." He rummages through the drawer. "But I don't want that between us. I don't want to start craving you in even more ways." He turns to me with a packet of gauze and a bottle of iodine. "I remember how good you taste."

I stretch out my hand so he won't have to come too close. "I probably taste like salsa after that breakfast burrito."

He tries to smile but doesn't give me the first aid stuff. "Lie down, it'll stop bleeding faster."

I recline on the couch on my unwounded side. Shane sits at my feet and peels the wrapper off the gauze, his hands trembling. Then he replaces the blood-soaked square of soft cotton with a clean one. "Hold it there."

I eye the bottle of iodine. "That'll hurt worse than the bite."

"Better to be safe, since we didn't clean your skin before Noah bit you."

After the ouch is over, Shane tugs my legs to rest in his lap. He slips my shoes off and starts to rub my feet. It soothes us both.

He squeezes my knee and speaks in a lighter tone. "So is this Ned guy cute?"

I shrug. "He's bald."

"Oh, okay." He goes back to rubbing my feet, secure in his status.

Guys with good hair are like thin girls—they think their opposites are automatically no competition. But give me a bald guy with a good body over a lumpy guy with good hair. I guess that makes me shallow in a different way.

I turn my head so I can see Shane's expression when he answers the question I'm about to ask. "You gave up biting women for me because it's such an intimate act. So why did you let Noah bite me?"

Shane smiles, his eyes soft. "Tasting your blood won't make him lust after you. The older we get, the more we can separate our nourishment from its source." He shrugs. "By the time I'm his age, I'll probably be able to see a human being as nothing more than a walking vein."

"Oh."

"Not you," he hurries to add. "Plenty of older vampires have human friends."

My mouth goes dry. "Just friends?"

He sighs and rubs the pale brown stubble on his jaw. "This is coming out wrong. When I say 'friends,' I mean any relationship. Vampires can still see people as more than livestock. Look at Monroe and David, for example. Mutual respect, common bonds, all that."

My heart feels like it could fit inside an espresso cup. When I'm forty-four, will I want more than mutual respect and common bonds with Shane? Will I even know him?

"Do older vampires fall in love with humans?"

"Or *stay* in love with them?" His face is shadowed by the halogen lamplight reflected off the ceiling. "Is that what you're asking?"

I nod, unable to speak.

Shane takes my hand. "Honestly, I've never heard of one. We get less human as we age, so it's harder for us to relate to you. But that doesn't mean it couldn't happen." His thumb caresses mine. "You keep me young and human."

"I try." I swallow the lump in my throat. "But you said you didn't want that. You said you'd rather fade than become someone you're not."

"True, but there's gotta be a middle ground between basket case and publicity puppet. I think you can help me find it." He kisses my hand softly. "Besides, I can't imagine ever not being in love with you."

I return his smile, because I can't help it, then put my head down and try to enjoy the foot rub while ignoring the fading sting in my side.

People speak of "emotional roller coasters" as if they're a bad thing, but those people are on the part of the roller coaster that makes you throw up, not the part that makes your blood sing and your heart leap into your throat, the part that makes you smile so hard your cheeks hurt.

And that part is why, when we stumble off, most of us run to the back of the line to ride again.

# 13

## Lunatic Fringe

"It makes me feel close to him." Lori twists her hands together and glances at the rest of the therapy circle. "I'm giving him something he needs. It feels like we belong to each other."

The group leader, Dr. Shelby, looks up from her notepad and regards Lori over her half-moon glasses. "Are you his sole donor?"

"I'm not a donor," Lori says with an edge to her voice.

"If he drinks your blood, that makes you his donor." Dr. Shelby taps her pen against the ends of her long silver braid. "Are you the only one he drinks from?"

Lori looks away from the therapist, at the third-grade classroom's display of shoebox dioramas. "You know the answer to that."

"I want to hear you say it."

Lori's jaw tenses. "Of course he has other donors. He's young, so he needs to drink a lot more than I can give him.

But I'm okay with that, because I know I'm special. He doesn't take those other people to dinner. He doesn't talk on the phone to them for hours."

"Does he have sexual intercourse with them?"

"I—" Lori flushes. "I don't know. We're not exclusive or anything."

I squirm in my seat, partly because the plastic chair is killing my ass, but mostly because Lori's pain is making me want to smack Travis seven ways to Tuesday.

We decided it would be easier for her to just tell the truth, with some exaggeration, so she wouldn't have to remember a fake story. She's the kind who wears her feelings all over her face.

Dr. Shelby removes her glasses and gives Lori a sympathetic look. "Do you want to have an exclusive relationship with this man? Do you want to be his girlfriend?"

"It's too soon to think of that." Lori crosses her arms and sits back in her seat. "We just started going out a few weeks ago."

"And look what it's done to you," says a strong, clear male voice.

I turn to see a young guy sitting next to Ned, a guy with shaggy dark curls and gleaming blue eyes. I remember him checking Lori out before the meeting.

He clears his throat. "Sorry, my name's Kevin." He looks at Dr. Shelby. "Can I try to help?"

I surreptitiously mark off his name from the list of Ned's cell phone contacts. With the doctor and other members who have already spoken, that accounts for six out of twelve names so far. Four others share Ned's last name and live in Chicago—family members, I presume. The remaining two are unlisted, and designated merely as *Stevenson* and *B.*

Dr. Shelby nods, and Kevin turns back to Lori.

"We don't have to be emotional slaves. I know he makes

you feel awesome, and it seems like you'd be lost without him." He taps his fingertips against his chest. "I've been there."

I look at Lori, who watches him with wide round eyes as his speech continues. My phone vibrates in my pocket, signaling a new text message. I slip it out, shielding it in my palm, and angle my head to read Travis's message:

Stevenson = FAN VP

My eyebrows pop up. Ned knows the vice president of the Family Action Network? Jackpot!

Dr. Shelby utters a soft "Ahem." I look up to find her glaring at me. I put my phone back in my pocket and focus on Kevin, who's finally wrapping things up.

"But we deserve better," he says. "We deserve to be treated with respect. We're human, after all." He says this last part with a curled lip, the way a whiny bigot might say, "We're white, after all."

"What do you mean by that?" I ask him.

His eyes narrow as they turn my way. "These monsters treat us like livestock. But they're the ones who should be rounded up."

"And then what?"

Dr. Shelby breaks in. "That's getting off topic. Lori, do you think Kevin's right? Do you think each of us has the power to reach for happiness, even if it means letting go of what we tell ourselves we need?"

Lori's brow furrows, and she glances at me. "I guess." She rubs her left shoulder. "But that wasn't all he was saying. Kevin thinks humans are better than vampires."

"We are." He looks at her with such intensity, I want to shield her. But she's not cowed.

"They were once human," she says. "Some of them you can't even tell the difference."

"They drink blood." He holds up his hands in a pleading gesture. "People don't do that."

"Everyone does something no one else does. My family's Finnish. We eat blood dumplings and reindeer. That doesn't make us better or worse than other families."

"Being a vampire is not like being from Finland." He raises and lowers his palms like he's weighing two objects. "They're metaphysically different creatures."

Dr. Shelby interrupts again. "We're not here for a philosophical discussion. We're here to help each other overcome emotional blocks that keep us from leading vampire-free lives."

I try not to laugh at the psychobabble. I'm not entirely successful.

The "doctor" turns to me. "What about you, Ciara? Are you ready to tell your story?"

I begin with the truth, to make my job easier. Besides, every lie has a truth at its creamy-nougat center.

"I discovered my boyfriend was a vampire the hard way. He bit me when we were, uh, intimate. Without my permission."

One of the men hisses. I hide my annoyance and continue.

"That got us off to a rocky start, but we worked things out, and I told him I never wanted to be bitten. Ever."

They all cock their heads, as if I've just started reciting Homer in the original Greek. They've never noticed that vampire bites hurt?

"Then one night, he got me really drunk." Yeah, like that would happen. "We were fooling around, you know, naked." I make brief eye contact with the three men in the group. "Next thing I know, he's biting me. I tried to push him off, but he wouldn't stop." I put my hands on my stomach, feeling sick for telling such a horrible lie about an imaginary Shane. "And then, all of a sudden, it started to feel good." I move my palms to my thighs in an "unconscious" gesture and slide them up and down. "Real good."

Possessing their rapt attention, I pause.

"Then what?" Ned says, jaw slightly agape.

"I liked it. But the next time, I was sober, and it hurt, so I made him stop."

"Did he stop?" Dr. Shelby asks in a clinical tone.

"He got me a glass of tequila. A big glass." I sigh. "So now blood and booze are all tangled up in my mind."

"Yes," she says. "You associate being bitten with a pleasurable chemical state of awareness." She chews on the end of her glasses, and I wonder if it tastes like scalp. "Do you consider yourself addicted to this man?"

I almost laugh, because I don't do addictions. I quit smoking because it bored me.

But then I wonder: could I live without Shane? The thought makes me feel heavy and cold.

"I need him." I stare at the floor. "I love him. But that's not the same as addiction."

The others—except for Lori—make disapproving noises, clicking their tongues and murmuring words like "slave" and "denial."

Dr. Shelby breaks in. "Ciara, our group was formed on the addiction model. Our very premise says that the notion of an equal relationship between a vampire and a human is absurd. If one being feeds off another, there can be no freedom, no true respect."

I look at Lori's stricken face. "But what if it's voluntary?"

Dr. Shelby shakes her head. "You know the power that lies in their eyes." She gives me a sympathetic gaze. "With vampires, there are no volunteers."

"So how'd you like your first meeting?" Kevin asks us across the diner's shiny white laminate table. He directs his second sentence to Lori, who's sitting next to me. "Hope we didn't scare you off."

She huddles inside her brown wool coat, like she always does after coming in from the cold, and says nothing.

I jump in, tapping the edge of the dessert menu on the table to grab their attention. "It's great to meet others who understand what we're going through. We can't exactly write to Ann Landers about this."

Across from me, Ned gives a warm smile, and I can't help thinking he'd be a nice friend if he weren't bat-shit crazy.

"When I met Dr. Shelby," he says, "it was like God threw me a lifeline. Like He was saying, 'Ned, I want you to live. You have a purpose.' "

"Wow." Elbows on the table, I rest my chin on the heels of my hands so I can give him an admiring gaze. "So what's that purpose?"

"To be a shepherd." He spreads his fingers on the table surface. "See, each of us has a choice. We can turn inward and drown in our own bitterness, or we can open our eyes and see others' suffering. At first, that just makes it hurt more, because it reminds us of the damage these creatures can wreak. But once we bring others into the fold, once we show them the way to freedom and the true path to God, we free ourselves all over again."

I want to look away, or better yet, run away. His words remind me too much of the lies my parents used to tell their congregations, the parade of suckers who'd give money in exchange for a promise of salvation. Mom and Dad would speak and sing of freedom and hope, and those people's eyes would shine just like Ned's.

"That's really nice," Lori says, turning the last word into two syllables in a failed attempt at sincerity.

"Yeah, it's inspiring." Kevin leans forward on his elbows, gesturing with his hands. "But it's only half the equation. We have to protect each other from these monsters, not just with words, but with actions."

Now we're getting somewhere. I sip my chocolate milk shake and ask in an innocent tone, "What kind of action?"

He gives me a suspicious glare. "Nothing illegal. We teach each other how to defend against an attack. We make sure none of us walks alone at night." He turns his dark gaze on Lori. "We act as each other's bodyguards."

He looks like he wants to do a lot more than *guard* her body. But it presents an opportunity to play connect-the-rhetoric.

"We can defend ourselves," I tell him. "We don't need big, strong men like you."

He shakes his head, making his curls bounce over his shoulder. "It's hard enough for a guy to fight them, even one trained in self-defense like me. But women are weaker." When I make an annoyed face, he says, "Your boyfriend overpowered you. You didn't have a chance."

I stir my milk shake with my straw, putting on a troubled look. "So you're saying it wasn't my fault?"

"Of course it wasn't. Vampires are predators. They take advantage of the weak, and compared to them, we're all weak."

I let my eyes soften, as if I'm having a sad epiphany. "Thank you for saying that. I'm so tired of pretending to be strong." I put my hands in my lap and lower my gaze. "Sometimes I wish—I mean, I think it would be kind of nice to have a man take care of me. Someone to make all the hard decisions. That way I could focus on what's really important in life." I fiddle with the clasp of my bracelet. "You know, like having kids."

Ned speaks softly. "Do you want children, Ciara?"

I send him a wide-eyed gaze. "Doesn't everyone?" I can't look at Lori, because I know I'll crack up. "That's all I've ever wanted. But these days, they tell us that's not enough."

"Yeah," Lori adds hesitantly. "I only went to college to find a husband. But none of the guys there wanted to get married until they were, like, thirty. Some don't want to get married at all."

"They don't need to," Kevin says. "They think, why bother

when girls will give it up for a couple of beers?" Lori looks down at her coffee, and he hurries to add, "Not you, I mean. You seem like a nice girl."

"I was." She tilts her head and frowns. "I guess that's why none of them bothered with me until Tra—uh, Trevor."

"Trevor," he snarls. "Is that your boyfriend's name?"

"He's not my boyfriend. He's just, you know . . ."

Kevin touches her hand. "A monster who drank your blood and took your virginity."

Her eyes go wide, and her mouth starts to tremble at the corners. She's about to lose it.

Just in time, she covers her face and heaves a fake sob.

"Lori, I'm sorry." Kevin yanks a napkin from the dispenser. She grabs it and stuffs it against her nose and mouth, choking back little hiccups.

"That was rather insensitive," Ned remarks.

"I know." Kevin drags a hand through his curls. "I was trying to make a point, but it was a stupid way to do it."

"No, it's all true." Lori's voice is even higher-pitched than usual. She lunges out of the booth and heads for the restroom. "I gotta go."

I watch her leave, then turn back to the guys and fold my hands on the table. "Lori's in a very vulnerable place right now."

Kevin clenches his fist. "That vampire's messed her up. They have no right to violate our women."

I'm about to deny the fact that we belong to them, but then I realize he means "our" as in "human."

I've stumbled into the Ku Klux Klan of vampirehood.

I scoot out of the booth. "I better go check on her." I hurry past the other tables and knock on the door of the single-occupancy ladies' room. "It's me."

The latch clicks, and Lori tugs me inside. Her face is bright red from laughing.

"Did you hear what he said?" She coughs and pats her

chest. "He thinks I was a virgin before Travis. I'm twenty-four years old!"

"Should we tell him your magic number and watch him pass out?"

We're laughing so hard we have to hold each other up, which is easy, thanks to the tight space. Finally we stop and blow our watering noses.

"It's a shame." Lori checks the mirror and drags a paper towel under her eye to wipe the smeared mascara. "He's really cute."

"Do you think he's a virgin himself?"

"No, he probably got totally screwed by some vampire bitch and is taking it out on the whole species."

"Female vampires can't have sex with human men."

"Why not?"

I explain the muscle-contraction dilemma, which resurrects her giggles.

"Maybe that's what happened to Kevin," she chokes out. "Maybe he got decockinated in a tragic vamp-fucking accident."

My laughter turns into a coughing fit as I choke on my own saliva. Finally I catch my breath and put a firm grip on Lori's shoulders. "We have to go back before they send someone after us. But first, I need to know: does your family really eat reindeer?"

"My grandparents, yeah, but just in restaurants. At home it's usually moose."

That comment does nothing for our sobriety.

Once our faces are the semblance of straight, I lead her back out to the table.

"Hate to cut this short, guys." I pick up my coat. "But I've got homework, and Lori's not feeling well."

Kevin stands up in a hurry and dumps a crumpled ten-dollar bill on the table. "We'll walk you out."

In the parking lot, Ned and I stand next to my car and keep an eye on Kevin and Lori.

"She's confused." Ned's mouth tightens in a frown. "Kevin can help her, but sometimes he's a tad aggressive."

I give his arm a gentle punch. "Not like you, right?"

"Right." He looks at his feet. "So, the next meeting is next week, same place, same time."

"I guess I'll see you then."

"Okay. Unless—" He glances away. "I mean, if you want to do something outside the Bitten . . ."

"I can't." I examine my own feet, all shylike, and tuck my hair behind my ear on his side. "I don't want to endanger you."

"From your sort-of boyfriend." He crosses his arms and stands with feet apart. "Don't worry, I can handle him."

I mute my laugh into a smile. "Let's just wait until things are less complicated."

"I understand. So I won't even try to kiss you right now." His tone is jokey casual, but his gaze traces the outline of my face. "Unless."

"No, best not." I look over his shoulder to see Lori get in her car. "I should follow her back to Sherwood. She has a bad transmission." I give Ned's elbow a quick squeeze, then hurry into my car and put the key in the ignition.

"Wait." Ned holds my door open and leans in. "I lied." He brushes his lips over mine. His mouth smells of coffee and ChapStick, and it's all I can do not to back out over his foot.

I force a smile. "Have a good week."

As I drive away, I look in the rearview mirror to see Ned and Kevin conferring beneath the diner's neon sign.

Instinct tells me never to see them again. But they might hold the answers we seek in their creepy little hands.

# 14

## Our Lips Are Sealed

I spend Thanksgiving Day cutting myself. Not on purpose, like Jeremy, or like that friend I had in high school. Since I have no flair for cooking, David has put me to scullery work in his kitchen. Ciara, peel this. Ciara, slice that. "This" ends up being my index finger, and "that" turns out to be my left thumb. There's enough blood in the candied yams to make it a part of any vampire's complete breakfast.

It keeps me out of David's way, which is where I've tried to be for the last week. We've trod gingerly around each other since that night I had The Dream, followed by Sexual Tension Moment. It's as if there's a force field between us, like we'll spontaneously combust if we get closer than ten feet. It reminds me of that Rutger Hauer prison movie *Deadlock*, where everyone wore collars, and if someone escaped, their collar and that of their secret partner would explode. Except it's the opposite.

Preparing Thanksgiving dinner together falls a little too

close to coupledom for my comfort. I'm not soothed by the fact that Franklin is attending with his boyfriend, thus giving the dinner a double-date configuration.

David comes into the dining room, where I'm setting the table, my heavily Band-Aided fingers fumbling with the utensils.

"Everything's ready," he says. "Remember, Aaron doesn't know the truth about the DJs, so treat him like any other member of the public." He looks into the living room, then hurries over and sweeps up the stack of mail from the coffee table. "This place is so cluttered, you can tell I'm not a vampire."

I laugh nervously and try to remember whether spoons go on the left or right of the plate. I'm sure Shane could tell me, and he'd probably also tell me to line up the bottom edges of all the utensils.

"Here's your mail." David brings over a rubber-banded group of envelopes. "Forwarded from your old apartment."

I toss the spoons in a pile and take it from him. I decided not to have my mail reforwarded to my new place, since there I'm officially Elizabeth Vasser.

It's mostly junk and a few bills. I flip over a tattered postcard. Who do I know is vacationing in St. Louis?

David snaps his fingers. "Almost forgot. I gotta call my mom." He disappears into the kitchen.

Cold sweat turns the postcard slick in my hands.

> *Dear Ciara,*
> *Obviously by the time you get this, I'll be long gone from here, but I wanted you to know I was safe, though you probably don't care at this point whether I live or die.*
> *I've been thinking about your mother a lot lately, and what I did to her life. I weep when I picture her sitting alone in that cell. I hope you won't make the same mistake.*
> *All my love,*
> *Dad*

"No, Mom, just a few people from work." David wanders in from the kitchen, speaking on the phone. "Of course I used real butter in the gravy. I know, Thanksgiving is no day for healthy living. Heart attacks are made of holidays."

He rolls his eyes at me, and I turn away into the dining room so he can't see my face.

I read the postcard again, resting my hands on the back of the antique wooden chair to keep them from shaking.

What does Dad mean by "the same mistake"? Ruining Shane's life, like he did my mom's? Or having it ruined *by* him? Which of us is the monster?

A knock comes at the door. I fold the postcard in half and stuff it in the pocket of my WVMP apron.

Still on the phone, David signals me to answer the door. "None of my friends my age are married," he says to his mom. "Thirty-three is not old."

My head spinning, I hold the banister on the way down the short flight of stairs into the foyer.

"I've been on a few dates, nothing serious." David pauses. "Yes, Mom. With women."

I open the door, and with one glance understand why the DJs don't impress Franklin. He's got his very own human god.

"You're Aaron?" I gape at the man's tall, J. Crew–clad frame. The breeze blows loose waves of short dark hair over his forehead, and the gray sky behind him sets off a pair of deep blue eyes framed with perfect black lashes. He couldn't be more than thirty—almost ten years younger than Franklin. "Seriously?"

He gives me a dimpled, knee-weakening smile. "Did you want to see some ID?"

I look at Franklin, who wears a deservedly smug expression.

"We brought wine." Aaron hands me two bottles of red, a Cabernet and a Shiraz.

"Thank you," I say with the gushiness of a game show winner.

We head for the kitchen, where David is trying to get off the phone with his mom.

"Yes, I'll absolutely come to Florida for next Thanksgiving. Okay, for Easter. Okay, I love you. Okay, bye."

The three men greet one another while I open the Cabernet. Maybe a glass of wine will help me forget the postcard in my pocket.

The most important ramification smacks my awareness. *Dad's not dead!* At least, not as of the postmark date two weeks ago.

With the rush of relief, hysterical laughter bubbles up. I cover my mouth and realize my hand is ice cold.

The guys give me a confused glance. I realize they were talking about the high price of heating oil.

"Sorry, I was thinking of something else." I hold up the bottle. "Wine?"

Over the next hour, I'm reminded that Aaron teaches at Sherwood College—in the history department, which I've managed to avoid. I'm definitely taking his History of Eastern Europe as an elective. I wouldn't mind looking at that face for three hours a week, and he says I can do my term paper on vampires.

We proceed to the table, my brain swimming from the two glasses of wine accompanied by nothing but light hors d'oeuvres. Normally I'm a one-drink woman, but my dad's postcard rubbed my nerves raw.

I sit next to Franklin and across from Aaron, to avoid being even superficially paired with David. If he could get a close look into my eyes, he'd see my disloyalty. My dad almost got him killed, after all, and Lanham ordered me to tell him if I heard from my father.

So they can hunt him down and kill him? Fuck that. He deserves punishment for his treachery, but I won't be an accomplice to my father's termination. He turned on his own family to save himself a few years in prison; I'm better than that.

"So where are your other coworkers?" Aaron asks. "I was hoping to meet these famous DJs."

We all answer at the same time.

"They're sleeping," I blurt.

"They're busy," Franklin says.

"They're visiting family," says David.

Aaron's mouth quirks, revealing just one dimple this time. "So they're busy sleeping at their families'?"

I laugh and pass him the mashed potatoes. "The DJs spend hours every night talking to the world, so it makes sense they'd want to hibernate."

I scoop a mass of cranberry sauce onto my plate. Its color and the conversation reminds me of what I've been trying to forget all day. The DJs aren't hibernating; on the contrary, they're holding their annual T-Day gathering with their favorite donors. All Shane would tell me is that it features a nice meal, followed by, well, a nice meal. He won't even tell me what the T in T-Day stands for—only that it's not "Thanksgiving" or "turkey."

Aaron hands me the gravy boat. "Any progress on the pirates?"

"We know who it is," David says. "It's just a matter of getting the FCC to take action."

Franklin grumbles. "The novelty is definitely wearing off for our advertisers."

"But you're safe as long as you only play men, right?"

"Right," I tell Aaron, "but our clients know that FAN can blot us out completely. It makes them not want to renew contracts. Why pay a bunch of money up front if their ads might be obliterated?" I omit the fact that we can disarm the translator at any time—it's hard to explain to a civilian the tightrope we're walking on.

Aaron cuts his turkey. "Maybe you ought to go on the offensive."

David gives me a warning glance before responding. "Offensive?"

"They say you're going to hell—assuming that sign at the Smoking Pig fire was meant for you, which would be consistent with the message in their broadcasts. So embrace it."

David squints at him. "Embrace going to hell?"

"People like that don't respond to rational talk. You can't *explain* why pretending to be vampires as a fun gimmick doesn't make you bad people. Denying their message only strengthens it."

David nods. "Like Nixon saying 'I am not a crook.' "

"Exactly. So take your hellbound destiny further than they ever dreamed."

I feel a smile coming on. "We could make it the centerpiece of a new marketing campaign."

"That's going a little far for my tastes," Franklin says.

"We could do a test rollout and see if we catch hell—I mean, flak." A sudden idea hits me, and I pound the table, rattling dishes. "The holiday party!"

Aaron raises his eyebrows at Franklin. "What holiday party?"

Franklin sighs. "Next Friday in downtown Baltimore. Our first remote broadcast." He turns to me. "Which makes it enough of a nightmare without rolling out a whole new theme."

I look at David, the tie-breaker and, ultimately, the boss. "What do you think? The WVMP Happy Hell-iday Extravaganza?"

David and Aaron laugh. Franklin puts his forehead in his hand. "Is nothing sacred?" he says.

"It's a brilliant idea on the surface." David trickles gravy over every item on his plate. "But we're definitely playing with fire."

After dinner, the men get all nineteenth century and retreat to the "library" downstairs to drink brandy and smoke cigars. The smell chases me to my former bedroom, too full of food to risk more indulgence and too full of wine to risk driving.

Alone, I pace the carpet, fighting the impulse to pull out my cell phone and call the person who'd be happiest to hear from me. Not Shane—he's, uh, busy with the T-Day feast. Not Lori—she's visiting her parents in Wisconsin.

I sit on the neatly made twin bed and dial a number I've never used.

After navigating the switchboard and speaking to a guard, I hold while five minutes tick by on the antique alarm clock, the kind with a mallet that strikes two giant bells in the loudest noise outside of a sonic boom. Then another five minutes. Is her cell really far from the phones, or does she just not want to talk to me?

I get up and start to pace again, sipping my wine, though my head is already pounding. Figures—only I could get a hangover while I'm still drunk.

Finally someone picks up on the other end. "Hello?"

The word almost sticks in my throat. "Mom?"

She gasps, and for once her melodrama might not be exaggerated. "*Ciara?* Is that you?"

"Who else calls you 'Mom'?" There was a time when that would have been nothing but a joke. These days I wonder.

She lets loose a high titter, the one that always used to grate on my nerves but today sounds like birds singing. "How long has it been? No, let's not waste time on the past. How are you?"

"I'm good." As the words leave my mouth, I realize they're true. I sit cross-legged on the bed and give her a short rundown of my job, eliminating the vampires-are-real part. She sounds like she's actually listening.

"That's fabulous, honey. You must send me a T-shirt."

"Don't you have to wear a uniform?"

"I'll hang the shirt on my wall. Of course, you can't send me a button, because I could stab someone with it."

"Are you sure it's not too profane?"

"I'm proud of you, no matter what unsavory elements you're consorting with. Are there any special men in your life? Come on, spill."

I tell her about Shane, keeping an eye on the clock. If I can draw out this part of the conversation, maybe the prison will cut us off before she can ask about Dad.

"Sounds nice enough for now," she replies. "Of course, in the long run I think you could do better than a disc jockey."

Yeah, maybe if I'm real lucky, I could nab myself a professional fraud like you did.

"Then again," she says, "I suppose I'm in no position to judge." Several seconds of silence follow. "Have you heard from your father?"

I close my eyes and picture the postcard at the bottom of my purse. "No."

"You're a poor liar, Ciara. Didn't we teach you anything?" After a pause, during which I hope an ice storm will tear down all the phone lines in Illinois, she laughs and says, "I'm only teasing. I'm sure you would have told me if he'd contacted you. We don't keep secrets from each other, right? Just from everyone else. I bet your boyfriend doesn't know about us."

"I told him everything."

"Oh, Ciara." She starts to cry. Maybe it's just the tin-can resonance of the cell phone speaker, but it sounds phony. "How could you bring that shame upon yourself?"

"I'm not ashamed of anything with him."

"I suppose that's a gift." She sniffles. "It sounds like the kind of trust I used to have with your father."

I crush the heel of my hand against my temple. She gave up so much for him, and he never even married her. But she doesn't know he told me that, because she doesn't know he's not still in jail, that he turned state's evidence on his own family in exchange for his freedom and an undercover job with the Control. I'm pretty sure it'd be a felony to tell her.

I pick up the wineglass and empty it down my throat. "I'm sorry you haven't heard from him."

"I guess I know how you feel now. I used to beg him to call you. I told him he had to forgive you or he'd regret it one day. Excuse me one moment." A nose-blowing sound comes from the line, and when she returns, her voice is clear. "Maybe that was why he stopped calling me. He got tired of me nagging him about you."

I set down the empty wineglass before my hand crushes it. She's not perfect by a long shot, but she doesn't deserve this.

A low-pitched female voice speaks to my mother. "All right," Mom says to her. "Ciara, my time's up. Thank you so very much for calling. It meant a lot to me."

Though I know it'll make her cry, and this time for real, I say, "I love you, Mom."

Instead of bawling, she falls silent, and I wonder if the prison has cut the call. Then she says, "I love you, too, sweet pea." Her whisper is tight around the edges, as if for once in her life she's holding back her feelings instead of exaggerating them.

She hangs up. I slump back on my pillow and watch the ceiling spin. Antoine leaps onto the bed with a *brraaap!*

"Hey." I stroke the cat's sleek white back. "I just drunk-dialed my mom."

My phone rings in my hand, startling me enough to drop it on the floor. My head swims as I bend over to pick it up. It's Shane.

I answer it upside down. "Crappy Thanksgiving, baby," I say.

"You have no idea how true that is."

"Aren't you supposed to be at that donor's house, having your little T-Day shindig?"

"I am. You and David need to get over here."

"Thanks, but I like my blood in my veins, not your belly. And if David goes, then I'm stuck doing the dishes alone."

"Ciara, this is serious." He pauses. "Jim brought the reporter."

# 15

## Dazed and Confused

The T-Day feast is in a large Colonial home on the outskirts
of town. Like a lot of houses this Thanksgiving evening, its
driveway is packed with vehicles. Probably where the similar-
ity ends.

Standing on the porch with David, I knock on the door,
afraid of what it'll reveal.

Shane opens it, looking worried.

"Are we too late?" David says.

"No. They're still eating." He lets us pass into the warm,
high-ceilinged foyer. The aroma of sage-slathered turkey
and stuffing greets my nose. In a room down the hall,
murmurs and laughter blend with the clank of dishes and
utensils.

Shane whispers, "The other donors know there's a newbie
among us, one who doesn't know the truth yet. That's part of
the fun."

I try not to cringe. "Let me guess: initiation is a T-Day tradition."

He nods. "Being surrounded by other humans who accept us helps the virgins adjust. It gives them an instant community."

"But virgins aren't usually reporters for national magazines."

"Which is why I called you."

Shane leads us down the hall into the dining area. The room is surrounded by floor-to-ceiling windows lined with white Christmas lights, setting off the darkness of the night sky beyond.

A holler of greeting goes up when we walk in. About a dozen people are sitting around the table—Travis and four DJs, along with an array of happy humans. The only one missing is Noah, who's at the station. I spy Jeremy sitting at one corner of the table, next to Jim, who is not smiling.

"Welcome." The woman at one end of the table slides back her chair. Her chin-length salt-and-pepper hair swings elegantly in a neat curtain as she approaches, hand extended. "I'm Marcia, Spencer's donor. Please join us."

I hesitate before shaking her hand. "Thanks, but I've already eaten. You have a lovely home, by the way."

"Oh, I adore entertaining, and T-Day only comes once a year."

The others laugh, some more slyly than others.

David shakes her hand. "Sorry to interrupt, but we just need Jim for a quick second."

Jim shoves back his chair and stalks over to us. He sneers at Shane as he passes him. "Thanks, rat."

Spencer stands up at the other end of the table. "Really, now, is this necessary?" He spreads his hands to encompass the table. "There's no harm being done here."

"Don't bother," Regina snaps at him. "Nothing's the same

since the fascist came on board." Her ebony-lined eyes send me a withering glare.

Jim turns to them. "Guys, it's okay. I know how to handle this." He sweeps past me and hooks his arm into mine. "Let's talk, just you and me."

I look back at Shane and David as Jim drags me away. Shane starts to move after us, but David stops him.

"Five minutes," David says to Jim, and checks his watch.

We go back down the hall, into a cozy sitting room off to the side of the foyer. Jim plops down on the loveseat and stretches his arm over the back.

"You can't bite the reporter," I tell him.

"Sorry, I can't hear you from all the way over there." He pats the cushion next to him.

I cross my arms and stand in the doorway. "If he writes about it, and someone believes it—"

"No one'll believe it."

"He'll have physical evidence." When he shrugs, I add, "Are you willing to risk the station?"

"You don't get it, do you?" he says softly. "Jeremy won't talk."

"He's a reporter. A truth-seeker. That makes him the enemy."

"He won't jeopardize what we have." His dark gaze falls to my throat. "He's addicted to the feel of my mouth against his skin."

"That's ridiculous," I say, but my voice comes out strangely feeble. "It's sick."

A corner of his mouth twitches. "You only say that because you've never tried it."

"I've been bitten. Twice."

"Not for pleasure." His palm sweeps across the cushion beside him, caressing it like the skin of a lover. "You look tired, Ciara."

My vision narrows to see nothing but his hand and his

eyes. Everything else—my surroundings, my past, my future—turns to fog.

Suddenly my feet are killing me. I recall how many hours I stood today, chopping and slicing Thanksgiving dinner. My ankles weaken, and I don't know if they'll support me long enough to get over to the couch.

I stumble on the last step, so that Jim has to catch me. He lowers me to the couch beside him, one hand on my elbow and the other on my waist.

"That's better," he whispers.

A low, steady hum plays in the back of my head, and I wonder if that last glass of wine is just now kicking in.

"I'll make you a deal." Jim slides my hair behind my shoulder, and a shiver skates over my neck. "I'll kick the reporter out after he eats, if that's what you really want."

What reporter? A vague worry pokes at my memory. It seems very important. "Yes. Yes, I want that."

"But you have to take his place."

My heart thuds, and I expect fear to turn my body cold. Instead, my skin heats as the blood vessels surge toward its surface, as if longing to be consumed.

My mind floods with panic. This is crazy.

I try to tear my gaze away from Jim's eyes, but he's paralyzed me, and now I know what it's like to be caught in the web. Does the butterfly secretly crave the spider's bite?

The tip of Jim's forefinger slides down my neck, tracing the vein down past my collarbone, inside my open jacket. Another finger joins it as the vessel widens to join my heart.

His hand stops, the other fingers curling around to trace my breast through my thin silk shirt.

"Don't." I force out the next word. "Shane won't—"

"Shane won't mind." He leans forward. "It doesn't count as cheating if all I do is taste you." He draws his lips near the corner of my jaw, just below my ear. "I want to taste you, Ciara."

I start to tremble as the cold fear sinks deep into my core, but still my skin burns. It feels like if he stopped touching me, took that mouth away from my skin, I'd burst into flames.

One of his fingers grazes my nipple, and a moan escapes my lips.

"Shh." His breath comes against my ear. "You know, since you've already eaten, we don't have to wait. We can go upstairs right now and—*aaaugh!*"

His yelp spikes my eardrum, followed by a hollow crack.

I leap off the couch, the spell broken. Shane has his hands around Jim's neck. He slams the older vampire's head against the back of the loveseat. The frame splinters at the impact, and blood spatters on the elegant fleur-de-lis wallpaper.

A shout comes from the doorway behind me. I recognize David's voice, but I can't turn to look at him.

"What the fuck?" Jim shrieks. "I was just playing around."

Shane rips a wooden shard from the back of the sofa frame and pulls it back as if to plunge it into Jim's chest. At the last moment he hesitates. The two vampires lock gazes.

I lurch forward. "Shane, don't."

"Yeah, man." Jim wipes the blood trickling from his nose, and I realize he's not afraid. "Give her the stake," he says in an even tone, "and I won't tear your fucking head off and throw it into the street." He smiles. "When all your blood runs out, your head'll come sliding back into the stump as you die. You want your little girlfriend to see that?"

"He can do it, Shane." David speaks from the doorway. "He's almost twice your age and strength. You'd be dead before the stake was halfway to his body. Now drop it."

Shane swallows, but his hand and his gaze remain steady. "Don't ever touch her again."

Jim gives me a sly look. "Or what?"

"Your car's getting old, isn't it?" Shane says. "Sometimes those antiques burst into flames without warning."

Genuine fear sparks in Jim's eyes. "You wouldn't touch Janis."

Shane tilts his head toward me. "Not if I don't have to."

"All right. I'll leave her alone." His gaze darts back and forth between me and Shane. "I promise, okay?"

I step forward and put my hand on the stake. "Okay." Shane gives it up without a struggle. He backs up and lets go of Jim.

I turn to see the sitting room doorway blocked by a crowd of onlookers.

Everyone backs up as the four of us file out into the foyer. I'm relieved to see Jeremy toward the back, standing with Monroe, who apparently interfered with the journalist's efforts to see the action.

"Sorry," Shane says to Marcia. "I'll buy you a new sofa."

"It was an antique." She peers into the room. "And look at my wallpaper. This room isn't set up for bloodletting." She hurries to shut the door.

"I'll take care of the repairs." Jim comes up behind Shane and pats his back. "I started it, after all." He slides his hand over Shane's shoulder and grasps the front of his shirt. "And I'll finish it."

"No!" I put out my hands before he can hurl my boyfriend through the window and across the street.

Jeremy clears his throat. "Jim, maybe we should go."

He glares at his new donor. "We can't miss T-Day. It only comes once a year."

Marcia crosses her arms. "I think you should leave before my insurance company gets involved."

Spencer steps up next to his donor, reinforcing the threat.

Jim reluctantly lets go of Shane. "Fine." He puts his arm around Jeremy's shoulders. "This scene has gotten too square."

When they're gone, the other guests file back to the dining room, all but Shane.

"You're welcome to stay for dessert," he tells me and David. "I mean, actual dessert, with coffee, not—you know."

"I just want to go home." I pull my jacket tight around my body. It's hard to look at him, for so many reasons.

David and I share actual dessert, with coffee, at his table. We haven't spoken since the car ride home, when David was on the verge of firing Jim before I convinced him it wasn't worth the fallout from our fans.

Finally he sets down his fork, his piece of pumpkin pie half eaten. "It's not your fault, what happened."

"That's the scariest part. When Jim was looking at me, and touching me"—my voice trembles—"I felt trapped in my own body. I would've let him bite me, but it wouldn't have been my choice." I rub my aching stomach. "It's like this summer, when Gideon was about to kill me, I was scared and sad and angry. I didn't want to die. But my blood *wanted* to be drunk. It wanted to be part of him." I put my forehead in my hand. "That's so twisted."

He shifts his coffee spoon on the table. "It can feel that way when it's someone you fear, like Gideon, or who you simply don't trust, like Jim. It's terrifying." His dark eyelashes cast long shadows on his cheek as he runs his thumb over the rim of his coffee cup. "But sharing your life force with a person you love isn't scary. It's, I don't know—"

"Sacred?"

He nods slowly. "Yeah. Sacred."

"Jeremy used that word, and he thinks it's just a kink. He doesn't know it gives them life."

"But he senses it."

"I'm worried about him."

"Are you worried about you?"

I poke at the remains of my pie. I really don't want to talk about it. But I really do want to talk about it.

"Shane asked to live with me."

"Already?" David looks at the clock, as if it's a calendar. "It's only been a few months."

"He likes to take things fast. He'd probably marry me if I wanted."

"You can't marry a vampire."

"Legally he's alive. He has his original social security number. Even when he gets old enough to change his identity, legally I could marry that person." I flatten the remaining piecrust with my fork. "Though I guess I'd have to divorce Shane first."

"I don't mean legally. It's just not done."

"And you've noticed my love of tradition and convention, right?" I sit back in my chair. "I'm not going to marry Shane or anyone else. Not yet."

"But you're going to live with him?"

"I don't know."

"Ciara, you should know something." He gets up and moves into the kitchen. As he passes, I catch the faintest hint of a sandalwood cologne. Has he been wearing that all day?

I hear him pull the coffee carafe out of the machine. "Remember that night you had the bad dream?" he says.

A cold sensation churns my gut. I set down my cup for him to refill. "Yeah. The one about—the one about Gideon." I hurry to take another bite of pie so I don't have to look at him.

He sighs. "I know the dream wasn't about Gideon. I heard you on the phone to Lori."

My jaw clenches around my pie morsel. It feels like it's going to stay in my mouth forever, because my throat is too tight for swallowing. A wave of heat starts at my nose and spreads over my face.

I wish Jim had eaten me dead. Anything would be better than this.

"How?" I choke out.

"The heating vents." He points to a small metal grate on the dining room floor. "The storeroom is under my bedroom. You can hear everything from one floor to the next if the house is quiet."

I set my fork down slowly. "Glad I moved out."

"Ciara." David sits at the table, which doesn't get me to look at him. "We never talked about the kiss."

"Why start now?"

"It put tension between us that hasn't been resolved."

"It doesn't have to be resolved." I finally swallow my bite of pie. "Some things in life are like the end of a European movie, where they just sort of fizzle out, you know, instead of some grand Hollywood climax." Oh, bad word choice. "I mean, some fight-to-the-death car-chase sequence."

David holds up his hands in a time-out configuration. "Can I just say something?"

"Depends on the something."

"Even before Elizabeth died, I had thoughts about you. Dreams not far from what you described to Lori." When my eyes widen, he adds, "But in my version Shane has no cameo."

The heat spreads from my neck down my chest and arms. I don't believe he's telling me this. The moment feels more dangerous than when Jim had his mouth to my throat. If David came around the table, took my face in his hands and kissed me, I'm not sure I'd pull away.

"But Shane is there in real life," David says, "and because of that, I would never act on these thoughts."

"Unless I asked you to."

He looks at me for a long moment, and in that stretch of time I can see a parallel universe, where the man I love walks in the sunshine, and eats pumpkin pie, and will someday have gray hair.

But even in that Never Never Land, where my fiercest wishes all come true, the man in the sunshine is the same as the man in the moonlight.

# 16

## Gimme Shelter

When I enter the hallway to the studio, I see Shane through the soundproof glass window, doing a crossword puzzle and nodding his head to the end of a Dinosaur Jr. song. Though his back is turned, he spins in his chair when I press my hand against the booth, as if he senses me.

He smiles and waves me inside. I slip into the studio and stand with my back to the door. Shane's gaze turns smoky, heavy-lidded as he absorbs my black lace camisole, high-heeled boots, and red silk miniskirt.

"Whoa." The song fades, and he pulls the microphone to his mouth. "Three forty a.m. at 94.3 WVMP-FM, the Lifeblood of Rock 'n' Roll. Mild night for this time of year. Fifty-four degrees"—he looks at the sky-high hem of my skirt—"and getting warmer. A lot like the weather in Manchester, England, where this band hails from."

He hits a switch to play "Fools Gold" by the Stone Roses,

then glides over to greet me. "Yes, miss. Did you have a request?"

I run my finger down the zipper of his faded jeans. "I'd like you to play the longest song in your arsenal."

"You're in luck." He pulls me into his arms. "This is the extended version."

In the few square feet of floor space, we dance in half-time to the funky rhythm, his left arm around my waist and his right hand entwined with my left. I press my cheek to his lean, solid chest and feel his heart beat against the pulse of my temple. His fingers lie warm against mine as his thumb caresses the tender spot inside my wrist.

He feels as human as I need right now. Maybe as human as I'll ever need.

His lips graze my forehead where it meets my hairline. His hand slips down my waist, fingernails gliding over my backbone, right to the base of my spine. The same nails he uses to strum the guitar.

My body responds in perfect tune. I lift my chin, searching for a kiss. It comes, deep but soft, exploring instead of insisting. I strain toward him with an urgent lust, but he pulls back—not enough to break the kiss, but enough to control our pace.

I came here for a simple fuck, but with Shane there's no such thing. He always has to seduce me, make me crave him so much it hurts.

I eschew subtlety and slide my hand over the front of his jeans, thrilled to discover him fully aroused despite his façade of self-control. He groans, and his grip on me tightens.

"God, Ciara." Both hands slip around my waist, pulling me tight against him. "I need every inch of you."

I smile against his neck. "When?"

"Now." Without letting go of me, he sits in his chair and tugs me onto his lap. Straddling him, I place my hands on

either side of his head and give him a deep, hard kiss. He
threads the fingers of one hand through my hair while the
other travels up my bare thigh, then underneath my skirt. He
discovers I'm not wearing any underwear and gives an appre-
ciative sigh.

"I love my job." He shifts my skirt up a few inches and
kneads the muscles of my ass. "And the fact that we're the only
ones in the building."

"Would you care if we weren't?"

"No." He slides down the strap of my camisole and bites
my shoulder with human teeth as his fingers slip between my
legs.

"Me neither." With shaky hands, I undo his jeans to release him. "Swear you've never done this before."

"I swear I've never done this before." Shane guides us together and pauses, gazing up into my eyes. "But I'll try to get
it right the first time."

He fills me, exhaling hard, and speaks no more.

Because of a loose spring, the chair rocks, and my boot
heels just reach the floor, giving me control over our rhythm.
I grind against him, greedy for that blinding moment when
I'll think nothing but one white-hot thought, when everything will become simple again.

Suddenly, Shane holds me still. I draw in a hard breath,
ready to scream in frustration.

"Sorry." He slides the chair to his left and swings the microphone near his mouth as the song fades out. "94.3 WVMP,
it's 3:51 a.m." As he continues to speak, imparting some fascinating fact about the band, he reaches around, adjusting my
angle and bringing me close to the edge. I bite my lower lip
hard to keep from crying out as the blood pounds in my ears.

"Let's take a few calls," he says. I try to smack his chest, but
he catches my wrist and mouths the words "Don't stop." He
hits another key. "Hello, you're on the air."

"Yeah, can you play some Foo Fighters?"

Shane traces the lace at the neckline of my camisole. "Are you a regular listener?"

"Uh-huh."

"Then you know I don't like Foo Fighters." His fingertips continue down to circle my nipples, then close in to caress them. "Why must you plague me?"

I fight to keep silent as my spine zings with the electric jolt of his touch.

"You don't like Pearl Jam either, but you still play them."

"That's different. Pearl Jam is from my time." He shifts his hips under me. I clutch the back of the chair. "Besides, I have a great deal of respect and admiration for them."

"You don't respect the Foos?"

Unable to stop, I move again, stroking his full length. He blinks fast, his concentration wavering.

"Damn." Shane's next breath comes hard, but he covers it with a light laugh. "Dude, it's just a thing with me, okay? Clearly you missed the sign on my door that says 'Absolutely No Foo Fighters.' "

There's an actual sign on the studio door that says that. Written in blood.

I close my eyes and focus on the feel of him sliding in and out of me, hard and hot.

The caller hesitates. "I can't see your door. This is radio. Maybe you should, like, announce it or something."

"Consider it announced." He peels up my top. "And I'm glad you can't see what I see right now. Next caller." He reaches over and punches a button. "You're on the air."

A deep, earnest voice comes out of the speaker. "God is watching you, young man."

My jaw drops, but Shane doesn't even blink.

"He is?" he says. "By all means, explain." He mutes his microphone and tells me, "I've gotten at least one call like this every night my entire career. Best to let them get it out of their system." He wraps his arms around me. "Don't let it distract you."

Right now, Bigfoot riding by on a unicorn couldn't distract me.

"God sees everything you do," the caller continues. "He hears every vile piece of depravity you play on the air. He knows how you corrupt our children."

I move against Shane again as he flicks the mike back on and speaks, his voice steady as ever.

"Sir, I'm sure He's got better things to watch than me. All I do is sit in a booth and push buttons."

His hands make him a liar. I close my eyes and let the red-orange haze of my imminent orgasm sweep over me.

"Except for the blood drinking," the caller says.

"Right. I keep forgetting I'm a vampire." He laces the last word with irony. "Now that you mention it, I am a little thirsty." He brings my breast to his mouth and slides my nipple inside. I arch my back and bite my lip again to keep from screaming. From the corner of my eye I see our reflection in the studio window, the light glinting off our hair as it shimmers with our movements.

"It's bad enough that you play that noise you call music, but to glorify demonic possession and blood drinking—"

"Whoa." Shane turns his head to the mike. "First of all, sir, I'm not possessed by a demon. I'm just a regular guy resurrected by magic." He holds up a finger to tell me to stop. I clench my fists, wanting to punch the console.

"And second," Shane continues, "Jesus asked his disciples to drink his blood to sustain their spirits, so how can it be wrong to do it to sustain our lives?"

I wrap my legs around the back of the chair, sinking him deeper inside me. His mouth opens, and his hand clutches the edge of the table.

The caller grunts. "He told them to drink wine, not blood. It was symbolic."

"Not according to the Catholic Church." Shane holds me still, then tugs me to rest my head against his shoulder. "We believe in transubstantiation, in which the Eucharist becomes the body and blood of our Lord and Savior." He strokes my hair, soothing my impatience. "Thirteen years of parochial school equipped me to argue the point with the most fervent but misguided Protestant." He tugs down my shirt to cover me and starts massaging my back, edging his thumbs into the tight spot inside my shoulder blade. "Care to try, sir, just for yuks?"

" 'Just for yuks'? The nature of the Christ is not a laughing matter, even for Romanists like you."

Shane snorts. "Romanist, now that's a word I haven't heard in a long time." Dragging the mike with him, he wheels us over to his CD shelf and grabs a new disc. "You're hard-core, aren't you, sir?"

"I don't know what that means, but I am here to challenge you and all your bloodsucking friends. You'll see us soon."

Shane's hand freezes in the middle of opening the CD. I sit up, wisps of fear leaking through my gut.

After a moment's hesitation, Shane speaks again, his tone the same as before. "I look forward to that. When and where will I have the pleasure?"

"There'll be no warning, and trust me, it won't be a pleasure."

Shane's gaze turns cold with anger. His voice comes clipped and fast, his lips nearly brushing the microphone. "Sir, I'm going to give you the benefit of the doubt because I realize you might not understand the context. This station has received numerous threats in recent weeks. The authorities are currently conducting an investigation." He pauses to let that return threat sink in. "I'll give you one chance. Would you like to retract your previous statement?"

The man scoffs. "I won't be retracting anything but a stake from your heart. I look forward to watching you shrivel up like a slug."

My shoulders relax a bit. This guy's a faker; he doesn't know that vampires don't shrivel up when they're staked. Well, they do, but that's before they get sucked through their own bodies.

The caller continues. "Guess where vampires end up after they go through the hole?"

Cold slithers over my neck. The true nature of a vampire's death isn't part of our marketing campaign.

Shane speaks low and somehow calm as he inserts the CD in the player. "Sir, I think our conversation is—"

"They go to hell, that's where. That's where you're going."

A sharp breath seizes my lungs at the sound of that phrase, at the memory of it slathered in red paint.

"Thank you for your comments, sir," Shane says, "and may I suggest calling your pharmacy and getting those prescriptions refilled. Your family and friends will thank you."

He strikes a key on the computer, and the music rumbles forth, the understated synthesized menace of Nine Inch Nails' "Heresy." As the relentless drum machine kicks in, Shane switches the telephone to play in the studio only.

"We're off the air," he growls at the phone speaker. "Now who the fuck are you?"

The man chuckles. "Someone who cares."

"What do you want?"

"To save the world from the likes of you."

"We just want to be left alone." He pulls me closer, as if to protect me. "We just want to play our music."

"In the past, maybe. Your anonymity kept you safe all these years, not worth our time. But you've brought yourselves into the light."

"It's just a marketing gimmick. We're not really vampires. What the hell is wrong with you?"

"You've made more humans want to be vampires. Before long, your virus will spread."

"But no one believes—"

"You must be stopped."

A loud click, then the dial tone fills the studio, shrouding the sound of Trent Reznor screaming that God is dead.

Shane touches the button to hang up the phone, then eases me carefully off his lap and onto my feet. We reassemble our clothes in silence.

"You were right." I sit in the other chair. "All those months ago, when you warned us this Lifeblood of Rock 'n' Roll thing would put you in danger." I look at the phone. "Gideon was right."

"It doesn't matter who was right." Shane leans back, arms folded over his chest. "That guy said, 'You'll see *us* soon.' Who's 'us'?"

"The Fortress? If they're antivampire crusaders, they'd know how you die."

He reaches out and takes my hand. "These people say they're after vampires, but I worry about you, too. I wish you could live here where it's safe."

"Oh." My stomach flips over as I remember the other reason why I came here tonight. "I thought maybe we could, uh . . ." I swallow hard. This came out a lot easier when I rehearsed it in the car.

He cocks his head and squeezes my hand. "We could what?"

I pull in a deep breath, then take the leap of my life.

# 17

## Bring It On Home

Shane unpacks quickly and decisively; he must have spent the last eighteen hours planning where he would put everything.

He hangs his clothes on the left side of Elizabeth's—I mean our—closet, then heads back out to the car for another box of stuff. The moment he's gone, I step into the walk-in closet and turn on the light.

His clothes are sorted systematically, the shirts by color and sleeve length, the jeans in descending order of fadedness. I hastily reshuffle my own shirts, skirts, and pants to create a semblance of order.

Before leaving the closet, I run my hand through his shirts, some flannel and some just plain cotton. I remember the way his shoulders and chest and arms feel beneath them, the soft material slipping over his muscles as he moves.

Then I imagine coming home to these clothes knowing he would never fill them again. My pulse leaps, and I want to rewind our entire relationship, back to the moment before I cared whether he lived or died.

I press my face into one shirt after another and breathe deep, searching for proof of life. He rarely sweats, except during sex, and even then only when he's recently drunk blood. Finally, on the fifth shirt, I find and revel in the faint, clean scent I recognize as Shane's.

I step back, then a weird impulse makes me pull out one of his sleeves and stretch it toward that of one of my blouses. Their cuffs barely meet at the center of the closet.

"Aw, that's cute."

I drop the sleeves and turn to see Shane. "Oh God." I put a hand to my face, which is warming rapidly. "You did not just see that."

"Careful with the blushing." He smiles and touches my cheek. "You know red makes me thirsty." Then his gaze trips past me to my clothes on the rack. "You don't have to sort your stuff on my account, but thanks." He angles a glance at me. "What'd you think of my 5:54 a.m. choice?"

I scour my memory for today's song secretly dedicated to me. "Nirvana's 'Breed.' Perfect moving-in-together song."

I follow him into the living room, where we stuff one of our empty boxes full of Elizabeth's CDs—mostly Broadway musical soundtracks and light jazz. Then Shane sets to work unpacking my CDs—which I finally took out of storage, along with my summer clothes, so I could save money on the rental—and putting them on the shelves in alphabetical order. His contentment is palpable—he's practically purring.

He left all his own CDs at the station, since he needs them for work. Instead, he's brought a box of mix tapes.

I sit on the floor, examining the edges of the plastic cassette boxes without touching them. They seem to be in chronological order, based on the cases' wear and tear. They're labeled in

many different handwritings, and some are elaborately decorated in faded colored pen inks.

Some have hearts on them.

"Did you make all these?" I ask him, knowing the answer.

"Most of them were made by friends or girlfriends. The
ones I made are probably stuffed in boxes in those people's
houses." Shane hesitates in the middle of sorting my CDs.
"The ones that weren't burned." He glances at me. "You can
look through them if you want."

I pull out one with choppy handwriting. " 'Music to Get
Legally Drunk to—March 1, 1989.' Your twenty-first birthday tape?"

He smiles and crawls over to join me. "My best friend
Steve made that for me." He cringes as he examines it. "Def
Leppard. Poison. Warrant. A walk-in closet's worth of musi-
cal skeletons."

I decide not to pick up the ones with feminine
handwriting—at least, not while Shane's here. Then I spy half
a dozen tapes with Shane's distinctive scrawl. I pull one out.

"Who's Meagan?"

"Senior year of high school." He takes it from me and
smiles at the case. "She gave it back and told me to add some
Janet Jackson. Meagan had crappy taste in music, but she
could really—" He glances at me. "Um, dance. She was a good
dancer." He averts his eyes and reaches past me into the box.
"Now, this is a great tape. Anne Marie, freshman year college." He shakes the case, rattling the tape inside. "She was
bad news—I should've listened to my mother about her. But
she introduced me to punk and indie music, saved me from
my heavy-metal hair-band wasteland."

"She cool-inated you."

His eyes crinkle when he smiles. "By some measures,
yeah." He slips the tape back into the box in its open slot.
"Does it bother you that I keep these?"

I hug my knees to my chest. "I try to erase my past as much as possible, so I don't understand the impulse to preserve it."

"These mix tapes aren't about the women, they're about the person I used to be. Like a musical autobiography." He runs his finger over the smooth case of one of the newer cassettes. "I haven't made once since I died."

"Make one for me."

His eyebrows pop up. "Really?"

I point to Elizabeth's stereo. "I have a tape player now."

"You wouldn't rather have another MP3 playlist?"

"I want a tape." I put my chin on my knees. "I want to be the next chapter in your autobiography." I close my eyes. "And that sounded so much less cheesy in my head."

"Okay." He takes my hand and kisses it. "You'll love it."

I try to return his smile. He seems so serene, so *at home* already. How can he not be terrified? If I tell him this scares the shit out of me, will he think I don't love him enough?

Dexter slides off the couch, then waddles over and pushes his enormous head between us. Shane scratches behind the dog's ear, producing a long, hearty groan of pleasure.

Despite their strength and ferocity, despite the fact that they could rip the throat from nearly any living creature, and despite their eternal youth, these two boys need me.

That's the scariest part of all.


I wait until I pull into the parking spot in front of my apartment building to dial Jeremy's number. The whole drive home after my Wednesday night class had too much crazy traffic to safely spend on the phone. Life in a major suburb does not please me.

Miraculously, he answers, with a heavy sigh. "What?"

"Jeremy, I've been calling you for almost a week. What's your deal?"

"My *deal* is that you interfered with a journalistic investigation."

"When?"

"T-Day."

I groan as I get out of the car and slam the door. "Trust me, you do not want that much weirdness."

"*Weird?* You sound like such a hater. Just because we're a little different from your clean-cut mainstream Barbie doll—"

"Hey!" That's the second time this month someone with facial piercings has called me a Barbie doll. "Can we forget T-Day for a minute and look to the future?"

"What about it?"

"Are you coming to the Hell-iday Party?"

"Of course. Just tell me which parts you plan to shield me from, so I can temper my disappointment in advance."

"It's a public event." I punch in the code to open the front door, which buzzes and clicks. "No shielding required."

"Ooh, I get to be part of the public. How special."

"Special enough to get an exclusive secret."

Paper rustles in the background. "Gimme it," he says, his hostility evaporated.

I unlock my apartment door. "David has found a way to prevent FAN's interference."

"How?"

"It's technical." I can't tell Jeremy about David pulling the plug on the translator, because that would tip him off to the cross and the Fortress and other real-real vampire issues. "But it'll be ready in time for the party. Regina's making her comeback, so we'll defeat the pirates in the most public fashion possible."

Dexter hops and dances when I enter the apartment, his forepaws bouncing against the floor. He comes over for a chin scratch. He's so tall, I don't even have to bend over.

"I gotta go walk my dog," I tell Jeremy. "See you Friday."
I hang up before he can ask any more questions.

"It's just you and me tonight, boy."

Dexter wags his tail and spins in a circle. He doesn't know vampires are supposed to brood.

Like the dog, I don't mind the fact that Shane splits his time between our apartment and the station. His show ends at 6 a.m., which is too close to sunrise for him to risk the forty-five-minute or two-hours-with-traffic drive home. He'll sleep in his old room on odd days and come home after sunset. So every other night I get the place to myself. Pretty sweet deal.

I find a note from Shane stuck to the refrigerator with a WVMP Lifeblood of Rock 'n' Roll magnet. Written in fine-pointed black ink, the words fit neatly within the margins of the lined yellow legal pad sheet.

> *Dear Ciara,*
> *You may have noticed I reloaded the dishwasher again. I know you didn't have one in your old apartment, so I figured you could use some tips.*
>
> *A) On the bottom rack, it's best to put the bowls on one side, plates on the other.*
>
> *i) and put the small plates together away from the big plates so you can grab them all at once when you put them away.*
>
> *B) On the top rack, you should put plastic things in between the glass/ceramic things so the glasses don't knock against each other and break from the turbulence.*
>
> *C) Ideally you shouldn't put the same kind of utensil in the same slot. Reasoning: if two spoons nest inside each other, then one might block the other from the spray, and it won't get clean.*
>
> *i) And there should be an even number of utensils in each slot.*

    *a) Unless you have a serving spoon or a spatula or something. That's worth two or three regular utensils.*

    *D) Per the manufacturer's instructions (attached), plastic always goes on the top rack so it doesn't melt.*

    *E) For God's sake, don't block the spout thing in the middle. Defeats the whole purpose, really.*

I turn over the sheet of paper to find another list of detailed instructions, followed by:

> *Hope you had a good day at work and school.*
> *Love you,*
> *Shane*

I toss the note, along with the attached manufacturer's instructions, into the paper recycling bin. As I lower the lid, I notice half a dozen sheets filled with iterations of the same note. Rough drafts.

    I give Dexter a grim look. It's begun.

# 18

## Bad to the Bone

"Nothing says Yuletide spirit like a bunch of walking corpses."

Franklin shouts above the pulsing music as he examines the vampire-themed holiday decorations adorning the walls of the Baltimore dance club. I'm especially proud of the eight fanged reindeer pulling Santa's flying coffin.

Standing next to him, Regina flips him the bird. "We're more alive than you'll ever be, dweebus."

"Until we're not." I point to the licking flames that frame our "Happy Hell-iday from WVMP" banner. "And then you know where we're going."

I can't hear Franklin's acid-tongue response over the opening drum beats of Jim's next song, the Beach Boys' "Little St. Nick."

The sixties DJ shouts over the music. "It's been a long, strange trip, and it ain't over." He holds up a replica of the original sign that was left at the Smoking Pig. "We're all goin' to hell!"

The people on the packed dance floor cheer and wave their red WVMP Lifeblood of Rock 'n' Roll candy canes. We decided to go with the plush version for our giveaway promo item, instead of hard plastic, figuring people would be hitting each other with them by the end of the night. Plus, they double as cinnamon-scented car air fresheners.

Franklin makes a disgusted face. "I'm going to recheck the sound again, make sure the broadcast is going out."

I watch him march off to his unnecessary task. Shane is already sitting on the side of the DJ booth with headphones, monitoring every moment of the FM signal. Noah and Spencer are back at the station, manning the audio board and receiving our remote broadcast.

Regina examines me. "Your devil horns are crooked." She reaches over and adjusts my diabolical headband, which matches the red trim on my elf's costume.

"Thanks." I glance at her face. Her jaw drops.

"Colin!"

I turn to see the flame-haired punk rocker bounce through the crowd to greet us. I can't help but smile to see him in one piece, considering how we left him in that alley.

Regina hugs him so hard his eyes bulge. "You sneaky bugger, what an awesome surprise."

"Wouldn't miss it, luv." He smiles at me, but tension tightens the corners of his mouth, and he seems too distracted to bother with the usual vampire dazzle.

Colin brings his mouth to Regina's ear and speaks words that are lost to me under the music. Her face freezes.

"No!" she says. "Fuck that. I'm not backing down. I have a job to do." She sees me watching them, then takes his hand and turns away. They retreat to a dark corner, where the dancing green and red lights can't find them. Being a lover of breathing, I don't follow.

I spy Jeremy sitting at a table on the next level, watching the partyers and taking notes. I zigzag through the crowd toward him, making sure no one steps on my shoes' jingle-bell curly toes.

"We put the 'X' in Xmas." I lean over his shoulder and tap his notebook. "You can quote me on that."

He glares up at me and says nothing.

I slip into the chair next to him. "So what do you think of our bonanza of blasphemy?"

He sighs. "The hype is wearing thin."

"Not for our fans." I sweep my hand over the throng. "They're soaking in it."

Jeremy points his pen at me. "Do you ever say anything that isn't completely empty?"

"Not on the job, no." The first tinkling sleigh bells of the Kinks' "Father Christmas" segue into its driving guitar chords. My shoulders sway to the music, unbidden. "You should go dance."

"Not now." He uncaps his pen and thumbs through the pages of his notebook.

"Did I catch you in the middle of a deep thought?"

He slaps the pad shut. "As a matter of fact, I was just ruminating on why it's impossible to get the truth from you people. There's always another layer, but each one turns out to be false."

"It's showbiz. What do you want?"

"I want something real."

"I don't even know what that means."

"I know you don't." Jeremy shakes his head in apparent sympathy.

My toe nudges the leg of his chair. "You and Shane could have an all-night conversation about authenticity."

"We have. I argued that even the nineties indie alternative whatever music he loves is more pretentious than he admits." Jeremy spreads his hands on the table's smoked glass surface. "Separating the artist from the audience is so twentieth century. The whole concept of the rock star is obnoxious and archaic."

"And what does he think of your emo music?"

"Don't call it that," Jeremy snipes, as I knew he would. "He thinks it's whiny, self-obsessive crap. He thinks he's a sensitive guy, but he's got his fortress like all the other macho men."

My spine jolts at his choice of word. "Fortress?"

"Around his feelings."

I give a nervous laugh. "Yes, luckily for me, or I'd never get anything done."

Regina's growl comes from the microphone. "Ladies and gentlemen, I am back. And I am one bitter bitch."

The crowd cheers, more aggressively than they did for Jim. I watch Shane's face for dismay. At the first sign of a broadcast interruption, he'll signal David, who's standing just a few feet away with Franklin. But it shouldn't happen, since David pulled the plug on the translator this afternoon.

"This is a live remote broadcast," Regina points out, "so you're hearing exactly what our listeners hear, except they get a seven-second delay in case I accidentally say 'fuck' or 'shit.'" She smirks and bleeps out the words on the delay. "But that means you'll be the first to hear if those pirate bastards interrupt me again." She goes silent for three or four seconds, which sounds like an eternity. "Nope. We've kicked their asses back to the Dark Ages, where they belong."

The crowd hoots and screams.

"First up is one of my favorite holiday tunes, featuring two of the craziest, loveliest men in the world." Regina angles her gaze to the light in a way that plays the shadows off her dark eyes and long lashes. "It's Peter Murphy from Bauhaus with Tom Waits. Don't ask me how those two hooked up, but they made this little monstrosity called 'Christmas Sucks.'"

Staccato chords in minor keys creep out of the speakers like a rat skirting the shadows. The vibe is one hundred percent Halloween and sounds like an R-rated version of *The Nightmare Before Christmas*.

I keep my eyes on Shane for any sign of FAN's shenanigans. At the end of the first macabre verse, he sends David a thumbs-up. No pirates.

"It worked," Jeremy says. "So far, at least."

"So FAN only had one translator. They could always build another one, but for now, we're free to be female."

"Nice." He watches Jim prowl the edge of the dance floor, mingling with his fans. The vampire doesn't even look this way.

"You're not his only one, you know." I didn't mean that as cruelly as it came out.

Jeremy shrugs. "And he's not mine." He looks back at the stage, where Regina sways and vogues like a diva.

Her, too? It's a wonder this kid has any blood left.

Suddenly an ear-shattering bell rings, dwarfing the music in its continuous drone.

"Fire alarm!" Jeremy shouts.

For a moment, no one moves. The partygoers glance around uneasily, putting on a façade of annoyance but no doubt thinking of other club fires where dozens were burned or trampled to death.

I look at Shane, a great gob of fear sticking in my throat. He and the other vampires will die if they burn. They'll disappear forever.

Then Regina yells into the microphone, "Holy shit, everybody get out!"

Panicked shouts erupt, and feet start to pound around us. The surge of bodies traps me and Jeremy against our table. If I join it, I'll be flattened.

Shane rips off his headset and leaps onto the stage. He snatches the microphone from Regina and cuts off the music.

"Listen," comes his calm, even voice. "Do not panic. Everyone stop for one second. Hear me? Stop!"

At the sound of his order, the crowd freezes.

"Look around," he continues. "Locate the nearest red exit

sign. Got it? Now please walk—do not run, okay? Walk toward the exit. Help those who are having trouble. Leave your purses and coats. Better to be too cold on the street than too hot in here. Now go."

The mob takes a collective breath, then splits off to move toward the exits on either side of the club, as well as the front door. The club manager and staff take over the evacuation effort.

Shane strides to the railing and holds out his arms to me. I reach out and let him lift me up, over, and down onto the dance floor level. Then he helps Jeremy clamber over the railing.

Monroe approaches the three of us, corralling David on the way, and ushers us toward the door on the right. We make our way toward the rear exit, which leads to the parking lot behind the building. I can hear two different sirens, their volume swelling as they approach.

The crowd carries us along to the street by the front of the club, which I expect to see engulfed in flames, just like the Smoking Pig on Halloween.

The wide squat building looks intact. Not a wisp of smoke curls up from its wood-and-concrete façade. A false alarm? Or maybe a small kitchen fire already extinguished.

David rubs his arms against the cold. "I hope the sprinkler system doesn't ruin our equipment."

I look up at Shane, who's scanning the crowd, his face on maximum alert—eyes flicking, nostrils flaring. He reminds me of Dexter, minus the perky ears.

"Something's not right," he says. "I smell fire, but not from the—"

A loud whistle pierces the air. I cover my ears, but not in time to block the *rat-a-tat* snaps of small explosions.

Something heavy slams my body, flattening me to the ground. I can't move. A wall of screams forms around me.

Two more whistles follow in quick succession, then more shots rattle the air. Oh my God, we're being attacked by vampire-hating terrorists. I kick with all my strength, but only manage to ring the bells on my toes.

"Hold still." Shane wraps his arm over my head, and I realize it's him covering me. I curl my lips over my teeth to avoid tasting blacktop.

The shrieks suddenly change to oohs and aahs.

"Whoa," Shane says.

"What is it?" I squirm under him, trying to get a limb out.

"Sorry." He rolls off and helps me up. "I thought they were gunshots."

"Me, too, but what is—Whoa."

Two Roman candles—a green one and a red one—explode in the sky about fifty feet above us, near the highway overpass. As the sparks bloom into graceful showers, they illuminate a twenty-foot black banner hanging from the overpass.

Giant yellow painted letters scream YOU ARE GOING TO HELL. The ARE is in red.

More fireworks explode, and applause breaks out. Half the crowd is smiling at us as they clap.

They think we did this as a stunt.

Two police patrol cars screech into the lot, red and blue lights flashing.

David looks at me sideways. "You didn't, by any chance—"

"No." I wave my hands, palms out, to ward off his accusation. "Even I wouldn't go this far for ratings."

"Just checking." He glances at Jeremy, then gives me a significant look. "So we just tell the police the truth."

Right. He means our version of the truth, which won't mention the aborted arson attempt on the station or anything else that would lead them to the vampires' happy home.

"Look on the bright side." Franklin stands beside me and stares at the overpass banner. "At least this time they used correct grammar."

# 19

## I Ain't Superstitious

Stakeouts suck. David lives on a hill, which means we have a great vantage point to watch the cross, but it also means the wind speed is about ten miles an hour higher than it is in town. The gusts cut through the unheated attic so hard, Lori and I might as well be outside.

Despite last night's pyrotechnical warning, WVMP has embarked on a weekend of all-women's programming, starting with Monroe's late-night Bessie Smith special. The DJs have recorded an extra set of original broadcasts to add to their regular lineup of live shows.

Our signal has yet to be pirated—not surprising, considering David pulled the plug on the translator. Last night Lori and Travis kept an eye (and binoculars) on the cross to see if any angry FAN personnel came to fix the disabled translator. This morning it's me and Lori, then David and Franklin. The off-duty DJs will take over tonight if no one has crawled into our trap by then.

Sitting cross-legged on a piece of thinly carpeted plywood, I peer through the tripod-mounted binoculars. Nothing to see yet, other than people putting up Christmas decorations in the development across the highway. This town loves its inflatable snowmen.

"I wish I could've been at the party last night," Lori says.

"Right, instead of here alone with Travis, playing detective. Or doctor, as the case may be."

"It was freezing, and he doesn't stay warm for long after he drinks." She shrugs. "Still, I don't mind."

"You should be glad you weren't there. That fire alarm nearly gave me a heart attack. The police questioning was almost as fun."

"Do they suspect you guys?"

"Of course. But there's no evidence. And we were all in plain sight when the fire alarm went off." I rub my eyes, which already ache from squinting. "So what do you think of the Bitten?"

"They're nice." She breathes on her fingers through her woolen gloves. "But only on the outside." She tightens her pale green scarf. "Sometimes the vampires seem more human than regular people do."

"Human in what way?"

"Less bullshit. They are what they are. Even someone like Travis, who isn't thrilled to be a vampire. He has a way about him." She wraps her hands around her mug of hot chocolate. "You know how most people are always looking around to see who's watching and what everyone else is thinking?"

"People are self-conscious sheep. It's in our genes."

"Vampires don't do that."

"Immortality boosts their confidence." I squint through the binoculars again. "When you have some version of forever to create yourself, you get comfortable in your own skin."

She slurps her cocoa. "Helps to have someone around like you who can save them."

I snort. "I can't save them. I just provide cosmetic enhancement. At most, I'm like an aloe vera salve."

"Letting Travis keep his hand wasn't cosmetic. You unstuck him from that cross."

"Yeah, good thing he didn't try to pee on it."

She almost snarfs her cocoa, then wipes her mouth. "So you think it's all because of your skepticism?"

"Maybe, but I'm skeptical about that, too."

This time she doesn't laugh. "So what would happen if you suddenly got religion? Would you lose your anti-holy powers?"

"I'm not going to get religion."

"But you know vampires exist, so how can you still believe in nothing?"

"Vampires as a species are older than some of the religions that scare them. So I don't see why believing in one makes me have to believe in the other." I stretch my back, which aches from hunching over the binoculars. "See, I think there's a huge truth behind it all, bigger than any mental box people can construct and label and put on a shelf. A bigger, bullshit-free truth."

"So maybe that's where your power comes from—that bigger truth, whatever it is." Her eyes widen, and her mug almost slips from her hands. "Ciara, what if your power comes from God?"

I scoff and turn back to the binoculars. "You're nuts."

"No, listen." She grabs my elbow. "What if God or the universe or whatever secretly hates religions, because they put God in a box. If God doesn't want to be in a box, He—or She or It—would find people who get it, like you."

"And put vampire-healing powers into their blood? Why would a big God care about vampires?"

Her eyes glow with an *X-Files* gleam. "Good question."

"Lori, even I'm not so egotistical to think the universe

gives a special shit about me. I'm just like everyone else." She raises her eyebrows. "Maybe not exactly," I add. "But you make me sound like a miracle worker. I'm just a recovering con artist trying to get her bachelor's degree."

"Fine. Be nonspecial. That way you'll never owe anybody anything." She checks her watch. "My turn to spy."

Resenting her dig but unable to deny it, I loosen the screws on the tripod to adjust the height.

Something moves within the field of view.

"Hold on." I press my eyes to the binoculars.

Two figures are approaching the cross. Their steps are urgent but confident—clearly they're supposed to be there.

"What is it?" Lori whispers, as if they might hear us from half a mile away.

"Two people, I think both men, based on the way they walk. But I can't see any detail. Open the window so the glass doesn't blur it."

Lori reaches forward and shoves open the tiny window, which swings outward like a barn door and lets in a rush of frigid air. Then she grabs Travis's camera with the mega-telephoto lens and scoots forward on her belly to the edge of the window.

I adjust the focus, but still can't bring the faces into resolution. The two men disappear into the trees surrounding the base of the cross. "Sorry, guys. It doesn't like you anymore."

The camera clicks and whirs in Lori's hands.

"What are you taking a picture of?" I ask her. "We can't even see them."

"Their car, and its license plate."

"Brilliant."

"I've learned a few tricks from Travis."

I poke her outstretched leg beside me. "I bet you have."

She doesn't reply at first. "I know you still don't approve of us."

"If Travis makes you happy, then go for it."

She turns to smile at me. "Thanks."

"But the moment he hurts you, I'll personally spike his Natty Boh with holy water."

I put my eyes back to the binoculars just as the two men come out of the trees, one waving his arms. They look like they might be yelling at each other. Lori snaps several shots.

"Can you see their faces?" I ask her.

"Almost." She fiddles with the settings on the camera, then points it out the window again. "Oh my God, you won't believe this." The shutter clicks again and again. "Go get David and have him bring Travis's laptop."

By the time David ascends to the attic, the men have driven off. Lori plugs the camera into the computer to download the photos, then clicks on the files to bring them up into a slide show.

"Look who's here," she says with pride.

I let out a gasp. "It's Ned."

"Is the other one Kevin?" David asks.

"Definitely not." I stare at the image of the tall blond man. "I don't think I've seen him before, but I wouldn't stake my life on it."

"Ciara's seen a lot of men," Lori says with a giggle.

David coughs as he turns the laptop to face him. "Uh, I'll forward these shots to Travis and have him check the license plate."

"I have an idea." I point to the keyboard. "Send it to Colonel Lanham, too. See if he gets the same results. Then we'll know if we can trust him."

He nods but gets a strange look on his face. "It goes both ways, Ciara. They have to trust us as well. Which means you have to be completely forthcoming."

Uh-oh. Something tells me he knows about my dad's postcard. Maybe he saw it in the bundle of forwarded mail.

Or maybe he's talking about Regina and Colin's mystery woman, Sara. How could he know what went on at Outlander that night?

I want to tell David everything, but if there's one thing I've learned, it's that secrets are made to be kept. I might not always be honest, but I can still be loyal.

I tried full disclosure once when I was sixteen, testifying about my parents' fraudulent activities. To show its gratitude for my service to society, the state took my folks away and put me in foster care. That's what I got for being a rat.

So I just give David a solemn nod with a straight face. "Forthcoming. Of course."

I hide my face in my giant coffee mug, thinking of my response to Jeremy's desire for something real. I've never known what "real" means, and I've built two careers on blurring the lines for everyone else.

The fact that the real thing is waiting for me at home makes me want to stay in this drafty attic all day and all night.

# 20

## Behind Blue Eyes

Dexter doesn't run to greet me when I walk into the apartment late Saturday evening. Lying on the couch next to Shane, he shifts his chin and flaps his tail.

"Hey." Shane lifts his hand from the guitar in his lap long enough for a quick wave. "How'd the spy mission go?"

"Productively." I hang my coat on the hook on the back of the door—the one with a C above it, to avoid a lecture.

"Catch any bad guys?"

"Ned and someone I've never seen before. We took their picture and their license plate." I lean over and kiss him. His lips are cool, and so is his hand when it caresses my face. I pull away. "I'm starving. David made me and Lori and Franklin eat his latest unrecognizable health stew."

I grab a box of mac 'n' cheese from the pantry and notice all the cans are facing forward, with their labels perfectly centered. To my relief, they're not alphabetized, at least not by any system I can recognize (maybe by third letter of the second ingredient, but I'm not going to check).

While the water boils, I creep back into the living room and sit near Shane and his never-silent guitar.

He pauses and looks at me. "What?"

"I never realized how much you play during your time off."

"How do you think I get so good? Vampire magic?" He smiles and strums a dramatic riff. "Practice, baby, practice." Then he sets the guitar on the floor, propping the neck against the arm of the sofa. "Does it bother you?"

I shake my head. "It walls you off from me."

His mouth opens and his brows pinch in a look of regret. "Sorry. I'm not ignoring you."

"No, it's a good thing. Sort of like adding another room to the apartment."

"Ah. It keeps you from having to deal with me." He cuts off my apologetic protest. "It's okay. I know you need your space. So do I. Whatever works."

I rub my sweaty palms against my jeans. "So you think it's working so far?"

Shane hesitates, his pale blue gaze shifting to meet mine. "Don't you?"

"No." I hold up my hands. "I mean, yes! I don't not think it's working." I shift closer to him, then closer again, right into his lap. "I love having you here."

His shoulders relax, and he wraps his arms around me. "So far."

" 'So far' is as much as I've lived through." I kiss him softly, then harder, as my appetite for food shifts to the back of my mind. My arms slide around his neck, and my back arches to meld my body against his.

He breaks the kiss. "Sorry, I can't right now." He brushes my hair off my face. "You might notice how cold I am."

I pull his hand to my mouth and breathe into his palm. "We can turn up the thermostat. I found the instruction manual."

He shakes his head. "It won't help. My blood's just not flowing. I haven't fed since Thanksgiving."

"Thanksgiving? That's almost ten days ago. I thought you needed to drink twice a week."

"This happens every holiday season." He rubs his eyes, which, come to think of it, look bleary and sunken. "Everyone's too busy to be bled."

"Can you get bank blood?"

"If I have to. But I'm seeing a donor tonight." He kisses my forehead. "I'll come home right after."

"Oh, good." I slide my finger down the buttons of his shirt. I'm not just looking forward to his improved health—the post-blooddrinking sex is particularly phenomenal.

A hiss comes from the kitchen—the sound of the boiling water splashing onto the stove.

"Are you using the small pot on the big burner?" he asks me. "It could melt the handles."

"Don't worry. I got the memo." I slide off his lap and dash into the kitchen.

"Turn on the exhaust fan so the steam doesn't warp the cabinets or set off the smoke alarm."

I do as he suggests, even though the noise blots out his subsequent guitar chords. I finally recognize the song—"Where Are You Going" by Dave Matthews Band—and can't suppress a smile. Even in his coldest moments, he's stretching himself into the twenty-first century.

I switch the exhaust fan to low so I can hear better, then turn to the wall-mounted spice rack for the red pepper flakes to add to my mac 'n' cheese.

The spices are out of alphabetical order. I didn't leave them that way, and why would Shane of all people rearrange them at random? Alphabetizing stuff makes him feel sane.

I look closer at the labels. Elizabeth's spice rack obviously came from a fancy bilingual or Canadian kitchen store, because each spice also includes the French spelling in small print under the English.

Sure enough, that's the new order.

I take the red pepper (*poivre rouge*) from the shelf and add it to the mix, wondering what's next. Rearranging the living room furniture alphabetically, clockwise one day and counterclockwise the next?

Shane's voice lilts through the air between us, swearing he's not a hero, for sure, but he wants to be where I am.

Even though it clearly drives him crazy.


I wake Sunday morning into total darkness—the new normal. Our blackout curtains maintain a permanent night, and even though my clock says 8:30, not a photon of light creeps into my room.

Shane sleeps beside me, his breath slow and even. Odd that he didn't wake me when he got home from the donor's. Maybe he knew I needed the sleep.

His soothing presence, combined with the deceptive, swaddling darkness, makes me want to succumb to sloth and wallow in bed for another lazy hour. But I have homework.

Instead of hitting the floor, my feet sink into fur. Dexter groans and gets up, brushing my legs. I hear him shake himself, jowls flapping, then he hops onto the bed, taking the warm spot I've left behind.

I make my way to the kitchen, hand against the wall, and finally reach a light switch. My eyes squint tight against the glare as I fumble for the door of the fridge.

Another note:

*Dear Ciara,*
*When you make toast, it really helps to use one knife to*
*put the butter on your plate and a separate knife to spread it.*
*That way you don't get crumbs in the butter.*
*Love, Shane*


I sigh and open the refrigerator in the vain hope that food will be inside. I haven't had time to grocery shop this week, and sexual frustration made me pig out on the entire box of mac 'n' cheese. Maybe a yogurt will be hiding behind the nothing.

A brown paper bag sits on the top shelf, its flap folded over tight. Aww, Shane got me a bagel from that place down the street. I could get used to this new living arrangement.

I snatch the bag, which is heavier than I expected (cream cheese, too? Or better yet, an egg, cheese, and sausage sandwich? Could he be that much of a god?), and switch on my new toaster oven.

Inside the bag, my fingers squish into thick plastic. Ew, I think as I pull it out, they didn't put the cream cheese into a tub, they just wrapped it in—

"Oh my God!"

The bag of blood drops from my hand. It lands on the stone tile with a *pop!* Cold red liquid spurts over my feet and shins. A crimson stain spreads across the floor. I let out another shriek.

Feet thud down the hall, and Shane skids to a halt outside the kitchen, Dexter at his heels. "Ciara!" He looks at my legs, spattered in blood. "Are you okay? What happened?"

I gape at him, unable to speak.

Then his gaze shifts to the paper bag in my hand. "Oh." His momentary relief turns into dread. "Oh."

Dexter steps forward, sniffing. Shane grabs his collar. "No." He leads the dog back to the bedroom. "This is one spill you can't clean up, buddy." The door shuts, and Shane reappears alone.

"I'm so sorry." I step away from the puddle, leaving bloody sock prints. "I thought it was my breakfast."

"No, it was *my* breakfast." He scratches his head and stares at the pool of red. "I was saving it for later."

"I thought you saw a donor last night."

"I did, but he was just getting over the flu. It wasn't safe for him to bleed." Shane sidesteps the puddle and grabs the paper towel roll on the counter. "I called all my other donors, but no one was available."

To keep from vomiting, I focus on his well-being. "Why didn't you drink it last night when you got home?"

"I don't know when I'll get to see another donor." Hands trembling, he sops up the blood with a clump of paper towels. "This time of year is crazy. So I figured I'd ration it."

I stare at him, so pale in the fluorescent kitchen light. "What are you going to do now?"

He gazes bleary-eyed at the blood on the floor, and I wonder if he's considering licking it up or sucking the paper towels. "This expensive tile of Elizabeth's is absorbing the stain. We'll need an area rug or something to cover it."

"I mean about drinking." I bend over to enter his line of sight. "Shane, call a female donor. This is a last-resort situation."

"You're probably right." He blinks hard and fast, as if to jolt his brain. "But first I should try the next-to-last resort."


I open our apartment door to David.

"Hi," is all I can muster.

"Good morning." His voice is smooth and level as he passes me to enter the apartment.

I take his coat, avoiding his eyes. "Shane's in the bedroom." I turn away with a nervous chuckle. Yes, it's a brilliant idea to remind us of my dream. "Oh, and there's bottled water in the fridge. He said you'd need to be hydrated first."

"I had some on the way, but I'll grab another." He goes into the kitchen. "Bleach'll get rid of this stain on the floor."

"Thanks." As he heads for the hallway, I blurt out, "I'm sorry."

"Don't be." He turns slowly to look at me. "I help them any way I can. Hopefully it makes up for their crappy salaries." His lips tug up as if he's trying to smile, to no avail.

"But here, of all places." I don't say Elizabeth's name. "And after Gideon attacked you—"

"Yeah, well." David runs his fingers inside the collar of his green turtleneck. "It is what it is."

Without another word, he enters the bedroom and closes the door.

I spend the next hour researching my term paper and pretending I'm not straining to hear noises from the bedroom.

I decided to take Franklin's brilliant suggestion and do my paper on identity theft. It's given me a great excuse to call up investigative agencies and ask them how they catch the bad guys, i.e., people like me. These agents are so smug, once I provided proof I was a real student and not a criminal—as if the two pursuits are mutually exclusive—they were thrilled to share examples of their semisecret techniques.

On the sofa next to me, Dexter raises his head suddenly and looks down the hall. I hold my breath but hear nothing over the background hiss of the forced-air heater.

My mind turns to that dream again, though I know that not even the tamest version of it could be taking place right now. Since becoming my boyfriend, Shane no longer fools around with the guys he bites. Some of them jerk off while he drinks them, which is their prerogative, but he doesn't lend a hand.

Still, curiosity drives me to set my laptop aside, then creep to the thermostat to shut off the heat.

In the ensuing silence I hear voices raised in what sounds like anger.

I tiptoe down the hall, then sit outside the bedroom door and press my ear to it. The voices have changed in tone.

"God, David," Shane moans. "You taste so good." The mattress creaks in a steady rhythm. "You like that?"

David murmurs "Yes" again and again, his pitch heightening. My mouth drops open slowly.

"That's it," Shane says. "I want to feel it when you come. I want to taste it."

I close my eyes against the dizzy sensation and rest my palm on the door. David's words turn incoherent, and I can see them in my mind, hands and teeth sliding over bare skin—

The door jerks open, and I pitch inward, nearly planting my face on the carpet. I look up to see Shane, fully dressed.

He smirks at me. "I knew you couldn't resist."

David laughs, sitting up in bed, also dressed.

I get to my feet. "I could tell you were faking it."

"Sure you could." Grinning, Shane examines my face, which must be red as a radish.

"But it was a good show." With a great effort, I glance at David, who looks slightly pale but otherwise hearty.

Shane offers his arm to David to help him stand. "Thanks, man. I owe you."

"What were you fighting about?" I ask them.

David scoffs. "Super Bowl Forty."

"He can't admit the Steelers won fair and square," Shane says.

"The refs gave it to them."

"Yeah, the refs and the Seahawks." He ushers us out of the bedroom, and in the low light I see him nearly glowing with energy, nothing like the shriveled shell of a man he was this morning.

In the living room, Shane switches on the satellite radio to the punk station. Dexter runs for the bedroom away from the noise, his sensitive ears no doubt assaulted by the wailing chords and relentless backbeat.

I fetch an energy drink from the fridge for David. "Are you okay to drive?"

"I'm fine, thanks."

"Are you sure?"

"He can't stay." Shane slides his hand over my shoulder and gives David his coat. "Much as he'd like to."

"Right." David avoids my eyes as he takes his coat and opens the door. "See you both at work tomorrow."

The moment the door shuts, Shane slams the deadbolt and chain in place. He turns to me, his eyes holding a predatory fever that starts a flame in the bottom of my belly.

I give a little squeak, then run.

Halfway down the hall he catches me, grabbing me around the waist. I scream and kick, laughter choking my protests.

Shane presses me face-first against the wall. "So you knew we were faking?" he says as he reaches around and unbuttons my jeans.

"Maybe."

"You liked it, anyway." He slides his hand inside, over my underwear, down to where I need it most.

I moan and angle my hips to meet his touch. "Yes."

"I knew you were there, listening. I heard you breathing." One finger slips under my panties. "I smelled you."

The first jolt arcs through me. I cry out, long past ready for him, and hope he doesn't make me wait.

Shane drops to his knees, slipping off my jeans. Then he turns me to face him.

When he looks up at me, the fangs are out. He wraps an arm around my legs so I can't move.

With a delicious mix of fear and desire, I watch his mouth move in on my hip. He bites through the strings of my bikini underwear, then hurls the material away.

"Come here." Shane carries me into the living room, sets me on the floor on my knees, and shoves my belly against the side of couch. His mouth brushes the back of my ear as he undoes his own jeans. "Should I tell you what it was like?"

My fingertips tingle, and I grind eagerly against him. "Yes."

"We took off our shirts." He tears his own off, then rips mine over my head, bra and all. "I held him in my arms until he stopped shaking."

My body goes still. "Shaking?"

"He was scared." His voice rasps against the back of my shoulder. "So we just talked for a long time."

"About what?"

"Music. Football. You."

"What about me?"

"Little things. Like the way you look in those sleep shirts, the ones with the buttons that go down to here." He traces his fingers between my breasts. "And big things, like the taste of your mouth." He slides his teeth—the human ones only now—against my back. I know he's probably making this up, but the thought of being between them, even just in conversation, makes me squirm and writhe against him.

"Then when he was ready," Shane says, "I held him down and bit him."

Shane enters me, smooth and slow. I give a long, throaty moan. He's never fucked me this soon after drinking. I didn't know a man could get so hard.

"His blood was hot." He strokes me deep. "And sweet and salty." He does it again, deeper. "He tasted like heaven."

My body jerks and spasms, every inch inside lit up like a firecracker.

"He loved it," he hisses, "just like always. I could've taken his life, ripped out his throat, and still he had his hands on me, begging for more."

My fingers crawl over the leather couch cushion, searching for an edge to clutch as I scream and snarl with the music throbbing from the speakers.

"David's a part of me now." Shane shifts his angle, planting one foot to the side. "He's inside me, fucking you."

I plunge over the edge, shrieking as he pumps fast and hard and deep enough to lift my knees from the floor. Shane's moan turns into a long, harsh growl. He finally collapses atop me, face damp with sweat between my shoulder blades.

When I can breathe again, I turn my head to the side. "Was that really what happened?"

"Of course not." He swipes his mouth over the back of my shoulder. "I'd be out of donors in three seconds if I told what happens during a bite." He caresses the side of my hip. "I just wanted to see if it would make you hot."

I feel my face warm. "Bet you're sorry you have your answer."

"Why?" Shane lifts himself up and helps me turn on my back to face him. "You think I'd be jealous?"

"A little."

He shrugs. "Maybe a little. But I'd be a hypocrite to take it personally, considering I keep myself alive with my mouth against other people's skin."

"David isn't just another faceless donor."

"True. He's our friend." Shane stretches out beside me on the couch. "So should I have asked him to stay?"

I stare at him until he starts to laugh. "Just kidding," he says. "He may be our friend, but he's also our boss. That's got about a million levels of wrongness." He swirls his fingertips in circles over my belly button. "In reality, at least." His eyes meet mine, tinged with mischief.

"Fantasy, I guess, is another matter."

"Entirely." He kisses me, teasing, his lips and tongue hot against my mouth as his fingers skate over my hips to my thighs, where they slip in between.

I gaze into his eyes, trying to find the courage to trust him enough to tell him about my dream. I could leave out the part where Shane was a murderer. The rest of it would probably turn him on, based on the things he just said.

But what if he's baiting me? What if I tell him I dreamed about David and he goes ballistic? Or worse, shuts down and stops speaking to me in any way but fridge notes? How much jealousy lurks under that cool exterior?

I can't take that chance. Total honesty might bring us closer, but in my experience, it usually rips people apart.

So I just close my eyes and murmur meaningless sexy phrases, urging him on the same as usual, as if this day has left no mark at all.

# 21

## Personal Jesus

Lori and I attend another meeting of the Munched—I mean, the Bitten. She has a fresh wound near her collarbone, which her shifting shirt reveals as she peels off her coat. The others (especially Kevin) give her a world of shit about it, and she gets defensive, and then we all eat donuts.

Afterward, Kevin stalks out without speaking to Lori. She hurries off to meet Travis, leaving me alone with Ned.

He invites me to go bowling. I tell him I'd love to, but the balls wreak havoc with my tendonitis. Then he invites me to a movie. I tell him I'd love to, but the flickering images wreak havoc with my epilepsy.

Like an angler who senses the fish losing interest, he tosses out the tastiest bait of all.

He invites me to the Fortress.

\* \* \*

Ned and I stand on the porch of a Victorian mansion in the swanky section of Frederick. The Christmas decorations in this part of town consist of tastefully draped white lights and wreaths with red velvet ribbons. Not an inflatable snowman in sight.

Ned pokes the lowest of three gilded doorbells with a trembling hand. Half a minute passes while no one opens the door. They're probably examining us via the closed-circuit camera over my left shoulder.

"Is this wreath real pine?" I reach toward the pale green branches on the door.

Ned grabs my hand. "Don't. Touch. Anything."

The sound of urgent feet approaches the other side of the door. Someone turns and slides a series of locks and chains.

A face appears in the six-inch crack between the door and the frame. "Who is she?" a tight-faced middle-aged woman asks Ned.

"A special friend."

She eyes me up and down, perhaps wondering if I'm *that* kind of friend. "Friend of yours?"

"Friend of the Fortress."

Ooh, can I get that on a T-shirt?

"Says who?"

Ned gives the woman a strong, level look. "Says Gideon Rousseau, the vampire she killed."

"Oh, her." She steps back and swings the door wide.

Ned motions for me to precede him into an enormous foyer, with a staircase on one side and a hallway leading to a dark room on the other. I step onto a thick Oriental rug. The sconces on either wall contain bulbs that flicker like flames. *Neat effect*, I think, before realizing they *are* flames.

The woman slinks down the far corridor without introducing herself or beckoning us to follow. I peek into the cavernous living room to my right. Its only light comes from the fireplace, but since the blaze is stoked high, the room is brightly illuminated. Shadowy figures sit in armchairs before the fire, a wisp of smoke rising from each.

Someone grasps the collar of my coat. I spin to see Ned.

"Relax," he whispers. "I'm just trying to be a gentleman."

I pull my coat tighter around me. "I'll keep it on. It's chilly in here."

He nods. "No electricity downstairs. It gives the illusion of old-fashioned values." He shrugs. "Things were better back then."

"Back when?"

"Eighteen ninety-nine. That's when the Fortress was formed."

*You mean the Citadel.*

"Come." He raises his arm toward a dark room in the opposite direction from the living room. "My brother will explain everything."

I follow Ned through the room, smacking my elbow into what turns out to be a baby grand piano, which I can only see from the streetlight leaking in through the sheer lace curtains. A tiny red beam glows in the room's upper corner—another video camera, no doubt, probably running on batteries.

Ned knocks on a door. After hearing no response, he cautiously slides apart the carved wooden doors.

The light of a huge fireplace streams over a wide oak desk. Ned leads me forward, hand on my elbow. On the desk, a closed laptop with a chrome case sits next to a quill pen and crystal inkwell. Beyond it lies an ornate set of French doors covered in sheer white curtains. My gaze flicks to all the shadowy places someone could lurk, and my finger clenches the pepper spray in my pocket.

"I thought he'd be here." He pulls out his cell phone and hits speed dial 2, which I remember as *B* from his contact list. Hmm, maybe *B* stands for "brother."

A voice comes on the other end of the line, speaking in a sharp, rapid tone that leaves no room for Ned to get in a word. He simply nods along and opens his mouth every few moments, to no avail.

Finally the voice stops, and Ned folds up his phone. "I've been instructed to ask you to wait, and in the meantime show you a short video presentation."

Is he kidding? Will the Fortress turn out to be some sort of pyramid scheme, where I'll be asked to sell scented soaps and garden gnomes to all my friends and recruit them, too, to make money money money?

"What's this about?"

"Please." He gestures to one of the chairs on the side of the desk nearest the door. "You'll want to sit down."

"That's okay. I've been sitting all day." Plus, I want to be able to run for it.

"Suit yourself." He opens the laptop and turns it around so that the monitor faces me.

An image lies frozen on the screen. I examine it, and suddenly my stomach feels like it wants to crawl up my throat.

In an empty, brightly lit room, my father stares into the camera.

My knees turn liquid. I shift my weight, searching for a stronger leg. I will not sit down.

Ned presses play, and the picture jumps to life. Someone nudges my dad from the side, and a male voice says, "Talk."

Dad glances at the unseen speaker, but his eyes hold no defiance, only despair.

He focuses on the camera. "Ciara, you have no reason to believe anything I say. I've let you down so many times. It broke my heart to betray David's secret to Gideon." He stops and rubs the back of his neck, looking older and thinner than ever.

I look at Ned. "Get me your brother. Now."

"Sorry, I can't do that." He angles the laptop screen to give me a better view as my father speaks again.

"These people say they're going to kill me. It's probably what I deserve." Dad looks directly into the camera, at me. "But I don't want to die. Not without seeing you again and telling you how sorry I am, how much I love you. Right now you're all I can think about."

I sit down hard on the edge of the leather chair.

Dad rubs his nose and says, "I missed you on Thanksgiving. If only I could spend one more holiday with you." He gives a nervous chuckle. "Remember how we'd always do Fourth of July with your aunt Lori? Those were such special times." His gaze suddenly intensifies, and his speech quickens. "Ciara, I don't know what they want, but don't risk your life for me. I'm not worth it." He glances to the side of the camera, then flinches as if someone's about to hit him. He looks at me again and turns his voice monotonous, like he's reading a prepared statement. "Do what they ask. They just want justice, like all of us. I know better than anyone the scourge of vampires. I lived with them for two years. Please, do whatever you can to help the Fortress." He puts his palm to his chest. "Remember, I'm your father."

The sound cuts off, and the video freezes his face, eyes open and pleading.

I look up at Ned. "That's it? What does it mean? Where is he?" I struggle to hide how much my mind is whirling with fear; no doubt someone is watching my reaction through the closed-circuit camera.

"I can't tell you where he is," Ned says. "But we have him, obviously."

"Since when?"

"I can't tell you that either." Ned puts a hand on my shoulder. "My brother will explain everything when he arrives."

"Is this a blackmail or a ransom? Does he want money?"

Ned laughs. "Money is the last thing he needs."

"And what's the first thing?"

He gives a sly smile—an expression I've never seen on his face—and leans over to whisper in my ear.

"Vengeance."

My cell phone rings, startling Ned into jumping back and slamming his hip bone against the desk.

I cram my hand into my other pocket and fumble for my phone, almost dropping it. "Hello?"

Lori's voice squeaks from the earpiece, tight with tears. "Ciara . . . help."


Police cars line the main street of Frederick's downtown historic district. The patrol vehicles' red and blue flashers blend with the white Christmas lights on the trees lining the road.

My car drifts past a tavern where patrons are gathered outside, many of them huddling without coats, breath steaming the air. They gawk at a man spread-eagled against a police car—Kevin from the Bitten meetings.

Two officers appear to be interviewing bystanders, who point down the street in the direction I'm heading, no doubt indicating the trajectory of the "acid splashing" victim.

I check the sign at the next intersection. Two more streets. I keep my speed slow to avoid attracting attention, but I've got to find Lori and Travis before the cops do.

I turn down a side street and park the car in a deserted lot reserved for a closed stationery store.

Before I get out of the car, I punch Lori's cell number to make sure they haven't moved.

"Where are you?" she whispers.

"Church Street and"—I crane my neck to see the little green sign at the corner—"Coppersmith Lane."

I get out of the car and try to look casual as I hurry down

the street, following her directions. Most of the shops are closed, but their cheery Christmas window displays seem to watch me, condemning my holiday horror.

Lori pops out of an alley ahead. Her blond hair glistens in the white streetlight as she waves her arms in a frantic gesture.

I run to her. She grabs my hand and tugs me down the alley.

"A whole bucket." Tears soak her reddened face. "Kevin had a whole bucket of holy water." The front of her coat is soaking wet. "How could he do this?"

We turn down a smaller alley, and I see a pair of sneakered feet sticking out from behind a big cardboard box. The chill air carries moans of agony.

When I reach Travis, he turns away and buries his face in his arms, then howls with pain.

I touch his hand gently. "Let me see."

Travis starts to lower his arms, and Lori whimpers.

"Ciara, it's real bad," she says.

"I'm sure I've seen— Oh God!" I leap back at the sight of Travis's face.

It's melted. His eyes are nothing but pools of red-and-white goop, and his nose looks like liquid Silly Putty. His lips are, well, gone.

"Go 'way," he slurs around his fangs. "Le' 'e alone."

Lori drags me a few feet down the alley. "He wants to die," she whispers, as if he can't hear her. "He wants us to leave him here and let the sun burn him." She clutches my arm. "We can't do that, can we?"

"Of course not." The cops would find him long before morning. They'd take him to the hospital, where he'd combust in public.

"Then you'll help him?" Lori wipes her eyes and swallows a sob. "Give him your magic blood?"

I look back at the oozing maw of Travis's mouth. "This isn't just a burn, like with Shane. His face is gone."

"I can see that!" Her whisper verges on hysteria. "We have to try." She digs her nails into my wrist. "I know it's gross here in the alley, but David can give you antibiotics."

Travis expels a gurgling cry. His breath rattles, sounding like it might be one of his last. My skin crawls as I wonder what happens when a vampire dies slowly.

"Ciara, please." Lori's voice pitches up. "He won't even make it to sunrise if we don't do something."

She's right. Travis might not be one of my favorite people, but Lori is. I can't watch her watch him die.

Before I lose my nerve, I march over to him, peeling off my coat. "I can't believe I'm saving you again," I mutter. "I don't even like you."

I shove up my right sleeve, lean over, and cram my forearm against his mouth.

Pain spikes through the tender flesh, just below my elbow. I suck in a hard breath and claw the brick wall in front of me to keep from screaming. It's a hundred times worse than Shane's bite, a hundred million times worse than Noah's. It feels like my veins are being yanked out through my skin.

Hot, thick liquid streams down my arm and through my fingers. It's too much. I try to pull away, but his grip on my elbow tightens, and his other hand slides up to grab my shoulder. He pulls me down against him until I'm slumped over his back, feeling him quake beneath me.

"No . . ." My voice sounds faint and feeble under the approaching sirens. Lori crouches on the other side of Travis, all of us hidden behind the giant box.

One block over, the sirens pass and start to fade. The alley falls quiet again, except for the sound of Travis slurping and gulping. With every swallow, a new wave of pain washes over me.

My head gets heavy, like a riptide is dragging me out to sea. I struggle to force out words:

"Lori . . . make . . . stop."

She speaks to him in an urgent voice. My mind pitches too hard to decipher anything beyond her pleading tone.

At last he releases me, but I'm stuck draped over his back, unable to move. Lori takes my shoulder and eases me off him.

"Oh God," she says. "Oh God. Ciara, I'm so sorry."

"What?" I want to examine my arm, but I can't lift it, and anyway, my vision has gone all swimmy. "Is Travis . . . does Travis have a face yet?"

Silence, then a soft, "Holy shit." Travis's voice, not the least bit slurred.

"Good sign," I whisper, as the world goes black.

I wake in the backseat of a car. I think it's mine, based on the smell of the upholstery crushed against my nose. There's a lot of lurching.

A white light shines in the darkness. I open my eyes to see upside-down block letters through the back windshield. Several of them are E's.

Lori speaks, louder than necessary. "Ciara, can you walk, or do you want me to have them bring out a wheelchair?"

"Where's Travis?"

"Right here."

I blink and try to focus on his face. He reaches up and turns on the cabin light.

His skin shows no burns, not even a scar. His eyes are once again round and back in their sockets. His lips are, well, there.

I did that. Or something bigger did it through me.

"I can't come in with you," he says. "If any of the people who were there tonight see me like this—"

"Go. Shane'll pick us up. Just get out of here."

Lori opens the back door, then steadies me as I get out of the car. "Are you sure you don't want a wheelchair?"

I look up at the Emergency Room sign, then ahead at the double automatic doors. "It's not that far." I take a few steps, then a few more.

My right arm throbs. I look down to see it wrapped tightly in Lori's dark red scarf.

Wait. Her scarf was pale green.

My knees buckle. "Wheelchair."

# 22

## Gotta Serve Somebody

My vision blurs and swirls, a little less with each minute. Sunlight creeps through the gaps between my eyelashes. To my left, a mechanical hum and intermittent boops create a soothing background for a pair of male voices.

"Please tell your agents to be careful," says David. "We don't want any more trouble than we already have."

My tongue tastes like salty sandpaper. I summon all my strength to whimper the word, "water."

"Ciara, it's me." David steps into my blurred view. "Sorry, they said you can't drink so soon after the surgery." A cool wet surface, maybe a paper towel, caresses my dry lips. "Better?"

I blink as hard as I can. "Muh."

David wipes my eyes with the damp cloth. "I met your surgeon. Nice guy." He draws a dry washcloth over my face. "Did you know he also treats the Ravens? The scalpel he used on you might have once been inside Steve McNair."

Several fumble-related jokes come to mind, but I just smile up at David's face, which is a lot less foggy without my eye gunk. Then I look past him at the other man. "Uh-oh."

"Ms. Griffin, good to see you again." Colonel Lanham steps forward so that David has to move out of the way. Even Lanham's civilian clothes are solid black, setting off the stark paleness of his smooth scalp under the ultrashort buzz cut. His footsteps are silent and deliberate, and his movements speak of a coiled power, completely under Control.

By now he must know what I did for Travis, what I can do for all vampires. My life is over.

"Wha' you want?" I ask him, trying to sound defiant despite the opium cloud that makes me want to agree with everyone about everything.

"We heard about what happened to Travis Tucker. I called David and offered to intervene on your behalf."

"I'm sorry, Ciara." Standing at the end of my bed, David touches my foot. "There was a Control agent at the bar last night where Travis got burned. Another one spied him later. Between your injury and Travis's recovery, they put two and two together about your powers. Colonel Lanham said he would broker a deal to let you keep as much of your personal liberty as possible."

I send the colonel a foggy glare. "*Let* me? 'S a free country."

Lanham gives a slight shrug, as if the Bill of Rights were a pesky technicality. "We've been monitoring these Fortress people for years, suspecting that they were a latter-day Citadel movement. One of our agents was shadowing that particular man."

"Holy-water guy?"

"Yes." He pulls out a small notepad and flips the pages. "Kevin Tarquinio, age twenty-nine. One of the Fortress's top lieutenants."

A dark object moves in my peripheral vision. A strapping

but unfamiliar young man in a black sweater stands just out-side my door. My bodyguard. Or my warden.

Colonel Lanham follows my gaze. "He's FBI, as far as the hospital knows. We have an agreement with the Bureau to let our agents use their forms of identification for cases like this."

I squint at my right arm and see it swaddled in bandages. A tube drains red goop near my elbow. I stop looking at it.

"Now what?" I ask Colonel Lanham. "I get to be your lab rat?" The morphine tangles up my lips so "lab rat" comes out "wabbit."

He shakes his head emphatically, making the window's daylight dance off his scalp. "All we ask is a pint every six weeks, the same as if you were giving to the Red Cross."

"I don't give to the Red Cross."

"I assure you we'll make it worth your while."

I reach for the wet paper towel, pretending my lips are too dry to speak. If they're willing to pay me or trade for some-thing I want, I should wait for them to up the offer.

Lanham folds his hands in front of him in a pious military gesture. "More important, Ms. Griffin, you'd be helping vam-pires in need."

I give the towel another suck. "Go back to the part about making it worth my while."

Colonel Lanham smiles—for the first time I've ever seen—then pulls up a chair. "The next time a vampire is burned with holy water, your blood could be administered without you having to be injured."

"Bullshit. You'll use it to build new weapons, not protect vampires from the ones already out there."

A petite dark-haired nurse strides in on sneakered feet. "How are we feeling?" she asks me with a smile.

"Zoomy."

She laughs. "I don't know what that means, but it sounds

good." She waves the men away from my bed. "Step back, fan club, while I take this lady's blood pressure."

I hold out my good arm. "Do I have to stay over?"

"I'm afraid so." She wraps the cuff and starts to pump. "But you're in luck. Tonight's our monthly non–Salisbury steak dinner." She glances at my bedside table. "Which one of these gentlemen callers brought the flowers?"

"I did." David puts his hands in his pockets. "But they're from Shane."

The nurse raises her eyebrows. "You have three men?"

Stoned, I giggle. "Not counting the one at the door."

The room falls silent as she assesses the pressure of my precious blood. I sleepily admire the dozen red roses sitting next to a scrubs-wearing teddy bear that Lori brought an hour ago, right after I got out of surgery.

Finally the nurse nods and rips off the cuff. She holds up a device that looks like a remedial remote control, with one red button. "To call the nurse's station." She gives me a balloon-looking thing. "For more pain meds."

"Cool."

"The young ones always say that." She slips around the other side of the bed and checks my IV setup. "You can have chipped ice now. I could have the nursing assistant bring it, but it'll be faster if one of your friends gets it from the vending area."

"I'll do it." David gives me and the colonel a nervous glance, then follows the nurse out.

Alone with Lanham, I become fascinated with the stitching on the crisp white bedsheet.

He eases his chair closer. "You're probably wondering what's in store for you."

"I'm wondering if I have a choice."

"There's always a choice." He leans his elbows on my bed railing, steeples his fingers, and rests his chin on his thumbs. "Your father made a choice."

I glance at an imaginary watch. "Wow, almost five minutes without bringing that up. Your restraint is admirable."
Or "ammable," if one hears it phonetically.

Another piece of brain wakes up and tells me I shouldn't
squander this chance to speak with him alone. "Am I the only
one you know of with this power?"

"Yes. But I only have the second-highest security clear-
ance. There could be others like you that I don't know
about."

"Others, locked up in an underground lab somewhere."

"Is that what you fear?"

"You're the guys who created vampire ferrets. But I can be
more useful to you outside."

He gives a single nod. "Infiltrating the Fortress."

"If I help you destroy them, will you leave me and my
blood alone?"

His thin lips tighten into an almost imperceptible line. "I
don't understand why you're not amenable to a periodic donation."

"Because it's not my choice. I should have control over what
happens to my own body." I shift my feet under the sheet.
"Plus, losing blood makes me woozy."

"We can minimize that reaction. If necessary to protect
your health, we'll take less than a pint at a time, and at first
we'd need no more than a few vials to study your blood's qualities." He stands, almost looming. "It *is* your choice. I hope
we can come to some mutually beneficial arrangement." His
eyes glint with a brief bitterness. "As for your father, you will
be notified when we locate him." Lanham turns crisply and
heads for the door. "As his next of kin."


I wake to the press of Shane's kiss. At least, I hope it's his.

I open my eyes and smile up at him.

"The nurse asked me to wake you for dinner." Shane pats his stomach. "I said no thanks, I'm full."

"That's tasteless, considering why I'm in the hospital."

"Speaking of tasty." He whips out a box of chocolates from behind his back. "You like them dark, right?"

"Dark and bittersweet, like the soul of my man." I grab the box and tear off the ribbon one-handed. Shane catches the teddy bear as it falls off my lap, then lowers the blaring volume on my wall-mounted TV set.

He pulls a chair up close to my bedside. "So what happened? You weren't very coherent in the ER last night. Lori told me about Travis, but you were mumbling something about the Fortress and your dad."

I describe my preempted encounter with Ned's brother "B," including the video of my captured father.

"Where do you think he could be?" Shane asks.

"No idea. He was in this totally blank room." I shut my eyes. "He sounded so scared. I don't think they were treating him well. He said the usual hostage stuff, like you see on the news." A memory knocks on the inside of my skull, and I open my eyes. "But something weird, too, about spending Fourth of July with my aunt Lori. I don't have an aunt Lori, and we never spent holidays with other family members."

He furrows his brow. "Do you think he meant your friend?"

"He didn't even meet her until this past August. Besides, we don't do Fourth of July together, because she's always up at Gettysburg for the battle commemoration."

We blink at each other as the realization hits us. Shane says, "Gettysburg? Did your dad know Lori was a Civil War buff?"

"If he could get David to tell him he staked Gideon's son, he could get Lori to talk about her favorite thing in the world. You think it was a secret signal to me? You think he's in Gettysburg?"

"Why else would he say that?" Shane shakes his head in amazement. "Clever. His captors would never make the connection, but he knew it would sound odd to you." He gives me a worried look. "I hate to say it, but we should tell the Control. They're the only ones with enough manpower for an operation like this."

I groan at the idea of getting further entangled with that bunch of thugs. But I might have no choice.

A soft knock comes at the door. "You awake enough to kill me?" says an all-too-familiar voice.

Shane stiffens at the sight of Travis. I put my hand on his arm to keep him from tearing off the younger vampire's newly restored face.

"Look who's here." My voice takes on an edge. "The erstwhile Elephant Man."

Travis creeps forward, carrying a bouquet of purple flowers. "I know this doesn't make up for it, but it was all I could think of."

"Come here." I beckon him with my left hand. "Let me look at you."

He skirts around Shane, sets the flowers on my nightstand, and moves close to my bed.

I reach up and touch his face, tracing the solid planes of his jawline and cheekbone, then glide my fingertips over his eyelids, remembering how his skin melted and oozed off his skull like candle wax. Now it's all real, all together.

He gazes at me with gratitude. I whack him hard across the face.

Travis jerks back. "Ow!" He puts a hand to his cheek. "I deserved that."

"You deserve worse." I gesture to my right arm, whispering. "Nerves, tendons, muscles. You fucking *chewed* me."

"I'm sorry."

"I told them it was a pit bull. I have to get rabies shots."

"I had no lips."

"Get out," Shane growls.

"I couldn't feel what my fangs were doing." Travis pulls at his own cheeks. "My whole face was gone. You got no idea how much it hurt."

"I was burned with that stuff, too," Shane tells him.

"Nothing like I was."

"He's right, Shane." I look at Travis, amazed it's the same person I saw in the alley last night. "You couldn't help it."

"Then why'd you hit me?"

"Because it felt good." My right arm is throbbing from the impact of my left hand against his face. But it was worth it. "Now tell me exactly what happened."

"Didn't Lori already give you the story?"

"She came this morning right after my surgery, but I was pretty out of it. Plus I want to hear your version."

He rubs his forehead, as if it'll erase the memory. "I met Lori for a drink after she got out of her support group. That guy Kevin came into the bar after us, started giving her shit for being with me." He crosses his arms. "I wanted to kick his ass, but Lori wouldn't let me. She said if I hit him, I might get arrested and not get out of the police station before sunrise. Finally, he was so obnoxious, the bouncer threw him out."

"Did Kevin say anything about vampires?" Shane asks him.

"At the end, yeah, when they were dragging him out. He said, 'He'll bleed you dry, Lori.' "

"That could be taken metaphorically," I point out.

"But then he said, 'Exterminate all vampires.' "

"Oh." I look at Shane, then decide to let Travis in on a little more of the situation. "That probably tipped off the Control agent."

His jaw drops. "What Control agent?"

"They had a guy tailing Kevin, who is apparently a high-ranking lackey in the Fortress."

The evening news comes on. I give the TV a distracted glance as the anchorman relates a story about an apparent gang killing.

"The victim, identified as Frederick resident Kevin Tarquinio, twenty-nine, was arrested last night for assault on Market Street, where he allegedly threw a bucket of acid in another man's face."

We gape at each other, then the television.

"After an extensive search throughout Frederick, that victim was never found," the anchor continues, "and Tarquinio was released, as the residue of the liquid was found to be nothing but water. Police say they have no suspects at this time."

They switch to another story. Shane pulls out his cell phone. "I'm calling David." Then he curses. "They won't let us use these things in here. Gotta go outside." He squeezes my foot as he heads out of the room.

A young woman in a ponytail passes him, entering with our dinners. My stomach churns with anxiety, but I haven't eaten a full meal in over twenty-four hours. I lift the metal plate coverings. Potato soup and a side salad.

Travis looks at the slip on my tray. "It's marked 'light.' You on a diet?"

"It's probably to keep me from barfing after the anesthesia." With some difficulty—not to mention shooting pain in my right arm—I sit up and pull the tray closer.

My left hand feels like it has too many fingers and not enough connections to my brain. The first spoonful of soup ends up in my lap.

"Here." Travis pulls up a chair and takes the spoon. He offers me a bite of soup, holding my chin steady with a napkin.

"Payback, huh? You feeding me?" I let him insert the food in my mouth. "Ow, it's too hot."

He sets the soup aside and cuts up some salad. "You got no idea what it felt like when that guy soaked me. Not just the pain. I put my fingers up to my face, and there was nothing there, just a lot of muck. You know when little animals get hit by cars, and there's more of 'em on the outside than inside?"

I look at him, then at the food.

"Sorry, that's gross," he says. "Anyway, I kept thinking, if I was still human, I'd just be wet. I wanted to die. But today I'm glad to be alive, or undead, or whatever. So if you ever need me to lay down my life for you, I'll do it in a second." He stabs a crouton. "For now, I'll just feed you salad."

I find myself strangely touched by his meandering confession. "Did you kill Kevin Tarquinio?" I ask him after the next bite.

"Thought about it, but figured Lori'd be upset if I did."

"She means a lot to you, huh?"

He stirs my soup. "Everyone I know acts like I'm a monster or a little kid. She treats me like I'm a man."

When Shane reenters the room, Travis gets up and lets him take his place.

"I couldn't reach David, so I called Lori." Shane shifts the chair closer. "She checked the news station's Web site." He looks at both of us. "It was an execution-style killing. Professional." He pauses. "They found Kevin Tarquinio's body near the police station. Wouldn't release the estimated time of death because of the investigation."

My stomach sinks. "The Control agent who followed Kevin might have killed him as soon as the cops let him go."

"Could be the Fortress," Travis points out. "That guy was babbling in public about vampires. Maybe that's against their rules."

I shake my head. "They might have punished him, but they're so pro-human they probably already had his certificate of achievement printed up for what he did to you."

"What about Ned?" Shane leans in closer as a quiet part of the news comes on. "Maybe you could call him, see his reaction to Kevin's death."

I suppress a shiver at the thought of consoling Ned. At least my arm gives me an excuse not to give him a long, touchy hug.

"Speaking of Ned, that was his car Lori photographed at the cross, so there's a dead end." Travis checks his watch. "I gotta go. I have a, uh, thing."

I hold up the teddy bear. "Tell Lori thanks for the stuffie. And sorry I fell asleep on her today."

He nods. "If she'll talk to me."

When he leaves, Shane picks up my soup spoon. "Still hungry?"

"Starving." With his help, I sit up a little straighter in bed. "I'll call Ned and see what I can find out. But I think Kevin's murder was the Control sending a message to the Fortress." I blink hard to clear my mind, even as the terrible thoughts flood in. "And to me. That's what they'll do to my dad when they find him." I mime a gun to the back of my head. "Colonel Lanham said as much when he left here."

"But the Fortress has him."

"For now. But if the Control is hot on their trail, they might find him. Or if the Fortress people have to go on the run, they might kill him instead of bringing him with them." I take a mouthful of proffered soup. "When my head clears from the morphine, maybe I'll remember another clue besides Gettysburg. Maybe we can find him ourselves."

Shane unwraps a dinner roll and breaks off a bite for me. "I can't believe I'm saying this, but I really think you should get the Control's help. This thing is too big for us. You might be able to strike a deal to protect your dad. After all, you have something they want."

As I realize he's right, I can feel my blood rebel. It wants to cruise through *my* veins, lurch through *my* arteries. It doesn't want to sit in a test tube, building the military machine.

"Blood for blood," I whisper, then lean my swimming head back against the pillow. "Get me Colonel Lanham."


Late Friday morning the hospital discharges me with a sling and a fistful of Percocet. When Lori drops me off at home around noon, Colonel Lanham is sitting at my dining room table with a scattering of papers surrounding his laptop. Shane looms behind him, arms crossed in a bouncerlike posture.

"I wouldn't let him look through your stuff until you got home." Shane takes my bag of pharmaceuticals. "Can I get you anything else before I go to bed?"

"No, but when you wake up I'll need a sponge bath."

He gives a low laugh and helps me take off my coat. "So much for me sleeping."

When he heads to the bedroom, I go to the kitchen. "Did Shane make this coffee?" I ask Colonel Lanham.

"I made it."

"Good." Left-handed, I carefully pour a cup and stir in three sugars. "He brews it superstrong so he can taste it, and then I have to add milk to keep from burning a hole in my stomach." I sip the black coffee and enter the dining room. "I hate milk in my coffee. It puts me to sleep." Yes, small talk will keep me safe. That and the vampire in the other room, who is no doubt listening behind the door.

"I brought more blood for your dog." Lanham gestures to a cooler on the table.

"Where do you get that stuff?" I'm almost afraid to ask.

"Dogs have blood banks, just like humans. And just like with human vampires, there are always samples that expire or can't be used because they test positive for a blood-borne disease." He pulls out a chair for me and points to an array of papers spread over the table. I recognize them as the names and addresses Travis fetched from Ned's cell phone contact list.

"I've eliminated his family members in Chicago," he says.

I stare up at him, turning cold despite the hot coffee. "You killed Ned's family?"

Lanham shakes his head. "I eliminated *their names* from our list of suspects, people who might be . . . keeping your father."

"What about Ned's brother, this 'B' person?"

The colonel's gaze shifts past my shoulder. "He might be a half brother. We're looking into it." For once, his words sound more rushed than deliberate. "As I was about to say, none of the contacts fit the profile of where your father might be."

"Didn't Shane tell you our Gettysburg theory?"

Lanham hesitates, then seems to come to a decision. He pulls a chair to the corner of the table and sits next to me. "Ms. Griffin, I'll be straight with you."

"That'd be a first."

He ignores me and continues. "Your father's not the Fortress's prisoner. He's their accomplice."

"Accomplice?" My head spins, but maybe it's just the drugs. "How do you know?"

"Internal Affairs has concluded that Ronan O'Riley escaped our custody with the aid of his bodyguard, whom we've determined to be a double agent for us and the Fortress."

"Did this bodyguard confess?"

"We have evidence." He folds his hands on the table. "It makes sense your father would turn to the Fortress. No one hates us more than they do. They'd be happy to protect him from us in exchange for information."

Information on the Control, on WVMP. On me. On everything and everyone that protects our most valuable assets.

"Your DJs are the most famous alleged vampires outside of Transylvania. It must irk the Fortress that they profit from their monstrosity."

"I get that part." I rub my forehead, as if that will make my brain more absorbent. "But why would they claim to hold my father prisoner?"

"Perhaps they think you'll make an exchange—a DJ's life for his."

My chest grows tight with rage. "And to think I felt sorry for my dad. He's using me. Again."

"I'm sorry." Lanham sounds like he means it, but no doubt it's just an act. "We won't know their ransom and therefore their angle unless you're willing to go back to the Fortress and speak to Ned's brother."

"I can't wait."

"And we can't wait to hear it." Lanham slides his brief-case over and opens it. He takes out a small clear plastic bag with half a dozen fuzzy black dots the size of his thumbnail. "When you return to the Fortress, we'd like you to plant as many of these listening devices as you feel safe."

I examine the contraptions through the plastic. They resemble earbuds with inch-long antennas. "The Fortress is full of security cameras."

"I'll teach you a few tricks. It should come natural to a sleight-of-hand master such as yourself." He glances at my sling. "Even with half the hands."

I don't let him flatter me. "Distraction only works on live humans. Cameras aren't fooled."

"Just do your best, and don't take any unnecessary risks." Lanham shuffles the lists of Ned's contacts. "Good thinking in getting these. You excel at thinking on your feet." I grunt in reply, and he adds, "Have you thought about where you want to work after you graduate?"

"You don't want someone like me." I give him a sullen glare

that I hope is sufficiently repellant. "I don't take orders, and I'm not a team player."

"Perhaps you'd consider contract work?"

"I wouldn't. I'm helping you too much as it is."

"Speaking of which, we must schedule your first donation."

I catch his use of the word "first." Somehow his gall surprises me. "I'm giving you a small, one-time sample. Not a donation. That's what we agreed."

His posture goes still and his eyes cold. "We could just take it from you."

"I thought of that. I've made arrangements with certain friends in the media that in the event of my death or disappearance, there are materials they would become privy to." I take a sip of coffee. "But all things being equal, I prefer that we work together instead of in opposition."

"So do I." Lanham regards me with a mix of respect and animosity as he stands and takes his coat from the back of the door. "Our other offer stands. I'm sure we could come to some mutually beneficial arrangement."

When he leaves, I turn the deadbolt, as if that will keep my soul safely locked here with me, and out of Darth Vader's pocket.

# 23

## Welcome to the Jungle

Ned meets me at the door to the Fortress, his face drawn and tense. I almost don't recognize him without his customary cult-glow.

He notices my sling. "Ciara, what happened?"

I shrug. "Just routine surgery for my tendonitis." Hey, that why-I-can't-go-bowling lie came in handy. "I saw on the news what happened to Kevin. I'm really sorry."

His lips tighten. "We had no idea he ran with that type of crowd. Shame."

He tries to slip across the threshold to join me on the porch, but I put my hand on the door.

"Can I use your restroom before we go?" When he hesitates, I bend my knees in a half hop. "Please? I drank a whole cup of coffee getting here. Traffic on 270 was a nightmare."

"Okay, okay." He leads me inside, then points down the far corridor. "Through the kitchen to the right."

I enter the kitchen, which strikes me as utilitarian compared to the house's grandiose decor. Then I remember that in Victorian times, only servants spent much time in this room.

I make note of the chocolate strudel in the glass cake dish sitting on the counter, then find the water closet, which is literally no more than a closet. The kitchen lantern's glow illuminates a candle and a lighter on the bathroom sink. No cameras in the corners—nice that they don't film each other peeing—so I light the candle and shut the door.

I pull the baggie of listening devices from my pocket. With a one-handed motion I've been practicing with my eyes closed, I activate the listening device's antenna and peel off its adhesive backing. Then I flush the toilet, run the water, and give myself a moment to "dry my hands," in case anyone's listening on the other side of the door.

I hurry through the kitchen, then come to a sudden stop a few steps beyond the cake dish, as if seized by an idea. I examine the strudel with undisguised avarice, caressing the glass cover. After a moment's "hesitation," I lift the lid and take a full whiff.

Cabinets sit against the wall to my right. Carefully balancing the bug on the tip of my curled finger, I open one, then another, until I find the plates. I reach up into the dark cupboard and pretend to lose my balance so that I have to grab the protruding edge. The listening device adheres, where it can't be seen from outside the cabinet. I grab a saucer.

"What are you doing?"

"Oh!" The saucer slips from my hand and clatters on the counter. I turn to face the mousy middle-aged woman who let us in the door last week. "I'm sorry. This strudel looked so amazing, I couldn't resist." I grimace. "I'm totally PMSing. It makes me crave chocolate."

She opens a drawer and pulls out a long, serrated knife. I take a step back.

"Relax." She slides the cake dish over and cuts a slice. "You should have just asked."

She hands me the plate of strudel, along with a fork. My stomach is twisting like a flag in a windstorm, but I take the dessert in exchange for a wide smile.

It's quite good, and I tell her so.

She looks down at her roughened fingers. "I made it."

"Wow. This crust is extremely flaky." *Just like me.* I extend my left hand. "I'm Ciara, by the way."

"I know." She pushes a blond-gray curl from her eyes as she shakes my hand. Then she turns to leave.

"So how long have you lived here?"

She stops and stares at me. "I, uh, it's been eight years. Since a vampire killed my mother."

The strudel goes lumpy in my mouth. "I'm so sorry."

She gives me a sharp look. "You're with that radio station, right?"

"Yes. But our vampires are good." *Good-ish*, I add mentally.

"There's no such thing as a good vampire."

"Do you have a radio in your room?"

She hesitates, then nods.

"Will you do me a favor and listen tonight? It's 94.3 FM." She glances at the kitchen door. "I don't think—"

"Just keep the volume low." I take a step toward her. "When I was a kid, I had to use headphones so my parents wouldn't hear."

She gives me a reluctant smile, then whispers, "Me, too. My daddy was a preacher."

"Mine, too! Only he was a fake." I set down my fork on the saucer, which emptied at an embarrassing rate. "But a lot of people were comforted by his words, so I guess he was real to them."

"That's all that counts." She inches closer to me. "My name's Luann. I was rude not to introduce myself before."

I wave off her apology. "So what kind of music do you like?"

She looks away and rubs the space under her nose. "When I was in high school, I once snuck off to go to a Cure concert. It was their first American tour."

"Then Regina's the one you want to hear. Her show's on tonight at midnight, then it'll be repeated tomorrow from three to six."

Luann glances at the door again. "I don't know . . ."

On a strange impulse, I dig into my purse for my MP3 player. "Here." I hold out the tiny silver contraption, its earbuds dangling from their ever-tangled wires. "Try our podcasts."

She gapes at me but doesn't take the player. "Why would you give me this?"

"I'm not. I'm lending it."

"But why?"

"I don't know. Because you make good strudel?" I shove it into her hands. "Just take it, all right? You're embarrassing me. Sheesh."

I walk out before she can protest, and find Ned waiting for me at the front door.

He looks at me, brows pinched. "I just found out—" He rubs the back of his neck. "Do you mind if we stay here a while?" He motions to the parlor. "We can sit in there and talk."

I follow Ned in and sit on one end of a silk-upholstered love seat while he stokes the fire in the fireplace. His shoulders are tight and slumped.

"I have good news," I tell him. "I've decided to break up with my boyfriend. After this is all over and my dad is safe."

"That's great." He shifts the log at the center of the fire. It breaks in half in a crackling shower of sparks.

"Especially for us."

He sets the iron poker back in its rack and turns to me.

"Ciara, there's something I need to tell you." He slides his hands into the pockets of his khakis. "I really like you."

Uh-oh.

He adds, "But I think I'd rather just be friends."

Oh. "Umm . . ."

"I just need to get my head together. Besides, I don't know about you, but when we kissed, I felt nothing. No spark. I think that's a bad sign."

"Probably." I want to laugh with relief, and to mock myself for assuming he was smitten.

"I'm sorry for leading you on," he says, "but I do really, really like you, and I want to keep hanging out, as friends."

I change the subject before he can detect my glee. "Is that why you're so nervous tonight?"

"No, it's—" He breaks off and stares at the foyer. "People are coming later. Elders of the Fortress."

"For a meeting?"

"No."

"Are you an elder?"

"Not yet. In this Fortress chapter, my brother decides who gets that rank."

"Didn't you say he was younger than you?"

"Benjamin has money, and a long antivampire history. People like me have to earn our way up."

I stand and go over to him so I can whisper. "How do you earn it, Ned?"

He hesitates, then takes my good arm. "I'll show you."


With the aid of a flashlight, Ned leads me down a dark staircase into a cool, musty cellar. To the left is a wide room with a stone floor.

"This is where they'll come tonight for the ritual," he says. "I don't know the details, since I've never been invited."

A rustle across the room makes me jump. "Who's here?"

"Not who." Ned shines the light at the far wall. "What."

A line of steel bars casts shadows on an enormous young man huddled on the floor in front of us. His face is grimy and his pale green eyes stare straight ahead.

"What's going on?" I choke out.

"Don't worry, it's safe," Ned says. "He's locked up."

The man blinks slowly, then shifts his gaze in the direction of our feet. I realize that what I thought was grime on his face is actually a mass of scars. The distinctive charred black of holy-water burns.

Beyond the scars, something about him seems familiar. I take a step closer and tilt my head. The sharp nose, pointed chin, and mop top brown hair remind me of—

A chill starts at my neck and courses down my spine, then flashes back up again.

"Jacob . . ." One of Gideon's bodyguards and progeny, who came to David's house and tried to kill us. Who no doubt has sworn an oath to kill me and Shane to avenge his maker's death.

"Gideon's right-hand vamp." Ned swings the flashlight beam to the back of the cage. "And there's the left hand."

Another hulking twentysomething man sits against the wall, arms locked around his knees. Like his blood brother Jacob, Wallace hails from the early sixties, but his dark hair forms a tight crewcut. He rocks fitfully but doesn't look up, even when Ned shines the light directly in his face, which is also crisscrossed with black scars.

I step back, ready to flee. "Why did you bring me here?"

"Don't worry." Ned's voice is solicitous. "They're starved, too weak to harm anyone. Hold the flashlight if it'll make you feel better."

I grab the long-handled contraption, reassured by its heft. "Shouldn't they be in Control custody?"

"Arrangements were made. To test my loyalty, the Fortress put me in charge of their care." He sniffs. "Such as it is."

"What do they want with them? Information?"

"We know all we need to know about vampires."

I shine the light to my left, where another cage sits empty. Unlike Wallace and Jacob's cell, this one contains a cot and a toilet.

Human accommodations.

"I gotta go."

To my surprise, Ned says, "Okay. I'd get in huge trouble if the elders know I brought you down here. Are you hungry? There's this great Thai place that just opened over on—" He stops and grabs my bad arm. I bite back a yowl of pain.

Footsteps—a lot of them—proceed across the floor above our heads.

"Uh-oh." Ned takes the flashlight. "Let's find the back way out."

In one dark corner, a short flight of stairs leads to a steel cellar door. Ned shoves against it, rattling the rusty latch, but it doesn't budge.

I point to the edge of the door. "It's welded shut. Can we hide somewhere?" Somewhere dark, where I can plant one of these bugs.

"This way." Ned runs to a door built into the space under the stairs, on the opposite wall from the cages. He unlocks it with shaky hands.

Inside the closet are chains, stakes, crosses, knives, and bottles of holy water. I've stumbled into the vampire Inquisition.

"There's no room for us!" Ned is on the verge of panic.

"Is this what they're using for the ritual?"

"I think so."

"Then let's put it all out, arrange it on the floor. They'll think you took the initiative to set up for them." When he hesitates, I say, "What choice do we have?"

"Right." He hands me the flashlight and goes to work. As I watch him set out the weapons in a line next to the wall, I notice a large white circle drawn on the floor. Twelve red hash marks are placed around it, like the hour delineations on a clock.

Finally, Ned draws out a ten-foot wooden stake twice the thickness of a flagpole. "I wonder where this goes."

I shine the light at the center of the circle. "In that hole?"

He jams it in, a perfect fit. Above us, the footsteps move toward the top of the stairs.

Ned and I hurry into the closet and sit on the floor. He pulls the door shut. I turn off the flashlight, plunging us into total darkness.

But not for long. Pinpoints of light appear, and I realize the drywall has rotted through—or been cut—in several eyeball-size places. Keeping far enough back to avoid detection, I peer through one hole to see the bobbing flames of two torches, carried by those at the beginning and end of a thirteen-man procession. Barefoot, they wear knee-length white linen robes tied at their waists with even whiter belts of silken rope.

All but one. A tall, muscular man with closely cropped sandy hair brings up the rear, his outfit identical to the others' except for a belt of scarlet. He looks roughly thirty and exudes a sinister self-possession not unlike that of an ancient vampire.

Benjamin, I assume. He's definitely the guy we photographed at the cross last week. He approaches the center stake, striding on bare feet with the crisp rigidity of a man in jackboots.

In their cage, Wallace and Jacob stare ahead with sunken eyes, catatonic. I look at Ned, who's watching through his own peephole. His hands twist together so hard, I worry his knuckles will crack and give us away.

A man with a dark goatee unlocks the cage. Two others

follow him inside. They strip off Jacob's shirt and haul him to his feet, while the first man holds out a cross in one hand and a torch in the other. He waves the flame at Wallace in the corner, keeping him at bay. None of the precautions seems necessary; the vampires look about as dangerous as sacks of flour.

As Jacob is dragged to the stake, two other elders pick up the length of chain that Ned laid out. The vampire suddenly twitches in their grip, as if the movement of his feet has returned the blood to his brain, along with the desire to live.

Two more men rush forward to subdue him with crosses, searing his exposed chest. He screams as his flesh sizzles, but his voice soon fades, and his unconscious body droops in their arms. They drag him to the stake, more slowly now due to his dead weight.

As four of the elders chain Jacob to the pole, the other eight position themselves around the circle, one at each hash mark. They begin to chant in a guttural language I've never heard before—it sounds like Latin spoken with a forked tongue.

"What are they saying?" I whisper to Ned, now that the room is loud enough to cover the sound of my voice.

He shakes his head, his face tight with worry.

"Is that Benjamin?"

He nods, hugging his knees. I wonder if he's ever seen a vampire staked, and how many of his 117 bites came from Wallace and Jacob.

Finally Jacob is secured to the pole, arms behind his back, chin drooped to his smooth bare chest. Benjamin advances with a sharpened stake. I take Ned's hand to comfort him. I'm ambivalent about this myself—after all, Jacob would kill me in a second if he could.

Benjamin plunges the stake into Jacob's heart. I startle—I was expecting more ceremony, or at least a new chant for this central piece of the ritual.

Jacob shrieks and jerks at the chains that bind him, but the thick metal links hold him fast. The vampire's body seizes and shakes, and his bare feet squirm and slide against the stone floor, as if he can run away.

Suddenly his efforts stop, and he slumps against the post. Passed out from the pain, I guess. He won't die until they remove the stake.

The chant ends, and a pair of elders steps up to the post. They loosen the chains around Jacob's upper body, keeping his legs tight against the pole so that he tilts forward, his head and chest out. The blood from his wound plops into a puddle.

The two men return to their places around the circle, but Benjamin stays at Jacob's side, watching the trickle of blood, blinking at the impact of each drop against the stone floor.

The goateed man enters the circle, carrying two clay bowls—one large and one small. Beside him pads a shorter fellow with a silver tray. The first man sets the smaller bowl under Jacob's dripping wound, catching the slow cascade of blood from his heart.

From the silver tray, Benjamin takes a long dagger with a curved blade. The knife's gilded hilt bears strange black markings that from here look like hieroglyphs. The guy with the tray bows and takes a step back.

A new chant begins, quicker and more intense than the last, with a low harmony that resonates in my bowels and makes my heart doubt its own rhythm. Beside me, I feel Ned shrink back from the wall. I let go of his hand and watch.

Benjamin slices Jacob's neck. Blood pours from the wound into the large bowl the other man holds up. The vampire's eyelashes flutter, but he remains unconscious, or so I hope, for his sake.

Within ten seconds the wound has healed, and the red flood slows to a halt. Benjamin cuts again, this time carving a half-moon shape into Jacob's left side. As it heals, he repeats the motion on the right side.

Steadily, methodically, Benjamin slices Jacob's skin—his upper arms, his chest, his neck again, his belly.

I shut my eyes hard. What do they want with vampire blood? To drink it in some twisted act of vengeance? They must have gotten nearly a gallon by now—there can't be much left. Maybe they just want to drain him dry.

The thick, coppery scent of blood assails me, and I slap a hand over my mouth and nose. I turn to look at Ned, whose face is buried in his arms as he sits with knees pulled to his chest.

I slip my phone out of my purse and nudge on the video function. In case Ned decides to open his eyes again, I lean forward to block the phone, then press its camera eye up to a crack near the floor that looks mouse-chewed.

Through my own peephole I see Benjamin replace the knife on the silver tray. He kneels beside the pole and lifts the small bowl of blood, joining the chant with a high, keening harmony that scratches my spine. His voice mesmerizes me the way no mere human's has done since I was a child listening to my father preach. I realize that this man is about the age my dad would've been at the height of his charismatic career.

The other elders—most of whom are a lot more elderly than Benjamin—watch him with a mixture of pride and fear.

The goateed man picks up the larger bowl and turns out to face the circle. He steps slowly, ceremonially, toward a middle-aged man with dark blond hair, taking care not to spill a drop of the blood sloshing near the rim of the punch-bowl-size vessel.

As one, the elders untie their robes and pull their arms out of their sleeves. Naked torsos of all shapes and shades appear as the robes fall back, tied at the waist.

The first guy dips his hands in the bowl of vampire blood.

It steams in the cool cellar air. I grimace, waiting for him to slurp.

Instead, he splashes it on his face, luxuriating in the liquid as if it were fresh, clean water. Blood clings to the hair at his temples and drips off his chin. He smiles.

The elder dips his hands again. This time he rubs the red liquid over his chest and shoulders, painting his skin in a literal bloodbath.

*My God.* I want to turn away, but fear that moving my head would make me pass out or throw up. My eyelids feel glued open, determined to witness this atrocity.

The man with the bowl shifts around the circle, letting each elder drench himself. I check to make sure Ned's eyes are still closed, then I ease my bad arm out of the sling, gritting my teeth against the pain. Quickly and quietly, I deploy another listening device in the corner of the closet wall. I tuck the last one inside my left palm, hoping to plant it in Benjamin's office later tonight. Finally I return my arm to the sling and look through the peephole again.

The red streaks on the men's pure white robes remind me of Christmas Day in Wisconsin when I was five. It had just snowed, so the roads hadn't been plowed. My parents and I were trundling along with chains on our tires, singing carols, when we came upon a deer hit by a car. Its neck was broken, and the blood from its mouth threw scarlet gashes over the fresh snow, stretching across our lane. I screamed for an hour.

Benjamin sets down the bowl and unties his own robe as the chant crescendos. Unlike the others, he removes it entirely and lets it fall to the floor. He kneels, now wearing nothing but a linen loincloth, like the kind they show in paintings of Jesus on the cross. Yet the effect of his taut muscles and smooth bare skin is more Daniel Craig–as–James Bond than a martyred messiah.

He raises the small bowl above his head, tilts up his chin, and closes his eyes. The blood from Jacob's heart tumbles over his face like a waterfall. It soaks his sandy hair, his skin, and his loincloth, then forms an expanding crimson pool around his kneeling form.

Benjamin smashes the empty clay bowl against the floor, shattering it into hundreds of shards. The chant cuts off with the impact, and the sudden silence accentuates the pounding of my heart in my ears and throat. I fold in my lips to keep my teeth from chattering.

I know what's next.

Benjamin stands, places one hand on the stake protruding from Jacob's chest, and raises the other palm toward the ceiling. He speaks alone now in the strange language.

It's too hard to watch directly, so I focus on my phone's screen to make sure my hand doesn't move and lose the image.

Benjamin's voice rises in pitch and volume. Around the circle, the other elders fall to their knees and spread their arms, palms up. Benjamin yanks out the stake.

Jacob's body twitches, and blood spurts feebly from his heart for half a dozen beats. Then it stops.

Finally, it goes backward.

Where it dribbled down his chest, it now flows up, returning to the wound. Every inch of his frame shakes—not spasming muscles or shivering skin, but each cell clamoring to be the first to leave this world.

The skin of his chest folds in on itself, sliding toward the stake wound, the only one that couldn't heal. I check to make sure Ned's not watching. The heels of his hands are crammed against his eye sockets.

Muscles tear and bones snap, and suddenly Jacob's eyes open. For one lucid moment he searches the circle for sympathy, then his neck bends to the left and finally snaps. His throat splits down the middle before sliding into the hole in his chest, dragging his wide-open eyes and mouth. The chains rattle, then fall to the floor with the twisted remnants of his body.

As his hands and feet scrape the floor in their descent, the room shimmers red. Every drop of blood coating the elders' bodies streaks toward the center of the room in a crimson wind. The liquid swirls into the last bit of hole-shaped flesh.

With a soft pop, Jacob is gone. No sound remains but Benjamin's hypnotic chant. The elders remain kneeling with palms upraised, skin pristine, robes as white as clouds. Their faces shine with an ecstasy I've only seen in one other place— after a baptism, when the preacher pulls the believer out of the water and they walk from the river, cleansed of sin.

That's what this is, I realize. A baptism in blood. These elders must think that their own sins fly off them and go swirling into the void along with the rest of the vampire. No water needed for this cleansing—just the magic of justice.

The practical part of my brain reminds me to send myself the video before the file becomes too huge for my server to accept. I stop the recording and quickly e-mail the world's most disturbing home movie.

Just as the message goes through, Benjamin ends his chant and lowers his hands, and the elders follow suit. They remain kneeling. Silence hangs over the room, and I hold my breath until my lungs ache.

And then, Ned pukes. Loudly.

Thirteen heads turn our way. The man closest to the silver tray grabs the curved knife. Torchlight glints off the part of the blade not covered in dull, drying blood.

Benjamin holds up a commanding hand to stop, then strides for the closet.

He yanks open the door, and his expression turns from

anger—when he sees Ned—to shock—when he sees me—and back to rage in the span of two seconds.

"Clean yourself, brother," he says in an even tone. "Upstairs."

Ned snivels and wipes his mouth. "Sorry." He scurries out of the closet.

I check my sleeve—the fact that Ned missed ralphing on me is my only lucky strike.

Benjamin looms in the closet doorway, his nearly naked form cutting a primal silhouette in the torchlight.

"You must be Ciara."

I unfold my stiff legs. "I'll go help Ned."

"No." He seizes my elbow. "You'll stay and help *us*."

The other men are gathering around, pulling their robes up over their arms, flexing their fingers as if they'd like to close them around my neck.

Benjamin drags me through the swarm of white-robed men to the empty cage. He jerks open the door and shoves me inside. I pretend to stumble, pitching forward and tossing the last listening device under the cot. The scuff of my shoes and my cry of alarm cover the *tink-tink* of the bug against the stone floor. At least, I hope they do.

One of Benjamin's henchmen grabs my purse, lifts it above his head, and with much drama turns it upside down to dump its contents. My cell phone makes a sickening bounce, and I'm relieved I gave Luann my MP3 player so it didn't meet the same fate. I'm even more relieved that nothing incriminating remains in my purse.

Benjamin picks up my cell phone and opens it. He jams down a few buttons with his thumb, then frowns. "Broken." He looks up at the purse dumper. "You idiot." In one swift motion, he rises and smacks the man in the head, cracking my phone against his skull.

The man cries out, stumbles back against the bars of the

cage, and touches his own temple. Blood coats his fingertips. "I'm sorry, Elder Zadlo. Forgive me."

Benjamin ignores him. "Leave me alone with her."

I take a step back and glance frantically at each man. Surely one of them will stop him.

The twelve men file out, their eyes lending me no sympathy, only hostility.

Benjamin stands in the doorway of the cage, arms spread across the opening, bare skin glowing. His robe still lies in a heap behind him near the center of the circle. A name is tattooed in a looping script on the bulge of his left biceps, but only the first letter is legible from here: S.

We're alone except for the surviving vampire.

"You're lucky you're injured," Benjamin says to me softly. "I never hurt anyone who can't fight back."

I lick my dry lips, searching for courage and finding only false bravado. "Like that vampire? You starved him until he was weak as a kitten."

"The struggle was a bit disappointing." He glances into the other cage at Wallace, who hasn't moved since before the bloodbath. "That one might not even last until the next ritual, much less provide a sporting battle." He smiles. "Which to him, makes you manna from heaven."

My blood runs cold from my neck, like someone just injected ice water into my jugular vein. I back into the far corner away from Wallace. "I'm not really big on being bitten. I know I'm in that group and all, but—"

"We won't let him bite you. At his level of thirst, he could chew right through your neck. The last thing we want is a vampire killing a human. We stick to our principles." He angles his chin toward the ceiling, the torchlight glinting off his golden hair. "Luann's a trained phlebotomist. She'll get your donation."

"And then what? What are you going to do with me?"

He tightens his grip on the bars, making his pectoral muscles flex and bulge. "I haven't decided yet."

"Where's my father? Is he still alive?" I know the answer to the second question. Cockroaches always survive.

Benjamin kneels on my cell floor to gather the stuff that fell out of my purse. He examines each object before placing it back inside. "What's this?" He rotates the amber pill bottle. "Pain meds?"

I bite back my cry of dismay. "Just in case. I don't really need them." I order my fingers not to twitch with the desire to lunge for the pills.

"Then you won't mind if I keep them." He tosses them into my purse, which he then tucks under his arm. "Suicide prevention is one of our missions."

I hate when people call my bluffs. No resort now but begging.

"Actually, I do need those pills. It was pretty major arm surgery."

He walks out of the cage and slams the door shut behind him. I hear a lock click automatically.

"Luann will bring you food and drink in the morning before you donate." He douses the torch in a basin of water near the bottom of the stairs and begins to climb. Now the only light shines in a dull yellow shaft from the kitchen.

"Wait!"

"Good night, Ciara." He shuts the door with a clang that resonates deep in my gut.

In all twenty-four and a half years of my life, I've never known complete darkness. I wave my hand an inch in front of my nose and see nothing. I open my eyelids wide, as if doing so will reveal some secret section of my eyeball that detects infrared.

The darkness seems to multiply the cold. I shiver violently, jostling my sore arm and making my teeth grit with the effort not to whimper. *Never show weakness in front of a vampire*, I remind myself, *even a catatonic one. Never act like prey.*

I fumble my way to the cot and lie on my side on the floor. Since I can't reach under with one hand without leaning on the other, I take off my boot and sweep my foot under the cot, pivoting on my hip like Curly from the Three Stooges, minus the *whoop-whoop-whoop*. The floor is so cold it hurts, but I move slowly so I don't kick the listening device out of the cage.

Finally I feel something small and solid through my sock. Hoping it's the bug and not a dead mouse, I curl my toes around the object and bend my knee to pull it toward me. Grimacing from the pain, I snatch it from under the cot.

I sit up and examine the device with the fingers of my left hand. The plastic shell feels unbroken, and the fuzzy microphone intact, but who knows whether the internal electronics survived my toss? I deploy the delicate antenna and pull the device to my mouth.

"If anyone can hear me," I utter in my softest whisper, "I need help. SOS." I describe my situation, relating the layout of the Fortress's bottom two levels. "Hurry. Bring Percocet."

I slide the bug back under the cot, hoping Wallace is too out of it to know what I just did—and that he's too far gone to know who I am.

I sink onto the thin mattress and press my back against the wall. Due to my injury, I can't even curl my arms around myself to keep warm. Wish I'd worn my long, heavy coat instead of this short blazer. I should start dressing for unexpected detentions.

A rustle comes from the other cage, stopping my heart. Wallace inhales deep through his nose, lets it out, then does it again. The second breath catches. He grunts.

Oh God.

"You . . ." he croaks.

I remain perfectly still, as if that will make me smell like nothing. As if I'm not oozing cold sweat that smells just like me.

"You. Killed." The vampire heaves a long, hoarse gasp. "My. Maker."

I want to protest that it was in self-defense, but my voice would just confirm my identity. So I bite my lips in turn— top, bottom, top, bottom—to keep from speaking. If I don't provoke him, he'll soon run out of strength.

Until tomorrow, when I feed him. Then he'll be able to speak and stare and reach through the bars and—

My skin crawls as I realize the other change my blood will provoke. Those holy-water scars all over his face? Gone, so fast no one will be able to deny the connection. The Fortress will know my secret, and unlike the Control, they won't even pretend to ask permission for my blood.

Or they might just kill me, to rid the world of a vampire healer.

Unless, between now and then, I can neutralize my own power, turn my blood into nothing more than food.

For the first time in almost ten years, I begin to pray.

# 24

## I Will Survive

They say there are no atheists in foxholes, that when desperate to save one's own butt from death or dismemberment, each of us will call on a higher power to intervene.

I tried, I really tried. But then, apparently, I fell asleep.

My throbbing arm just woke me up, with my face pressed against the mildewy mattress. I have no idea what time it is, but Wallace is silent and so is the house above me.

I sit up slowly, wincing at the spasms shooting down to my fingers and up into my neck. How can one chewed elbow hurt such far-reaching bodily geography?

I draw in deep, slow breaths to control the pain and notice how much clearer my brain feels off the Percocet. Time to analyze the situation.

I can't get out on my own. Even if I could open the cage, the only path to the outdoors lies through the house, where the cameras see all. I check the corners—no gleaming red camera lights, which makes sense. No permanent evidence of their brutality for a disgruntled ex-member to use against them.

Except the video I took last night. I wish I'd sent it directly to Shane or Colonel Lanham instead of to myself.

What if my message never got through to the Control? Maybe I didn't deploy the bug's antenna, or maybe the device was broken. But Shane knew where I was going last night, and what time I should have checked in. He's probably called Lanham already.

I remember a conversation I had with the colonel earlier this year, about why they couldn't storm Gideon's compound to rescue me. An extraction is a delicate, intricately planned operation that poses risks to their agents, not to mention innocent bystanders. With the Fortress in the middle of the city, any firearms would draw the attention of the civilian authorities.

So I could be waiting a long time.

A single set of footsteps crosses the ceiling, in the direction of the kitchen. I remember last night's chocolate strudel, and my stomach gurgles in a strange combination of hunger and nausea.

My mind spins with the ramifications of last night's ritual. Clearly the Fortress isn't related to Christianity or any other mainstream religion. I wonder what FAN would think of the basement activities of the men funding their expansion. Maybe they already know, and they figure it's better to be secretly occult and evil than openly occult and benign.

An even bigger realization hits me: despite their professed hatred for vampires, the Fortress will never drive them to extinction. They wouldn't even endanger their existence by proving to the public that vampires exist. They need their blood for their twisted rituals.

So why the attack on the station? Is it the prelude to a kidnapping? Does Benjamin have special plans for our DJs? Ned mentioned something about vengeance.

I sit up straight, my mind scrambling for the other place and time I heard that word uttered with such urgency.

It was dark and cold, like here. But loud, and—

A bell goes off in my head. Colin! The voice of Regina's friend plays out in his Cockney accent. "There's talk of revenge, for Sara."

Another image falls in my inner vision, like a slide show shifting to the next frame.

Benjamin's tattoo. A name inked in a script on his left biceps, a name starting with S.

The door at the top of the stairs creaks open, letting in a shaft of light. Legs appear, followed by the rest of Luann, carrying a tray of what looks like food, as well as a blanket draped over her arm.

When she gets to the bottom of the stairs, she leans over and brushes her shoulder against the wall. A recessed ceiling light flicks on.

"Ow." I shut my eyes against the glare. I guess last night's torches were just for effect.

Luann comes closer, and her hands are shaking so hard, the dishes rattle. Her glance is glued to Wallace on my left. I look over to see him sitting cross-legged in the corner, forehead resting on the wall, as still as a stone. Our brief "conversation" last night must have worn him out.

"Good morning," Luann whispers as she sets the tray on the floor. She unlocks a small door at the bottom of the cage and slides the tray through. "I brought you breakfast."

"Thanks, but I'm on a strict no-poison diet. Doctor's orders."

"You need to eat before you donate, or you'll pass out. Here's an extra blanket." She pushes it through the bars.

"Thank you, but I'll pass out either way. I hate needles."

"No, I'm really good." She closes and locks the little door. "You won't feel it. And Benjamin will be there, so you better act brave."

So much for escaping by beating up Luann with one hand. Time to try a different tack.

I lift the lid on the plate. "Did you make these pancakes?"

"Yep. They've got blueberries."

"My favorite. Thank you." I take the tray back to the cot. "Did you listen to WVMP last night?"

"I heard Regina's show." Luann whispers the DJ's name and throws a nervous glance back at the stairs, thus feeding my Sara-related suspicions.

"Did you stay tuned for Shane?"

"Oh no, I had to get some sleep so I could get up early."

"What time is it now?"

She looks at her watch. "Five forty-five."

I set the tray aside and go right up to the bars. "Can I ask you a favor?"

She backs up and twists a long gray-blond curl around her finger. "I don't know."

"I just need to know the last song Shane plays during his show. It'll come on in about ten minutes."

"Why's it so important?"

"It's just a stupid little thing we have between us. It'll distract me." I rub the side of my neck. "I'm pretty scared, locked up in here."

"I understand." She looks down at her wringing hands. "More than you know."

I wonder if she's at the Fortress of her own free will, but something tells me that asking her directly will scare her away. For someone who looks over forty, she seems almost childlike.

She turns for the stairs. "Eat your breakfast. We'll be back soon."

She leaves on the light, which turns out to be rather dim, not even reaching the shadows in the far corners of the room. I sit on the cot and turn my back on Wallace while I try to eat. Objectively the pancakes are moist and fluffy and the orange juice sweet-tart perfection, but in my mouth the food turns to cardboard and the liquid to acid.

I keep chewing, keep swallowing, keep trying to forget that the strength I gain from this food will soon belong to the vampire who wants to kill me.

"Needle phobia?" Benjamin says as I turn my head away from the things Luann is doing to my left arm. The scent of the alcohol swab stings my nose.

Lying on the cot, I look straight at Benjamin as he stands in the doorway to my cage, now fully clothed in tailored black trousers and a blue silk shirt that calls out the arresting shade of his eyes.

I suppress a wince as Luann tightens the rubber tourniquet and keep my focus on Benjamin. "We never had a chance to talk last week after Ned showed me the video of my father. You were about to make some dastardly demand while twirling your metaphorical mustache." That came out better than I thought it would. "Ned said you wanted vengeance. How am I supposed to help you with that?"

He shifts his feet and leans against the side of the doorway in a clear attempt to look casual. "Things have changed, now that you're here, now that you're . . . informed."

My neck prickles. He means *now that you'll never get out of this place alive.*

"Who's Sara?"

Luann lets out a little gasp as she taps my inner arm, searching for a vein.

Benjamin's stillness speaks louder than any flinch. "No one who matters."

"She obviously mattered when you got that tattoo."

A tiny muscle twitches in the corner of his jaw. "We all make mistakes, Ciara. Some of us are big enough to not only admit them, but examine them daily so we can look in the mirror and say, 'Never again.' "

I can picture him doing that each morning. If I hadn't seen his unblemished bare back last night, I'd take him for a self-flagellator.

"Were you married?"

"Make a fist," Luann says in a shaky voice. I swallow hard and obey.

Benjamin rests his ink blue gaze on me. "I said, it doesn't matter."

"Was she murdered by a vampire?" I almost add, *like Luann's mom*, but realize that now would be a bad moment to upset her. Her hand trembles on my elbow, but she takes a deep breath and inserts the needle. Just a pinch—she's good.

"Not all killing is murder," he says. "For example, it would be the epitome of mercy to take a life to save a person from a fate worse than death."

I pause, trying to catch up to his slight non sequitur. "What kind of fate?"

"Damnation."

I glance down at my arm, where things are proceeding in an orderly and despicable way. "So someone made Sara a vampire. I can see why you'd hate them." I remember how David's voice shook as he told me about hunting down Elizabeth's maker, Antoine. "Did you get revenge?"

He crosses his arms and leans back against the bars of the cage. "Not yet."

I start to ask him what he's waiting for, and then it hits me. He's no longer waiting.

Regina turned Sara. She's been the main target of the piracy. Maybe the relentless blocking of female singers was just a feint, or a FAN improvisation. But why hasn't Shane ever mentioned his blood sister?

"What happened to her?" I ask Benjamin, since I might

never get a chance to ask Shane, or see him again or speak to him, or—my brain cuts off that thought before I start to cry.

Benjamin shrugs in a poor show of indifference. "It doesn't matter. What matters is what didn't happen. The Control was too interested in the technicalities of the case to enact justice." He waves a hand. "Issues of volition and consent, and then, of course, the reality that in this world, accidents do, in fact, happen."

Accidents. Regina told Colin, *It was an accident.* But vampires are made on purpose—by the maker, at least.

Then I remember something Shane told me about Regina the night before daylight savings time ended. *Being underprotective didn't work out so well for her once.*

Oh. Shane hasn't mentioned a blood sister because he no longer has one.

"The Control wouldn't rule in favor of extermination." Benjamin breaks my gaze and watches his own fingers run along the smooth black cage bar. "As if a woman's life, and the lives she could have carried inside her one day, were equal to the desperate, pathetic existence of a walking corpse."

I glance at Wallace, who has no reaction to this insult. Right now he just looks like a regular corpse.

But not for long.

I deliberately provoke Benjamin to see what he'll spit out. "I don't see much difference between the Fortress and the Control. You both lock up vampires seemingly at random."

His neck is tight as he turns to pierce me with his glare. "The Control holds no principle. They do the bare minimum to keep order, but don't be deceived—if they wanted, they could wipe out every vampire on this planet."

"So why don't they?"

"They would lose their budget. Like most bureaucracies, they exist merely to justify their own existence." Benjamin rakes his gaze over the ceiling. "The Fortress stands for the old ways. If anything, the Fortress is the true Control. We stand for right and wrong."

"And vampires are always wrong?"

"They are an abomination of God." He utters this proclamation as if it's self-evident, like the blueness of the sky. "How can you deny that, after Gideon almost killed you, and your own boyfriend drugged you into becoming a donor? How can you work with them, live with them, sleep with them?"

I realize Ned has shared my false confessions. "I thought those Bitten therapy sessions were private."

"Ned's worried about you. He wants you to know that vampires aren't romantic. They're monsters. To destroy one is extermination, like one would do to a rat raiding the larder or a wolf that slaughters the lambs."

"You're a very sick puppy."

"What Ned doesn't realize," he continues, as if I haven't spoken, "is that some sheep are forever lost to the wolves."

"I'm not any kind of sheep."

"That's enough blood," Benjamin snaps at Luann. "We only need to keep him alive, not well."

Luann withdraws the needle and holds gauze against my wound, since my right hand can't do it for me.

Benjamin slides a stainless steel dog bowl sideways through the bars of Wallace's cage and sets it on the stone floor. Watching the vampire closely, he reaches through the bars and turns the bag of blood upside down to squeeze out its contents.

I turn away, my stomach pitching. Luann places a gentle hand on my shoulder.

I hear Wallace turn, sniffing, then the cloth of his trousers shifting against the stone floor as he drags himself toward the bowl. I close my eyes but can't cover my ears.

The slurping, the chop licking, and the grunt of satisfaction are not what I dreaded most. That's coming up in about—

"Good God." Benjamin's feet shuffle back away from the cage. "Luann, look at him."

She turns away from me and gasps. "His scars. He was— they were all over his face. Where'd they go?"

"Unbelievable." Benjamin's voice is filled with awe. "In all the annals of the Fortress, I never read about anything like this."

"What about when you were in the Control?"

"Not there either. I—" His teeth clack together as he shuts his mouth.

They both go silent. I keep my eyes closed, pretending I didn't hear Luann's big oops.

"Out," he tells her. "Bring the extra blood. Leave her with nothing but water."

"Yes, sir. I'm sorry, sir."

"Just do as I say. I need to think."

Luann quickly places an adhesive bandage over the hole in my arm. They exit my cage and shut the door behind them. On the way upstairs, one of them shuts off the light. I open my eyes to utter darkness.

Ten feet away, Wallace begins to laugh.


I ponder all the things I've done, the decisions I've made, that brought me to this moment. For some reason, I keep going back to that trip to the discount store to buy cheap housewares. If I'd let myself use Elizabeth's money to furnish her own kitchen, I'd have gone to a better establishment. I can't imagine running into Ned Amberson at Neiman Marcus.

Then again, he was probably following me, trying to draw me into the Fortress, where I could be tricked into trading the life of one of my friends for that of my father, whose own life was never in danger.

Or, failing that, I could be stuck in a cage at the bottom of a Victorian mansion listening to a psychotic seventy-year-old vampire describe in Technicolor, three-dimensional, high-definition detail how he will kill me, how very long it will take, and which special pre-death activities I can expect to enjoy.

When Wallace finishes the story—which always ends the

same way—he begins again, adding a new adventure with each iteration. If I interrupt, pleading for him to stop, or shouting that I killed Gideon in self-defense (and boss-defense, and lover-defense) and that hey, my blood just literally saved Wallace's own skin, he begins again, adding *two* more installments to the story instead of one. I eventually learn my lesson and shut up, tuning out his macabre imagination by humming advertising jingles in my head.

I'm using the local Toyota dealership's one-line ditty to blot out the proposed scene where Wallace peels off my skin with a barbecue fork, when the door at the top of the stairs opens. That precious shaft of light slips in, and I swear I could eat it.

Luann trots down the stairs on her tiny feet, turns on the overhead light, then hurries across the room. She shoves a small silver object through the bars. "I thought you could use a distraction."

"Thank you!" I snatch the MP3 player out of her hand. "This is better than food."

"I couldn't get your pain pills, but here's some ibuprofen." She hands me a white plastic jar and a fresh water. "I'll bring your lunch soon." She backs away, staring at Wallace, who's sporting an evil grin I thought only clowns could wear. "By the way, Shane's last song? 'Message in a Bottle.' "

"By the Police?" My fingers tighten on the bars. "Are you sure?"

She nods, still backing toward the stairs. "I remember because I thought it seemed more like Regina's time."

"They have a lot of overlap." Worried she might be suspicious, I hold up the player. "Hope you enjoyed it."

She gives me a secretive smile. "I did." She disappears, leaving the light on. Which, it turns out, just gives Wallace more visual cues with which to describe my dismemberment.

I curl up on my wafer-thin mattress and jam the earbuds tight inside my ears, cranking up the volume on Shane's latest podcast, about the Riot Grrrl movement of the early nineties.

Bands like Hole, naturally, and some I'd never heard of before meeting Shane. Their strength lends me the comforting delusion that I might survive.

If I squeeze my eyes shut, I can imagine Shane's here with me, murmuring all these fascinating facts into my ear. His arms are around my waist, and he's using his magical supersecret-mega-unicorn healing powers to soothe the shooting pains in the right side of my body. (Hey, as long as I'm nurturing the pipe dream of getting out of here alive, I might as well go all the way.)

But maybe it's not just delusion that he'll rescue me. Surely his 5:54 a.m. song was a signal that my SOS was heard, that help is on the way.

After less than an hour, I realize how much Luann enjoyed my MP3 player. She enjoyed the battery right down to oblivion. The sound cuts off in the middle of an L7 song, and Wallace's voice is once again the loudest in the room.

I start singing to drown him out—Courtney Love, Shirley Manson, Bikini Kill—at the top of my lungs. At first he talks louder, but I just belt out the songs even more off-key, second verse same as the first.

Finally he shuts up, ending his litany of destruction. I reward his silence with my own. I doze.

The sound of shouting wakes me, and I hear footsteps pound on the floor above.

My rescuers? Yes?

I jump up and move to the door of my cage, ignoring Wallace smacking his lips at my approach.

The door hits the wall at the top of the stairs, and three men hurry down, the first and last pushing the middle one between them.

Oh.

Not my rescuers. Instead, they appear to be two of Benjamin's henchmen.

With Jeremy.

# 25

## Nobody Told Me There'd Be
## Days Like These

The Prince of Pain won't stop staring at Wallace.

"I can't believe they're real." Sitting in the far corner of our cage, Jeremy blinks through his cracked glasses at the fully fanged rictus grin of the ancient vampire. Wallace is pressing his face between the bars separating our cages, like Jack Nicholson's "Heeeere's Johnny!" moment in *The Shining*.

"I wanted to believe," Jeremy says, "but now that I'm actually looking at one—"

"Yeah, it's a real paradigm shifter." I wince and press my hand to my aching gut. Ibuprofen is no friend to an empty stomach. But at least now I can move my arm without screaming. "So how did they get you?"

He drags his gaze away from Wallace to look at me. "I was on my way home after meeting Regina—"

"I thought you were Jim's donor."

"They share me. Anyway, on I-95 a car with a blue flashing

light started following me. I was speeding, so I pulled over, figuring it was an unmarked police car." He hugs his arms, rubbing the crescent moon tattoo near his inner elbow. "Guy had a gun, told me to get out of the car and into their van."

"You didn't notice a license number, did you?" I pull out the Control listening device sitting behind the far leg of the cot.

He looks at it, confused. "I did. Why?"

I hold the bug up to his lips. "Say it here. Loud and clear." My unintentional rhyme makes me giggle. "Better yet, quiet and clear."

He takes the device and examines it. "Is this for real?"

For a moment I can't be sure. "Tell the good guys on the other end what happened to you."

Jeremy speaks slowly and clearly, but I can see the doubt in his eyes. He probably thinks I'm delusional. Maybe I am. Wallace's storytelling was so convincing, part of me wonders whether I'm still alive or have already entered hell.

"Do your kidnappers know who you are?" I ask him.

"They didn't say anything about the magazine. They just said they'd destroy, quote, 'something she cares about.' "

" 'She'? Regina?"

"I guess. What did they mean, destroy? What are they going to do with us?"

"Me, I don't know." I sit next to him on the cold stone floor, our backs against the steel bars. "You, they'll probably feed to him."

"What?!"

"They'll just extract your blood. They won't let a vampire kill us. They're people of principle." I pat his knee. "They'll kill us themselves."

He stares at me. "You're insane."

"Unfortunately, no, I'm all too acquainted with reality."

He takes off his glasses and draws his hands down hard over his face. "Well, I wanted to get inside the story."

"You're certainly embedded." I offer him the rest of my water bottle. "Are you going to write about this if we get out?"

He shakes his head. "My editors have a whole stable of fact-checkers who'd never be able to confirm this stuff. I'd be laughed right out of the industry." He takes a sip of water. "If I'm lucky, I'd spend the rest of my career writing for tabloids."

"In that case, I have a long story for you. But first, come here. It's freezing on the floor."

We sit on the cot together, our backs against the wall, huddled under one shared blanket. I tell him everything, figuring we're in this together now, and our lives might depend on each other. Wallace adds editorial comments about the superiority of vampires and the so-good-it's-good-for-you nature of my blood, but the last twenty-four hours have made me an expert in pretending he doesn't exist.

Jeremy absorbs it all with surprising equanimity. "I guess it all makes sense," he says when I'm finished, "that stuff about the Control and the Fortress. If vampires exist, someone has to make sure they don't run rampant."

I snort. "I doubt world domination is on their agenda. Mostly I think they just want to be left alone."

"Alone is best." Wallace snickers. "It allows for lingering over the tastiest bits. For example . . ."

He begins to list the parts of my body in order of tenderness. I keep talking to Jeremy, saying whatever comes to mind about the weather and politics and TV shows, as my companion's eyes bulge with fear.

Eventually he falls asleep with his head on my shoulder. I guess the shock and terror have sucked away all his energy. Wallace gets bored and returns to his corner.

Jeremy starts awake when the door opens at the top of the stairs. "What's happening?"

"Judging by the smell? Breakfast."

He rubs his stomach and winces. "I can't eat."

"You need your strength for when they take your blood. Besides, Luann's a really good cook."

"Aww, thanks." Luann gives me a shy smile as she comes down the stairs. She crosses the room, skirting the outer edge of the ritual circle. "I brought you strudel this time."

"Yes." Wallace hisses the word at Luann. "Fatten up little Hansel and Gretel." He leers at us. "I don't, as a rule, eat the flesh of my prey, but in your case I'll make an exception."

I give him the finger as I go to the trap door to receive the tray.

"Shane's show was great this morning." Luann passes the food through the hatch. "I just caught the last hour."

Scratching my head, I look at Jeremy. Shane was on the air two nights in a row? Or have I lost track of an entire day?

"What was the last song, do you remember?" I ask, as casually as I can.

"I'd never heard it before. Something like 'Black New Year'? Lots of screaming about suicide and something about hair dye."

"You mean, 'Jet Black New Year'?" Jeremy asks.

"That's it!" She points at him. "But Shane didn't say the name of the band."

"It's—" Jeremy cuts himself off as his eyes go wide. Then he blurts, "It's Fall Out Boy."

"Oh. Well, I don't care. It was too weird for me." Luann locks the trap door and stands up. "I'll be back in a couple hours to draw your blood," she tells Jeremy. "Now eat, and drink your whole glass of orange juice."

He nods quickly. "Yeah, okay. Thanks." He seems eager for her to leave.

She keeps a careful eye on Wallace as she returns to the stairs. Then she dashes up and slams the door behind her.

Jeremy whirls to face me. "Ciara, that song."

" 'Jet Black New Year'? I don't know it. Why would he play that for me?"

"He didn't. He played it for me." Jeremy taps his chest. "He knows it's one of my favorite songs. The lyrics inspired two of my tattoos." He rolls up his sleeve and displays the slit-wrist tattoo, then turns his arm over to show me a small black heart on the back of his hand.

I gasp. "So Shane knows you're here. Which means our second message got through, and last night's song wasn't a coincidence." I point to the listening device under the cot. "The song was a signal that they heard us."

"That's not all." Jeremy grabs my shoulders. "I lied to Luann. Fall Out Boy didn't do that song. It's by a band called Thursday."

I stare at him for a moment, wondering if I'm supposed to have heard of them. Then my jaw drops. "Today is Thursday. They're coming today to rescue us!" I hop up and down on my toes and struggle to keep my voice to a whisper. "But when? How? Are there clues in the lyrics?"

"Let me think." Jeremy lets go of me and starts to pace, mumbling under his breath. He stops suddenly. "Shit. The first verse talks about cyanide in the air."

I put a hand to my chest. "They're going to gas the place?"

"Shh." Jeremy goes to the far corner of our cage, muttering to himself.

I leave him alone and pick up my glass of juice. My mouth is dry as sand. From the corner of my eye, I see Jeremy strum an air guitar to jog his memory.

Wallace watches him with the cold, unblinking stare of a snake. While not exactly on our side, he must know that a raid on the Fortress is his only hope for survival. By going back to Control custody, he can at least live out his days in a safe place with decent meals and a complete lack of being staked.

Jeremy stops, smacks his palms together, and looks at me, his eyes gleaming. "Ten seconds to midnight."


December 20, one of the shortest days of the year, feels to me and Jeremy like the longest of our lives. In what we think is the late morning, Luann collects Jeremy's blood under the watchful eye of a well-muscled Fortress thug who could probably break both our necks in the middle of his own nap.

Then nothing happens for so long, we run out of small talk and are forced to move to Big Talk.

"You and Shane are pretty serious, huh?" Jeremy asks from the other end of the cot, where we lie head-to-foot under the fuzzy yellow blanket.

"I guess so."

"You guess so? You live with the guy."

"That's temporary, while—uh, while I'm apartment-sitting for the station's owner until she gets back in the country." I'm definitely not sharing my identity theft with a reporter, in case we do make it out alive.

"What about long term?" he asks. "Are you going to have him turn you into a vampire?"

"No way! I'd miss food and sunshine." I tug the blanket up a few inches to cover my shoulders. "Besides, he wouldn't do it even if I asked."

"But if you stay human, your love is intrinsically tragic."

"Only in the extreme long term. How can I think about twenty years from now when I don't know if I'll survive the week?"

"It's times like this when you *should* think about it, figure out what's important." Jeremy shifts his weight under the blanket, pulling it in his direction. "Let's say the Fortress locks us away somewhere forever to keep their secret. What would you be most loath to leave behind?"

"Shane, of course." Though Dexter is becoming a close second.

"But as you age, you *will* leave him behind. You'll change, but he'll stay the same. He'll, uh—what's the word you used?"

"Fade," I whisper, pulling the blanket up to my chin. "He'll fade."

"So why not become a vampire and fade with him? It'd be like growing old and crotchety together, like humans do. Kind of romantic."

"Kind of depressing." I think of Jeremy's suicidal tattoos. "But I guess that's your specialty, huh?"

"I don't run from life's pain."

"No, you sprint right into its arms." Frustrated with my efforts to get comfortable, I sit up, keeping the blanket over my legs. "What about you? Planning to trade in this nice warm skin?"

"I'd love to," he says, with no apparent irony or embarrassment. "It'd be the story of a lifetime. A story I'd only tell myself, of course."

"You realize it's a one-way trip, right? Eternal night, monotonous diet—"

"It'd be worth it." He folds his hands behind his head. "I bet they're more alive than we are."

"Regina said that once."

Jeremy's eyes light up. "She'd probably turn me."

"I wouldn't bet on it." I explain my theory about Sara and the whole personal nature of Benjamin and the Fortress's vendetta against the station.

"Jeez." He takes off his glasses and rubs his bloodshot eyes. "I had no idea."

"Bringing a new vampire into the world is a huge responsibility. You have to feed them, shelter them, protect them. You leave behind families who mourn them, and sometimes lovers who want to avenge them, like Benjamin." I look at Wallace, who lies curled up at the back of his cage. Asleep, his ruddy face is smooth and slack, almost childlike. For the first time, I wonder what he was like before Gideon turned him. "I'd never ask Shane to do it. He'd have to kill me, and I wouldn't want that on his conscience."

"But it's not taking life," Jeremy says, "it's giving life, especially between lovers. The way I see it, you and Shane can't make it in the long run unless you're the same. Right now, he's human enough that you can pretend he's like you, that he's not a monster."

"He's not a monster."

"See? It's working."

"Shut up." I press what I hope is a smelly foot into his face.

"My point is, he can't become like you. That option's off the table." He smooths the swoop of blond hair out of his eyes. "But you can become like him. If that's what you really want."

"I just want things to be simple."

"Then you've got the wrong guy."

I groan and slump back on the cot. "You don't know what you're talking about."

"Maybe you love him because you know it can't last forever. He's got temporariness built in. When you finally break up someday, you can blame it on the human-vampire thing instead of your inability to commit."

"You don't even know me."

"I know the type."

"Why? Because you think you dated someone like me once? Someone who ditched you or just wasn't perfect enough? The person you think of whenever you listen to that sad, pathetic music?" I jab his ankle with my good elbow. "I just want to be happy, and you think that's pathological because all you want is to be miserable. Which one of us is more fucked up?"

Jeremy utters a tight sigh, and his leg tenses beside me. I can tell he wants to shift away, and I do, too, but we need the warmth. So we lie there pressed together, our bodies close but our minds a million miles apart. I wonder if we'll ever be friends after all this is over.

The door opens suddenly, and Benjamin walks briskly down the stairs, followed by Luann, who proceeds slowly, carrying a large tray laden with plates and glasses.

We sit up, and Jeremy takes my hand, though whether it's to comfort me or himself, I'm not sure. I check our captors' wrists—no watches. It could be near midnight, or it could be five o'clock.

Benjamin claps once. "Dinner is served!"

Luann sets the tray carefully on the floor and opens the hatch in our cage. Before she pushes it through, Benjamin takes off two red plastic straw-cups, then goes to the closet and unlocks it.

He reappears holding what looks like a three-foot-long metal forceps. He uses it to set one of the cups just outside Wallace's cage while standing back at a safe distance.

The vampire lunges forward and grabs the tool. A sizzling sound, followed by his scream, makes us all jump. He jerks back his hand, which is scorched, like he just grabbed a hot poker.

"Coated with holy water. Can't have you seizing our weapons." Benjamin points the tool at the cup on the floor. "Drink that. It'll make you feel better."

The vampire gives him a suspicious look, then uses his uninjured hand to reach through the bars and pick up the cup. He sniffs the edge of the lid, and his eyes roll up in ecstasy.

Wallace turns to me. "This won't be the last of you I taste." He wraps his tongue around the straw and takes a deep gulp. A long sigh escapes him.

He lifts his hand, whole and healed again. His laughter booms out, echoing against the stone walls.

"Shut up and finish it," Benjamin says. "When you're done, give it back, and you can have another."

Wallace hurries to drink the rest of my blood, slurping loudly at the bottom of the cup. I resist the urge to plug my ears, knowing my disgust would just enhance the taste.

He tosses the cup through the bars and lets out a gut-rippling belch. Benjamin uses the long forceps to set the second cup outside the cage.

Wallace waits for him to withdraw the contraption, then seizes the second cup. He sniffs it first and frowns.

"Not from her." His hungry gaze alights on Jeremy. "The new one, yes?" He lifts the cup to Jeremy in a toast, then takes a long sip.

In the corner of my eye, Benjamin steps forward. I turn to see Luann backing away and covering her face. What the hell are they—

"Urgh!"

Wallace drops the cup. The lid pops off, and blood splashes across the floor into our cage. Eyes bulging, the vampire clutches his throat. It looks like he's trying to scream.

Then his tongue protrudes, black and steaming. Burned.

One of Wallace's hands slides down his shirt to his stomach, and his face crumples in agony—eyes popping wide, mouth contorting into a crooked red slash.

Jeremy squeezes my arm hard enough to leave a bruise. His face has turned chalk white. "My blood's not poison," he says. "None of the other vampires—"

"Of course it's not poison," Benjamin cuts in. "Unlike Ciara, you're nothing special."

Wallace collapses onto the floor and curls into the fetal position, choking and gasping.

I untangle my own tongue to ask Benjamin, "What did you give him?"

He puts his hands behind his back in a professorial posture. "We've secretly replaced the plasma in each of your blood samples with holy water." He points his chin in Wallace's direction. "I think he noticed the difference."

"You monster," I spit out.

"Me?" He laughs. "Lord, the perversity. This is the same vampire who'd love to rip off your head and use your carotid artery as a drinking fountain."

I step back, my face twisting at the image. "If he tried, I'd kill him if I had a weapon. But this is cruel. If you think humans are so superior, then show some humanity."

"How?" Benjamin's deep blue eyes flash at me. "Put him out of his misery? Stake him? Burn him?"

"What are you talking about?" Jeremy's voice verges on hysteria. "He's burning up right now, from the inside!"

"Holy water doesn't kill like fire," Benjamin tells him. "It just burns and leaves permanent scars." He glares at me. " 'Permanent' until you came along." He steps up to the bars of Wallace's cage. "How are you feeling there, li'l fella?"

Wallace spins and surges to his feet. Benjamin lurches back just in time to avoid becoming the aforementioned fountain. Wallace's arm strains through the bars, fingers stretched toward his captor's throat.

Benjamin straightens his shirt and rubs his neck. "Heh. Not nearly dead yet."

Wallace's heaving breath carries the stench of singed flesh. I cover my nose and realize that he has yet to make a sound louder than a gasp.

"His throat's burned out, isn't it?" I ask Benjamin.

Luann answers. "His stomach, too, I bet."

"So you're going to let him starve?"

Benjamin nods. "Once he's weak enough to be handled, we'll use an endoscope to see the extent of the internal damage." He rests his hands on his hips, assessing Wallace's tortured form as if he were a stalled car. "A fascinating coda to a worthy experiment. I'm glad we'll get good use out of him before the next ritual."

I realize the implication of his words. "If he can't feed, then you don't need us anymore. We can go home, right?"

He snorts. "Of course. Because I can trust you to keep your mouths shut about everything you've seen." He pulls out his cell phone and places a call. "The prisoners are ready for transfer." He hangs up.

I look at Luann, who's twisting her hands together, staring wild-eyed at the floor like it's going to bite her.

"Transfer to where?" I ask Benjamin, though I'm not sure I want the answer.

"Truth? I don't know." He slips the phone back into his pants pocket. "I prefer to stay out of the loop on matters of disposal."

My fingers turn to ice. "Disposal?" Please, midnight, get here fast.

"Though I'd like to study the qualities of your blood, we can't take the chance of letting a vampire healer survive. Not one with friends and allies looking for her." He shrugs. "Besides, we have your father."

My heart pounds. Even if my dad thinks he's in league with the Fortress, they might still take his blood, lock him up forever in a lab. "My father can't heal holy-water burns."

"Are you sure?" He gives me a long, penetrating gaze, then shifts his regard to Jeremy. "You're normal, but still a witness."

"You can't do this." I flail for an argument to stall. "I thought you liked humans."

"*Human?*" Benjamin's handsome features twist into an ugly mask. "You're less than human. Vampires are what they are—evil creatures who feed off us—but they have no choice. They're just doing what comes natural." He takes another step closer. "Vampire lovers, on the other hand, make a very unnatural choice. What deer would lie down for the cougar, what rabbit would hop into the fox's mouth? None. But you people, you willingly bare your throats for these monsters. You're a traitor to your species."

"That's bullshit." I stalk toward him. "We're not animals. Besides, donors save human lives. Without volunteers, vampires would be forced to hunt."

"Yes, and then *be* hunted by the righteous. That's the old way. The way of nature. The way of God."

"What kind of god wants more death and misery?"

"The one true God. The God of blood and sacrifice."

"What would the Bible say about your rituals?" I scrape my mind for the old memories. "Paul would call them 'deeds of darkness,' and—and, Deuteronomy says they're 'detestable to the Lord.' " At least, I think it says that.

"The devil can cite Scripture for his purpose." He tilts his head. "*Merchant of Venice*," he adds piously, as if a footnote makes it all better.

Benjamin glances at the ceiling. "Where are they?" He checks his naked wrist, forgetting he's not wearing a watch, then opens his phone. "Figures. Midnight shift change."

I look at Jeremy, who stares at me as he puts his hand over his nose and mouth and rubs in what looks like a deliberate gesture. A signal? He removes his jacket and drapes it over his arm. Ah, yes. I take off my coat.

Benjamin dials the phone again, muttering to himself. Luann glances anxiously among me and Jeremy and Wallace. The vampire stands frozen against the bars, his eyes distant in an expression of absolute vigilance.

Suddenly Wallace's gaze darts to the ceiling. For a moment I hear nothing. Then a dull thud, from a room not directly above us, maybe the living room. The moment stretches on, taut and brittle as cold taffy.

Another thud, this one in the foyer right above us.

Benjamin looks up. "What the—"

The door at the top of the stairs slams open. Splinters of wood fly down the steps, followed by a clanging, hissing metal canister. A white cloud pours out as it bounces end over end.

"Ciara, hold your breath!" Jeremy shoves his coat against his face. I follow suit, jamming the rough wool against my nostrils.

Luann screams. "It's poison gas!"

Benjamin grabs her and drags her toward the open weapons closet. He shoves her inside, hurries to follow, then slams the door shut behind them.

A tall figure in flannel appears through the white cloud.

Shane.

He shoves two gas masks through the bars. Jeremy grabs both, then straps one over my head before securing his own.

Two more men in black Control uniforms streak down the stairs—vampires, obviously, since they have no masks.

"Look out!" I point to the closet, my eyes already burning from the gas. "They have weapons. A man and a woman."

Jeremy tightens the straps on my mask, since it's a job for two hands. "How are we getting out of here?" he yells to Shane.

Shane puts his finger to his lips and kneels in front of the lock with a short thin metal instrument.

Through the thickening cloud of gas, I see the two Control vampires open the closet. In another moment, they enter and disappear.

"Got it." Shane jerks open the door, reaches in, and pulls me out. We leave Wallace in the capable hands of the other agents and make our way upstairs.

On the main floor, men cry and cough as they crawl over the Oriental rugs, eyes squeezed shut. I double-check the rubber seal of my gas mask as Shane pulls me through another thick white cloud.

He shields me as we make our way down the hall toward the foyer. We sidestep a man on his hands and knees, puking. By the open front door, where the air is clearer, a black-clad Control vampire and a stake-bearing Fortress guard are fighting hand to hand. The thud and crack of fists and feet sound nothing like they do on TV. Each impact feels like a punch to my own gut.

Shane steers us to the right, through the piano room. "We'll go out through Benjamin's office."

I hurry toward the open double doors, relieved I gave the Control such a detailed layout in my original plea for help. I hear Jeremy's footsteps close behind me.

Shane slows abruptly as we approach the office. "Wait, someone's in there."

Ned steps into the doorway, a dull black pistol in his trembling hand. His eyes are bloodshot, his face soaked in tears.

Time seems to stand still as my gaze adheres to the darkness at the end of the gun barrel.

"You killed Gideon." He waves the pistol. "Both of— Augh!" He yelps as Shane tackles him in a blur of motion.

A deafening crack, then a whistle past my ear. I scream and drop to the floor. Jeremy lands beside me, his arm over my back.

Another crack, not as loud but just as sickening. Then the crash of broken glass.

"Come on." Shane helps us up. "Hurry."

My legs wobble as I try to run across the office, the sling on my arm throwing me off balance. I focus on putting one foot in front of the other instead of the fact that five seconds ago, my head almost got blown off.

"Watch the glass." Shane leads me through the splintered frame of what used to be the French doors of Benjamin's office. I step around Ned's twisted body onto the back patio. I look back into the house and realize Shane just tossed my would-be murderer over thirty feet through the glass doors.

"Oh my God." Jeremy peels off his mask and gapes at Ned, then at Shane. "Is he dead?"

"Not yet." Shane picks the pistol out of the rubble. "He wasn't bluffing, Ciara." He raises the weapon to point at Ned's chest. "He was going to kill you."

"Shane, no!" I put out my hand, resisting the urge to grab his arm. "We're safe now. Let's just go."

He hesitates for a long moment, holding the gun steady as he aims. Finally he takes a deep breath, then clicks the pistol's safety and lowers it to his side.

"No." He drags his gaze up to the Fortress's turreted façade. "We'll never be safe."

# 26

## Mysterious Ways

"I knew I'd get you to listen to that emo crap," Jeremy says to Shane across the back of the Control van, which sits down the block from the raided Fortress.

"I'm not listening to it, but it seemed like the best way to get the message across, especially after I realized we were extracting you on a Thursday."

"It was perfect." I snuggle against Shane's side as he strokes my hair. The residual fear of almost getting killed has left me shivering despite the van's cranked-up heat. "Except for the part about the cyanide."

"You really thought we'd risk your lives with poisonous fumes? The tear gas was bad enough." He uses his thumb to wipe a bit of nonexistent wetness from my cheek.

"So tell me about Sara."

Shane tenses. "I swear, Regina and I had no idea the guy doing all this was Benjamin Zadlo."

"I assumed his name was Amberson, like Ned's, though Lanham did say they could be half brothers."

His mouth twists in a bitter scowl. "The Control knew, since they were monitoring the place. This might've been avoided if they'd just shared more of their information."

"And ruin an investigation they've been conducting for years? Besides, you're one to talk, keeping secrets about Sara. So spill."

He lets out a heavy sigh. "Sara was the reason I finally broke up with Regina."

"This was a couple years ago, right?"

He nods and runs a heavy hand through his tangled hair. "Where to start . . . they met at a club in D.C."

"Was she Regina's donor?"

"No, they were just good friends. Sometimes when Sara's boyfriend got really bad, she stayed with us at the station."

"In your apartment?" What happened to no humans allowed? "Wait, what do you mean, when Benjamin got really bad?"

"He hurt her. When she met Regina, it was mostly pushing and arm twisting, but things got worse fast. The first time he punched Sara, it took all five of us to keep Regina from killing him. A homicide watch, you might say. This guy was an asshole, but he was still human, not to mention an up-and-coming captain in the Control. If she'd hurt him, it would've jeopardized the agency's protection of the station."

Jeremy folds his arms. "Why am I not surprised this guy was a girlfriend beater?"

My mind fuses another connection. "So Regina changed Sara to a vampire so she could defend herself?"

"That was a big part of it." His eyes narrow. "And Regina wanted a new pet." He shakes his head, as if dismissing his own accusation. "No one could deny it was what Sara wanted. She even signed a VBC form."

"A huh?"

"Vampire By Choice. That's not the official name, but it's what we call it. It's a Control form."

"So if she gave her consent, what was the problem?"

His lips tighten into a thin line. "Just because someone wants to die doesn't give anyone the right to kill them. Making a vampire is murder."

"According to who?"

"According to me." His eyes are dead serious, and he taps himself in the chest. "I'm Catholic, remember."

The irony of a pro-life vampire does not escape me. "Is that why you broke up with Regina?"

"It's why I finally gave up on us. We hadn't been a real couple for years, but once in a while—" He glances at Jeremy, and I sense he wants to say more.

I prompt him. "So Sara became a vampire. Then what?"

"Then the soap opera began. Sara was powerful and hot and could suddenly have any guy she wanted. And she wanted all of us."

"Did you—"

"No." He puts up his hands. "I knew how toxic that would be, with me and Regina's breakup. But Sara kept trying. And one day Regina walked in on . . . Sara trying."

My chest tightens. "Regina killed her?"

"Of course not. But she started letting her go her own way. I guess you could say Regina turned into a negligent parent." He lowers his gaze. "We were all to blame for not taking care of her. Infant vampires can be so annoying, but that was no excuse to let her go out alone the night daylight savings time ended."

"Oh God," Jeremy says. "Sunrise an hour earlier."

Shane gives a faint nod without looking at him. "Sara wasn't getting enough to drink, and sometimes she'd pass out or fall asleep. So she'd set her cell phone alarm to wake her in time to come home, like I used to do at your apartment."

"Oh my God." The cruel truth dawns on me. "The cell phone reset the time but not the alarm. That happened to me last year."

"Miracles of modern technology." He grimaces. "Regina called her, but it was too late. Sara was driving back to the station, racing the sun. She lost." He closes his eyes. "We heard her screaming."

I touch his arm gently. "I'm sorry."

The back door of the van opens to reveal Colonel Lanham.

"Did the medics check you both over?" he asks me.

"We're fine now," I tell him. "How's Ned?"

"Early signs indicate swelling of the brain. He'll probably be in a coma for a while."

I put a protective hand over Shane's knee. "Ned shot at me."

"Don't worry. We have people at the state's attorney's office. No charges will be filed."

"Did you ever find Benjamin and Luann?" I'm afraid to ask about my dad.

Lanham frowns. "They escaped, but not for long. We'll need to debrief both of you ASAP, separately." He includes Jeremy in his glance. "Maybe you'll remember something that can help us find them."

We both nod, then Jeremy says, "Sir, I have a lot of questions."

Lanham nearly laughs, then catches himself before he can commit this unnatural act. "That is, no doubt, the understatement of the day. Major Ricketts will collect you in a few minutes. She'll answer your questions and take your statement." Lanham turns to me. "We'll be speaking soon."

"No doubt."

I wince as he slams the door shut.

"So dude," Shane says to Jeremy, "after all this, what are you going to write?"

"No idea." Jeremy pushes back his limp curtain of blond hair. "I sure as hell can't write the truth."

"Don't worry," I tell him. "We'll come up with something better."


Lanham waits exactly twelve hours to track me down for our "speaking soon." Friday afternoon finds him in my apartment suggesting that I should repay the Control for saving my life by giving a year of said life to their employment.

"I told you, I'm not a team player." I shove aside the contract he puts in front of my face. It's ruining my appetite for this bowl of mac 'n' cheese (something I swore I'd never again deny myself if I got out of the Fortress alive). "My blood's not enough, you want my sweat, too?"

Lanham frowns, then seems to remember something. He reaches for the long black coat draped over the dining room chair. Out of the pocket he pulls a black pleather square, which he opens with the flick of a thumb.

"The badge of an active Control agent."

"Ooh, pretty." I examine the silver sun insignia, surprised it's not in the shape of a fist. Then I notice the green flashing lights above a tiny keypad embedded near the bottom edge. "What's with the bling?"

He snaps shut the badge holder. "A dynamic security system. An agent's codes are refreshed every seventy-two hours, sometimes more frequently. This way if a badge is stolen, it can't be used as a forgery. Or if an agent goes rogue, their security code can be nixed immediately."

"Wow, you must have some high turnover rates to warrant such a complicated system." I take another bite. My mac 'n' cheese is getting cold, which makes me cranky. "You can't win me over with super-sweet spy toys, if that's what you're thinking."

"I wasn't expecting to. But if you encounter someone who claims to be a Control agent, now you'll know whether he or she is a fake."

"Do the lights go out when they don't put in their new code?"

"They turn red."

I wonder if somewhere in the back of a drawer, David has a red-lit blinky badge.

"As for your employment," Lanham continues, "I assure you we could make it worth your while in other ways than—"

"Stop." I hold up my fork. "If that's all you came here to talk to me about, you may leave."

Lanham puts his hands behind his back. "Very well. I'd like to show your video of the Fortress bloodbath to the executives at the Family Action Network. Not the supernatural part, of course. The rest of the ritual ought to be enough to scare them straight."

"And they'll leave the station alone?"

"I imagine they'll cut ties with the Fortress immediately. Without the extra funds from this source, they can't afford new translators to override radio signals. And I suspect they'll want to run as far away from any connection with WVMP as they can, lest the public discover their association with Satanic-looking rituals. Not to mention arsonists, as we believe the Fortress to be behind the going-to-hell threats as well."

"Tell FAN that Jeremy and I will make up a reason why they've abandoned their crusade, one that will let them save face. They'll confirm it with the *Rolling Stone* fact-checkers."

He nods. "Good. That should sew things up on that end."

His ensuing silence forces me to ask the question. "No word about my father, I suppose."

Lanham hesitates. "He wasn't at the Fortress at the time of the raid. We had the place surrounded, and there were no other escape corridors except the hidden door in the back of the basement closet."

Which I really wish I'd found while I was sitting in there—not that I would've had the key. "If my father has the same power I do, he's not safe in the hands of the Fortress."

"We understand that."

I stab the macaroni left-handed, trying not to show my burgeoning concern. "Any leads on where he might be?"

He blinks slowly. "I'll let you know."

I grit my teeth around my fork. He's not telling me every-thing.

"The vampire Wallace has been returned to our custody," Lanham says. "With your permission, I'd like to investigate if your blood can cure his injuries. It would be delivered in-travenously, of course, since he can't currently swallow." He pauses. "Without your blood, he'll likely starve to death."

"If you can give him my blood by IV, why not feed him that way the rest of his life, with bank blood?"

Lanham frowns. "Part of the purpose of this operation is scientific inquiry."

"An experiment."

"Yes."

I drop my fork in the empty bowl with a clatter. "I have a request."

I beckon Lanham to follow me into the kitchen, where I turn on the stove's exhaust fan to shroud our voices from Shane in the bedroom, who may or may not be asleep.

"What's this about?" Lanham asks.

I lean against the stove and meet his steel-blue gaze.

"Let Shane go home for Christmas."

He doesn't blink. "Absolutely not. A ruling was made when his father died. I couldn't overturn that if I wanted to."

"Don't be such a Scrooge."

"We both know it's not about one holiday. If his mother

were his sole remaining relative, his case review might have had different results. She would die before he aged much further, or would at least be deemed senile if she told anyone her son was a vampire. But his sister is young and has children. If he doesn't cut off contact with them now, it will be that much harder in ten or fifteen years when we need to change his identity and location."

"Everything could change in ten or fifteen years."

"Nothing changes when it comes to humans and vampires."

*Wanna bet?*

I take a deep breath.

"I'll work for you." My hand tightens on the edge of the counter. "After I graduate. I'll sign a year's contract today. Just don't make Shane hurt his family again."

He folds his arms. "Be careful."

"I'm not afraid of you."

"That's not what I mean. You're willing to make this sacrifice, become something you hate, for the sake of a vampire."

I consider defending my feelings, telling Lanham that Shane would do the same for me, if not more, that he's already sacrificed and given more of himself than I ever could.

Instead, I just hold his gaze and say, "Yes. I am."

In the midst of figuring out how to find my father, and in the midst of recovering from arm surgery and a brush with death, and in the midst of offering a sample of my blood to a paramilitary organization, who may or may not be satisfied with a few vials . . .

I have a paper to write.

It's 3 a.m. now, seven hours before this assignment is due. I stretch my back over the edge of the dining room chair and look at Shane, who quietly tunes his guitar on the sofa. He's wearing a WVMP baseball cap backward, so for once his face isn't obscured by his pale brown hair. He twitches his jaw as he tunes, and the action sets off his sharp, high cheekbones.

Shane stops tuning and shifts some sheet music on the coffee table in front of him. He's teaching himself to play Buffalo Springfield's "A Child's Claim to Fame," in response to folk-rock requests from the hippies at his gigs.

My computer boops to signal a batch of incoming e-mail. One of the messages takes longer to download than the others. I freeze when I see Colonel Lanham's address with the subject line "An Offer". I swallow hard as I open the attachment.

A contract. A year's employment with the International Agency for the Control and Management of Undead Corporeal Entities.

At the click of a mouse, it comes out of the printer to my side.

1. My tenure at the Control will start within thirty days of my graduation or thirty-six months from today, whichever comes first. Damn. I was hoping I could weasel out of it by never getting those last three credits.

2. As a consultant, my boot camp attendance is encouraged but not required. Yay, no one calling me a maggot.

3. Starting salary: more than I make at the radio station. Bonuses for hazard pay.

No clauses saying I have to travel extensively or that I can't sleep with a vampire. I uncap my pen and ease my right arm out of the sling.

Shane's voice trickles through the air between us, singing something about lullabies and make-believe.

I look into our kitchen at my spice rack, at the automatic dishwasher, at the refrigerator, where he's left so many notes.

None of his compulsions will improve with time; in fact, they'll get worse, until Shane's life is so regimented we'll have to schedule our spontaneous sex. I can slow down his fading, reverse some aspects of it (music, for instance), but ultimately I have to accept what is and what can never be.

Eyes wide open, I sign the contract. Then I take it down the hall to the study and fax it to Colonel Lanham's office.

As the last sheet jerks through the machine, transmitting my future, I wonder if I'll get to wear one of those bitchin' black uniforms.

I come back to the living room and lean on the wall at the corner. "What's it called when the Catholic Church gives you special permission for something that goes against the rules?"

Shane looks up. "Dispensation. Why?"

"You want some?"

He tilts his head. "What for?"

"Colonel Lanham had your case reviewed. You can go home for Christmas."

His mouth falls open.

"The Control won't mess with your family." I shift my feet when he continues to stare at me. "It's not permanent permission yet. You can't reveal you're a vampire, not until the agency does deeper background checks on your family."

"That's incredible." He sets aside the guitar and slowly crosses the room to me. "What changed their mind?"

"I begged. Pleaded. Argued. Cajoled." The lie won't sit inside me without causing heartburn. I hold up the contract. "I said I'd work for them."

"What?" He yanks the papers out of my hand. "Ciara, no."

"It's just for a year."

He scans the contract, eyes flashing left and right. "I don't believe this. How could you sign your life over to those thugs, even for a day?"

"Those thugs just saved my life. With your help, of course."

"You have no idea what they'll ask you to do. They have no limits. Everything's a means to an end."

"Now you sound like Benjamin."

"That's not fair. Hating the Control doesn't make me a Fortress sympathizer."

"What's not fair is expecting me to share your hatred. I'm not exactly a principled person. Maybe the agency is the perfect place for me."

"No, Ciara." His voice is soft, and so are his eyes as they look at me like I just died. "You're not like them."

"Then you have nothing to worry about." I touch the front of his shirt. "I won't let them change who I am. Please have enough faith in me to believe that."

"I trust you. It's them I don't trust."

"So keep an eye on them and guard my nonexistant virtue."

"Don't worry, I will." He takes my hand. "I can't believe you did this for me."

"I love you." I shrug, still getting used to those words after all these months. "And anyway, it's not for you. It's for me. When you're miserable, I'm miserable. Therefore, you missing Christmas with your family was really bumming me out." I hope the addition of old slang helps my case. "It's a completely selfish act."

He kisses me. "I don't know how to thank you."

"You can start by playing that guitar until I finish my paper, even if your fingers fall off."

Shane caresses my face. "My mom'll be so thrilled, she's going to freak." He kisses me again and heads back to the couch.

The glow of making Shane happy fades quickly as I calculate how many words I have to write and revise—with one hand—in six and a half hours. I'll be lucky to pass this class.

I tried to get an extension by telling my professor about the "pit bull" attack and subsequent surgery, but he pointed out

that in the real business world, we have to meet our obliga-
tions, no excuses. I thought that instead of handing in a paper
on the effect of identity theft on small business, I'd just give
him a list of all the life- and revenue-threatening challenges
I've overcome in the last six months. The "real business world"
has tried to eat me alive, thanks very much, Mr. Ivory Tower.

"I can't believe I have another two and a half years of this,"
I whine to Shane over my seventh cup of coffee. "Is this why
you quit college? Life got in the way?"

"Nope." He adjusts a string, then plucks it with his pick.
"Drugs got in the way."

My fingers freeze above the keyboard. I knew he had a
habit when he was alive, but I didn't know it was the end of his
academic pursuit of music theory. I didn't know it ruined his
life. We never talk about the past. Maybe we should start.

"I'm sorry," I tell him.

"Yeah, well." He shifts his weight on the couch and plucks
the intro to a Steve Earle song. I can't place the title until he
sings the mesmerizing first line, soft and unapologetic. It's
"CCKMP," which stands for "Cocaine Cannot Kill My Pain,"
but, ironically, it's not a song about cocaine.

The notes create a shroud around him, one I might never
penetrate. At the same time, the very acknowledgment of "the
only gift the darkness brings" somehow diminishes its power
over him.

I try to imagine him in a dark, seedy apartment, jonesing
for his next fix, or blissed out with a needle in his arm. That
picture in my head hurts a lot, partly because I love him, but
also because it stretches my imagination to the breaking point.
He's so full of life now—thanks to the music—that the sad,
despair-ridden part of him lurks too deep for me to glimpse.

But it's there and always will be. As bits of truth color in
the tapestry of his past, it's harder for me to fill in the empty
spaces with the things I want to believe.

When he finishes the song, I close my laptop lid. "Can I ask you a personal question?"

He sends me a crooked smile. "You're my girlfriend. You can ask me anything."

"So." I fidget with the frayed edge of my sling. "How many female vampires have you slept with? Besides Regina."

His left eyebrow quirks, but otherwise he takes it in stride. "A couple. Maybe several."

"Are they better?"

"Better than what?"

"Me."

"No one's better than you," he says without smiling.

"Are they better than humans? In general."

"No." He breaks my gaze and glances at the wall over Elizabeth's stereo. "Just different."

"Different how?" My heartbeat quickens as I think of what David told me, about why human men can't risk sex with a female vampire.

"Colder." Shane taps his fingers against the wood of the guitar. "Stronger. Rougher. There's usually biting."

I wipe my forehead. The honesty is making me sweat. "Do you miss it?"

He turns back to me. "You know what I miss?"

My throat has frozen shut, so I just shake my head.

"Sometimes in the middle of the night," he says, "when I'm in the studio, a song will remind me of you. One line of lyrics, or even just a riff that travels up my spine the way your fingers do. And suddenly I'll miss the way your skin smells in all the hidden places. I'll miss the way you sigh when I slide inside you, and the way your eyelashes flutter. Or I'll just miss the way you laugh at one of my stupid jokes. And sometimes this happens in the middle of the day when I'm at the station, and I know you're upstairs in the office, and I could walk up and see you in less than a minute."

I somehow find my voice. "Why don't you?"

His gaze meets mine, stealing what's left of my breath. "Because I want you to miss me, too."

The look on his face makes me forget about my paper, about pretty much the rest of the world. I cross the room to sit beside him.

Shane sets the guitar on the floor and takes me in his arms. I kiss him with the bottomless need of the almost nearly dead. He pulls away a few inches to look at me.

"Shane, I—"

"Shh." He leans in and whispers against my ear with a soft breath. "Don't say anything. Don't do anything."

Shane undresses me carefully, brushing his lips and fingertips over every inch of my skin, reclaiming the body we almost lost.

Then he makes love to me slowly and gently, just the way I need it. I feel no twinge of pain, in my arm or anywhere else, and in his eyes I see no regrets, no disappointment with my fragile human form.

That's when I realize the truth doesn't always have to hurt.

# 27

## Heart Full of Soul

Just after twilight on the night before Christmas Eve—what my mom used to call Christmas Eve Eve—Shane and I begin our drive to Youngstown. I'm relieved he doesn't want to listen to seasonal music, instead flipping the satellite radio among eight or nine rock stations.

Halfway to Pittsburgh, we hear the first haunting piano notes of Evanescence's "Bring Me to Life."

"Oh! I love this song." I turn up the volume. "I know, what vampire-lovin' female doesn't? Forgive the cliché." Not that he'll even recognize the tune.

"Is that . . . ?" Shane focuses on the radio display before turning his eyes back toward the road. His grip on the steering wheel tightens, and his brow crinkles as if every neuron is sparking.

I keep quiet, hoping his memory will stretch forward to 2003, when the song was released. But maybe it's like wishing a dinosaur would remember when humans started walking the earth.

He suddenly switches the station to the blues channel. I frown at his temporal hiccup, then make a mental note to download the Evanescence track next time I'm online.

Ten, maybe twenty seconds pass, then Shane's shoulders ease their tension a bit. "That was Sara's favorite song. Regina let her play that CD all day in our apartment, I guess because it's sort of Goth. Then one night it accidentally got 'lost' under the wheel of Jim's car."

"Do you really think Regina's a murderer for making Sara a vampire?"

"It's not Regina's soul I worry about. Sara's the one who asked to die." He chews his lip for several seconds. "I know you think I'm an idiot for believing in souls and sin."

"I'm okay with souls."

He gives me a rueful glance. "What if I told you I thought those signs the Fortress painted were right? About me, at least."

"That you're going to hell?" I decide now is not the time to discuss the nonexistence of said realm. "Because you're a vampire?"

"No. Not all vampires are damned. Just the few who get turned on purpose."

"But Regina made you against your will."

"No, I'm not being clear. It's not about vampires. It's about suicide. That's what I wanted from Regina—death. Just because she gave me something more doesn't mean I didn't try to die."

"But you'd tried to kill yourself before. Were you damned after those attempts?"

"As long as I was alive, there was the chance for salvation and redemption through repentance. Once I died, that chance was gone forever."

I speak carefully. "Shane, I respect the fact that you believe that, but isn't it possible you could be—"

"Wrong? Yeah, except for one thing." Shane's pale skin

shines blue and haunted in the glow of the radio display. "Most vampires say that when they were turned, when they died, they saw a bright light waiting for them." The shadows shift on his face. "All I saw was darkness."

A cold sensation sweeps over me, lodging in my throat.

"I'm dead, Ciara. You won't admit it, because it means things for us that we never talk about. But I don't age. I don't change."

I argue, to keep from crying. "Your heart beats. Your blood flows." I count off on my fingers. "You blink. You breathe. Sometimes when we have really wild sex, you even sweat."

"It's not life. It's reanimation." He puts his hand on mine. "Feel how cold I am. The warmest my body ever gets is ninety-seven degrees, right after I drink, and even then it's another human's warmth flowing through me. It's not real."

"You're not dead. You're just alive in a different way than I am." When he starts to protest, I smack him in the shoulder. "I am not a necrophiliac—"

"Technically you are."

"—and you're not a suicide. Don't you see? You've been pissed all these years at Regina for turning you against your will. But she saved your soul. You can kick the despair that made you want to kill yourself. The rest of your existence— which'll be a really long time if I have anything to do with it—you can have hope. You can even have faith."

"Faith in what?"

"Anything. Faith in yourself, or in the future, or"—I point at the radio—"good old-fashioned Tennessee blues. Just never hole up in fear like Gideon. If hell exists, he's in it."

"Great. I put him there."

"He would have killed you. He would have killed me, and David. Gideon's despair wasn't your problem." I take his hand again. "Only yours is."

We're silent for several minutes, during which I turn up the volume.

Finally he says, "How do I confess to a priest that I killed myself?"

"Fudge the facts. Say you tried, but someone saved you, and that you're sorry and you'll never do it again." Wincing, I rest my right elbow on the window frame. "That's true, right? Promise me? Never again?"

He appears to think about it for several long moments, then brings my hand to his lips. "Never again."


The moment we step out of the car, Shane's mom smothers him with a hug. It lasts approximately a year, while I pretend to do something abstract with my keys.

I wave at the trio of people on the porch. Only one of them, the tall teenage boy on the lowest step, returns my gesture. He looks back at Eileen, who stands with one hand on his shoulder and the other on the shoulder of the younger boy, a blond kid who's chewing his thumb.

"Come on, Mom," the older one says. She lets go of him and he bounds down the walkway. "Uncle Shane!"

Shane releases his mother and turns to him. "Is that Jesse?"

Eileen's sharp voice cuts the cold night air. "He's gotten big in the last twelve years, huh?"

Jesse gives Shane a quick, hearty hug. "I downloaded your podcasts? They were *so* awesome, I listened to them, like thirty million times. I told all my friends I knew you, and they wouldn't believe me. So I bought a WVMP T-shirt. Can you autograph it and say 'To Jesse, my favorite nephew'?"

"You gotta earn it." Shane ruffles the boy's shaggy brown curls, then looks at the porch. "You must be Ryan."

The blond boy, who's maybe ten or eleven, takes a half step backward and casts a nervous glance up at his mom.

"Go on." She lets go of him. "Say hello."

Shane greets him halfway up the walk, where they solemnly

shake hands. "Glad to meet you." Ryan just nods in reply.

"You weren't even born when he left," Eileen tells her son. She looks at me. "Boys, this is Ciara."

"Hey," they say in unison, Jesse just as shyly as Ryan.

"Let's get inside," Mrs. McAllister says. "It's freezing." She pats Jesse's faded black My Chemical Romance "DEAD!" T-shirt. "How can you be in short sleeves?"

Shane taps my elbow. "I need to get stuff."

I open the trunk, and Shane pulls out a bag of gift-wrapped boxes. As I close the lid, he gives me an odd look.

"Don't you need to get something?"

I look at his bag, and my eyes widen. "Were we exchanging gifts this year?"

His lower lip goes out in the world's briefest pout. "Uh, I guess not. I mean, I got you something. Several somethings."

"Sorry." I squeeze his arm. "I guess I could hit the mall tomorrow, if it's that important to you."

His gaze falls to the driveway. "Whatever."

We go into his mom's tiny house, into the front room, where snacks and cocoa are waiting for us next to a sparkling tree. It's like a TV special: *A Very Normal Christmas.*

We set about opening gifts. Shane gives me a box set of CDs with every 5:54 a.m. song he's ever played for me. Each disc has a cover with original artwork and a list of songs. The last disc is all him, playing acoustic. In a separate package is the best gift of all: a mix tape of music I've never heard, entitled "Not Fade Away".

I lean over to kiss him thanks. "It must have taken forever to put all this together."

"Lotta time to kill while you were imprisoned," he murmurs low enough for only me to hear.

Mrs. McAllister hands him a present and pats his cheek. "I can't get over how young you look."

He shrugs. "Must be all those blood transfusions."

We gape at him. I'd kick his shin if I could reach.

Shane pops up his eyebrows. "You know, from Dick Clark."

Even Eileen laughs a little. Then Ryan says quietly, "I don't get it."

Jesse punches his arm. "Then why'd you laugh, loser?"

"You didn't get it either."

"I know who Dick Clark is." He looks at Shane. "Did Mom tell you I play guitar? Last year Dad took me to see Eric Clapton."

Eileen frowns and shifts in her seat at the mention of their father. I guess they're divorced.

"So what bands do you like?" Shane asks Jesse.

"I like a lot of old stuff, but I also like, um"—he counts off on his fingers—"let's see, My Chemical Romance, AFI, Fall Out Boy, Good Charlotte, Jimmy Eat World, Chevelle, the Killers, Dropkick Murphys—"

I glance at Shane, whose brows pinch tighter as his nephew rattles off bands he's never heard of. I bet he feels every one of his thirty-nine and three-quarters years.

"—and Green Day, I really like Green Day."

Shane's posture relaxes. "Green Day, yeah, they're awesome." He turns to Ryan. "What about you?"

Jesse rolls his eyes. "Don't even ask. Ryan likes country."

"Country's cool, too," Shane says. "It all comes from the same place. It's just a different way of expressing it."

"Yeah, a hella lame way." Jesse pounds his fist on his knee and gives me a pointed look. "Can we do it now?"

"Jesse!" Mrs. McAllister glares at him.

Shane glances between us. "Do what?"

I reach into my pocket and pull out a slim package, wrapped in metallic red paper. "I just realized I tucked this into my purse."

He takes it from me with a smile of relief and rips off the paper. "Oh. A new pick." He turns it over. "It's really nice."

His mom lets out a giggle. Jesse bounces on the sofa cushion, more like a toddler than a teenager.

"What's so funny?" Shane asks us.

"There's another part to the gift." I give his mom a hopeful glance. "Right?"

She jumps up from the sofa. "I thought you'd never get to it. Shane, it's in the den."

He looks at her, then at the pick, then at me. "You didn't."

He leaps up, forgetting to hide his supernatural speed. His mom sucks in an astonished gasp. We follow him to the door of the den, which he slides open.

"Oh my God."

Shane moves zombie-slow toward the pure white electric guitar that waits for him in the center of the armchair.

He kneels before it and reaches out tentatively, as if it will burn him with its beauty. Before he touches it, he turns to me. "You did this?"

"Yep." I can't wait to tell him later that I bought it with my own money and not Elizabeth's. Of course, living in her apartment for free really loosened my budget.

Jesse leaps over the corner of the coffee table to get to him. "I set it up. It's already tuned. Dude, it's so sweet."

"It's a Gibson SG," I tell Shane, "just like on our logo. I hope that's okay."

"It's a miracle." He spies the cord leading to the amplifier. "You got me an amp, too?"

"It's a used one. But the guitar is new, and you know, if you'd rather have a Les Paul, or another brand, we can trade it in. I still have the receipt."

"Are you crazy? This is the most amazing gift I've ever gotten in my life." He looks quickly at his mom. "I mean, except all the ones you gave me. Those were just as good."

She waves her hand. "Nonsense. Now go on and play, would you? It's not a museum piece."

This time, he only pauses a moment before picking up the guitar. He strokes the curves and the signature SG points at the top of the guitar that remind me of bat wings.

Then he pulls the strap over his head and flicks on the amp. The power thrums out from the speaker, waiting for his call.

I hand him the pick. "You dropped this."

As he takes it from me, he pulls me closer and gives me a kiss of promise and passion. "Thank you," he whispers as he lets me go, then caresses my face.

"You know how to thank me." I point to the guitar.

He licks his lips and touches the pick to a couple of the strings, making them hum. "Whoa," he whispers.

"Would you get on with it?" his mom says finally.

I smile. Clearly she's forgotten that her son can't be hurried. In response to her urging, he fiddles with the amp some more and adjusts the strap around his shoulders.

Finally he plucks a few strings, then pauses. All at once he launches into the opening licks of Aerosmith's "Walk This Way." The notes stream flawlessly from the speaker. If Regina were here, she'd have her finger in her throat in a fake gag at the music choice. But to me it sounds like angels singing.

Jesse punches his fist into the air in a gesture that reminds me of Shane's football victory gloats. When Shane stops, the boy goes, "That was awesome! Let me try."

"Jesse, don't be a hog," Eileen says, though her face glows at the sight of her son and brother together.

Shane and Jesse take turns slobbering over the guitar for about an hour, while Ryan and I talk dogs. He wants to be a veterinarian. He shows me the picture of his own two mutts on Mrs. McAllister's end table.

Eventually I find myself playing video games with the two boys. They kick my ass in a thousand ways, but it gives Shane some time alone with his mom and sister. The living room next door is quiet, with an occasional feminine sob, drowned out by the sound of my avatar getting his brains splattered.

It's the noisiest Christmas ever. Also, the best.

# 28

## Do You Hear What I Hear?

On Christmas Eve, I stand on David's deck, craning my neck to search the star-studded sky for that exploded comet. But my night vision is seared by the white lights strung over the railing, along with the candles arranged atop the wooden banister. Dexter wanders through the yard, reacquainting himself with his favorite old rabbit holes. His blinking red LED collar makes him look like a walking Christmas tree, or a patrol car.

The door slides open behind me. "You can't see the comet anymore," David says.

I turn to him. "It moved that fast?"

"No, it faded away, lost its mass." He points to the sky above the trees. "It's still there, you just can't see it without a telescope now."

The thought makes me kind of sad. I wish I'd looked at it more often.

A raucous cheer comes through the sliding glass door to the dining room. I turn to see Travis and three of the vampire DJs—Spencer, Monroe, and Shane—pointing and laughing at Jim. He downs a shot of whiskey. Shane and Travis nod their heads to Noah's reggae rhythms from the stereo. Regina's also at the station, ready to take over at midnight.

"They're still playing quarters?" I ask David.

"Chase quarters. Two people have the cups, one on each side of the table. When you bounce the quarter into the cup, you pass it to your right. If you've still got your cup when the other one catches up to you, you have to drink."

"Add a sleigh ride and caroling, and you've got a regular Norman Rockwell Christmas."

"At least we can safely share this holiday with them, unlike Thanksgiving."

I twist my mind away from the T-Day ordeal. It's still hard to look at Jim, even though he's kept his eyes, mouth, and hands to himself since that day.

"This must be their favorite time of year. Long nights, short days."

David nods and rubs his hands together to warm them. "For vampires, winter *is* summer, the time when they have the most freedom. The sun turns everything backwards."

I reach in my coat pocket, wincing as my right arm gets used to being out of the sling. "Mrs. McAllister gave me this last night when he wasn't looking." I hand David an old photo of Shane. It shows a skinny kid with a battered secondhand guitar strapped over his shoulder. "From the summer of '86, when he was between high school and college."

"Wow. I was only twelve."

"I was three." I take back the photo. "You know what makes this shot so beautiful? The sunlight reflecting off his hair. I've never seen that, and I never will."

David gives me a grim smile, then reaches inside his jacket and pulls out his wallet.

He hands me a worn photo of Elizabeth, the corners bent and the back date-stamped July 1997. She's standing on a brick sidewalk in front of a boat, maybe at Baltimore's Inner Harbor or the Annapolis waterfront. Tanned and grinning, blond hair streaming in the sun and breeze, she blows a kiss to the person behind the camera.

David shifts his feet. "Her twenty-seventh birthday."

I stare at the picture, trying to see the hard, cold Elizabeth I knew. This woman disappeared into her.

David retrieves the photo from my hand. "They say winter solstice is the time when light returns to the world to conquer darkness, because the days start to lengthen again. It's supposed to be a time of hope and renewal."

He offers the photo to one of the candles, lighting the top left corner.

"David, what are you doing?"

"Renewing." He holds up the burning photo. We watch Elizabeth's face blacken and curl. When the fire nears his fingertips, he sets the photo in the ashtray full of the vampires' cigarette butts. A cold breeze whisks the last black shred up into the sky, where clouds are creeping in to blot the stars. The air suddenly smells like snow.

"What brought that on?" I ask him.

He taps the toes of one shoe against the wooden railing's vertical slats. "When you were held hostage at the Fortress, I was really worried about you. I wanted to charge in there myself, guns a-blazin', and carry you out."

I shift away from him a little, wondering where this is leading.

"But then I realized," he continues, "that my thoughts were not along the lines of 'If Ciara survives, I'll tell her how I feel, because life's too short.' "

"Huh?"

"I was scared for you as a friend, and nothing more. That's when I knew I was over Elizabeth, when I was over you."

Dexter joins us on the deck, his yard-puttering project complete. He leans against my leg, and I commence ear scritchies, grateful for a break from the awkward moment.

"Any word on your father?" David asks me.

"No." I can't add anything further without revealing the intensity of my fear and anger.

"Do you miss your family at Christmas?"

"I miss Jesus." I shake my head. "Not Judge Jesus, separating the sheep from the goats. I miss Little Kid Jesus, the one who understands everything and loves everyone. Like Santa Claus, kind of, except that everybody's on the Nice List, or could be, if they just had faith." I scratch under Dexter's collar, making the dog thump his foot against the deck in joy. "I know he's just a stand-in for my lost innocence or some shit like that, and that's what I really miss. The ability to believe in my parents."

"Just because they lied for a living doesn't mean they never told the truth. You believe they love you, right?"

"They're good at faking emotions."

"But I saw the way your dad was with you. He wasn't faking."

"You didn't see that video from the Fortress. His fear looked so real, I could feel it in my gut." My stomach tightens at the memory. "But he's not a prisoner, he's an accomplice, to the people who would've killed me, the people who'd love to kill my friends."

David adjusts the string of lights on the wooden railing. "How do you know he's an accomplice?"

"Lanham said there was evidence against his bodyguard, who let him escape so he could go join the Fortress."

"Why do you believe Colonel Lanham and not your dad?"

"Because . . ." I struggle to get out a coherent thought

amid the rising queasiness. What if I'm wrong? What if my father really is in danger? "It makes sense. All the pieces fit together."

"Nice and neat. Plus it confirms what you want to believe about your dad. Then you can tell yourself you don't miss him on Christmas Eve."

I have to laugh, since the alternatives are crying or puking. "Between you and Lori and Shane, I must be the openest book on the shelf."

"Yeah, for a con artist, you're pretty transparent."

"Only to a few." I give Dexter a light shove with my knee. "Mommy's hands are tired, and Uncle David wants to pet you."

The dog shifts in front of David and sits on his feet.

"I'm not sad this Christmas," I assert. "It's nice just being with friends." I gesture to the vampires through the door. "No drama whatsoever."

The DJs and Travis raise their glasses in a collective toast I can't hear. They laugh and start to drink.

Then they pause before the glasses touch their lips. As one, the five vampires turn to stare at the radio.

"I have a bad feeling about this." David strides for the door, me and Dexter on his heels.

Inside the dining room, no sound comes from the speakers except a quiet *thup . . . thup . . . thup.*

"What's that noise?" I ask them.

Spencer looks at me. "It's the needle hitting a record's center label."

"I've never heard that before."

"Darlin'," he says, "you're not supposed to hear that."

David picks up the phone. "I'll call the studio. Shane, try to reach Regina at the station apartment. If something's happened to Noah, she can take over."

The rest of us watch the two men press the phones to their ears. No one's picking up.

The *thup . . . thup . . . thup . . .* gets louder. It stops for a moment, followed by the shriek of a needle across vinyl.

We all cry out in pain at the high-pitched noise. Dexter barks at the stereo.

Which is now silent as death.


The station's parking lot is empty when we arrive. As the oldest, strongest vampires, Spencer and Monroe approach the door first. I hang back with Dexter, who sniffs the wind, the hair along his spine erect. The first flakes of snow blot his smooth black fur.

Spencer and Monroe open the door cautiously and step inside. In a moment, they beckon the rest of us—Shane, Jim, Travis, me, Dexter, and David.

The main office looks untouched. Hearing cries of dismay from the lounge below, David and I follow the vampires down the stairs.

In the dim light of the fallen halogen lamp, the lounge looks like it was hit by a combination of a tornado and the Texas Chainsaw Massacre. The shelves and credenza lie on their sides. Broken glass crunches under my feet. Splashes of blood accent the wall, and bloody footsteps cover the shabby rug leading to the hallway and the back door.

Spencer, Monroe, and Jim are gathered around something on the floor in the center of the room. Travis paces, holds his head, and moans the words "oh God" over and over.

David sets the lamp upright, and suddenly I see what lies at the center of the silent chaos.

Noah, on his back amid chunks of the shattered table, his limbs twisted around the piece of furniture like he's clutching it to keep from drowning.

Dexter yanks me forward, and now I see a long thin shard

of wood protruding from Noah's chest. A piece of the broken table? No, it's too thin and smooth and perfect.

An arrow from a crossbow.

"No . . ." I let go of Dexter and kneel at Noah's feet. "He never hurt anyone." *That you know of,* says a small voice inside me. "How could they do this?"

Spencer pulls back Noah's lid and examines his eye. "He's unconscious but alive, at least until we pull that arrow out." He rubs his own face. "Son of a bitch, I never thought it'd be him."

"Filthy fuckers," Jim growls. "I can't wait to eat their brains, and I don't even eat brains."

Shane lurches out of the hallway. "Regina's gone. There's a whole body's worth of human blood on the studio walls."

"At least we know Regina's not dead," David says to Shane. "You would have felt it."

"Right." Shane rubs his chest, as if anticipating the sudden tightening, ripping feeling that would come at the moment of his maker's demise.

Travis moans again. "You don't ever want to feel that. It's like ten heart attacks piled on top of each other." He turns to David. "What are we gonna do?"

"First," Spencer says, "we have to pull this out." His fingers slide over Noah's chest, flanking the arrow. "We have to let him go."

My own heart feels punctured. I clutch Noah's sneaker, rubbing my thumb over the worn-out sole.

"I'll do it." Monroe kneels at Noah's side, across from Spencer. "Everyone come and say good-bye."

As his hands tighten on the arrow's shaft, the others gather around—Shane on my left next to Spencer, David and Travis on my right beside Monroe, and Jim at Noah's head. Everyone lays a hand on our friend's body. Even Dexter squeezes between Jim and Spencer to lick Noah's face.

Monroe whispers a prayer, and I close my eyes, hoping there's a place beyond that accepts vampires—at least the good ones like Noah.

"Ready?" Monroe whispers.

I want to tell him no, because I'm not ready to watch our friend's body turn in upon itself, inch by inch of tearing skin, splintering bone, oozing flesh.

Tears spring from my eyes and stream down my cheeks. I don't wipe them away but let them plop onto the cuffs of Noah's jeans.

Monroe says, "Good-bye."

He yanks out the arrow. Noah's body lifts and flops back to the floor. Blood seeps in a circle from the wound. I wait for it to flow backward, bringing everything with it that used to be Noah.

The bleeding stops. We hold our breaths.

Noah's eyes open, staring into the void, watching the approach of his second and final death.

Then he blinks. His gaze wanders until it settles on Monroe. "What's happening?"

I squeeze his ankle. "Noah, they shot you. You were hit in the heart."

He brushes his hand over his shirt and thumbs the hole. "They missed."

Spencer unbuttons Noah's knit shirt. No wound remains under the layer of darkening, drying blood. "I'll be damned. But why were you out cold?"

"The pain." Noah eases himself to sit up, wincing. "They shot me, then one of them twisted the arrow. Regina got him."

I look through the open door to the hallway. Half of the studio's glass window is opaque red, like it's been power-washed with blood. My stomach tilts, even as my heart races with relief at Noah's continued unlife.

"Where's Regina now?" David asks him.

"They took her. One of them wanted to pull that out." He looks at the arrow in Monroe's hand. "The other say to let me suffer for all the pain I cause. 'Let him pull it out himself,' they say. Then I fainted." He rubs his face in what looks like embarrassment, then suddenly notices Shane. "You're okay. So she's not dead yet."

"Not ever," Shane says, "if I can help it."

"Shh!" Jim points to Dexter, who's staring at the door at the bottom of the stairs, ears straight up and pricked forward. Then Jim jerks his chin. "I just heard it, too. Engine."

The other vampires listen, then start at a sudden noise I can't hear. Monroe creeps to the lounge door on stealthy feet. A few moments pass, then he holds up two fingers, which I guess signals the number of people upstairs.

Silent as snakes, the rest of the vampires move toward the door. I grab Dexter's leash, in case it's someone we don't want to kill.

Footsteps scurry down the stairs, and Spencer whips open the door.

A woman's voice shouts. "Don't hurt us! We're on your side."

Luann?

"Wait, I know her." I push through the vampires at the bottom of the stairs. "She was at the—"

The word "Fortress" dies on my lips when I see who's standing beside Luann, dressed in black like her.

"Hello, pumpkin." My father raises his arms halfway, then lets them drop to his side. "Merry Christmas?"

A deep growl shakes my body, and for a moment I think it's my own throat making the noise. Then I realize it's Dexter, at the other end of the taut leash. His snarling muzzle is pointing right at our intruders, ready to deploy his inch-long fangs at my command.

I look at my dad, then at Dexter, then my dad again. Ronan O'Riley's face turns as white as his hair.

"Angel, I can explain."

"There's no time," Luann says. "We know where the Fortress took Regina. Let's go before it's too late."

I squint at her, unable to reconcile her commanding tone with the meek little mouse who gave me breakfast and took my blood. "Why should we believe either of you? You're with the Fortress."

"Not exactly." She and my dad exchange a nod, then hold up a pair of badges with green blinking lights. "We're with the Control."

# 29

## I Don't Like Mondays

We squeeze into David's car, Dexter between me and Shane in the back, and my dad in the front passenger's seat. David's driving, since we don't trust my father as far as we can throw him—which, come to think of it, would be pretty far in Shane's case. Luann goes with Jim, Spencer, Monroe, and Travis, while Noah stays behind to put his show back on the air.

"Have you been with the Control all along?" I shout to my father over the clank of the driveway's gravel under the lurching car.

"Only since they caught me," he says, "which was about two days after I escaped back in August." He turns his head so I can see half his frown. "I thought I was good, but they're better."

"I figured they'd kill you."

"They weren't happy. But we came to an agreement. If I

worked undercover with the Fortress, as someone who shared their animosity toward the Control, at the end of the operation I could simply finish my original sentence in federal prison."

"You mean the sentence you had cut short by working for the Control the first time. The one for fraud?"

"Yes." At least this time he doesn't rub in the fact that my testimony put him and my mom in prison eight years ago.

"What was your other option?"

"Never seeing daylight again." He looks at David, whose face is tight with rage. "I'm sorry I ratted you out to Gideon. You probably want to kill me."

David turns off the driveway and onto the highway, jamming down the gas pedal so hard that my back slams the seat, jarring my sore arm.

"Put your seat belt on," he tells my dad.

"Huh?"

"Put it on, because I'm this far from slamming the brakes just to see you go through the windshield."

My father hurries to pull the strap across his chest. I wrap a protective arm around Dexter, as if I could prevent his own projectile flight.

I turn back to my dad. "Why didn't Lanham tell me they captured you? Why let me worry about you all this time?"

"Because I was undercover." Ronan turns to me with a magnetic grin. "You were worried about me?"

"Shut up." I rub my temple and look at Shane. He puts a hand on top of mine on Dexter's shoulders.

"Turn right," my dad tells David. "We're going north."

David turns, then punches the radio power button. Noah's reggae rhythms provide a weird contrast to the snowflakes bouncing off the windshield. David clicks on the wipers.

"Where were you all this time," I ask my dad, "if not at the mansion in Frederick? And what about that postcard?"

"I was at the Fortress's headquarters in Gettysburg. The

Control had me write that postcard to help maintain my cover." He hesitates. "And it was a loyalty test for you, to see if you'd tell Lanham I'd contacted you."

Bastards. "I guess I failed the test."

"Not to me you didn't."

I try to ignore the pride in his voice and the way it still makes me glow inside. A sudden thought occurs to me. "Dad, did you know I was being held prisoner?"

"Of course I knew. Luann's my, uh—my partner. She kept an eye on you for me."

"Would she have kept Benjamin from killing me if it meant risking the mission?"

"Ciara, don't you get it?" He points a thumb back at me. "When you were captured, you *became* the mission. The Control wasn't ready to raid the place yet. But once civilians were endangered, we had no choice."

"So I ruined the operation."

"Not entirely. We got some of the bad guys. And you probably saved Wallace's life."

"Great." My short list of those whose lives I'd fight for doesn't include Gideon's psychopathic progeny. "But Benjamin got away."

"For now." My father turns in his seat to face me. Instead of his usual slathered-on charm, his lined and dimpled face wears a deadly grimness. "But not for long."

Peering through the trees into the wide torchlit clearing below is like looking through a window in time. A window opening onto a Klan rally, circa 1925.

Three tall crosses lie on the ground, about fifty feet apart. Snow-dusted wood is piled at their bases. The largest one in the center appears to be made of white metal instead of wood. The Big Honkin' Cross, junior edition.

About fifty Fortress members—all male, from what I can tell—stand in rows in front of the crosses, like an audience. The wind whips the hems of their long white robes around their ankles. They each hold a four-foot-long wooden staff which they pound against the earth in a primal rhythm that spins my innards.

They begin to chant, low and hypnotic, just like the elders in the Fortress basement. The swell of voices amid the whistling wind and snow sounds like a call from another world. I glance at the thick woods around us, half expecting the trees themselves to reach for our throats.

Dexter growls low in his chest, and I wrap my hand around his muzzle. "Shh. No bark."

He shifts his forefeet and pulls back his ears in dismay, but his shoulders relax.

Another dozen men are gathered in one corner of the clearing, outside the assembly rows. The angles of their bent postures tell me they're restraining three prisoners.

"Who else did they capture?" I ask my dad.

He rolls up the sleeves of his black Control uniform. "I have no idea." He nods to the fire extinguisher at my feet. "You'll be okay using one of those, with your hurt arm?"

"I can't just wait here while Regina's life is in danger."

His bright blue eyes examine me. "The vampires are getting under your skin, aren't they? It was one thing to risk jail for them, but you could get killed." He juts his thumb in the direction of the clearing. "These people don't mess around."

"I know all too well, Dad. That's why I have to save her."

"Loyalty is such a quaint concept." He squeezes my shoulder, and I step away, out of his grip. "I'm kidding," he says.

I turn back to the clearing to see a guard next to each cross, long guns slung over their shoulders. They pace in front of the crosses, marching in time to the chant, like hell's color guard.

Maybe Dad's right. Maybe I shouldn't risk my life for Regina. I have no training in these brawn-over-brains operations. I'm useless.

"How long before the Control gets here?" I ask Luann, hoping the decision will be made for me.

She checks her watch. "ETA ten minutes."

"We don't have that long." David adjusts the focus on a pair of long, black binoculars. "They're moving the prisoners." He lowers the binoculars and turns to us. "We'll have to do it ourselves."

In the center of the clearing, Regina marches on her own, chin held high, wrists bound behind her back. The other two people, heads covered in black hoods, are being dragged, the chanting hordes nearly drowning out their high-pitched screams.

Luann and my dad, along with me, Shane, and the other four vampires—Monroe, Spencer, Jim, and Travis—gather around David while he draws the battle plan in the inch-thick snow.

"The vampires will be the first line of attack," David says, "to disarm those guards and protect the prisoners from the crowd." He assigns Shane and Spencer to the first cross, Jim and Travis to the middle one, and Monroe (the oldest and therefore strongest) to the third. "Then the rest of us move in and release the prisoners. Once the fires are lit, it won't be safe for the vampires to do that part."

"What about Dexter?" I ask David.

He gives me a solemn look. "He's a vampire. He goes with them."

"They're raising the prisoners!" Shane announces.

On either side of Regina, several men are pulling up the crosses with long ropes. Screams come from the figures tied to them. White robes cover their struggling bodies, but their arms and legs are bare.

"Let's go," David says.

We skirt around the edge of the hill, keeping just inside the tree line, out of the glow of the torchlight.

Regina goes up, without a hood. She doesn't scream.

The Fortress members dump more wood around the crosses' bases, the piles reaching past the women's feet. The snow keeps falling, but it's too dry and wispy to dampen the wood.

We reach our launch point behind the crosses, just in time. Three men step forward ceremonially, each carrying a torch toward a cross, the flames snapping and sparking in the wind.

The woman on Regina's left shrieks again.

"Oh my God." Shane stops short and stares in horror at the clearing. "That's my mom."

# 30

## Miss Murder

My stomach goes cold. "Are you sure?" I ask him. "Her head is covered."

"I know her voice." His own voice is strained near breaking. "The other one must be Eileen."

"Someone from the fortress followed us to Youngstown?"

Luann hands me my fire extinguisher. "Before I got away from Benjamin, he swore revenge on Shane for putting Ned in a coma."

The torches are lowered, lighting the wood.

Shane turns to me. In his eyes I see determination to save three of the women he loves most, even if it means losing his own life.

"Go." I clutch the front of his shirt. "I'll take care of myself."

He kisses me hard and quick. Under his lips I can feel his fangs.

"I love you," he says, and begins to run.

I unclip the leash from Dexter's harness. "Go on, boy. Follow Daddy."

The six vampires—five human and one dog—stream down the hill, the three oldest in front. I gasp at the sight of their speed. It's like watching lions chase down a herd of startled wildebeests.

The armed guards turn and fire. None of their opening shots hits, but the man guarding Shane's mother gets off another round before Monroe arrives and disarms him. Literally.

Shane stumbles and falls. I cry out as I realize he's been shot.

He rolls down the hill, his shirt coated with blood, then pushes himself to his knees. Two or three seconds pass while I hold my breath, then he staggers to his feet and keeps running.

I search in vain for Dexter. Is he in the middle of the crowd? Or did he run off? For his sake, I hope the latter.

Jim charges past Regina's cross and grabs the barrel of her guard's gun. He slams the butt into the robed man's head, producing a burst of blood. Spencer dispatches the guard at Eileen's cross in a similar manner. My knees weaken at the bowel-shaking brutality.

"That's our cue." David turns to me. "Last chance to back out. No one would blame you."

I hoist my trusty fire extinguisher. "I would blame me."

We dash down the hill, David and Luann to the left, Dad to the right, and me straight ahead, ignoring the pain that shoots up my right arm with every step.

In front of Regina, Travis points the guard's shotgun in a wide arc at the encroaching throng. "Get the fuck back. Now!"

They obey, but only when the weapon is pointing straight at them, so Jim acts as a backup to keep them away from the cross. I yank the pin from the fire extinguisher, aim at the base of the flames, and pull the trigger.

A huge white cloud bursts from the extinguisher, and the trigger sticks in the "on" position. The wind shifts suddenly, blowing the ice-cold chemicals back in my face. Choking, I circle to the front of the cross, as close as I dare to get to the screaming crowd.

The fire extinguisher stops. I squeeze the handle, trying not to panic.

"Hurry!" Regina screams. The roaring flames have almost reached her feet.

Jim grabs the fire extinguisher from me and tries to get it working.

"Empty," he yells.

A white-robed man runs up behind him, a stake raised high. "Look out!" I shriek.

Jim whirls, slamming the fire extinguisher into the face of his would-be assailant. An explosion rocks the air, and I turn to see Travis pointing the smoking barrel of the shotgun at the sky. The pack recoils.

Determined to put out Regina's fire any way I can, I kick the burning branches aside, separating them to slow the spread of the flames.

Finally I clear a path to Regina's cross. Jim climbs over the smoldering wood and shoves on the base of the metal pole in an attempt to push it over.

Something whistles past my ear. Regina screams in what sounds like pain. I look up to see an arrow protruding from her gut.

Then Jim shrieks, and I realize he's worse than shot. His sleeve is ablaze. He leaps off the pyre, drops to the snowy grass, and rolls to extinguish what's left of his arm.

The cross is tilted back, almost far enough to fall. I scramble through the burning wood and give it a hard shove. The hot metal sears my hands through my thick leather gloves, but I hang on. I shift around to the back, pulling instead of pushing. I can almost . . . get it.

My right hand, weakened by injury, slips off the cross, and

I fall backward into a pile of blazing wood. A shriek rips my throat, and the smell of singed hair fills my nostrils.

"Ciara!"

Travis appears above me. He grabs my shoulders and drags me from the fire, then tears off his coat and snuffs out my hair.

Regina screams again. In his haste to save me, Travis left the front of the cross unattended. Two Fortress members run forward with torches, toss them into the brush pile at the base of the cross, then leap back into the safety of the mob. The flames lick inches from Regina's feet, while another arrow whips over our heads.

"I got it," Travis says.

"No!" Smoke fills my lungs. I sit up, coughing and hacking, trying to tell Travis he can't step into the fire, not even for a moment. "Don't . . ."

He gets a running start, then charges through the burning wood to hurl his weight against the bottom of the cross. It creaks, then stops. He does it again, and it falls at last. I scramble out of the way just before the bar slams the ground beside me.

Another scream cuts the air. Travis is burning.

The flames move up his legs, devouring them in an instant, as if he were made of tissue paper. I crawl toward him, lungs aching, but without legs, his body falls into the flames. I reach for his hand as it stretches toward me.

It disappears.

"Travis?" I stagger to my feet, hoping someone pulled him out from the other side. Nothing remains but his clothes, curling and sparking in the flames.

He's gone. Into nowhere, like Elizabeth, like his maker Gideon, like his blood brother Jacob.

"No!" I kick one of the burning logs, trying to dissipate the fire. Maybe he rolled off when I wasn't looking. If there's anything—

A heavy weight slams me to the ground. The impact knocks out my breath. I can't get it back, because someone in a white robe is sitting on my chest.

Benjamin.

"Monster-loving bitch." He punches me in the mouth, sending waves of pain reverberating through my head, matched only by the agony in my arm. I still can't draw a breath to scream or even speak.

He hits me again, and I taste my own blood on the back of my tongue. It flows down my throat, drowning me.

His hands wrap around my neck. Orange and black spots dance in front of my eyes as his thumbs press my windpipe.

My legs kick, trying to buck him off, but he's too heavy, too strong. My left fist shoots out and catches him in the chin. One of his hands leaves my throat, and my heart surges with hope.

Then I hear it: the low, sharp *shing!* of a metal blade.

"Let's make this quick," Benjamin hisses.

*No.* I kick harder. *Hate sharp things. Please, God, no death-by-sharp-thing.*

From my left comes a low roar that sounds straight from hell. The call of the Grim Reaper? Could I have been wrong about the afterlife?

Suddenly Benjamin's face is full of black fur and yellow teeth. He screeches and lets go of me but doesn't get off. I choke in a shallow, desperate breath as Dexter steps on my face in his effort to save my life.

The dog squeals and leaps out of sight, revealing Benjamin holding a long, bloody hunting knife. He wipes his own blood from his eye with the long cuff of his robe.

"I know that won't do the trick on your pooch." He shifts the knife to his left hand and pulls a long wooden stake from a holster on his right ankle. "But this will."

Dexter gives a rumbling growl, ready to pounce again.

Benjamin tightens his grip on the stake, waiting. Their eyes meet like a bull and a matador in the ring. A matador holding a grenade behind the red flag.

"No!" I flail at the ground around me. My right hand hits something hot and hard. If only that arm would work. . . .

Dexter's growl turns into a roar as he hurls himself toward us, not knowing his opponent holds his certain death.

Shrieking in anger and agony, I grasp the burning log and smash it into Benjamin's face. He yelps and pulls up his arms.

Dexter slams him from the side, and they fly off me. Breath comes back to my lungs in gasping, agonizing waves. I force myself to sit up.

Benjamin flops in Dexter's giant jaws, which are wrapped around his neck. The wooden stake lies beyond the unconscious man's grip.

"Dexter, no!" I shout with as much volume as my bruised throat will muster.

The dog stops, his feet on Benjamin's chest. Slowly his jaws open, and he turns to look at me.

"Good boy." I hold out my palm in a *stop* gesture. "You stay." I crawl toward the stake, trying to get it before Benjamin wakes up.

Someone grabs my shoulder, making me scream.

"Sorry." Shane kneels beside me. "You okay?" He reaches to touch my face, then pulls his hand back. "Holy shit, what did he do to you?"

"I'm okay," I choke out, so happy to see him I can barely speak. I try to embrace him, but he seems to be holding me away from his body. "What about everyone else?" I ask.

"We got my mom and sister down. They're scared and sore but not hurt. David and Monroe are guarding them with the shotguns." He points to the field. "And the cavalry's coming."

Control agents in dull black riot gear are swarming the

assembly. From the looks of it, they've been here for a few minutes, which must have been why the Fortress thugs didn't attack me when Travis died.

"We've gotta save Regina." Shane helps me up but shields me from the crowd. "Stay in front of me in case—" Another arrow snaps the air above us. "In case of that."

We scuttle over to Regina, hunched like soldiers under sniper fire.

"Get me off this thing," she yells at us from the fallen cross.

Shane unties the metal cords binding her wrists and legs, but she still doesn't move. The skin of her legs and arms and shoulders is stuck to the cross.

"It's a goddamn vampire trap," she says. "And it's hot."

Wisps of smoke are already rising from her skin. A shotgun blasts, and I duck instinctively, feeling like a battlefield medic.

I tear off my glove and roll up my sleeve, dreading the pain of her fangs. "You'll have to drink from me."

"Wait." Shane points to my face. "Plenty in there."

I realize my mouth's full of blood, thanks to Benjamin's punches.

Regina gazes at my lips, eyes heavy with desperation. "Hurry. I won't hurt you."

I hesitate only a moment, then lean over her face. Before I can bring my lips to hers, her tongue snakes out and licks my chin, following the trail of blood up to its source.

Our mouths meet, pressed deep in one life-giving moment. She moans beneath me, and a great tremor passes through her.

I draw back to let her swallow. Her eyes slam open, wide with what I hope isn't pain.

Then her hands are at my neck, pulling me into another kiss. She laps at my tongue, her own mouth cool and alien and strangely delicious, like freeze-dried ice cream.

"That's enough," Shane says. He slides a hand between us and gently extracts me from her grip.

"Huh." She lets go and stares at me, then looks at Shane. "Tasty."

I sit back, my head swimming from the punches and the smoke and yes, the kiss.

Regina rolls off the cross. "Well, now I know how Joan of Arc felt."

For some reason, Shane gives a gruff laugh. He points to the arrow in Regina's stomach. "Do you want me to—"

"I got it." She yanks it out as casually as one would tear off a Band-Aid, then tosses it aside. "We better help Jim."

I turn to see the DJ curled up on the ground about ten feet away. His burned right arm has sealed into a ragged stump above the elbow.

Regina crawls over to him. She shakes his shoulder, and he starts, as if she just woke him up. His whole body is quaking.

She looks at what's left of his upper arm, then back at me. "Can you try?"

I check my mouth for blood. It's still flowing out of one side, where Benjamin gave me the second, harder punch.

Still shielding me from the crowd, Shane helps me scramble over to Jim.

With a trembling hand, the injured vampire cups my chin and brings my mouth to his. It's even colder than Regina's, with a shining silver core of magic that sends a shiver down my neck, all the way to my fingers and toes.

Jim draws away, his mouth red with my blood. He swallows. We watch his arm for signs of regeneration. It stays the same, which doesn't surprise me. Nothing cures fire.

"Sorry," I tell him.

Jim looks at my mouth, the pained expression somewhat ameliorated. "Maybe if we tried it again—"

"Fat chance." Shane puts a hand between us, as if I'd agree to kissing Jim again ever in my life.

We survey what remains of the battle. Control agents are

still wrestling a few Fortress members to the ground to hand-
cuff them, but everyone appears to be disarmed.

Standing apart from the multitude, Spencer and Monroe are
examining each other's injuries. It looks like they've each lost a
couple of chunks of flesh from their limbs—none as bad as Jim,
though, and theirs will heal faster anyway due to their age.

Oddly, my father is sitting on the ground next to what was
Eileen's cross. He waves at me, flashing the brilliant smile I've
learned to love and hate. I return the greeting, half wishing I
had the strength to run to him, and half glad I don't.

"What happened to him?" I ask Shane.

"Cross fell on his foot."

"Someday I'll find that funny." I point to the explosion of
blood on Shane's stomach. "That guard shot you."

"Yeah, but it's healed." He rubs his belly and winces.
"Which means I've got a gut full of buckshot."

I study the front of his shirt and jacket, noticing other
splashes of blood near the collar and on his sleeves. I reach
out. "What happened to—"

"Don't touch me!" Shane backs up quickly, lifting his
hands. "It's not safe for you."

"Why?" As a vampire, he can't carry diseases.

"It's not my blood." He averts his gaze. "It's . . . some human's."

"Did you—"

"No." He shakes his head. "At least I don't think I killed
anyone. I tried to hold back." His fists clench and his eyes
blaze with a rekindled fury. "But they had my mom." He looks
over his shoulder to where his family is huddling in borrowed
coats, then wraps his arms around his chest. "I can't have her
see me like this."

The energy drains out of me all at once, and I turn away.
My man is a killing machine, or at least a maiming machine.

"Where's Travis?" he says.

I raise my gaze to meet his. "He's dead."

"Dead?" Shane looks at me as if he doesn't understand the meaning of the word.

"Burned up," Regina says, "saving our lives. I guess he thought he owed us."

"Goddammit." Shane puts his head in his hands. "Goddammit." He stalks over to Benjamin's unconscious body, which is still being guarded by Dexter. "This is all his fault."

"Shane, no." I stumble forward. "Get away from him."

He comes toward me. "He tried to kill you. Twice."

"I know, but he'll be in custody soon. If you hurt him when he's helpless, you'll be joining him there."

"She's right."

We turn to see Regina lifting Benjamin by the shoulders, as easily as I could lift a loaf of bread.

"Besides"—Regina turns her back on the clearing and the Control agents—"this one's mine."

She seizes Benjamin's chin and twists his head to the side. A sickening snap cuts off my protest.

Regina carefully lays the body on the ground and straightens Benjamin's robe. "That's better."

My stomach lurches. I sit down hard and jam my head between my knees. After everything I've seen, all the blood and the burning and the violence, this simple act of deliberate extinction puts me over the edge.

"Jesus, Regina," Shane says.

"If the Control ever let him go, he'd be after us in a minute. We have enough enemies in this world."

He scoffs. "And you probably just created more."

"I don't care." She looks over at me, and her lips tremble. I touch my battered, bleeding face and realize Sara must have looked like this after meeting Benjamin's fists.

She stares down at his broken body. "He'll never hurt anyone again."

# 31

## A Long December

At the Control headquarters in the hills of northern Virginia, Colonel Lanham unlocks a large steel door and leads me into a bare gray room.

"Angel." Using one of his crutches, my father tries to stand up from behind the metal table.

"Don't get up." I come over and give him a quick, awkward hug. "Sorry you have to spend Christmas in jail. It sounds like a country-western song."

"I've worked hard to get where I am." His smile shines as bright as ever, white teeth gleaming from his ruddy face. Maybe it's his pain pills.

He folds his hands on the table between us. "Ciara, thank you for visiting me before they ship me back to Illinois."

"You said you had something important to tell me."

"That's right." He clears his throat. "I want to give you a piece of truth you've deserved your whole life."

This ought to be good.

"When I was in Gideon's compound, as you know, several of the vampires drank my blood on a regular basis."

I nod and try not to blanch at the image.

"You probably know what's next," he continues. "Their old holy-water scars began to heal." He leans forward. "It was very gradual, though, not instantaneous like your miracles."

I flinch at his word choice. "Did they figure out it was because of you?"

"Gideon did, eventually. I honestly don't know if he passed on this knowledge to the other vampires. It gave him a great deal of power."

I heave a frustrated sigh. "I would really love to know if there are vampires out there hoping to make me their personal skin care regimen."

"I understand, but I honestly can't tell you. What I can tell you is why you're like this."

"I thought it was my skepticism."

"Partly, yes. You have a high resistance to other people's explanations of reality."

"Like religion."

"Yes, but it's more than that." He takes a deep breath. "As far as we can figure, the real determinant is the ability to create one's own reality."

I squint at him. "Let me get this straight: healing holy-water burns depends on being a bullshit artist?"

"Within our family, at least. There's a genetic element that seems to be made of some sort of Old Country magic. Or more precisely, anti-magic, which is a magic in its own right."

I rewind to one of his earlier statements. "Wait, you said 'as far as *we* can figure.' Who's 'we'? You and the Control?"

"No." He hesitates. "Your mother and I."

My eyes pop open. "You called Mom? It's about time.

Does she know you're out of jail? Did you tell her all that classified stuff? I felt so bad I couldn't let her know I'd seen you, and—"

"Ciara, stop. Listen. Your mom isn't in jail. She's right here." He turns and nods to the guard.

"You got her out?" I watch the guard knock on the door. "Why didn't she call me?"

The door swings open, and Luann walks through, escorted by another guard. I'm surprised to see her also in the pale blue garb of a federal prison.

"Hello, Ciara. How are you feeling?" For the first time, her voice contains a strong southern accent.

I give her a tentative smile. "Do you have my mom?"

"Well, you might say that." She tucks a pale curl behind her ear. "My full name is Luann O'Riley. I'm your dad's wife, from the Travellers. Down in South Carolina?"

I sit up straight and stare at my father. "This is the one you told me about? The one you left for Mom but never divorced?"

Luann clears her throat. "Ciara, honey . . ."

The back of my neck prickles. Why is she calling me 'honey'?

"Ciara, I'm your real momma. The one who gave birth to you."

I gape at her without blinking. In fact, I may never blink again.

"That little thing you can do for vampires?" she says. "It runs in the clan. Some of us got it stronger than others. With you, it's the right combination of genes and—well, you might say, frame of mind."

"Wait. Stop." I put my face in my hands. "Go back to the part where you're my mother."

"I'm sorry, angel," Dad says.

"You lied to me." I raise my eyes, wishing they could shoot

lasers into his skull. "I asked you point-blank if you had children with your wife, and you said no."

"I did, but . . ." He spreads his palms on the table. "That's because it wasn't a good time to explain."

"You're goddamn right it wasn't. A good time would have been twenty years ago." I take two deep breaths and try to process the implications. "Wait a minute." I turn to Luann. "You said the power was strong in our clan. Am I some kind of inbred mutant freak?"

"No, no, no." My father gestures to Luann. "We're only distantly related, third cousins."

"Once removed," Luann adds, with an inordinate amount of pride.

"Still." I shake out my hands like they've been touching earthworms. "Ew!"

Luann takes a cautious step forward. "I don't expect you to accept me as your mother. I wasn't good enough for you when you were a little baby." Another step, not so cautious. "But I want to make up for all those lost years."

I put out a hand to ward her off as my head starts to clear. "This is another scam, isn't it? An experiment by the Control? They—they want to see if what I believe about my blood makes a difference in how it works." I slide back my chair, making it squeak on the waxed linoleum floor. "This isn't a family thing. This power comes from me and me alone." I stare into the closed-circuit camera in the corner. "That's what I believe, okay? That's all I can trust."

"Nonsense." My father shakes his head. "Nothing comes from oneself. Everything ultimately comes from God."

"Oh, spare me. Why would God care whether vampires have a few scars? Why would God care about vampires at all?"

"Mmm. That's a good question," Luann says gravely, as if I've uttered a Zen koan.

I stand up and move away, though this tiny room won't let me go far.

"Ask me anything." Luann's voice rings clear with sincerity, or the facsimile thereof. "I have all the answers you need."

"I bet you do." I need truth, which I'll never get from this pair of charlatans. "Happy Holidays," I mumble as I grab my purse and head for the door.

"Wait, Ciara," calls the woman who claims to be my mother. But I don't turn around, and she can't follow me as I walk out the door. Out of all of us, I'm the only one who's free. Sort of.

In the next room, Colonel Lanham turns from the desk where he's speaking with a guard.

"I'll walk you out." He joins me without asking if it's okay. Not surprising, considering how skillfully he manipulated me into signing away a year of my life.

"How long has she been with you?" I ask him when we enter the last long corridor leading to the outside. "Either tell me the truth or just say 'pass.' I can't take any more lies."

"She joined us eighteen months ago, after your father turned state's evidence against his family. Her profile indicated she would excel in undercover work, so we struck a deal similar to the one we have with your father. She went into the Fortress right out of training, about six months ago."

"Is she going back to jail?"

"Yes, with a greatly reduced sentence. She should be out in a year."

"Fabulous." I ask the sixty-four-billion-dollar question. "Is she really my mother?"

"It appears so."

"Appearances aren't everything." I resist the urge to grab Lanham by his starched black lapels and shake him until his sinuses collapse. "You let me worry about my dad's life, when all along he was working with you."

"Undercover work is not selectively secret."

"I wish I'd known this before I agreed to work for the Control."

"First of all, you and I arrived at a mutually satisfying arrangement. Second, I believe our methods and philosophy will suit your general outlook. And third." We reach the final outer door, which Colonel Lanham unlocks by tapping in a code on a panel to the left. "You have up to three years to get used to the idea." He pushes open the door and motions me through. "I'll be in touch."

The farther I walk through the parking lot, and the farther I get from my father, the more my spine straightens and my lungs expand. When I finally reach my car, I stand there with the door open, letting the cold afternoon wind whip my hair forward over my face, scraping the skin that's just beginning to heal.

I look back at the Control's gleaming headquarters building, surrounded on all sides by electric fences disguised as vines and trellises.

Maybe Dad was right. Maybe I can't decide what my powers mean or where they come from. But I can decide how to use them.

For now.


Elaine the bank manager—a woman with hair of a brassy red not found in nature—gives me a friendly nod and shuts the door, leaving me alone with my safe-deposit box.

I sift through my birth certificates, all six of them, searching for the real one, the one that says "Ciara Marjorie O'Riley." When I turned eighteen, I changed my last name to Griffin for reasons both silly and serious.

I find the original birth certificate and hold it up to the fluorescent light. Having acquired five forgeries, I should know a fake when I see it.

In the space for "Mother's Name," the blue mottled paper ends in a halo around the typed letters of the woman I've always called Mom. As if someone has whited out the original name, replaced it, then photocopied the result and given it a fresh stamp. The background behind my father's name remains uniformly blue.

"Son of a bitch."

I fold it up and slip it into my purse. For a second I think Travis can tell me for sure whether it's a forgery, but then I remember he's dead.

Outside the bank, I open my brand-new phone and dial my mom. Not the real one, but the one who feels real.

Like on Thanksgiving, it takes a while for the guards to fetch her. I'm unlocking my car by the time I hear her voice.

"Two calls in five weeks," she says brightly. "To what do I owe this honor?"

"Mom?" I resist the urge to call her Marjorie. "If I told you I needed a kidney transplant, and it could only come from a blood relative, could you give it to me?"

She starts to cry, and this time I don't doubt the sincerity of her tears.

I sit down hard in the driver's seat and pull the door shut. "How? How could you not tell me who my real mother was?"

"She didn't deserve you," she hisses. "She was always drinking. Never gave you baths. Your own grandmother said Luann would leave you alone in the house while she went to the liquor store. When she went to jail for her third check-kiting conviction, your dad sued for custody. The judge said it was the easiest case he'd seen in years." She pauses. "She didn't fight it. I'm sorry, Ciara, but she didn't want you. We did. We loved you so much, we would've kidnapped you, if that's what it took."

I squeeze the steering wheel so hard that the leather creaks in my grip. "I don't remember any of this."

"You were only eleven months old."

Too young to remember. But it seems impossible not to. How can someone not know, deep down in the core of her heart? How could I look at Luann and not feel the tug of instinct? "My whole life, I thought you were my mother."

"I am."

"You're not even my stepmother, since Dad never married you."

Her silence sends a chill across the back of my neck. Oops.

"How do you know that?"

I structure my response to be as technically truthful as possible. "I spoke to Dad yesterday. He's in prison."

"Why hasn't he been in touch with me?"

"I don't know, Mom."

She draws in a quick breath. "You'll still call me that?"

"You're the only mother I've ever known." I run my thumb over my apartment key. "The only one I'll ever want."

She lets out a long sigh, then sniffles. "I suppose I wasn't a total failure in raising you."

"Thanks. I guess."

A knock comes on my windshield. I jump. Outside my car, a white-haired lady huddles in a pink quilt coat.

"Are you leaving?" she yells through the window.

I glance back to see a car idling behind me. All the other spots are full in this tiny, built-for-a-past-era bank parking lot. I nod and mouth the word "sorry."

"They're telling me I have to go now," my mom says. "You'll call again soon?"

"I will," I tell her, and mean it. "Mom . . . when you get out of jail, you should move to Maryland. I'll find you a job."

"Really?" she whispers. "I could live with you?"

"No. But nearby." At least an hour away. Maybe two hours. "Think about it."

"I will. Merry Day-After-Christmas." Her end of the call cuts off.

"Not yet it isn't." I pull out of the parking space, keeping my eyes dry long enough to avoid hitting the adjacent cars. I wave at the patient lady, who toots her horn in response.

I drive under a banner that hangs across Sherwood's narrow Main Street, advertising the town's First Night New Year's Eve celebration. It makes me reflect on the last two months, how three major holidays have turned my life—which was not terribly stable to begin with—into utter chaos.

Halloween: station gets attacked by FAN, and Dexter enters the picture.

Thanksgiving: I realize how dangerous even the "good" vampires can be, and somehow still invite Shane to live with me.

Christmas: almost get killed (again), then find out my mom isn't my mom.

Maybe for New Year's, I'll just stay in bed.

# 32

## Heart-Shaped Box

In the business world, the week between Christmas and New Year's is notoriously slow. Everyone's on vacation and out of the office, or goofing off in the boss's absence. Phone calls aren't placed or expected to be returned. Deals don't get made this week, especially not the sort that change lives.

But WVMP is the exception to every rule.

Right now I'm standing in the freshly rebuilt Smoking Pig, at WVMP's private party, tapping my feet to some rousing Chicago blues and admiring the life-size cardboard poster of *Rolling Stone*'s first cover of the New Year. Regina and Jeremy pose next to it as Lori snaps photos. The DJ successfully re-creates her cover stance—snarling face and middle finger extended toward the camera. In real life, the gesture doesn't have a black box over it.

Below her defiant pose, the cover reads WVMP TAKES BACK THE NIGHT. Jeremy and I decided to go with the feminism angle, how a band of twentieth-century "vampires" overcame a seventeenth-century worldview. We added just enough subtle allusions to the "real vampire" subculture to titillate the public.

Tipped off to the article, the two major satellite radio providers entered a bidding war for weekly broadcasts by each of our vampire DJs. We sold the rights as a six-piece package, for more than the sum of its parts.

The contract was lucrative enough to let the DJs jointly purchase the station. Spencer's T-Day-hosting donor, Marcia, is a corporate lawyer specializing in transfer of property. She'll make it all look copacetic, then arrange for Elizabeth to disappear with minimal attention from the authorities.

The man who will benefit most from the overdue demise of the station's owner is currently passing out a box of cheesy plastic sunglasses shaped like the numerals of the New Year.

When David reaches me, I catch a whiff of a distinctive smell on his breath. I wrinkle my nose. "Stuart got absinthe for the party?"

"Jeremy's idea. It's an experience you really should . . ." David seems to fumble for the correct word. ". . . experience." He picks out a pink pair of sunglasses and tries to fit them on my face. Instead he pokes me in the eye with the plastic frame. "Sorry."

"I don't care how trendy and vampiric absinthe is, I hate licorice." I put on the sunglasses, wanting to ask him if the rumors are true, that the liquor makes you see green fairies.

"Besides," I add, "tonight I'm sticking to the drink of the man of the hour." I raise my bottle of National Bohemian beer and take a wistful pause to think of Travis.

David's face sobers, if not his brain. "How's Lori?"

"Better now that she's back in Sherwood. When I called her at her parents' house to tell her, she couldn't even grieve in front of them. She can't tell them her boyfriend died—they'd want to know his name and look up his obituary and learn all about the man who loved their little girl." I watch Lori immortalize Regina with Travis's camera and realize that for the first time, she doesn't seem afraid of the leather-drenched vampire.

David frowns. "Public mourning is a luxury for people like us."

I try to see his eyes behind the plastic zeros of his sunglasses, to no avail. Behind him, the front door opens to reveal Shane.

My boy saunters over and kisses me. "Happy New Year." He says it like he means it.

"How'd it go with your family and the Control?"

"Good news and bad news." He takes off his jacket and lays it over a chair. "Bad news: we can't tell my nephews about my true nature. The Control thinks they'd tell all their friends at school, what with the current popularity of vampires."

"And the good news?"

He shrugs. "The Control will give Mom and Eileen an incentive not to tell anyone that they were snatched out of their home and almost burned at the stake."

"How big an incentive?"

He gives me a cryptic smile. "More than a TV network would pay them for their story."

When it rains manna from heaven, it really pours.

"How's your mom taking all this?" David asks him. "Does she want to send you to an exorcist?"

"Not after I told her what holy water will do to her baby boy's face." He rubs his cheek, but his smile falls flat. "She cries a lot when we talk, and blames herself."

I take his hand. "Does she think you're going to hell?"

"That's the promising part. She figures if vampires are hated by truly evil people like the Fortress, then we can't be all that bad."

"Keep her away from Regina and Jim so she holds that thought." I lift my Natty Boh. "Want a beer?"

"I'll wait for the champagne." As the song changes to a slow, sensuous blues tune, he gives my hand a gentle tug. "Dance with me while I ask you something."

David salutes us with an orange pair of sunglasses. "Sounds like my exit cue."

I let Shane pull me into the open space between the bar and the stage. As we start to sway together, he says, "I was thinking—"

"Uh-oh."

"—now that Elizabeth will be dead for good, we'll have to move out of her apartment."

"I know. I'm sorry. But at least we'll have a shorter commute. You'll be at the station and I'll be . . . I don't know where."

He slows, almost missing a beat. "I saw an ad for a basement apartment in downtown Sherwood. Three bedrooms, fully furnished, washer/dryer, and they take pets."

"I probably can't afford it. I'd never pass the credit check on something that nice."

"No." He squeezes my hand. "Not by yourself."

My feet freeze. This is much bigger than holing up together in another person's place. This is sign-our-names-on-a-piece-of-paper-together big. I try to remember how to breathe.

Shane tilts my chin up. "Since it's in Sherwood, I could come home every morning after my show, except in summer when it gets light real early. We wouldn't be living together part-time anymore."

I fumble for a stalling question. "Does it have a dishwasher?"

"It doesn't matter." He holds my gaze. "I have a method for hand-washing dishes, too. I have methods and routines for things you can't imagine. Over the weeks or months or,

God willing, years, you'll discover them, one by one. There'll be blood in the fridge, and notes and charts *on* the fridge, but there'll also be music in the living room, and the bedroom. I'll never bring a donor home, and I'll never forget to walk the dog when it's my turn. Sometimes I'll even walk him when it's your turn. I promise you all of this."

I break eye contact and look around the room, as if the answer will be written in the freshly cut wood of the walls. Regina is dancing with Jim, who will have only one arm for the foreseeable future.

"Kissing them wasn't like kissing you," I tell Shane. "Not warm and real. They kissed me like I wasn't a person." I look up at him. "How long before you get that way?"

"I don't know." He lets his hands slide down my arms, releasing me until we're only touching fingertips, but still standing close. "Is that your answer?"

I think of Ned's broken body lying in a pool of glass, and the blood and who knows what other substances splattering Shane's shirt on Christmas Eve. My boyfriend is a monster. I can't deny that anymore. I can't pretend he's a normal human or ever will be.

But his ferocity reared its head so he could protect the four women he loved most—his mother, his sister, his maker, and me. If he's a monster, he's our monster. He's mine.

"This is my answer." I yank him close and kiss him hard. My head spins and pitches, like I'm falling from a cliff. No, not falling—waltzing on a tightrope, with no more looking down.

Shane folds me in his arms, then pulls me away a few inches so he can look me in the eye. "Is that a yes?"

I nod. "We'll sign a lease together, like real grown-ups."

He cringes. "Don't use the G word. DJs don't like it."

"Neither do con artists." I kiss him again, reveling in the warm-enough heat of his mouth. I try not to wonder how much maturity—and which other qualities—I'll need to be a Control contractor. That's many months' worth of worry away.

"Five minutes to midnight!" shouts a loud voice behind us. I turn to see Stuart, proud owner of the new-and-improved Smoking Pig, brandishing a trio of champagne bottles.

We join the others at a side table, where champagne flutes are lined up like dutiful soldiers.

Shane looks around. "Where's David?"

Jim points his cigarette at the double doors to the bar's deck. "Out there in the smoking lounge." Which, I notice, Jim's not using, and probably won't until the ban takes effect in one month and four minutes, and maybe not even then.

I pick up an extra glass of champagne and carry it to the door. Before opening it, I peer through to see David standing alone outside, leaning on the railing. His chin is tilted up, as if he's searching the sky.

I walk over to Lori, who's standing to the side of the party, examining Travis's camera.

I put my arm around her, careful not to drip champagne down her back. "How's it going?"

"I'm thinking of taking up photography. Travis taught me a lot about it when he was alive. I mean, when he was, um, around." Her shoulders sag for a moment. "Anyway, he said I had talent."

"That's great. You've got some killer equipment there."

She tries to smile, and I notice her eyes are rimmed with red. "Maybe it's time I did something with my life besides chase ghosts and schlep drinks."

I look at the extra glass in my hand. "Then this is terrible timing, but could you take this champagne out to David? I don't think he wants to be with the crowd right now."

"I can understand that." She takes the champagne flute and picks up her own.

I watch her exit through the glass doors and approach

David. He turns and accepts the champagne with a smile. I wait, expecting them to return to the bar but hoping they won't.

Finally, Lori and David turn away from us to look out over the railing together at the darkness. Though it's not midnight yet, they clink their glasses and sip.

"Happy New Year, guys," I whisper, then turn back to Shane, a sudden bubble of hope swelling inside me.

The countdown begins. I gaze around at all the young-looking faces and realize how many New Years some of them have greeted. For Monroe, nearly a hundred. Yet at this moment, none of them look jaded, not even Regina and Shane, who have raised coolness to an art form, a moral imperative.

We hit zero, and Shane kisses me. I hold tight to him as the others sing "Auld Lang Syne," a few of them horribly off-key.

A squealing harmonic comes from the speaker, joined by a saxophone, and then Roy Orbison implores us to let the good times roll.

We obey, dancing and singing (me and Regina on backup) and, of course, drinking until we can't stand up.

I've always believed in now, and that's always been good enough. But for the first time, tonight, I believe in what comes after.